Outstanding Praise for Richelle Mead and SUCCUBUS BLUES!

"Mead cooks up an appetizing debut that blends romantic suspense with a fresh twist on the paranormal, accented with eroticism."
—*Booklist*

"*Buffy* meets *Sex and the City*. Guilty pleasures don't get much better."
—David Sosnowski, author of *Rapture* and *Vamped*

"This is an excellent paranormal."
—*Romantic Times*

"Sexy, scintillating and sassy! Richelle Mead is now on my must-buy list."
—Michelle Rowen, author of *Bitten & Smitten*

"One of those books that had me engrossed from the very first page."
—*Romancejunkies.com*

"Take a beautiful, sassy immortal. Mix in suspense, murder and plenty of hot sex. Pour yourself a great read and enjoy the hell out of this story."
—Mario Acevedo, author of
The Nymphos of Rocky Flats and
X-Rated Bloodsuckers

"*Succubus Blues* is great fun."
—*The Romance Readers Connection*

"Writing this good tempts me to believe in angels . . . or deals with the devil. *Succubus Blues* is original, exciting, seductive stuff, filled with characters I'd sell my soul to meet."
—Rachel Caine, author of *Firestorm* and *Glass Houses*

Books by Richelle Mead

SUCCUBUS BLUES

SUCCUBUS ON TOP

SUCCUBUS DREAMS

SUCCUBUS HEAT

STORM BORN

THORN QUEEN

Published by Kensington Publishing Corporation

SUCCUBUS
ON TOP

RICHELLE MEAD

KENSINGTON BOOKS
http://www.kensingtonbooks.com

KENSINGTON BOOKS are published by

Kensington Publishing Corp.
850 Third Avenue
New York, NY 10022

All Kensington titles, imprints and distributed lines are available at special quantity discounts for bulk purchases for sales promotion, premiums, fundraising, educational or institutional use.

Special book excerpts or customized printings can also be created to fit specific needs. For details, write or phone the office of the Kensington Special Sales Manager: Kensington Publishing Corp., 850 Third Avenue, New York, NY 10022. Attn. Special Sales Department. Phone: 1-800-221-2647.

Kensington and the K logo Reg. U.S. Pat. & TM Off.

ISBN-13: 978-0-7582-1642-7
ISBN-10: 0-7582-1642-4

First Kensington Trade Paperback Printing: January 2008
10 9 8 7 6 5 4 3

Printed in the United States of America

*To Heidi and John, for your unfailing friendship,
generosity, and internet access.
You are quite possibly the finest people I know.*

Acknowledgments

As always, no book could be written without the consistent love of my family and friends. Many thanks go out to my awesome beta readers: Michael, David, and Christina. Your patience and enthusiasm have kept me going through the Valley of the Shadow of Writer's Block, and no words I write can express what your support has meant to me.

Thanks also to my publishing team, agent Jim McCarthy and editor John Scognamiglio, who excel at (good) reality checks and flexible deadlines. You guys keep me on the straight and narrow, despite my best efforts.

Finally, I'll always be grateful to my darling eighth graders who were so generous about letting me retire from teaching in order to finish this book. I wish you all the best and can't wait until you're old enough to actually read the stuff I write.

Chapter 1

Demons are scary.

No matter what religion or walk of life you come from, this remains pretty constant. Oh sure, they have their absurd moments—especially in the circles I run with—but all in all, people have good reason to fear and avoid hell's diabolical servants. They're cruel and merciless, delight in pain and suffering, and torture souls in their free time. They lie. They steal. They cheat on their taxes.

Yet, in spite of all that, I couldn't help but think I was about to witness the most terrifying demonic act yet.

An awards ceremony. For me.

Horatio, vice demon of such-and-such division of Infernal Affairs, stood before me, trying to impart an air of solemnity to the moment and failing miserably. I suspected his sky blue polyester suit and matching paisley bow tie were largely to blame. The sideburns didn't help either. He probably hadn't left the inner circles of hell in about six centuries, back around the last time sky blue polyester was in style.

With a too-long clearing of his throat, he glanced back and forth between those gathered, verifying we were all paying attention. My supervisor Jerome stood nearby, looking utterly bored, occasionally glancing at his watch. Beside him, Horatio's impish assistant Kasper grinned from ear to ear. A briefcase sat on the floor near him, and he clutched an assortment of papers. The eager, suck-up, lapdog look on his face indicated a burning desire for promotion.

As for me . . . well, I was fighting a hard battle to look excited too—and failing. Which was unacceptable, of course. I'm a succubus. My entire existence relies on making people—men in particular—believe and see what they want to in me. I can switch from simpering virgin to sultry dominatrix in a heartbeat. All it takes is a bit of shape-shifting and a dash of playacting. I'd picked up the former ability when I traded away my human soul; I'd acquired the latter over time. After all, you can't spend centuries telling every guy, "Yeah baby, you were the best I've ever had" and not learn a little something about schmoozing. Myths may paint us as ethereal, demonic creatures of pleasure, but honestly, being a succubus just comes down to a convincing poker face and a good sales pitch.

So, really, this awards thing shouldn't have been a problem for me. But Horatio wasn't making it easy to keep a straight face.

"Verily, it gives me great honor to be here today," he intoned in a nasal, baritone voice.

Verily?

"Hard work is what makes us great, and we gather here now to recognize one who has shown dedication and given her all to the Greater Evil. Such individuals are what make us strong, what will allow us to win in this immense battle when all tallies are counted at the end of time. Such individuals are worthy of our esteem, and we strive to reward their commitment, letting all know just how important it is to push hard against the odds and fight for our objectives in these difficult times."

He then added: "Whereas those who do not work hard are cast into the fiery pits of despair, to burn for all eternity and be ripped asunder by the hounds of hell."

I opened my mouth, on the verge of noting how that

would be more cost effective than severance pay, but Jerome caught my eye and shook his head.

Meanwhile, Horatio had nudged Kasper, and the imp hastily handed over a gold embossed certificate. "It is therefore with great pleasure that I present unto you this Award of Achievement for Excellently Exceeding and Surpassing Requisite Succubus Quotas in this Most Recent Quarter. Congratulations."

Horatio shook my hand and handed me the certificate, which had been signed by about fifty different people.

This Certifies that:
LETHA (alias Georgina Kincaid), Succubus in the
Archdiocese of Seattle, Washington, United States of
America, North America, Earth, has hereby Excellently Exceeded and Surpassed Requisite Succubus
Quotas in this Most Recent Quarter, demonstrating outstanding performance in seduction, damnation, and corruption of human souls.

Everyone looked at me when I finished reading, so I supposed they expected some kind of speech or something. Mostly I was wondering if I'd get in trouble for trimming this down to fit an eight-by-ten frame.

"Um, thanks. This is . . . cool."

That seemed to satisfy Horatio. He nodded smartly, then shot a glance to Jerome.

"You must be so proud."

"Exceptionally," murmured the archdemon, stifling a yawn.

Horatio turned back to me. "Keep up the good work. You might find yourself in line for promotion to the corporate level."

As if giving my soul away wasn't already bad enough. I forced a smile.

"Well. There's still so much to do here."

"Excellent attitude. Most excellent. You've done well with her." He gave Jerome a chummy pat on the back, something my boss did not look happy about at all. He didn't really like friendly pats. Or being touched, period. "Well, if there's nothing more, I should probably—oh, I nearly forgot."

Horatio turned to Kasper. The imp handed over something else to his master.

"These are for you. As a token of our appreciation."

He gave me a gift card for Applebee's, as well as some Blockbuster free-rental coupons. Jerome and I both stared for a moment, dumbstruck.

"Wow," I finally said. The runner-up for this award probably got a gift card for Sizzler. Never doubt that second place really is the first loser.

Horatio and Kasper vanished. Jerome and I stood in silence for a few moments.

"You like riblets, Jerome?"

"Droll, very droll, Georgie." He strolled around my living room, pretending to study my books and artwork. "Nice job with the quota thing. Of course, it's easy to excel when you're starting at zero, huh?"

I shrugged and tossed the certificate on my kitchen counter. "Does it really matter? Still gets you the laurels. I figured you'd like that."

"Of course I do. In fact, I've been rather pleasantly surprised at just how well you've kept your promise."

"I always keep my promises."

"Not *all* of your promises."

My silence made him smile. "So what now? Going out to celebrate?"

"You know where I'm going. I'm going to Peter's. Aren't you?"

He avoided the question; demons excelled at that. "I thought perhaps other plans had arisen. Plans with a certain mortal. You do seem to be doing that an awful lot lately."

"It's none of your business what I do."

"All of your business is my business."

Again, I didn't answer. The demon stepped closer, dark eyes boring into me. For inexplicable reasons, he chose to look like John Cusack while walking the human world. That might seem like it would reduce his power to intimidate, but I swear, it only made things worse.

"How long are you going to keep up this farce, Georgie?" His words were a challenge, trying to draw me out. "You can't honestly think you have a future with him. Or that you two can stay chaste forever. For Christ's sake, even if you can keep your hands off him, no human male's going to stay celibate for long. Especially one with a large fan base."

"Did you miss the part where I said it's my business?"

Heat rose to my cheeks. Despite knowing better, I'd recently gotten myself involved with a human. I wasn't even entirely sure how it had happened since I've always gone out of my way to avoid that kind of thing. I guess you could say he sort of snuck up on me. One moment he was simply a warm and comforting presence at my side; the next I realized how intensely he loved me. That love had blindsided me. I hadn't been able to resist it and had decided to see where it might take me.

As a result, Jerome never failed to remind me of the potential disaster I courted daily in this romance. His opinion wasn't entirely unfounded. A small part of this was because I didn't have a good track record with serious relationships. The larger part was that doing much more than hand-holding with a human would inevitably lead to me sucking away some of his life. But hey, all couples have their stumbling blocks, right?

The demon smoothed down the jacket of his perfectly tailored black suit. "Just friendly advice. It makes no difference. I don't mind if you keep playing house with him—denying him a future, a family, a healthy sex life. Whatever. So long as you keep up the good work, it's all the same to me."

"Are you done with the pep talk? I'm late."

"One more thing. I thought you might like to know I just made some arrangements for a pleasant surprise. One you'll like."

"What kind of surprise?" Jerome didn't really do surprises. Not good ones, at least.

"Wouldn't be a surprise if I told you, now would it?"

Typical. I scoffed and turned away. "I don't have time for your games. Either tell me what's going on or leave."

"I think I'll leave. But, before I do, just remember something." He put his hand on my shoulder and turned me around to face him again. I flinched at his touch and his proximity. The demon and I were not as buddy-buddy as we had once been. "You only have one man who's a constant in your life, only one man you will always answer to. A hundred years from now, *he* will be dust in the earth, and *I* will be the one you keep coming back to."

It sounded romantic or sexual, but it wasn't. Not in the least. My tie to Jerome ran deeper than that. A binding and loyalty that literally went straight to my soul. A connection I was bound to for all eternity, at least until the powers of hell decided to assign me to a different archdemon.

"Your pimp routine is getting old."

He stepped back, undisturbed by my rancor. His eyes danced.

"If I'm a pimp, Georgina, what's that make you?"

There was an ostentatious poof of smoke, and Jerome disappeared before I could reply.

Fucking demons.

I stood alone in my apartment, turning over his words in my mind. Finally, remembering the time, I headed for the bedroom to change clothes. As I did, I passed Horatio's certificate. Its gold seal winked up at me. I flipped it over, face down, suddenly feeling queasy. I might be good at what I did, but that didn't mean I was proud of it.

I ended up only being about fifteen minutes late for my

friend Peter's shindig. He answered his door before I could even knock. Taking in his billowing white hat and KISS THE COOK apron, I said, "I'm sorry. No one told me *Iron Chef* was being filmed here tonight."

"You're late," he chided, waving a wooden spoon in the air. "So what, you win an award and think you can forget all about propriety now?"

I ignored his disapproval and swept inside. It was the only thing you could do with an obsessive-compulsive vampire.

In the living room, I found our other friends Cody and Hugh sorting large piles of cash.

"Did you guys rob a bank?"

"Nope," said Hugh. "Since Peter's trying to provide us with a civilized meal tonight, we decided a civilized pastime was required."

"Money laundering?"

"Poker."

From the kitchen, I could hear Peter muttering to himself about a soufflé. It sort of diminished my image of a bunch of shady characters huddled around a backroom card table. "I think bridge would be more appropriate."

Hugh looked doubtful. "That's an old-person's game, sweetie."

I had to smile at that. "Old" was kind of a relative term when most of us could boast centuries. I had long suspected that among my circle of lesser immortals—those who were not true angels or demons—I had more years than any of them, never mind the optimistic claim of being twenty-eight on my driver's license.

"Since when do we even play games?" I wondered aloud. Our last attempt had involved a game of Monopoly with Jerome. Competing with a demon in a struggle for property and ultimate control is kind of futile.

"Since when don't we play games? Games of life, games of death. Games of love, of hope, of chance, of despair, and of all the myriad wonders in between."

I rolled my eyes at the newcomer. "Hello, Carter." I'd known the angel was lurking in the kitchen, just as Peter had felt me coming down the hall. "Where's your better half tonight? I just saw him. I thought he was coming too."

Carter strolled in and gave me one of his mocking smiles, gray eyes alight with secrets and mirth. He wore his usual transient ware, ripped jeans and a faded T-shirt. When it came to age, the rest of us couldn't even compare to him. We had all once been mortal; we measured our lives in centuries or millennia. Angels and demons . . . well, they measured their lives in eternity. "'Am I my brother's keeper?'"

Classic Carter answer. I looked to Hugh, who was, in a manner of speaking, our boss's keeper. Or at least a sort of administrative assistant.

"He had to take off for a meeting," said the imp, stacking twenties. "Some kind of team-building thing in L.A."

I tried to imagine Jerome participating in a ropes course. "What kind of team building do demons do exactly?"

No one had an answer for that. Which was probably just as well.

While the money sorting continued, Peter made me a vodka gimlet. I eyed the bottle of Absolut on his counter.

"What the hell is that?"

"I ran out of Grey Goose. They're practically the same anyway."

"I swear, if you weren't already an abomination before the Lord, I'd accuse you of heresy."

When all the money was sorted, including my contribution, we sat around the vampires' kitchen table. Like everyone else in the known world right now, we started playing Texas Hold'em. I could play okay but fared far better with mortals than immortals. My charisma and glamour had less effect on this group, which meant I had to think harder about odds and strategy.

Peter scurried around during the game, attempting to play and watch his meal at the same time. It wasn't easy, since he insisted on wearing sunglasses while playing, which then had to be removed while he checked the food. When I commented on how this would be my second fancy dinner in two nights, he nearly had a fit.

"Whatever. Nothing you had last night will even compare to this duck I've made. *Nothing.*"

"I don't know about that. I went to the Metropolitan Grill."

Hugh whistled. "Whoa. I wondered where you got the glow from. When a guy takes you to the Met, you can't really help but put out, huh?"

"The glow's from a different guy," I said uncomfortably, not really wanting to be reminded of a tryst I'd had this morning, even if it had been pretty hot. "I went to the Met with Seth." The memory of last night's dinner brought a smile to my face, and I suddenly found myself rambling. "You should have seen him. He actually didn't wear a T-shirt for once, though I'm not sure it made a difference. The shirt he did have on was all wrinkled, and he couldn't really tie the tie. Plus, when I first got there, he had his laptop out on the table. He'd shoved everything else aside—napkins, wineglasses. It was a mess. The waiters were horrified."

Four sets of eyes stared at me.

"What?" I demanded. "What's wrong?"

"You are," said Hugh. "You're a glutton for punishment."

Cody smiled. "Not to mention totally love struck. Listen to yourself."

"She's not in love with him," said Peter. "She's in love with his books."

"No I'm—" The words died on my lips, mainly because I wasn't sure what I wanted to argue. I didn't want them to think I only loved the books, but I wasn't entirely sure I loved Seth yet either. Our relationship had blossomed with remarkable speed, but sometimes, I worried what I actually loved was the idea of him loving me.

"I can't believe you guys are still doing the sexless-dating thing," continued Hugh.

My temper flared. I'd already taken this from Jerome; I didn't need to hear it here too.

"Look, I don't want to talk about this if you guys are just going to nag me, okay? I'm tired of everyone telling me how crazy it is."

Peter shrugged. "I don't know. It's not that crazy. You always hear about these married couples who never have sex anymore. They survive. This would be almost the same thing."

"Not with our girl." Hugh shook his head. "Look at her. Who wouldn't want to have sex with her?"

They all looked again, making me squirm.

"Hey," I protested, feeling the need to clear up a point. "That's not the problem. He *wants* to, okay? He's just not going to. There's a difference."

"Sorry," said Hugh. "I'm just not buying it. He can't be with you in the clothes you wear and not crack. Even if he could, no guy could handle his woman seeing as much action as you do."

It was a well-worn point in my mind, the same Jerome had made, the one that worried me more than our ability to keep our hands off each other. One of my greatest nightmares involved having a conversation akin to: *Sorry, Seth. I can't go out tonight. I have to go work this married guy I met, so I can get him to sleep with me, thus leading him further and further down the road to damnation while I suck away part of his life. Maybe when I'm done, you and I can catch a late movie.*

"I don't want to talk about this," I repeated. "We're doing just fine. End of story."

Silence fell, save for the sound of cards and money hitting the table. Glancing around, I saw Carter watching me levelly. Only he had stayed out of the Seth bashing. This didn't surprise me. The angel usually just listened until he could interject some sarcastic or esoteric quip. This used to infuriate me, but recent events had changed my attitude toward him. I still didn't fully understand him or know if I could trust him, but I had come to respect him.

Troubled by the scrutiny, I glanced back down and discovered I finally had a respectable hand after several rounds of shit. Three of a kind. Not the greatest but passable. I raised high, wanting to get the others out before more cards came into play and made my hand less passable.

My strategy worked on the vampires. The next card fell. Seven of spades. Hugh scowled and folded when I raised again. I waited for Carter to drop out as well, but instead, he reraised further.

I hesitated only a moment before calling. As the last card was about to play, I puzzled over what the angel might have and whether I could beat it. A pair? Two pair? Ah. The last card came out. Another spade. There was now a strong possibility he had a flush. That would beat me. Still hoping I could bluff him out, I raised even more. He reraised me again, more than doubling my initial bet.

That was a lot of money to add, especially considering what I'd already put in. Centuries of investments kept me pretty comfortable, but that didn't mean I had to be stupid. What did he have? It had to be the flush. Balking, I folded.

With a pleased grin, he swept in the massive pot. When he tossed his hand over to the discard pile, the cards' edges caught, making them flip over. Two of diamonds. Eight of clubs.

"You . . . you bluffed!" I cried. "You had nothing!"

Carter wordlessly lit a cigarette.

I looked to the others for confirmation. "He can't do that."

"Hell, I've been doing it for half this game," said Hugh, borrowing Carter's lighter. "Not that it's done me any good."

"Yeah . . . but . . . he's, you know. An angel. They can't lie."

"He didn't lie. He bluffed."

Cody considered, twisting a piece of his blond hair around one finger. "Yeah, but bluffing is still dishonest."

"It's implied lying," said Peter.

Hugh stared at him. "'Implied lying?' What the fuck does that mean?"

I watched Carter stack his money and made a face at him. You'd think an angel who hung around with employees of evil would be a good influence, but at times, he seemed worse than we were. "Enjoy your thirty pieces of silver, Judas."

He gave me a mock hat tip while the others argued on.

Suddenly, like a row of dominoes, conversation steadily dropped. Carter felt it first, of course, but he merely arched an eyebrow, as indifferent as ever. Then came the vampires with their heightened reflexes and sensitivity. They exchanged glances and looked toward the door. Finally, seconds later, Hugh and I sensed it as well.

"What is that?" Cody frowned, staring across the room. "It's sort of like Georgina but not."

Hugh followed the young vampire's gaze, face mildly speculative. "Incubus."

I had already known that, of course. The signatures we all carried differed by creature. Vampires felt different from imps, just as imps felt different from succubi. If one knew an immortal well enough, one could also pick up on an individual's unique attributes. I was the only succubus who inspired sensations of silk and tuberose perfume. In a room full of vampires, I would have been able to quickly determine if Cody or Peter were present.

Likewise, I immediately knew there was an incubus approaching Peter's door, and I knew exactly which incubus it was. I would have known his signature anywhere, even after all this time. The fleeting feel of velvet on the skin. A whispered scent of rum, almond, and cinnamon.

Not even realizing I'd gotten up, I flung the door open, staring with delight at the same fox-faced features and mischievous eyes I'd last seen over a century ago.

"Hello, *ma fleur*," he said.

Chapter 2

"Bastien," I breathed, still disbelieving. "Bastien!"

I threw my arms around him, and he lifted me up like I weighed nothing, twirling me around. When he gently set me back on my feet, he looked down at me fondly, his handsome face cracking into a grin. Until I saw it, I hadn't realized how much I'd missed that smile.

"You look exactly the same," I noted, taking in the curling black hair that touched his shoulders, the eyes so dark a chocolate brown they almost looked black as well. Unlike me, he liked to wear the shape he'd been born with, the body from his mortal days. His skin was the color of the mochas I consumed regularly, smooth and lovely. His nose had been broken when he was human, but he never bothered to shape-shift the signs away. It didn't detract from his looks any; in fact, it sort of gave him a dashing scoundrel persona.

"And you, as usual, look completely different. What are you calling yourself these days?" His voice carried a faint British accent leftover from many years spent in London after leaving the slave plantations of Haiti. He kept that accent and the French expressions of his childhood only for effect; when he chose to, he could speak American English as flawlessly as I could.

"Georgina."

"Georgina? Not Josephine or Hiroko?"

"Georgina," I reiterated.

"Very well then, *Georgina*. Let me see you. Turn around."

I spun around, like a model, letting him get the full effect of this body. When I faced him again, he nodded with approval.

"Exquisite—not that I'd expect any less from you. Short, just like every other one, but the curves are in all the right spots, and the coloring is very nice." He leaned closer to me, studying my face with a professional eye. "The eyes I especially like. Catlike. How long have you been wearing this one?"

"Fifteen years."

"Barely broken in."

"Well," observed Hugh dryly, "it sort of depends on how you define 'broken in.'"

Bastien and I both turned, remembering we had an audience. The other immortals watched with bemusement, the poker game momentarily forgotten. Bastien turned on a high-beam smile and crossed the room in a few quick strides.

"Bastien Moreau." He extended a polite hand to Hugh, every inch of him polished and deferential. Incubi, after all, have just as good a sense of customer service and public relations as succubi. "It's a pleasure to meet you."

He made equally polite introductions with the rest of the group, pausing momentarily when he reached Carter. A brief flicker of surprise in Bastien's dark eyes was the only other indication that he found an angel in our midst odd. Otherwise, his surface charm remained perfect as he smiled and shook Carter's hand.

Although clearly surprised at Bastien's presence, Peter stood up dutifully. "Have a seat. You want a drink?"

"Thank you. You're too kind. Bourbon on ice, please. And thank you for allowing me to show up so unexpectedly. You have a stunning home."

The vampire nodded, mollified at someone finally appreciating his hospitality.

I, however, had other concerns and wondered what had

caused the incubus to "show up so unexpectedly." I suddenly remembered Jerome's taunting surprise. "Jerome knows you're here, doesn't he?"

"Of course. Long since arranged." Our kind could not cross into another's territory without making arrangements with the local supervisor. For a group that had allegedly rebelled against the system, we had a staggering amount of rules, regulations, and paperwork. We made the IRS look juvenile. "He told me where to find you tonight."

"And you're here because . . . ?"

He flung a playful arm around me. "You're pushy. No "Hello, how are you"? Can't I just stop by to see an old friend?"

"Not in this business."

"How long have you known Georgina?" asked Hugh, shifting his solidly built body into a more comfortable sitting position.

Bastien turned thoughtful. "I don't know. How long has it been? Ages?"

"You have to be a little more specific than that," I reminded him, my mind slipping back to a London of long ago, recalling rough-hewn streets redolent with the scent of horses and unwashed humans. "Early seventeenth century?" He nodded, and I let my tone turn teasing. "Mostly I just remember how green you were."

"I have no idea what you're talking about."

"Whatever. I taught you everything you know."

"Ah, older women." Bastien glanced around at the others, shrugging his shoulders with feigned haplessness. "Always so sure of themselves."

"So, explain how this works," Cody urged eagerly, young eyes on Bastien. "You're like the male equivalent of Georgina, right? You shape-shift and everything?" Having been an immortal for less than ten years, Cody was always learning something new about us. I realized he'd probably never even met an incubus before.

"Well, there's really no equivalent for Fleur, but yes, something like that." I think he preferred calling me Fleur because it was easier than trying to remember the names I kept acquiring over the years.

"So you seduce women?" pushed Cody.

"Exactly."

"Wow. That must actually be hard."

"It's not so—wait a minute," I said. "What are you implying over there? What's this "actually" business?"

"Well, he's got a point," insisted Peter, handing Bastien the drink. "It's not like your job's all that difficult, Georgina. By comparison, I mean."

"My job's very difficult!"

"What, getting men to have sex with a beautiful woman?" Hugh shook his head. "That's not hard. That's not even remedial."

I looked at them incredulously. "It's not like I can just jump into bed with anyone. I have to get quality guys."

"Yeah, as of a month ago maybe."

Bastien shot me a sharp look at that remark, but I was too annoyed to acknowledge it. "Hey, I just won an award, you know. Got the certificate and everything. And anyway, contrary to your pathetic love lives, not all guys will immediately give in to sex. It takes work."

"What, like horns and a whip?" suggested Peter slyly, referring to a particularly embarrassing incident from my past.

"That's different. He wanted it."

"They all want it. That's the point." Hugh turned to Bastien reverentially. "How do you do it? Got any pointers you can share with the rest of us?"

"Several lifetimes' worth," chuckled Bastien, still watching me. "Those are trade secrets, I'm afraid. Although, really, in Fleur's defense, the techniques are the same for both of us. You should have been paying more attention to her."

"Low-cut necklines aren't exactly a trade secret."

"Much more to it than that, my friend. Especially with Georgina. She's one of the best."

Hugh and the vampires looked at me as though they'd never noticed me before, apparently attempting to figure out if what Bastien said was true.

"No need to start that up," I pointed out hastily.

"Come on, weren't you just bragging about how you taught me everything I know? You and I used to run some good rackets back in the day."

"What kind of rackets?" asked Peter.

When I wouldn't answer, Bastien merely shrugged. "Oh, you know. The kind that require a partner."

Cody's eyes widened. "Like . . . group sex?"

"No!" I protested, unable to stay silent at that. Not that it wasn't in my curriculum vitae. "Partnerships to suck somebody in. Play husband and wife. Or brother and sister. Or . . . or . . . whatever it takes to nail your mark."

Bastien nodded along with me. "Men really like the thrill of winning over someone's beautiful young wife. Women too, for that matter. The forbidden always has a certain allure to it."

"Wow." Cody and the others pondered this new development and tried probing us a bit more for details. Bastien, sensing my reluctance to elaborate about the past, gave vague answers, and conversation soon drifted to other topics—as well as to Peter's amazing dinner. It wasn't Met good, but maybe the company had biased me.

"Are you going to tell me what's going on?" I murmured to the incubus later, as our group finally rose from the table and began making motions to leave. I was dying to know what could have drawn him here and earned Jerome's approval. Hell's denizens could take vacations, but this smacked of business.

Bastien patted me on the back, giving me his trademark grin. "In good time, my sweet. Is there somewhere we can talk?"

"Sure. I'll take you back to my place. You can meet my cat."

When Bastien left me to once again thank Peter for dinner, Carter strolled over.

"Are you seeing Seth soon?"

"Later tonight." Seeing his amused expression, I scowled. "Just get it over with, okay?"

"Get what over with?"

"The part where you tell me how stupid it is to try to have a serious relationship with a mortal."

The mirth faded from his face. "I don't think it's stupid."

I studied him, waiting for the punch line. "Everyone else does."

"Does Seth? Do you?"

I looked away, thinking about Seth. That funny, distracted look on his face when inspiration seized him. His goofy T-shirt collection. The exquisite way he could capture the world on paper. How warm his hand was when it slid into mine. The way I just couldn't stay away from him, despite the million reasons that said I should. Suddenly, caught in Carter's penetrating eyes, something inside of me let loose. I hated how the angel could do this to me.

"Sometimes I do. Sometimes I look at him . . . and I remember how it was when I kissed him and felt that love. It makes me want that back. I want to feel it again. I want to return it. Other times, though . . . other times, I'm so scared. I listen to these guys . . . and to Jerome . . . and then the doubts gnaw at me. I can't get them out of my head. We've been sleeping together, you know. Literally. It hasn't been a problem so far, but sometimes I lie awake watching him, thinking this can't last. The longer it does . . . I feel like . . . like I'm standing on a high wire, with Seth at one end and me at the other. We're trying to reach each other, but one misstep, one breeze, one side-glance, and I'll fall over the edge. And keep falling and falling."

I took in a shaking breath when I finished.

Carter leaned toward me and brushed the hair away from the side of my face. "Don't look down then," he whispered.

Bastien had returned, catching the end of my soliloquy.

"Who's Seth?" he wanted to know later, once we were back at my apartment.

"Long story." Yet I found myself spilling it anyway.

Of course, telling Bastien about Seth meant telling him about a lot of other things too. Like a recent encounter with Jerome's half-human, half-angel son—a stunningly beautiful man with a twisted sense of social justice who had been on a semipsychotic mission to make other immortals pay for the shoddy treatment of him and his kind. The fact that he had been a good dancer and a phenomenal lover had not really been enough to make up for his wanton killing of lesser immortals and subsequent attempt on Carter.

That, of course, led me to next explain how Seth had witnessed the inevitable showdown and had been injured when I kissed him to get an emergency fix of energy. Jerome had wanted to erase Seth's memory of the whole event, as well as the writer's love for me. I had begged the demon not to, finally getting him to agree when I offered to devote all of my efforts back to seducing and corrupting decent men like a good little succubus should. Horatio's visit had been the ultimate testimony to my "new and improved" self.

Bastien, sprawling on my sofa, listened thoughtfully and frowned when I finished. "What do you mean? Why weren't you going after decent ones already?"

"I got tired of it. Didn't like hurting them."

"So what? You were going after bad ones?"

I nodded.

He shook his head, knowing as well as I did how little life energy an ignoble mortal yielded compared to a good one. "Poor Fleur. What a miserable existence that must have been."

I gave him a bittersweet smile. "I think you're the first person that's ever sounded more sympathetic than incredulous. Most people think I'm idiotic for getting by like that."

"It's a pain, yes," Bastien agreed, "and requires more frequent fixes, but hardly idiotic. You don't think I have days when I feel the same way? When I just want to throw my hands up and leave decent women alone?"

"Why don't you?"

"Not our lot. You and I are glorified prostitutes—courtesans, if you want to be more genteel, but it's all the same thing. Switching to bad ones won't change our fates. Won't even do anything in the long run, really, except relieve our guilt a bit, and even that relief doesn't last forever."

"Christ. You aren't really making me feel better."

"Sorry."

"No, no, it's okay. Whatever. I mean, it's nice to have someone to talk to about this. No one else—none of the other immortals—really get it."

He snorted. "Of course they don't. How could they?" My silence agreed for me, and Bastien gave me a kindly look. "Not that your friends weren't nice. Are there other immortals in the city you can talk to? Any succubi or incubi?"

"A few more vampires and minor demons, but that's it. They're less social than the ones I run with. I have some good mortal friends too. Still. They're not the same either." I smiled gently. "They're not you. I've missed you."

Bastien tousled my hair, earning a critical glance from my cat Aubrey. "I've missed you too."

"So will you tell me what's going on now?"

His serious mien turned jovial. "Not sure what you're going to think about it, now that I've heard all of this."

"Try me."

Sliding off the couch, Bastien settled next to me so we could speak face-to-face. "You ever heard of Dana Dailey?"

"I live on this planet, don't I? She's always my first choice when I'm driving in my car and feel like listening to some highly commercial, conservative rhetoric." I didn't make any attempt to hide my disdain. In addition to touting worn-out family values, radio host Dana Dailey also enjoyed working thinly veiled racist, homophobic, and even sexist insinuations into her talk show. I couldn't stand her.

"I imagine that mood strikes you quite a bit. Did you know she's Seattle based?"

"Of course. It's a wonder she hasn't dragged down the property value."

"Funny you should mention that. A house in her neighborhood just came up for sale."

"So?"

"So, our employers have purchased it."

"What?"

Grinning, knowing he had me hooked, Bastien leaned in eagerly. "Pay attention, Fleur, because here's the good part. We got wind of some rumors concerning Mrs. Dailey's ex-pool boy in San Diego. He claims to have been 'romantically involved' with her."

I racked my brain, recalling a promotional picture I'd seen of her and her politician husband on a billboard. "Have you seen Mr. Dailey? I'd opt for a pool boy too. What became of the rumors?"

"Oh, you know. The same thing that always happens to rumors with no proof. They faded away; nothing happened."

I waited expectantly. "Okay, and the house fits in how?"

"Well, like you said, her husband's no prize. Of course, she isn't going to get divorced or anything, not when it could potentially tarnish his political future and her whole prissy, on-air family-values campaign. But . . . the naughty streak is still there. If she's strayed once, I bet she could be lured into doing it again."

I groaned as the pieces fell together. "Like with a handsome, debonair neighbor?"

"Debonair? Really, you're too kind."

"So what happens after that?"

"Then we just let the evidence do its work."

"Evidence?"

"Well, yeah. We're not going to go the way of the pool boy. When I manage to lure the illustrious Mrs. Dailey into physical pleasures surpassing her wildest dreams, there'll be a camera rolling. We're going to record this for posterity, then go to the press. Full exposure, full takedown. No more radio empire preaching to the masses to return to pure, decent ways. Even her husband's political campaign will be marred, thus opening the door for some liberal upstart to take his place and help get this area back into the corrupt rut it so desperately longs for."

"Gee, it's all so neat."

He eyed me. "You doubt the plan's brilliance?"

"I don't know. I appreciate the ballsy factor here, but I think this is kind of out-there, even for you. I can't imagine Dana Dailey'll go down so easily."

"Leave the going down to me."

"Your ego's out of control."

He laughed and pulled me to him. His arms felt good around me. Familiar. Reassuring. "Admit it. That's why you love me."

"Yeah, you're like the brother I never had. One that doesn't set my hair on fire."

His eyes sparkled wickedly. "And once again, you've jumped ahead of me. I want you to see me in action on this—not to mention keep me company while I'm in town. You've got to come visit—as Mitch's sister."

"Who?"

Bastien suddenly stood up and shape-shifted. The familiar features morphed, leaving no trace of the rakish incubus I knew. Six-two and broad-shouldered, he now had dark blond hair and sky blue eyes, his face only just losing its pretty boy aspect and giving way to the sizzling promise of an experienced, confident man in his early thirties. When he smiled, those perfect teeth lit up a room.

He winked at me. "Mitch Hunter," he explained in a suave, movie-star voice. No accent now.

"You got an equally cheesy title to go with that? 'Mitch Hunter, MD' or 'Mitch Hunter, Private Investigator?' Seems appropriate."

"Nah. I'm a consultant, of course. Everyone's favorite nondescript yet well-paid white-collar job."

"You look like you need a golf club in one hand and a burger flipper in the other."

"Tease all you want, but Dana won't be able to resist this. Now"—he gestured for me to stand up—"let's see what you can do."

"Are you joking?"

"Do I look like I'm joking? If you're going to come visit me, you've got to put on some family resemblance."

I rolled my eyes and stood up. After a moment's study of his features, I shape-shifted my petite body into a taller, more athletic one with long blond hair.

He scrutinized me, then shook his head. "Too pretty."

"What? This is perfect."

"That body's unreal. No one looks that good. My God woman, that ass."

"Oh, come on. You don't think Special Agent Mitch Hunter's sister isn't the type to spend two hours a day on a stair-climber?"

Bastien grunted. "You've got a point there. At least lose some of the hair. These suburban types go for boring and practical."

"Yeah, but I'm not suburban. I'm your hipper, more stylish—"

Someone knocked at my door. He glanced at me questioningly.

"Oh! It's Seth."

I changed back to my normal body, and Bastien did the same. I opened the door.

Seth Mortensen, best-selling author and professional introvert, stood outside my apartment. Clad in a Frogger T-shirt and corduroy jacket, he seemed to have forgotten to brush his hair again. It was messy and brown with a faint coppery cast, mirrored in the perpetual five o'clock shadow across his lower face. His lips turned up in a smile upon seeing me, and I couldn't help but briefly ponder how soft and kissable they looked.

"Hey," I said.

"Hey."

Despite whatever attraction burned between us, the engine of our conversation always took a little while to turn over. I led him inside, and his expression faltered a bit when he saw Bastien.

"Oh. Hi."

"Hello," boomed Bastien, extending his hand. "Bastien Moreau."

"Seth Mortensen."

"A pleasure. I've heard all about you. Your books are fabulous. I mean, I've never read any of them—just don't have the time for that anymore—but I'm sure they're *magnifique*."

"Um, thanks."

"Bastien is an old friend," I explained. "He's going to be in town for a while on . . . business."

Seth nodded, and silence dropped in between all of us like a fourth companion. Finally, Bastien cleared his throat. I could see from his face that he was already losing interest, dismissing Seth as too quiet and unexciting. The incubus craved action.

"Well, I should take off. I don't want to interrupt your plans."

"What are you going to do?" I asked. "You can't have any plans of your own yet."

He winked. "I'll improvise."

I gave him a knowing look.

Ruffling my hair again, he embraced me and kissed each of

my cheeks. "I'll be in touch, Fleur. Make sure you keep an eye on the news."

"I'll never leave my television."

Bastien gave Seth a friendly nod. "Nice meeting you."

When the incubus was gone, Seth asked, "When you say 'old friend,' are we talking, like . . . since the Ice Age?"

"No. Of course not."

"Oh."

"It's only been about four hundred years."

"Ah. Yes. Only four hundred." A wry expression spread over his face. "Being with you is a continual experiment in perspective. Among other things." He considered. "So what is he? Werewolf? Demigod?"

"Nothing so exciting. He's an incubus. You must have heard of those."

Seth nodded, frowning. "Sure. Like a succubus only . . . he has to go after women to survive?"

I nodded.

"Wow. For all eternity. *Wow*." His eyebrows shot up as true wonder played over his face. "That's got to be . . . wow. That's really rough."

My eyes narrowed. "Don't even start down that road."

Bastien had said he didn't want to interrupt our plans, but we didn't really have any, short of spending the evening together. I suppose most couples, running out of options, could have resorted to sex or at least making out, but the nature of our relationship required a full itinerary. We mustered some ideas.

"You want to rent a movie?" I offered. "I've got some coupons."

We ended up renting *Gladiator*, at which time I discovered Horatio's free rental coupons had expired long ago.

"That son of a bitch!"

"Who?" asked Seth.

But of course I couldn't explain. Fucking demons.

Back home, Seth and I snuggled on my couch as we watched, warm and close yet still safe from any detrimental succubus effects. He listened with bemusement as I pointed out historical inaccuracies, most of which involved how much dirtier and smellier the Roman Empire had been.

When it finished, we turned off the television and sat together in the dark. Seth stroked the side of my face, sifting through the strands of my hair and occasionally brushing my cheek with his fingers. A small gesture, yet when that was all you could do with another person, it became startlingly erotic.

I looked up at him. I knew what I saw when I studied him. He was everything I could want and everything I couldn't have. The steady, loving companion I'd pined for all these years. I wondered what he saw with me. The expression he wore now seemed fond. Admiring. And a little sad.

> *"But thy eternal summer shall not fade*
> *Nor lose possession of that fair ow'st;*
> *Nor shall Death brag thou wand'rest in his shade,*
> *When in eternal lines to time thou grow'st;*
> *So long as men can breathe or eyes can see,*
> *So long lives this, and this gives life to thee."*

"Sonnet Eighteen," I murmured, thinking he recited beautifully. Hell, forget his recitation skills. How many guys in this age of instant messaging even knew Shakespeare anymore? His amused little half-smile played over his face.

"Clever and beautiful. How could any man settle for a mortal woman?"

"Easily," I returned. My friends' misgivings suddenly loomed up in me. "You could, you know."

He blinked, and his rapt look faded, giving way to exasperation. "Oh. Not this discussion again."

"I'm serious—"

"And so am I. I don't want to be with anyone else right

now. I've told you that a hundred times. Why do we keep talking about this?"

"Because you know we can't—"

"No buts. Give me some credit for being able to control myself. Besides, I'm not with you for sex. You know that. I'm with you to be with you."

"How can that be enough?" It never had been for any other man I'd known.

"Because . . . because . . ." He tipped my chin up with his hand, the emotion in those eyes making my insides melt. "Because being with you feels so right . . . like it's always been meant to be. You make me believe in a higher power for once in my life."

I closed my eyes and put my head on his chest. I could hear his heart beating. He wrapped me to him, his embrace warm and solid, and I felt like I couldn't get close enough to him. Probably I should have let the discussion go then, but one more thing was still on my mind tonight. After all, I had a gold-embossed certificate sitting on my counter.

"Even if you can control yourself . . . even if you can stay celibate, you know I won't be."

The words hurt coming out, but my mouth's control switch didn't always function so well. Besides, I didn't want anything standing between us.

"I don't care." But I felt his hold on me stiffen a little.

"Seth, you will—"

"Thetis, *I don't care*. It doesn't matter. Nothing matters except what happens between you and me."

The fierceness in his voice—a contrast to his normal placidity—thrilled me, but it was not that that made me give up the argument. It was the word "Thetis." Thetis. Thetis the shape-shifting goddess. The shape-shifter wooed and won by a steadfast mortal. Seth had coined the name for me when he learned I was a succubus, when he'd first insinuated that my infernal standing was not a deterrent.

I pulled him closer. *Don't look down.*

We went to bed shortly thereafter, Aubrey snuggling up at our feet. The feel of Seth's body curled by mine under the covers was tantalizing, a cruel whisper of the restrictions around us.

I sighed and tried to think of something other than how nice he felt or how great it would be if he slid his hand up my shirt. I grinned as a most unsexual sentiment came to mind.

"I want pancakes."

"What? Right now?"

"No. For breakfast."

"Oh." He yawned. "You'd better get up early then."

"Me? I'm not going to make them."

"Yeah?" His sleepy voice carried mock sympathy. "Who's going to make them for you then?"

"You are."

It was a well-known fact—at least to Seth and me—that he made the best pancakes known to mankind. They always came out perfect, light and fluffy. Through some kitchen magic, he even managed to put smiley faces on them when he made them for me. Once he'd even put a *G* on one. I'd assumed it was for my name, but later, he'd sworn it stood for "goddess."

"Am I?" His lips brushed my earlobe; his breath was warm against my skin. "You think I'm going to make you pancakes? Is that how you think it's going to be?"

"You're so good at," I whined. "Besides, if you do, I'll sit on the counter in a short robe while you cook." Oops. Maybe pancakes could become sexual after all.

His soft laughter segued into another yawn. "Oh. Well then." He kissed my ear again. "Maybe I'll make you pancakes."

His breathing grew slow and regular, the tension in his body easing. Soon he slept, not troubled or tempted in the least by having me in his arms.

I sighed again. He was right; he did have self-control. If he could do this, surely I could too. I closed my eyes and waited for exhaustion to take over. Fortunately, it didn't waste any time; staying up late will do that to you. Maybe that was the real key to sleeping chastely.

I woke up in his arms hours later, hearing the ever-so-faint sounds of bad seventies music drifting through the wall. One of my neighbors felt the need to do aerobics to the Bee Gees every day around lunchtime. Certifiable insanity.

Wait. Lunchtime?

I sat bolt upright, panic jolting me into full consciousness as I assessed the situation. My bed. Seth sprawled beside me. The full roar of traffic outside. Clear, winter sunlight pouring through the window—a lot of sunlight.

Fearing the worst, I looked at the nearest clock. It was 12:03.

Groaning silently, I groped on the floor for my cell phone, wondering why no one had yet called me in to work. Looking at the phone's display, I realized I'd turned the ringer off during the movie. *Seven new voice mail messages*, the phone read. So much for pancakes. Tossing the phone back down, I looked over at Seth, the cuteness of him in a T-shirt and flannel boxers momentarily allaying my frustration.

I shook him, wishing I could just crawl back under the covers with him. "Wake up. I've got to go."

He blinked up at me drowsily, further increasing his appeal. Aubrey wore a similar look. "Huh? Too . . . early."

"Not that early. I'm late for work."

He stared at me blankly for a few seconds and then sat up nearly as rapidly as I had. "Oh. Oh man."

"It's all right. Let's go."

He disappeared into the bathroom, and I shape-shifted my appearance once more, turning the pajamas into a red sweater and black skirt, my loose hair into a neat bun. I hated doing this so often, much preferring to rifle through my own closet. Shape-shifting also burned through my energy stash that much more quickly, requiring more frequent victims. Unfortunately, time-crunches call for certain sacrifices.

When Seth returned, he did a double take at my appearance and shook his head. "Still can't get used to that."

I expected him to go home and sleep, but he went with me to the bookstore. Its coffee shop was his favorite place to write. As we walked into Emerald City Books and Café, I breathed a sigh of relief that neither my manager Paige nor Warren, the store owner, appeared to be around. Still, business had already opened for the day without me, and my chipper, morning-people coworkers made it impossible to sneak in without notice.

"Hey, Georgina! Hi Seth!"

"Georgina and Seth are here!"

"Good morning, Georgina! Good morning, Seth!"

Seth left to take up his writing station upstairs, and I made my way to the back offices. All of them were dark, which I found odd. No managers at all. Someone should have opened before me. I flipped on the light in my own office.

I was so fixated on figuring out what was going on that the demon took me completely by surprise.

Red-skinned and multihorned, he leapt out at me, waving his arms and making unintelligible grunting sounds. I yelped and dropped the things I'd been carrying, recoiling.

A moment later, my senses returned, and I walked over and smacked him on the side of the head as hard as I could.

Chapter 3

"You're such a dork, Doug!"

"Fuck, that hurt!"

Doug Sato, the other dysfunctional assistant manager here and one of the most entertaining mortals I knew, pulled off the rubber mask he'd been wearing, revealing the beautiful features he'd inherited from his Japanese ancestors. He rubbed his forehead, giving me a wounded scowl. Upon closer inspection, I saw that the mask was not that of a demon but rather Darth Maul from *The Phantom Menace*. I should have known. No self-respecting demon would have had that many horns.

"What are you doing?" I leaned down to pick up my scattered belongings. "Halloween was, like, a week ago."

"Yeah, I know. Everything's on sale. I got this for three dollars."

"You got ripped off."

"Boy, you're one to nag, Miss I-Show-Up-When-I-Feel-Like-It. You're lucky it's just me here."

"Why *are* you here?"

Doug and I held the same position. On days when we overlapped, we usually worked different shifts, not identical ones. It was for the best. We usually distracted each other enough to accomplish the work of one person. Sometimes less.

He grabbed the back of the rolling desk chair and impressively flipped his body into it, the impact of which caused the chair to roll half-way across the office. "Paige called me in. She's sick."

Paige, our manager, was about six months pregnant. "Is she okay?"

"Dunno. If she gets better, she'll come in later."

He spun around the room a few times, then rolled up to the desk and beat out a fast rhythm on it with his hands. I presumed the cadence was from one of his band's songs.

"Jesus, you're wound up today. You get lucky last night?"

"I get lucky every night, Kincaid."

"Whatever. Your demon mask was more believable than that."

"Okay, maybe I'm not getting lucky *every* night right now, but that's going to change. The group's getting fucking amazing."

"I've always thought you guys were fucking amazing," I stated loyally.

Doug shook his head, dark eyes almost feverishly bright. "Oh no. You can't even believe it now. We got this new drummer, and suddenly . . . it's just like, I don't know . . . we're doing things we've never done before."

I frowned. "Because of one drummer?"

"No, I mean, it's all of us. He's just one of the good things that's happened. It's like . . . everything's just clicking into place. You ever have days like that? When everything is perfect? Well, we're having weeks like that. Songs. Gigs. Style." His enthusiasm was palpable, and it made me smile. "We're even playing the Verona."

"Seriously?"

"Yup."

"That's a major venue. I mean, it's not like the Tacoma Dome or anything, but then, they wouldn't let you play there anyway if you didn't have a monster truck worked into the act."

He spun the chair around again. "You should come see it. A bunch of the other staff is. It'll be the greatest night of your life."

"I don't know. I've had a lot of great nights."

"Second best then. Unless you're thinking of joining my groupies. I'd let you be their leader, you know. You could always have first dibs on me."

I rolled my eyes, then turned pensive as the sex jokes reminded me of my recent Seth issues.

"Hey Doug, do you think men and women can date without having sex?"

He had been tipping way back in the chair and suddenly snapped forward. "Oh my God. You *are* thinking of joining the groupies."

"I'm serious. Two people dating without sex. Fact or fantasy?"

"Okay, okay. For how long? A week?"

"No. Like, months."

"Are they Amish?"

"No."

"Are they ugly?"

"Er, no."

"No."

"No what?"

"No, they can't do it. Not in this day and age. Why do you want to know?"

"No reason."

He cut me an arch look. "Of course not." He didn't know about Seth and me, but he did know me.

Our phone's intercom came to life just then, asking for backup on the registers.

"Paper rock scissors?" Doug asked, spinning the chair around again.

"Nah, I'll go. I should make up for my tardiness. Besides, I think you need to come down from your caffeine high. Or your megalomania high. Not sure which."

He flashed me a grin and turned to the paused game of Tetris on our shared computer.

Truthfully, I didn't mind going out anyway. I worked for the fun of it, not the money. Immortality was long, and vocation and daily work sort of regulated human existence, even if I wasn't technically human anymore. It just felt right to be doing something, and unlike so many other unfortunate souls in this world, I actually liked what I did for a living.

I checked in on Seth a few times as I worked throughout the day, drank a lot of white-chocolate mochas, and dealt with what was becoming a heavy flow of business as the holiday season grew ever closer. At one point, I finally did have to pull Doug out with me. I found him in our office, still playing Tetris.

I opened my mouth to make a joke about his work ethic and then caught sight of the computer screen. He played Tetris on a regular basis, so I was familiar with the game and his prowess, but what I saw now blew my mind. His score was the highest I'd ever seen, and he was at such an advanced level now that the pieces zoomed down the screen. I couldn't follow them. Yet, he caught and placed them all, never missing a beat.

"My God," I muttered. There was no way his hands and reflexes could be responding like that. The computer would probably implode at any moment. "I guess everything really is clicking into place for you lately."

He laughed, either at my pun or my astonishment. "Need me out there?"

"Yeah . . . though it seems so wasteful now compared to this . . . mastery. Like interrupting Michelangelo."

Doug shrugged obligingly, shut down the game, and followed me out. I think the computer was relieved. He and I worked together cheerfully for the rest of my shift. His good mood over the band's success kept him chipper and lively, making the day fly by. When it was time for me to go, I offered to close for him since he'd had to come in unexpectedly early. He waved me off.

"Forget about it. Go do something fun tonight."

As I was leaving the store, I passed a rack of magazines and saw a copy of the latest issue of *American Mystery*. In big letters, one of the headlines read: *Cady and O'Neill Return! Seth Mortensen gives us an exclusive novella.*

Eek. What a bad girlfriend I was. Seth had told me about this story's upcoming appearance, and I'd completely forgotten about it. It had just come out yesterday. Apparently being with him regularly was distracting me from his art. Before the publication of his last novel, I'd literally marked off days on my calendar until its release. Longing washed over me, but I knew I couldn't read this story tonight. Bastien had left me a cell phone message saying he'd stop by my place later, and I had a feeling he'd distract me for most of the evening.

Tomorrow, I promised myself. I'd read the story tomorrow.

I'd just settled in back home when Bastien showed up bearing Thai food.

"How was the literary world today?" he asked as we had a picnic on my living room floor. Aubrey watched sharply from a discreet distance, her eyes fixed covetously on a container of green curry. Pad Thai did nothing for her.

"Weird," I reflected, recalling sleeping in late, Doug's behavior, and the frenetic pace of early holiday shopping. "Yours?"

It was clear from his expression he'd been dying to tell me this from the moment he'd cleared my door.

"Fantastic. I moved into the house today. You should see the neighborhood. It's the American Dream and then some. Big appliances. Manicured lawns. Three-car garages."

"Three cars? Do you even have *a* car?"

"Sure do. Company car."

"Hmphf. No one ever gave me a company car."

"That's because you aren't on the verge of the Seduction of the Century. I even met her already."

"Dana?"

"First day, and she comes to me! Can you believe it? It's

like I don't even have to do anything. This operation just runs itself. I am its tool. Its plaything even—or rather, Dana's plaything."

"I don't know about that," I noted dryly, "unless you're going to add that she jumped on you and ripped your clothes off today too."

"Well, no. She actually just came by to welcome me to the neighborhood. But, she did also invite me to a party she's hosting. 'A Barbecue in November.' Charming, huh?"

"Adorable. Nothing I love better than eating hot dogs in the cold."

He elbowed me. "It's a theme, Fleur. It's fun. And it's all indoors. You know, you're turning into a regular cynic lately."

"Not cynical. Just still skeptical of this whole thing. It seems overly elaborate for what it is. A lot of work for one lay."

"One lay?" He tsked me and shook his head. "Let me see your laptop."

I retrieved it from my bedroom and returned to find Aubrey licking the edges of my plate. I shooed her away and handed Bastien the computer. A few quick clicks, and he soon had the Committee for the Preservation of Family Values' website open. Dana's organization. Most of her radio broadcasts were archived and available for download. He picked one, and we finished the rest of our meal to the sound of her rich, melodic voice.

The first broadcast concerned homosexuality. The CPFV maintained an appearance of sugarcoated goodness, a desire to help people and improve American life. Consequently, because being openly racist or sexist was not good for one's image anymore, the organization only espoused views slanted in those directions in subtle ways. Blatantly condemning homosexuality, however, was not entirely taboo yet—unfortunately—and the bulk of this broadcast involved Dana oozing on about the importance of "helping" those people to understand the true way both nature and God intended love to be. Toleration of such misguided lifestyles, she claimed, would lead to a breakdown in our families. The children. For God's sake, think of the children.

Her next broadcast damned the abominable state of today's clothing. School uniforms and fashion censoring were the only ways to go. How could we expect young girls to grow up with any self-respect when they walked around dressed like sluts? It led to sexual acts they weren't ready for, not to mention instilling in them the idea that their value came from appearance, not character.

I thought of the lacy purple thong I wore under my jeans just then. What was wrong with character *and* sex appeal?

The third one we listened to concerned the futility of teaching teenagers about safe sex and contraception. Abstinence training was the way to go. Keep them in pure ignorance. End of story.

"Enough," I said at that point. Her shallow, prejudiced values cloaked in so-called love and kindness unsettled the food in my stomach.

Bastien grinned. "Still think it's just one lay?"

I stretched back on my carpet, resting my feet on his lap. He massaged them for me. "I hate hypocrites, good or evil. Doesn't matter what they're touting."

"You should hear some of her background, some of the past issues she's advocated for with her group. Lovely stuff there—I researched her all day. I can pull it up for you."

I held up a hand. "No, please. I believe you. The bitch must fall, okay? If I had a sword, I'd tap your shoulders and send you off with my blessings."

He lay down beside me. "Well, why don't you take a front-row seat then? Come to the party with me. I'm sure no one would mind if Mitch brought his sister."

"Party on the Eastside? My blessing only goes so far."

"Oh, come on. Admit it. You have a perverse desire to

meet her in the flesh. Besides, it's been a while since you've seen me in action. You might pick up on a few things. Get some pointers."

Laughing, I rolled over on my side to better study him. "Like I need pointers from you."

He rolled to his side as well, smirking. "Yeah? Then prove it. Let's go out tonight. Let's go hunting."

My smile diminished. "What?"

"Just like the old days. We'll find some club, work up a sweat, then tag respective fixes for the night."

Bittersweet memories flashed into my brain, recalling the French cabarets of the nineteenth century. Bastien and I would go out in fine form, separate, and meet back in the morning to laugh and brag about our conquests. The game no longer held much appeal.

"I don't do that anymore. I told you that."

"Yeah, but you've still got to survive."

"I am surviving. I got a fix just a couple days ago. I'm set for a while."

Bastien scowled. "A few days ago? Bleh. This writer guy's making you boring."

"Hey, it has nothing to do with him. It's my choice."

"Sure."

"What's with the tone?"

"Not sure. I mean, I thought the whole writer-dating thing was amusing at first—even if he seems kind of dull and will probably only end up causing you pain. But now I'm starting to think it's indicative of a larger issue with you. I mean, there's the whole nice guy hang-up to begin with. Then you're, what? An assistant manager at a bookstore? Not to mention the fact that you have a cat."

Aubrey glared, and so did I. "There's nothing wrong with having a cat. And Seth isn't dull."

"I suppose you'd know better. He just didn't really strike me as much, that's all. If you wanted to obsess about a mortal, I could find you a better one."

"I don't want a better one. I mean, there is no better one. I want him."

"Suit yourself. You're just becoming ordinary, that's all. You used to be extraordinary."

"Ouch. All this because I won't go out with you tonight?" Bastien shrugged.

"Okay then. We'll go. But no victim for me."

"Fair enough."

We went down to a club in Pioneer Square, both of us groomed to the kind of sexy, beautiful perfection that only an incubus and a succubus could achieve. I had pulled my hair up in messy, sex-kitten glory and wore a baby blue tank top with a V-neck that almost went to my belly button. The opening was covered in very sheer lace and made wearing a bra utterly pointless. So I didn't.

The tension between us evaporated as we hit the dance floor. The rhythm pulsed through me, the movement and sweat intoxicating. Bastien and I danced together for a while, both of us aware of the admirers we drew, even in a packed room like this. Physical attraction was about so much more than just superficial appearance. It was about eye contact, outgoingness, and movement too. Incubi and succubi learn this early on, and the good ones move with a grace few mortals can match. I, who had danced well before becoming a succubus, knew I was among the best when it came to body language. Watching us was irresistible. A turn-on in itself.

After a while, we split up. The results of the succubus game distressed me sometimes, but the game itself was fun. Very fun. I moved from partner to partner, thriving on the effect I created, on the desire I could see mounting in those whose bodies mine toyed with. It was why, despite my frequent bitching, I had given up my mortal soul for this vocation.

I confess, that the thought of going home with someone grew tantalizing, my body warming to the idea of someone's hands upon me, but then I thought about Seth and his determined adherence to the arrangement we'd entered into. No. No superfluous victims for me tonight. I could be good. I wanted to be good. I'd wait until I actually needed a recharge.

From across the room, Bastien inclined his head to me when he left the club, his arm around a small, entranced blonde. When he turned, I noticed a brunette in his other arm.

Overachiever.

It was two in the morning when I finally made it home. I woke aching and tired the next day, the weather making me feel worse. Rain formed a steady gray curtain as I walked to work. Everything seemed colder. I had been raised in a warm Mediterranean climate; I could never quite accept these kinds of temperatures.

When I showed up at the bookstore, it had once again opened without me. Oddly, though, despite exactly the same staff working today, I didn't get the same boisterous greetings as yesterday.

Casey and Janice, on the registers, paused in their work to watch me walk in, their expressions enigmatic. Janice leaned over, murmuring something in the other woman's ear. When they noticed my curious look, they both forced smiles. "Hey, Georgina."

"Hey," I responded, puzzled and slightly uncomfortable.

Passing by the information desk a moment later, I found Beth regarding me with an equally peculiar look.

"How's it going?" I asked when she didn't say anything.

"Fine." She hastily turned to the computer screen in front of her.

Now, I'd been subjected to my share of strange looks upon coming into work before, but this was weird even for me.

Sometimes, after being with a lover, their absorbed life energy gave me a glamour that unconsciously attracted mortals. It was the same glow that Hugh had teased me about during poker. That was not to blame now, however. My last fix, as I'd told Bastien, had occurred a few days ago. The glow would have weakened by now. Besides, I know entranced looks when I saw them. These were not it. These were curious, what-is-she-doing looks. The kind of looks you get when you have food on your face or a missing button. The likelihood of either of those seemed low, but I ducked into the restroom anyway, just to check.

Nope. Flawless. A long denim skirt and a navy, off-the-shoulder sweater. Both smooth and perfect. Makeup in place. Unbound hair hanging to the bottom of my shoulder blades. A typical look for me. Nothing to warrant this attention.

Assuming I was reading too much into things, I continued on to the café, getting a friendly nod from Seth as he worked in his corner. At least he was behaving normally.

A new barista bustled at the espresso bar, and she nearly dropped the cups she held upon seeing me.

"H-hi," she stammered out, wide-eyed, looking me over from head-to-toe.

"Hi," I returned. This woman didn't even know me. Why was she acting weirdly too? "Medium white-chocolate mocha."

It took her a moment to churn into action, writing my order on a cup. As she rang it up at the register, she asked curiously, "You're Georgina, right?"

"Um, yeah. Why?"

"Just heard of you, that's all." She looked back down.

She said no more to me after that, simply making and handing me the mocha. Taking it, I walked over to Seth and sat across from him. The barista continued watching us with interest, though she immediately turned away upon catching my eye.

"Hey," Seth greeted me, eyes and fingers busy.

"Hey," I returned. "Everyone's acting really weird today."

He glanced up. "Are they?" I immediately recognized the thrall he fell into when his writing seized him. He became even more distracted and scattered than usual under such conditions. A succubus should be so lucky to have that kind of effect on a man.

"Yeah. Have you noticed anything? I feel like people are staring at me."

He shook his head, stifling a yawn before returning to typing. "Things seem the same to me. I like your sweater. Maybe it's that."

"Maybe," I conceded, slightly mollified by the compliment, even if I didn't believe it. Not wanting to distract him further, I stood up and stretched. "I should get back to work." Glancing over at the espresso bar, I noticed Andy, one of the cashiers, buying coffee. "There!" I hissed to Seth. "Did you see that?"

"See what?"

"Andy just smirked."

"No he didn't."

"He *did*. I swear it."

When I went downstairs, back to the main part of the store, I passed Warren. Mid-fifties and strikingly handsome, the store's morally questionable owner had once been a regular for me before I'd promised Jerome I'd go back to seducing good men. Warren and I had not had sex in some time. Considering my current regiment of decent souls, I kind of missed having an occasional guilt-free one.

"Hello, Georgina." I was relieved to see he at least didn't give me any of those gaping looks. "Been up talking to Mortensen, I presume?"

"Yes," I agreed, wondering if I was going to be chastised for not getting to work right away.

"Pity you had to take the stairs. We do have an elevator, you know."

Now I stared open-mouthed. Of course we had an elevator. It was key operated, there for handicapped customers and shipment transport, and was almost never used otherwise. "Yes. I know that."

Warren winked at me and continued on his way upstairs. "Just making sure."

Shaking my head, I went back to the main floor and took over a register, giving Andy his lunch break. Janice and Casey remained stiff with me at first, eventually warming somewhat as time progressed. Other staff, moving in and out around me, continued to give me wondering looks, occasionally whispering to each other when they thought I wouldn't notice.

When Seth passed by at one point to tell me he had to run errands but would see me later, I thought Beth—dropping off a book—might pass out.

"All right," I exclaimed once Seth was gone, "what's going on here?"

Casey, Beth, and Janice all turned sheepish.

"Nothing, Georgina, honest." Beth gave me what was apparently supposed to be a winning smile. The others remained silent, faces perfectly innocent, nigh angelic.

I didn't believe any of it, of course. Something weird was going on. Weirder than usual. I needed answers, and there was only one person in the store candid enough to give them to me. Shutting down my register, I stormed back to my office where Doug sat occupied by the computer.

Bursting in, I opened my mouth, ready to rant and rave. He jumped about two feet in the air at my sudden arrival, reflexes kicking in with astonishing speed so as not to slosh coffee from the cup he had just raised to his lips. There was a funny look on his face, almost like guilt. No doubt another Tetris game was in progress.

But it wasn't that that delayed my tirade. A strange feeling was creeping along my flesh—a feeling that brushed my immortal senses, rather than the usual five that accompanied a human body. It felt weird, almost uncomfortable. Like nails raking down a chalkboard. Nothing I could identify or had even ever felt before. I looked around the room, half-expecting to find another immortal lurking, even though that strange sensation didn't quite touch me like the signature I'd usually feel off of an individual.

Doug drank from the cup and then set it down, watching me with bemused calmness. "Something I can help you with, Kincaid?"

Blinking, I gave the office another once-over and then

shook my head. The feeling disappeared. What the hell? I could have blamed it on stress-induced imagination, but after over a millennium of succubus life, I doubted my immortal senses would start falling prey to hallucinations now. And yet the only thing in here that could possibly be construed as supernatural or divine was Doug's Tetris mastery. That, I thought wryly, had more to do with hours of skirting work than any sort of magic.

Remembering my righteous fury, I pushed aside that momentary weirdness and ratcheted my anger back up to the *other* weirdness in my life.

"What the fuck is going on?" I exclaimed, slamming the door.

"My sweet Tetris skills?"

"No! With everyone! Why is everyone treating me so strangely today? They keep staring at me like I'm a freak or something."

Doug's expression stayed baffled, and then I saw understanding flood his face. "Ah. That. You really don't know?"

I could have grabbed his neck and shook him. "Of course I don't know! What's going on?"

Casually, he moved some papers around on the desk and lifted up a copy of *American Mystery*. "You read Seth's story yet?"

"I haven't had time."

He tossed me the magazine. "Do it. Go take your dinner break somewhere—not here—and read. I won't leave until you get back."

Looking at the time, I realized his shift was nearly over. "But what's that got to do with—"

He held up a hand to silence me. "Just read it. Now."

Scowling, I took the magazine and left the store, settling myself at one of my favorite cafés down the street. With clam chowder secured, I turned to the first page, wondering what in the world Doug expected me to find.

As Seth had explained a few weeks ago, the story was

more of a self-contained mystery, dealing little with the over-arching psychology and development of his characters. Cady and O'Neill worked for a fictitious institute based out of Washington, D.C., one that researched and secured archaeo-logical and artistic relics. Thus, the two often found them-selves liberating art from international thieves or uncovering mysterious code on a piece of pottery. In traditionally gen-dered styles, Bryant O'Neill worked as a sort of field agent, doing most of the physical work, getting into a lot of fist-fights and whatnot. Demure Nina Cady focused on the re-search, often staying up late to unravel some key piece of evidence in an ancient text.

This particular story contained a lot of those same ele-ments, but like always, Seth's beautiful writing and quick, witty dialogue kept the material captivating. In another trend consistent with his characters' behavior, O'Neill almost al-ways got involved with some beautiful woman, though Seth's last book had turned this pattern on its head, letting Cady fi-nally see some action. The story I read today fell into old ways, and O'Neill, in his ever suave manner, made the moves on a stunning museum curator:

Genevieve sauntered through the halls, a queen among subjects, surveying people and displays with both calculation and command. With those green-flecked hazel eyes, she put him in mind of a cat siz-ing up its next meal. He felt exactly like prey as she paused in front of him, favoring him with a languid look that oozed over his body, her tongue lightly moistening bee-stung lips.

Oh God, to be a mouse, he thought.

"Mr. O'Neill," she purred, brushing a lock of that shining hair away from her face. Faint streaks of honey laced those pale brown strands, like gold veins in ore. He wanted to bury his face in it. He wanted to taste it. "You're late."

Despite nearly a foot separating their heights, he felt like the underling here, like he should do penance for his tardiness and kneel in her presence. Not that he would mind that so much, he decided, trying not to stare at the way her dress's thin material molded itself to her hips and full breasts. Those breasts, he decided, were perfect. Definitely impressive in size, but not grotesquely out of control. And their shape . . . ah, even a master sculptor could never have duplicated those exquisite curves . . .

Realizing she expected a response, he filed his base thoughts away under *L* for *Later* and gave her an unruffled smile.

"My apologies." Now probably wasn't the time to mention the attack back at his hotel. "But I never rush anything. At least not when a woman's involved."

With that being only the mildest of the suggestive dialogue, I wasn't surprised when things escalated between them near the end of the story. After all, I thought dryly, it wouldn't be a true Cady and O'Neill experience if someone didn't score. And man, did he score. The feline comparisons were right on because Genevieve was a cat in heat. She ended up tying O'Neill up in an elevator, performing an array of kinky acts on him that made even me raise an eyebrow. I was surprised *American Mystery* hadn't edited them out, though I'd be lying if I said it wasn't sort of a turn-on to realize such sordidness had come from mild, complacent—

Elevator?

We do have an elevator, you know, Warren had told me.

Light brown hair. Hazel-green eyes. Petite. Nice breasts.

"Ahh!" I cried, dropping the magazine as if it might bite me. It landed next to my now-empty bowl, and a passing waitress gave me a startled look. Hastily leaving a wad of cash on the table, I grabbed my coat and purse and sprinted back to the bookstore. Doug was still playing Tetris in our office, but I was too upset to speculate much on what was again an amazing performance.

All those looks. The whispers and smirks. It all made sense now.

"They think it's me!" I told him, making him jump for the second time that day. "Genevieve. They all think I'm some sort of horny, rope-wielding, elevator-fetish dominatrix!"

Doug raised an eyebrow. "You mean you aren't?"

Chapter 4

"Doug!"

He shrugged. "It's not a big deal. I mean, it's pretty hot, really."

"But I didn't do those things. It's not really me."

"She sounds just like you. Her name begins with a *G* too."

"But it's not . . ." I swallowed, noting the similarities as well.

Doug watched me appraisingly. "You can't really blame them. Description-wise, you two match, and everyone knows you and Mortensen are chummy—not to mention what a zealous fan you are and all. After they read the story, Casey even made the brilliant observation that you guys came in together yesterday. You should have seen the speculation that started."

"But . . . that was nothing." No one at work even knew Seth and I were dating. I hadn't wanted that widely known. "We hadn't done anything."

Doug shrugged again, rising from the computer. "Too bad. I wouldn't have thought less of you if you had, you know. It's your business anyway."

I groaned. "Not when it's in print for everyone to see."

"I thought it was all fictitious," he reminded me with a sly grin, putting on his coat.

"It is! Doug, what am I going to do?"

"Don't know, Kincaid. I'm sure you'll figure something out. Maybe start with asking Mortensen why he's putting his fantasies on display for everyone to see." He tweaked my cheek, and I squirmed out of his reach. "As for me, I've got a rehearsal to get to. Big night tomorrow. Later."

My shift proceeded miserably after that. Now that I knew what the looks were for, the experience moved into a whole new realm of humiliation. I hated idle speculation, hated people thinking terrible things about me. I mean, it wasn't like I *hadn't* ever tied someone up before or had sex in an elevator, but come on. It wasn't the kind of thing I wanted people to consider publicly. I liked to keep my intimate affairs discreet.

I therefore stayed in the office as much as possible, only going out to help when absolutely necessary, and to check if Seth had returned yet. Finally, a couple hours before closing, I saw him back at his table. I sat down opposite him in a rage, not even caring what others would think of us being together.

"Why did you do it? Why did you write me in like that?"

Seth looked up from his laptop, his expression clearly implying whatever writing he was working on still held his attention more than I did. For all I knew, I was at the center of an orgy in some novel now. "What?"

"The story!" I threw *American Mystery* onto the table loudly. "You wrote me in. I'm Genevieve."

He blinked. "No you aren't."

"Oh yeah? How come both our names begin with a *G*? How come we look alike?"

"You don't look anything like her," he countered.

"That's not what half the store thinks. They think she's me! They think you've written up a fling we had in an elevator."

Realization flashed across his face, and to my horror, he actually smiled. "Really? That's funny."

"Funny? It's terrible! They all think I'm a bondage freak."

"Thetis," he began gently, still damnably serene, "I—"

"Don't 'Thetis' me. It won't work."

"I wrote that story, like, six months ago. Long before I met you. The publishing world doesn't move that fast."

"Well, the others don't know that." I hovered on the verge of tears.

"I'd never write in anyone so blatantly."

"Yeah? Well, they don't know that either," I said, slouching back against my chair miserably, arms crossed.

Seth sighed, his amber brown eyes compassionate as he regarded me. "Look, do you want me to say something? Tell them that it wasn't you?"

"Lord, that would just convince them even more that it was me. Besides, what are you going to do, call a press conference to clear my name?"

"I'm sorry," he told me seriously. "I never thought anything like this would happen." A hesitation. "Do . . . do you still want to go out tomorrow night? I mean . . . if you don't . . ."

The old adorable shyness fell over him, and I couldn't stay mad.

"No," I told him. "I still want to go, but . . . I think we should, you know, show up at the concert separately. Most of the staff will be there, you know."

He opened his mouth to speak but then reconsidered. I suspected he had been about to accuse me of overreacting, but apparently my radiating fury made him think better of it. Seth wasn't exactly the confrontational type. Or, considering the mood I was in, perhaps he just wasn't the stupid type.

"Okay," he finally said. "We'll meet there."

"Georgina?"

Looking up, I saw Paige standing over us, disapproval all over her face. I hadn't even noticed her approach. She wore another of her beautiful power suits, this time in an electric violet that looked stunning with her dark skin.

"Can I speak to you for a few minutes?" she asked, tone grim. "In private?"

I followed her to her office, letting her close the door behind us. Not surprisingly, a copy of *American Mystery* sat on her desk.

"So," she began crisply, "I've been hearing some rumors—"

"Damn it. It's not me."

I proceeded to relate to her my own recent discoveries, pointing out Seth's observation concerning how long it took for works to come out in print. When I finished, I think I had mostly convinced her of my innocence, though sordid stories flying around the workplace still obviously distressed her.

Studying nothing in particular, Paige drummed her lacquered red nails against the desk as she thought about what to do. "This will get cleared up with the staff in time. That, or they'll just get over it. What I don't like is the idea of any outsiders drawing conclusions. You *do* sound like that character, and anyone else who reads the story could make the same mistake. I don't want rumors starting that half of Seth's reason for working here is that he gets sexual favors on the side, courtesy of our employees."

"Oh Lord." I covered my face with my hands, wondering how celebrities dealt with truly large-scale scandals. This small one was bad enough. I wanted to disappear. It tainted the beauty of what Seth and I were trying to build.

"I think the best way to approach this is—"

Her words dropped off as a grimace crossed her face and one hand clutched her stomach.

I started toward her. "Are you okay?"

She nodded, forcing a strained smile. "It . . . it's nothing."

"The hell it is. You should call your doctor . . . or at least go home."

"No, it'll pass. Besides, I've got too much to do. I need to make the new schedule and go over some inventory stats."

"That's crazy. I can do that stuff."

She shook her head, arguing again, and I argued right back. At last, Paige yielded, which only verified something must be seriously wrong. Those who went head-to-head with her rarely won.

So, I finished my shift doing her extra jobs and serving as backup. It was exhausting, but I was happy to do it, still worrying about her and her baby. When we closed, I headed straight over to the suburbs, following the directions Bastien had given me.

When I pulled up to his house, I could only sit in my car and stare for a few minutes.

Now, I had a few well-formed ideas about the American Dream. After all, I'd been alive in the days when the term was first coined. I'd seen it arise, seen the mythology that surrounded it, seen the white picket fences and cute, well-kept neighborhoods. I'd even watched *Leave it to Beaver*. Seth's brother, for example, lived north of the city and had a pretty nice chunk of it carved out.

But this? This was an American Wet Dream.

Bastien's house went on forever, expanding ostentatiously beyond its marble and taupe façade. Even if he'd had a wife and family, I doubted they could have filled it up, and anyway, the kind of people who lived in these places didn't have large families. After all, this was the generation that had, what, 1.75 kids?

The garage had three doors, as advertised, and tasteful shrubs and ornamental trees decorated the lawn. Since it was dark now, I couldn't see the rest of the neighborhood in detail, but I suspected I'd find more of the same. One house, next door, was lit up and busy with people. It was even bigger than Bastien's and probably the location of the party.

"Are you compensating for something?" I asked when the incubus opened his door.

Mitch Hunter flashed me the million-dollar grin. "My sweet sister, you and I both know that's not true. Love your haircut."

I'd come as Tabitha Hunter, lean and blond, though I'd conceded to his earlier complaints and given myself shoulder-length hair. He kissed my cheek and ushered me inside for a quick tour.

After a few rooms, it all started blurring together. Cherry hardwood floors. Gorgeously painted walls. Sleek black appliances. Wainscoting. A hot tub out back. Enough guest bedrooms to house a Girl Scout troop. And cute, cleverly placed knick-knacks everywhere.

"Isn't this going a bit far?" I asked, pointing to a framed copy of the Lord's Prayer in the foyer.

"Tabitha, my love, man cannot survive on bread alone. We can, however, survive on delicious appetizers and hamburgers, so let's head over."

We arrived considerably after the starting time, since I'd been at work, and the party was in full swing. Maybe I shouldn't have been so quick to dismiss these suburbanites after all.

"Mitch!" called a loud voice as we shouldered our way through the people. Most were dressed for the barbecue theme in shorts, T-shirts, and Hawaiian prints.

"Hey, Bill," returned Bastien, extending his hand to a plain yet well-groomed man with silver-streaked black hair. I recognized him from his photos. Dana's husband. "This is my sister, Tabitha. Hope you don't mind me bringing her."

"No, no! The more the merrier, I say." He allowed a small, artificial laugh and smiled at me, making his eyes crinkle. "Especially ones so pretty. Makes me wish I was a younger man," he teased with a wink.

Unable to resist, I looked up at him through my lashes and said demurely, "I've always thought age was kind of irrelevant, Bill." I held onto his proffered hand. "I know I'm always happy to learn from those with more . . . experience."

His eyes widened slightly, lighting with both intrigue and alarm.

"Well," he said after an uncomfortable moment, "I should

probably spread myself around." He remembered to let go of my hand. "Feel free to find something to eat, and don't forget to try the pool."

He glanced at me and my come-hither smile consideringly, hesitated, and then reluctantly departed.

"Don't ever do that again," hissed Bastien, steering me toward the kitchen by the arm.

"Do what?"

"Flirt with this group! You're supposed to be bolstering my wholesome image, not leading on my target's husband."

"I wasn't leading him on. Besides, what's it matter? Scandalize them both."

"No. Dana only. My show."

I cut him a look but said nothing. He wanted me as an observer but not a participant. It figured. All the glory for himself, praise from those above. He'd always had this competitive need to make himself shine. It was one of the things that I liked about him—an eager desire to prove himself the best. I guess I'd had it once too, but not anymore. As far as I was concerned, he was welcome to all the fame and fortune of this gig.

"Just play my sweet, angelic sister," he continued in a whisper. "Possibly my sweet, angelic, and *frigid* sister."

Moving through the house gave me a chance to take in more of the party's theme. Faux palm trees. Glittering, decorative suns everywhere. Small appetizer tables set up here and there, laden with deviled eggs, cocktail wieners, and cubed cheese. It was silly in some ways, but someone had obviously paid a lot of attention to detail. I appreciated that. All of the guests looked like Bill—and Bastien and me, I realized. Clean-cut, with every hair in place. High quality, conservative clothes (in a tropical sort of way). Upper-class. White.

They freaked me out.

The kitchen proved to be the true hub of food, and I decided to simply gorge myself rather than risk more conversation that might upset Bastien. I loaded up a paper plate with a hamburger, potato salad, and some kind of weird Jell-O-fruit-whipped-cream hybrid dessert.

My efforts to simply eat unnoticed proved futile, as I soon found myself surrounded by a group of women. I didn't know where they'd come from. One minute I was just eating, the next minute six perfect faces were smiling at me. They were like a pack of wild dogs, yipping nonstop, honing in on lone prey. They'd even managed to separate me from Bastien, all the better to tear me apart. The incubus now stood across the room with a similarly ravenous group of men, no doubt discussing cigars and lawn mowers. I shot him a panicked look, but he merely shrugged.

"Mitch's sister," oozed one of the women. "I should have known! You guys look exactly alike."

"Well, not *exactly* alike," tittered another. She wore an appliqué sweater vest. Yikes.

"We were just talking about stamping. Do you stamp, Tabitha?"

"Um, like use stamps?" I asked with a frown. "I mean, I mail things . . ."

The Stepford Wives giggled again at this. "Oh! That's so funny."

"We mean rubber stamps. Arts and crafts stamps," explained one of them. She'd introduced herself as Jody—the only name I could remember among the group. Probably because she seemed to have a slightly higher IQ than the rest. And was the only one of us without blond hair. "You use them to decorate things."

She dug into her purse and produced a small invitation on beautiful ivory cardstock. Scrolling vines and flowers decorated the front.

"This is the invitation Dana made for this party."

I stared. "Seriously?"

Somehow I'd imagined the "Great Job!" kind of stamps

that teachers used on well-written papers. This was beautifully inked and in different colors. It looked professional, like something from Hallmark.

"Mitzi's having a stamp party next week," exclaimed one of the other women. "We could show you how to do it."

"Ooh . . . that would be so fun!"

"Yes! Let's!"

"Gee, it looks kind of time-consuming," I told them, wishing desperately that I was somewhere else. I was sure I could have held my own in a cigar and lawn mower conversation better than a stamping one. "I don't think I have the time."

"Oh, but it's so worth it," one assured me earnestly. She wore earrings that spelled *ALOHA* in dangling letters. "Betsey and I made bridal-shower invitations for her sister all day yesterday, and the time flew by."

"Did you use those cute dove stamps?" cooed another, not unlike a dove herself. "I spent all Tuesday looking for those at the mall."

"Don't you guys work?" I asked, wondering at their frequent use of "all day." A century ago, I wouldn't have given it a thought. But this was the age of the so-called modern woman. We weren't supposed to lounge around in parlors anymore and pass out from wearing corsets.

They turned to me, mouths agape.

"Well, there's so much to do around the house," Jody finally said. "Most of us are too busy with those things."

Like stamping?

"Besides," laughed Bitsy or Muffin or whatever the hell her name was, "it's not like we need to. Do you have a job?"

"Well, yeah . . ."

"What's your husband do?"

"Oh. I'm not married."

This got more stares, and then suddenly they erupted with ideas and suggestions of "perfect single men" who worked with their husbands.

I *had* to get out of here. Either that or render myself unconscious with the wrought-iron pig wearing an apron that sat on the kitchen table.

I turned anxiously to Jody. "Didn't I hear there was a pool somewhere?"

She brightened. "There sure is. I'll show you."

We extracted ourselves from the others, and she led me toward the back of the house.

"Sorry if they're a little overwhelming," she apologized. "I sort of feel responsible for their stamping frenzy."

The fact that she'd used the word "frenzy" to describe them made me laugh. "How so?"

"I got them into it." Her dark eyes twinkled. "Never thought it'd go this far, though. I used to be an elementary art teacher, and sometimes they remind me of the kids. They're all good souls, though."

"Why don't you teach anymore?" Drawing pictures with children sounded like a wicked cool job to me. If nothing else, the grading had to be easy.

"Well, Jack likes me at home, and this way I get to take out my artistic urges on the house—and enable the neighbors. Every time I get hooked on a new project, our house takes the brunt of it: pottery, beading, watercolors . . ."

"And stamping?"

She laughed. "And stamping."

"Could you, like, teach part-time and still get everything done around the house?"

"Maybe. But I've also got my CPFV duties, so my schedule's pretty packed."

CPFV? Damn. For a minute there, Jody had seemed like a pretty cool person. "You're a member?"

Her expression registered mild surprise. "Yes, of course. We all are. You should come to a meeting someday. I know Dana would love to have you."

"Where *is* Dana?" I hadn't even seen the main attraction tonight. "I mean, I'm such a fan and all. When Mitch told me we were coming, I couldn't even believe it."

Pursing her lips, she glanced around with a cute frown. "I'm not really sure where she is. She's probably just mingling. Everyone wants to talk to her. But don't worry—you'll see her before you leave."

"That'd be great."

She smiled and gave my hand a quick squeeze. "I hope we get to see you around. Oh—here we are."

We arrived in a massive, glass-encased sunroom containing a crystal blue pool. It looked lovely and inviting. When Jody asked if I had a suit, I assured her I had one under my clothes and thanked her for helping me. She returned to the main party, and I slipped into a bathroom where I shapeshifted into a turquoise bikini.

Some people eyed me curiously, probably wondering who I was, but they left me alone once I was in the pool. I dove under, swimming laps, enjoying the solitude water offered. It had been a long time since I'd been able to do this. I knew Seth swam at a local health club; he said it helped clear his head sometimes. He and I would have to go together one of these days. Or better yet, swim in the ocean somewhere. Yes, that was the way to go. Moonlit beaches and tropical air, away from this crummy rain. Maui. Cancún. Hell, why did we even have to constrain ourselves to North America? We could go to the French Riviera, the Greek Islands . . .

I was so caught up in my fantasies that when I climbed out of the pool, I didn't notice the woman in front of me. I sidestepped, ever quick on my feet, just barely avoiding collision.

"Sorry," I said. "I didn't see—"

I froze. It was Dana.

She looked exactly like her promotional pictures. Slim, average height, shoulder-length black hair, and penetrating blue eyes. Her bio placed her in her forties, but she looked a lot younger than that. The result of all that clean living, I supposed. She wore khaki shorts and a green T-shirt, modestly covered by a white button-up blouse tied in a knot over her stomach.

A smooth, cool smile settled on her face, and those eyes reminded me of a hawk seeking out prey.

"No harm done," she said in that same hypnotic radio voice. "I don't think we've met. I'm Dana." She extended a hand, and I took it.

"Yes. Of course you are. I mean, I know you are. I've seen your pictures. Er, I mean, I'm a fan and all . . ."

"And you are . . . ?"

"Oh. Sorry. I'm Tabitha Hunter. Mitch's sister. Though maybe you knew that. Everyone says we look alike. I guess we do. I've never really thought about it . . . much . . ."

Ye gods, why was I rambling like this? I had worked dukes and bishops who were ten times scarier than her. They hadn't turned me into a blathering idiot. What was it about one radio bigot that should prove so unsettling?

The eyes, I decided. They reflected no warmth. They were shrewd. Conniving. The kind of eyes that warned she had not risen to where she was today without hypervigilance. The kind of eyes that had an agenda.

"It's nice to meet you," she said, still maintaining that too-perfect smile. "I didn't know Mitch had a sister. You seem to be . . . enjoying the pool."

Her eyes glanced down over me and back up, suddenly making me feel self-conscious. Water dripped most unflatteringly off of me, and I uneasily wondered if this suit showed too much skin. At least it wasn't white. Bastien's warning about wholesome image came back to me for real, and I understood his concern now. Looking like a strumpet could be bad for his reputation. If he drew whispers and disdain, he might be ostracized from this group and lose access to Dana. Suddenly, Dana's frostiness didn't seem so weird. It was disapproval. She had, after all, delivered a whole spiel on the abominable state of today's fashions. Here I was embodying it.

"It's very nice," I said. "One of the, um, best pools I've swam in."

I stopped before I could say something else even more asi-
nine, and silence fell. She looked as though she expected me
to continue and could wait all night until I did. Unfortunately, I had no idea what to talk to this weird woman about.
My alleged hatred of homosexuals? Ask if she had recom-
mendations for a more modest swimsuit?

"So, um . . ." I began. "This barbecue theme . . . it's really,
uh . . ."

I was saved just then—sort of—by Bastien. He strode up
to us, appearing very excited to have found Dana. A sharp
look in his eyes said he was less thrilled to see me, especially
in this state, but he kept it masked from the other woman, instead coming off as amiable and charming as ever.

"Ah, Tabitha, I see you've met our hostess."

"Yes," agreed Dana. "We've been having a most stimulat-
ing conversation. Your sister's quite the wordsmith."

I flushed. Bitch. When I was in my zone, I could outtalk
her any day.

"Glad to hear it. My Tabby Cat here is nothing if not stim-
ulating."

Oblivious to my horror over my new nickname, Bastien
steered her into some pleasant conversation about the creativity of the party and the beauty of her home. Her demeanor warmed up only a bit from what it was with me. She
still came off cool and watchful. Maybe she was always
chilly around people, and it wasn't just me. In fact, I thought
optimistically, this slightly elevated interest in Bastien might
indicate that she wanted to throw him up against a wall.

They conversed a bit longer about something I lost interest
in, and I tried to stay inconspicuous, though I could tell I
never dropped off Dana's radar. She was studying me, trying
to figure me out. Finally, Bastien said good-bye, and we
began our retreat toward the front door—once I'd changed
back to decent clothing, of course. Our exit proved more difficult than expected since apparently it was customary to say

good-bye to every single person you passed and get continually delayed by meaningless small talk.

"My God," I exclaimed once we were safely back at his place, "that was annoying."

He turned on me, anger flashing in those movie-star blue eyes. "Are you completely out of your mind?"

"Okay, you're right. I've been in more annoying situations. Remember that marquis' party back in Marseille?"

"That . . . that getup! When I first saw you two together, Dana looked ready to explode. Thank goodness this body's more flat chested than your other one. It saved you from looking like a complete pinup."

"I'm sorry," I told him. "I was just trying to escape those stamping women and headed for the pool without thinking. I have a suit just like this at home. It was stupid . . . but I don't really think it caused long-term damage." I hoped.

His expression darkened, and he threw himself into one of the living room's exquisite armchairs. It was covered in white suede. Breathing on it would probably get it dirty.

"I don't know. She was distant with me—you saw it."

"I was hoping that's how she always is. And she was a bit more responsive with you than me," I offered helpfully.

"No. You should have seen her when we spoke earlier tonight. Much friendlier. She definitely clammed up with you around."

"I'm sorry," I said again, feeling idiotic. "I guess I shouldn't take a front-row seat to this after all. I'm cramping your style. Or rather, destroying it."

His stormy expression lingered a bit longer, then disappeared like clouds swept away by wind. That was my Bastien. Quick to anger, quick to love. "No matter, Fleur. Takes a lot more than you to 'destroy my style.'" He patted his lap and grinned. "Come here, sis, and I'll tell you the rest of my brilliant plan."

I rolled my eyes. "Are we *that* kind of family?"

His smile broadened, and I sat down, unable to resist that goofy charm. He slung his arm around me in an old, familiar way, and I leaned into him. It was nice to have the touch and comfort of another living thing, romantic or not.

"So there's another part of this wacky plan?"

"Not so much another part as an entirely different plan. A backup plan, if you will."

"Oh no. Here it comes."

"Naturally, I'd much rather disgrace Dana in a horizontal kind of way, but in the very unlikely event that doesn't work, there's a much less exciting—yet effective—way to do it. And you're going to help me."

"How so?"

"We're going to break into her house."

Chapter 5

I jerked my head away from him.

"What?"

Bastien didn't miss a beat, obviously amused by my reaction.

"You heard me. We're going to break in. I overheard Bill saying the whole family would be out the night after next."

"And pray tell, how are we going to lead her to scandal through violating her home? By proving to the world that her security system isn't as good as she thought it was?"

He laughed. "No, by rifling through her paperwork and finding some sort of incriminating evidence. Money laundered from the CPFV. Illegal means of carrying out the group's goals. Maybe even love letters from the infamous pool boy. You know there's got to be something."

"Bastien, this is—"

"Ingenious?"

"Ridiculous. Even for us."

"Hardly. Like I said, it's a backup plan. Probably not even necessary, since I suspect she's probably in the shower right now masturbating to fantasies of me."

"Yeah, she sure looked like it back there," I said nastily. "More likely she's sanitizing her pool after my defilement of it. Well, backup or no, you're going to have to do this break-in on your own."

"Come on! We'll be invisible. Nothing to lose."

"That's not the point. The point is I don't do this kind of thing."

"We're agents of evil. We lead innocents into temptation and suck away their life. How is breaking and entering that much of a leap?"

I tightened my lips and shook my head.

"I thought those broadcasts pissed you off. Don't you want to see her fall?"

"Not enough, apparently."

He fixed me with a sharp stare. "Did you know that the CPFV recently kicked out a woman for leaving her husband? He had been beating her incessantly—sent her to the hospital twice. When she finally got the nerve to walk out on him, Dana condemned her for violating the sanctity of marriage. Said the woman hadn't tried hard enough to make things work."

I groaned. "Don't tell me this stuff."

"So are you in or out?"

"You sure are pushy, you know that?"

He kissed my cheek and hugged me. "I learned from the best."

I went to Doug's concert the following night, showing up about halfway through the opening act's set. I found several of the bookstore staff occupying a corner but saw no sign of Seth yet. Part of me regretted the whole separate-arrival mandate, but then I remembered the part in Seth's story where Genevieve had spanked O'Neill. Suddenly I didn't feel so bad anymore.

While waiting at the bar for a vodka gimlet, a familiar shape slid up next to me.

"Hey, hey, pretty lady."

I flashed a smile at Doug's bass player, Corey. "Hey yourself. You guys ready for this? You're in the big time now."

He returned my smile, eyes alight. Intimidating and fierce

looking, he wore a lot of black and had piercings everywhere. He was also one of the nicest guys I knew.

"Hell yeah, we are. We were born for this night. This is the night that's going to define our existence! The night that's going to define existence for everyone in this room!" He extended his hands over his head and whooped with delight, emitting something like a cross between Tarzan and a B movie Apache chief. The silvery glitter of those piercings added to his savage persona.

He was as exuberant as Doug had been the other day. Maybe more so. As much as I wanted to see the band succeed, there was no telling what true fame would do to them. They'd be bouncing off the walls. Setting things on fire.

When I got the gimlet, Corey tugged at my arm. "Come on. I'll give you a sneak peek backstage. You can say hi to Doug."

I glanced back at the corner, saw no sign of Seth, and followed him.

In the dressing room, the rest of the band was in similar form. They all knew me and cheered my arrival, holding up their drinks in a giddy salute. Doug was dressed in a spectacularly gaudy manner, sporting black spandex biker shorts, a Thundercats shirt Seth would have envied, and a sweeping red velour cape. His shoulder-length black hair was tied back in a sleek ponytail. He scooped me up as I entered, hoisting me so that I nearly sat on his shoulder. Min, the group's saxophonist, waved the instrument over his head in barbaric approval at my capture as Doug roared a cry of victory.

"Here she is! Kin-fucking-caid! You ready to rock, babe?"

"I'm ready to dump this drink on your head. Put me down."

Doug laughed and eased me down to the floor. I stumbled a bit but not from being set down.

It was here again.

That weird tingling feeling I'd felt with Doug in our office.

Only this time, it was stronger. Much stronger. It pulsed around me, almost making me squirm. I peered around stupidly, trying to figure out where it came from, but it was impossible to tell. The sensation was everywhere, an abrasive vibration singing through the air that only I seemed affected by.

Wyatt, a redheaded guitarist, grinned at me. "How much have you been drinking out there? You look a little glazed over."

"Starry-eyed's more like it," said Doug, teasing. "Not every day a girl can be around this much sexy action, huh?"

"Whatever. I think her sexiness is a little more lethal than ours," Wyatt said. He gently turned me around. "You met Alec yet?"

The new drummer, presumably. He stepped forward and bowed before me with a flourish, just as goofily wound up as the rest. He was a little younger than they were, a bit lanky, and had fading blue streaks in his blond hair. He seemed only slightly less keyed up. Still clueless about what was making me feel so weird, I attempted to push it out of my mind and offer Alec a normal smile.

"Hi," I said. "You sure you want to hang with this group of misfits?"

"I've seen worse."

"In an asylum?"

He laughed and nodded at my drink. "What are you having?"

"Vodka gimlet."

"Nice choice," he said coolly, though I suspected he'd probably never heard of one before. There was a total look of fumbling inexperience about him. "Order your next one on me. Tell the bartender to put it on my tab."

I worked hard to keep a straight face. He was attempting suave movie-star lines, but they lost some of their effectiveness coming from someone who was barely old enough to drink himself. He probably hoped Wyatt's earlier assessment of my inebriation was accurate.

"Hey," said Doug, grabbing hold of me. "Stop flirting with my Groupie Queen. Only when you can snatch the fly with the chopsticks, Grasshopper, can you accumulate the groupies. For now, the student must leave the groupies to the master."

Doug marched me around the room in a—very bad—mock tango. The jerking motion, combined with that grating buzzing in the air, made me lightheaded. "Is the rest of the gang out there?"

"Waiting with bated breath," I promised. I cocked my head at him. "Shouldn't you be a little more nervous than this?"

"Sure. If I had anything to be nervous about. Which I don't."

I felt just as astonished now as I had at work. Doug knew his own talent, but I'd seen him before shows in the past. While always joking and in a good mood, there had been a nervousness to him before, a private sort of ruminating while he mentally braced himself to put on the best show he could. I knew he'd said the band had hit some sort of peak recently, but the change was dramatic, to say the least.

After a few more jokes and sexual innuendoes, I finally left them. Just like that, the discordant feeling disappeared as soon as I cleared the door. It was like breathing fresh air after a sandstorm. Glancing behind me, I stared into the room, trying to find any indication of what had just happened. Nothing revealed itself. The band had forgotten me already. They were laughing at something else, drinking their beer or pop or whatever, and roughhousing in what must have been some male tension-reliever. Puzzled, I walked away.

Seth had joined the others when I finally made my way back to the main floor. I felt a smile creeping up on me in spite of my concerns. His hair was as unkempt as ever, and he wore a Thundercats shirt.

"Hey," I said when I saw him, conscious that everyone was watching us, apparently waiting for me to pull out my handcuffs.

"Hey," he returned, hands casually in his pockets, posture relaxed and easy like always.

"You know, Doug's wearing a shirt very similar to that."

"I know. I lent it to him."

We all shared a good laugh over that, and Beth turned to me. "You saw Doug? Is he ready for this?"

"The question, actually," I told them with a small frown, "is 'Is the world ready for Doug?'"

A half hour later, they saw what I meant. Nocturnal Admission burst onto the stage, and suddenly all that pent-up energy and enthusiasm was channeled into their music. Like I'd told Doug, I'd long been a fan of the group. Their style combined hard rock with a bit of ska, and the fusion always hooked me. After centuries filled with repetition, innovation was a treat. They regularly performed with flair and passion, making them as much fun to watch as to listen to. My biased affection for Doug didn't hurt either.

Tonight was unbelievable. All of their songs were new; I'd never heard any of them before. And Christ, what songs they were. Amazing. Incredible. Ten times better than the old ones—which I'd hitherto found hard to beat. I wondered when Doug had had time to compose these. He wrote most of their stuff, and I'd last seen them perform about a month and a half ago. He must have had help to write all of those in so short a time. I knew he usually took a while to compose one, refining lyrics over and over. He never treated the process lightly.

And the performance itself . . . Well, Doug was always flamboyant; it was his trademark. Tonight, I swear, he never stopped moving. Pure energy in human form. He danced, he sauntered, he did cartwheels. His between-song monologues were hilarious. His singing voice surpassed anything I'd ever heard from him, rich and deep. It resonated in my body. The audience couldn't get enough. They loved him, and I understood why. No one, even the people who worked there, could take their eyes off the stage.

Except one.

There, along the far edges of the crowd, was a man casually making his way toward the exit. By his stride and apparent lack of interest, he didn't find Nocturnal Admission as compelling as the rest of us. While this was intriguing enough to draw my own gaze from the band, his attire struck me even more strongly.

If *GQ* magazine had been around in the days of Victorian poets, he would have been their cover model. He wore beautifully tailored black slacks paired with a long, black coat, the tails of which almost touched the backs of his knees. Underneath the coat was a gorgeous, billowing white shirt that might have been silk. Whatever it was, it made me want to touch it and see how soft it was. Unlike Horatio, whose demonic wear had simply been out-of-date, this guy had taken the past and made it his own. His own hot historic couture. The kind the modern day "goth" movement so longed to achieve. He'd opened the first few buttons to reveal smooth, tanned skin. That skin tone paired with the glossy black hair that flowed halfway down his back made me think he must be of Middle Eastern or Indian descent.

When he reached the door leading out, he paused and turned toward the stage, watching the band for a few moments. A small, pleased smile played along his lips, and then he was gone.

Weird, I thought. I wondered who he was. Prospective agent maybe? Or perhaps just someone who didn't get down to this type of music. He had looked like the kind of guy who owned Chopin's complete works, after all.

I considered the man for a few more moments, then turned back toward the stage. The group was taking a momentary reprieve from their new stash and doing a cover of one of my favorite Nine Inch Nails songs. Nothing like hearing Trent Reznor's lyrics paired with a saxophone.

"I can't believe this," I told Seth later, moving to the back of our group so I could stand near him. Our friends were so hypnotized by what was onstage that Seth and I could actually talk without drawing attention. "It's . . . unbelievable."

"That it is," he agreed. "I take it this isn't the norm then?"

"No. Absolutely not. But I hope it becomes the norm. Jesus."

We fell silent then, our eyes and ears drawn back to the band. As we watched, however, Seth rested his hand on my back in a friendly, innocent gesture that made me promptly lose interest in the music. And that was saying something. The shirt I wore was hardly a shirt at all. It was a glittering tunic type thing that covered the front of me only, then tied behind my neck and once below my shoulder blades, thus letting his fingers stroke bare, exposed skin.

Less than a week ago, I'd been in a hotel room with a guy who'd massaged scented oil all over my body and then gone down on me in a way that left me gasping. And yet, I swear that didn't do as much for me as Seth's fingers on my bare skin did now. The rest of my body jolted to life, suddenly ravenous for more of him. When he trailed his fingertips down to my lower back, I could perfectly discern every place he had touched me and every place he hadn't, as though his fingers left scorch marks in my flesh. Magic fingers. Seductive fingers. My nerves pulsed hungrily, demanding I take action and give them more.

When his hand finally came to rest by my tailbone, right at the edge of my jeans, I murmured, "You can go lower if you want."

"No," he returned. His voice seemed huskier than usual, holding an unfamiliar intensity. But it was laced with wistfulness too. "I really can't."

The audience whooped and demanded an encore when the show ended, which the band was only too happy to give— multiple times. Talk about stamina.

As I watched them wrap up the song and make their bows, an idea suddenly struck me. Excusing myself for the bathroom, I headed back in the direction of the dressing room.

Once out of any passerby's eyesight, I turned invisible and slipped back into that room, still perplexed about that burning, crawling sensation.

It was gone. Everything felt perfectly normal in the room. Jackets and instrument cases lay in unceremonious heaps on the floor, and empty red plastic cups vied with overflowing ashtrays to cover up other flat surfaces. I paced around slowly, peering in corners, looking for something—anything—that would explain what I had felt. And again, I came up empty-handed. All was quiet and still. No person or creature waited to leap out, though I was pretty sure what I'd felt hadn't come from anything living. Yet, it also hadn't resembled any charm or enchanted object I knew of either. If anything, that tingle had felt like something in the middle: half sentient, half not. But that made no sense.

Returning to my friends, I saw them making preparations to leave. None of us could stop talking about the show. We separated and met up again at Doug's place for a post-show party he'd invited us to. I'd been to similar gigs of his but saw more people here than ever before. They packed the place. Alcohol and pot flowed like milk and honey, but I stopped after a couple shots since I had to open at work in the morning.

Through the smoky, decadent haze, the band worked the crowd like they'd done this sort of PR all their lives. They talked to everyone, charismatic and outgoing, though never too proud or conceited.

As this went on, Seth and I kept a respectable distance from each other in order to maintain the illusion we were nothing but friends. While I still believed that was a good idea, it sort of seemed like rubbing salt into open wounds. Bad enough we couldn't touch each other; now we couldn't talk either.

Alec found me at some point, attempting to resume the conversation we'd been having when Doug spirited me away. The drummer handed me a plastic cup.

"This guy over there knows how to make vodka gimlets," he said happily.

I sniffed the cup. It smelled like pure vodka. Probably a cheap kind at that.

"Thanks," I said, literally keeping it at arm's length.

Alec leaned against a nearby wall, propping his elbow against it to create a more enclosed sense of space between us. "So, did you like the show?"

"Yes. Absolutely. You guys were amazing."

His chest puffed up with pride. "Thanks. We've been working really hard. We've got some other big shows coming up soon—I hope you'll come see us."

"I will if I can. I seem to be working a lot lately."

"Over at that bookstore with Doug? I can't figure that out. Neither of you seem like that type. Especially you. You look like someone with a wild side. Someone who likes to party."

I kept my smile up and took a step back. "Sure. Just not on school nights, you know?"

Ignoring what I thought were obvious "back off" signs, he took a step toward me with a smile he probably believed was seductive. His clumsy attempts at flirtation suddenly seemed less endearing. "Come on," he laughed. "Call in sick tomorrow. I know somewhere . . . somewhere we could go if you really wanted to have a good time. A more intense scene than this."

"No. I can't. Sorry. Um, thanks for the drink, but I've got to go ask Doug . . . uh, something about work. I'll see you around."

Clear disappointment flashed across Alec's face at my rejection, but he didn't push the matter as I made a hasty retreat toward Doug. When I found him, he and I didn't really discuss work, but we hashed out a number of other amusing topics, made more so by his increasing intoxication and the fact that he really did now have an entourage of groupies. It looked like he'd be getting lucky after all. If he was still running on the same energy tonight, he'd probably keep a bunch of them happy.

Finally, tired of the scene, I told him good-bye and found Seth on the other side of the room. Not surprisingly, he was by himself and not drinking. He'd been born without the small-talk gene, and I knew for a fact interacting with others at parties made him uncomfortable. I had teased him in the past that he might actually be pleasantly surprised if he just made an attempt at talking to new people. He wouldn't have any of it, however. He seemed fairly entertained by people-watching, eyes twinkling and lips quirked in a half-smile as if he were in on some kind of joke the rest of us didn't know about. I wouldn't have been surprised if he was logging all of this for future novels.

"Hey," I said.

He brightened upon seeing me. The twinkling eyes took on a warm, knowing look. Something inside of me heated and tightened. "Hey."

"I'm ready to go. You want to come over to my place?" He deserved it after the way I'd neglected him tonight.

"Sure."

We were discussing who would leave first when I looked across the room and saw Alec handing Casey a drink. She looked like she'd already had more than enough, and Alec was doing the same closing-in maneuver he'd tried on me.

"What's wrong?" asked Seth, seeing my frown.

"That new drummer. Alec. He hit on me earlier, and now he's moving in on Casey. I think he's one of those guys who thinks plying girls with liquor is the only way to get laid."

"Wait. I thought I was the only guy who knew that secret."

I chastised him with a dry look before turning back to Alec and Casey. "I don't like it. I don't like him thinking he can do that to women."

"You don't even know he's thinking that. Besides, look around. Every guy here is trying to get laid. Alcohol is par for the course. Casey's old enough to know that."

"I'm going to go over there."

Seth gave me a warning glance. "She won't thank you for playing mother hen."

"Better she's mad at me than does something stupid."

"Thetis, don't—"

I'd already left him behind, weaving through the people as I honed in on my target.

". . . look like someone who likes to party," Alec was saying as I approached.

"Hey," I said loudly, sort of wedging my way in between them.

They both turned to me in surprise. "Hi, Georgina. What's up?"

"I'm heading home," I told her. "Wondered if you wanted a ride."

Casey smiled, glanced at Alec, then back to me. College-age, Casey was Hawaiian and Filipino, with high cheekbones and sleek black hair. Very pretty. "Thanks, but I'm gonna stay here for a while."

Alec looked very pleased with himself. I turned back to her.

"Okay, but can I ask you something real quick, Case?" I smiled sweetly at Alec. "It'll just take a minute."

I steered her away, catching her as she stumbled. Closer inspection revealed she'd been indulging in more than just alcohol.

"Casey," I told her, once we were out of earshot, "I don't think you should be hanging around with him."

"Why not? He's a nice guy."

"I don't know about that. He just used the same pick-up lines on me. I think he's trying to get laid."

"Every guy here is trying to get laid. I know the game."

"Yeah, but—"

"Look," she said, "I appreciate the big sister thing, but I'm not stupid. I can handle this." A mischievous look crossed her face. "Besides, I never would have thought *you* would be the one preaching sexual caution."

Like I didn't know what that was a reference to. Damn O'Neill's libido. I made a face and attempted a few more logical pleas. She rejected them all, indulgence soon giving way to annoyance. By then, Alec hadn't been able to control himself. He came back over and put a possessive arm around her. She looked up at him adoringly, and I knew a lost cause when I saw one.

Seth and I met up back at my place, and he listened with admirable patience while I vented about men preying on women.

"Isn't that what you do though?" We were sitting on my living-room floor, setting up a game of Scrabble.

"I . . . no. It's not the same at all."

"How so?"

He held my eyes for a moment, and I finally looked away. "It just isn't. Do you want to go first?"

He let the matter drop. Another nice thing about being with a nonconfrontational guy.

I quickly discovered playing Scrabble with Seth was like playing Monopoly with Jerome. A losing battle from the first turn. Admittedly, my knowledge of more than two dozen languages gave me a large vocabulary, but I didn't craft or manipulate words on a regular basis. Seth was a master. He could study the board, spend a minute calculating, and then play some word that was not only worth tons of points but interesting too. *Maize. Hexagon. Tawdry. Bisque.*

That last one was just cruel.

Meanwhile, I was spelling words like *as*, *lit*, *ill*, and *tee*. And almost never on high-point spaces.

"Wait," he said. "That's not a word."

I looked down to where, in a moment of desperation, I'd played *zixic* on a triple-word-score space.

"Uh, sure it is."

"What's it mean?"

"It's sort of like . . . quixotic, but with more . . ."

"Bullshit?"

I laughed out loud. I'd never heard him swear before.

"More zeal. Hence the z."

"Uh-huh. Use it in a sentence."

"Um . . . 'You are a zixic writer.'"

"I don't believe this."

"That you're zixic?"

"That you're trying to cheat at Scrabble." He leaned back against my couch, shaking his head. "I mean, I was ready to accept the whole evil thing, but this is kind of extreme."

"Hey, it's not cheating. Just because your limited vocabulary doesn't include this word doesn't mean there's anything sinister going on."

"Care to back that up with a dictionary?"

"Hey," I said haughtily, "I don't appreciate your zixistic tone."

"If you weren't such a zixy woman, I'd be angry."

"Your zixicism is infuriating."

The game forgotten, we spent the next twenty minutes coming up with as many *zix* variations as we could. Interestingly, it seemed to function just as well as a suffix as a prefix. I suspected that if Bastien had heard this conversation, I'd be accused of more boring geekiness.

Seth and I finally went to bed on the verge of hysterics, both of us still giggling once we were wrapped up in my covers.

"You smell good," I told him, my face close to his neck. "What cologne is that?"

He stifled a yawn. "I don't wear cologne. Too strong."

"You must." I pressed my face closer.

"Hey, be careful. You're giving me funny ideas."

He had skin and sweat smells unique to him and him alone, deliriously delicious. With that, however, was a faint scent of something else. Almost like apples, but not in a girly, boutique sort of way. It was fleeting and lovely, mingled with musk and soft leather.

"No, it's something. You must. Is it your deodorant?"

"Oh," he mumbled, yawning again. "I bet it's this soap Andrea and Terry got me. Came as part of some set."

"Mmm. It's perfect." It made me want to eat his neck— among other things. "You know, you still owe me pancakes. I think I could go for . . . apple cinnamon ones now."

"Apple cinnamon? You sure are demanding."

"It's all right. I think you're man enough for it."

"Thetis, if I actually believed you had either apples or cinnamon in your kitchen, I'd make them for you right now."

I didn't answer. I was pretty sure I had some year-old Apple Jacks, but that was about it.

Seth gave a low laugh at my silence and then kissed my temple. "I don't know how anyone could think you were Genevieve. I couldn't make up someone like you in a thousand years."

I considered that, not entirely sure if it was a compliment or not. "How do you come up with your characters then?"

He laughed again. "If I didn't know any better—and I'm sure I do—I'd say that sounds suspiciously like 'Where do you get your ideas from?'"

I blushed in the darkness. When he and I had first met, I'd taken a haughty high ground over that question, making fun of the fans that so often asked him that.

"Hey, it's a totally different question."

I could sense his amusement as he contemplated an answer. Part of the reason he stumbled in conversation sometimes was because he didn't like to blurt things out. He chose his words carefully.

"They come from my head, I guess. The stories too. They live there, screaming to get out. If I didn't write them down, they'd eat me up. Give me less of a grip on the real world than I already have."

"Not that I'm complaining . . . but, if there's so much inside, do you even need to care about the real world?"

"Well, that's the paradox. The stories are born in my head, but my inner self is fueled by my outer self. Symbiotic relationship of sorts. The stories' ideas wouldn't come if I didn't have experiences to draw on. Jealousy. Love. Lust. Anger. Heartache. All that stuff."

Something pulled inside of me. "You had your heart broken much?"

He paused. "Of course. Everyone does. Part of life."

"Tell me her name. I'll kick her ass. I don't want anyone hurting you."

He rested his face against my hair, his tone even and gentle when he spoke. "You're wondrous and powerful and gifted, but even you can't save me from hurting. No one can do that for anyone. I can make things perfect in the fictions I create, but the real world isn't so kind. That's just how it is. And anyway, for every bad thing in life, there are more good things to tip the balance."

"Like what?"

"Like little blonde nieces. And royalty checks. And you."

I sighed and relaxed into him. His grip on me shifted into something more comfortable, and in a few minutes he was asleep. Amazing.

I lay snuggled with him for a while, but sleep proved more elusive for me this time, as I turned over his words. I thought about someone breaking his heart and wondered if I'd be the next culprit, intentionally or otherwise.

When sleep came, I immediately dropped into a steamy dream in which Seth and I were having mad, passionate sex. He'd tied my hands to my bedposts, and naturally, he was huge. Each thrust made my headboard bang against the wall, so much so that my neighbors complained.

I woke up with a start, suddenly thinking being so entwined with him wasn't such a great idea. Of course, I was apparently the only one who had a problem with it. Seth slept on peacefully and heavily, like I wasn't even there, no doubt having properly chaste dreams. A paradigm of virtue and resolve.

I watched him for a long time, admiring the way the soft

lighting fell across his features. The fit muscles of his upper body. Eyelashes I wished I could have had as a mortal. Biting my lip, I resisted the urge to reach out and touch him. It was lust and something else, something that just wanted to be close to him. It scared me. Maybe he wasn't the only one who could walk away from this with a broken heart.

I wiggled my own weak self away to the other side of the bed, putting what space I could between us. As I lay there, my back to him, Aubrey jumped up and lay next to my stomach. I stroked her black-speckled white head and sighed.

"They were all wrong, Aub," I whispered. "There's at least one guy in this world not trying to get laid."

Chapter 6

One thing about working in a bookstore is you have immediate access to print media:

> Nocturnal Admission is a treat for the senses, one of those rare jewels that emerges from the dark obscurity of small clubs and restaurants. Of course, after last night's performance at the Verona, it's unlikely they'll be playing shoddy venues again. Nocturnal Admission is well on its way to becoming a household name—not only at the local level, but the national one as well.

The opening staff and I oohed and aahed over the concert review in the *Seattle Times*, all of us clustering around the information desk, rereading our favorite quotes over and over. The writer had even provided a few words of Doug's bio—after several other lines praising his voice and onstage persona—adding that he worked at a "local bookstore." We loved that; the nondescript reference almost made us feel like celebrities too.

I let them chat on a bit longer, reveling in my own pride and pleasure for Doug, before finally breaking things up. "All right, kids, I hate to crack the whip, but I see customers at the door."

They dispersed reluctantly, but I saw Andy smirking when he thought I didn't notice him whispering something to Casey. The only word I caught was "whip." Charming. One would think having a dominatrix reputation would at least make me a more formidable authority figure, rather than a source of ridicule.

And today, I was the only authority figure. Paige was out sick again, so I had to unofficially work both her job and my own. At least the staff was in good form despite the late night, which made things easier.

Casey seemed unaffected by last night, which I found remarkable. Maybe it was the resilience of youth. After drinking and smoking that much, I doubted I'd have been in as good a shape as she was—and I had the advantage of supernatural healing and recovery. My misgivings about Alec must have been premature, I decided, considering what a good mood she appeared to be in.

She smiled every time I saw her during the day and was always ready with a friendly comment to customers and coworkers alike. When I stopped by to take something from a neighboring register, I heard a customer ask her if she knew offhand whether his books would total under twenty-five dollars or not. She flipped through the stack expertly and had an answer within ten seconds.

"With tax, $26.57. Put this one back, and you'll be at $22.88. Closest you can get without going over."

"Did you do that all in your head?" I asked her later.

Dimples showed in her pretty cheeks. "I'm an accounting major."

"Yeah, but my accountant sure as hell doesn't do my taxes in his head."

"Of course not. But this stuff's easy."

Doug came in at noon, much to the delight of the others. Practically strutting, he couldn't stop crowing about the review and kept asking me if I'd read such-and-such in the article. I had to assure him repeatedly that I'd read it all.

Like Casey, he too acted untouched by last night's party-ing. He worked and bounced around with what was becoming his trademark energy. Compared to the two of them, I felt downright curmudgeonly, not to mention inadequate. Sheesh. What were immortality and shape-shifting next to superhuman computations and dazzling stage performances?

When I returned from my lunch break, he practically sprinted up to me. "Kincaid, Kincaid—you gotta help me out."

"What's wrong?"

He inclined his head toward one of the registers. Alec stood leaning against it, flirting with Casey. She smiled and nodded enthusiastically at something he said.

"Alec came by to tell me he got us a *major* audition over at the *Blue Gallery*. We have *got* to go practice. *Stat*."

"Good grief. Slow down on the italics."

"Kincaid, I mean it! You have to cover for me. No one'll know I left. These guys don't care, and Paige and Warren won't be in."

"How long do you need?"

"The rest of the day."

"The rest of the—that's going to be over twelve hours for me! Besides, I can't close. I'm going to a play downtown." Seth had just secured us some last minute tickets.

"Then . . . stay as late as you can. Janice'll handle closing."

I hesitated. Warren preferred that the manager or one of the assistant managers close, but Doug was right. Janice could handle it.

"Kin-*caid*," he begged. "Please. I need this. You know I do."

Doug had always been charming and irresistible. Something about him today particularly appealed to me. A master working another master, apparently. When I gave in to his pleas, he picked me up and spun me around in a most undignified way. Two minutes later, he and Alec left, and I settled in for a long day.

When it finally neared its end, I felt certain the store would burn to the ground in my absence. Dragging myself away at last, I drove downtown, found parking, and sprinted into the theatre just as the lights were going down. Breathless, I slid into a seat between Seth and his thirteen-year-old niece Brandy. On the other side of him, Seth's brother and sister-in-law waved to me.

Brandy grinned. She'd been shy the first time we met but now seemed to regard me as the older sister she didn't have. I adored her too. If Seth and I ever split up, I wasn't sure I was going to be able to handle keeping away from his family.

"I didn't think you'd make it," she told me, her features faintly discernible in the dim lighting. In days long past, people would have said she and her mother had "flaxen" hair, but no one really used that term anymore. Still, I always thought it appropriate when I saw that pale shade of gold.

"Just making a fashionably late entrance," I whispered back. "Remember that when you're older. It keeps men guessing. Once they start presuming anything, there's no living with them."

Brandy giggled. Seth only smiled, but his eyes radiated approval, as he assessed me. I wore wine-colored silk and had my hair in a French twist. His eyes, I'd long since discovered, could be as eloquent and expressive as his pen. The messages they sent me now hardly seemed decent for a public setting. He moved his hand over to cover mine, so that both rested on my thigh, and as the night progressed, I found myself thinking more about that hand placement than the excellent play.

Afterward, he and I stood with his family in the lobby for a while, catching up. Terry and Andrea Mortensen were great people who always treated me with genuine kindness. From what I'd learned of Seth's antisocial habits, I think they regarded me as some sort of last hope for him. Brandy affirmed as much when she and I dashed to the restroom together.

"Dad told Uncle Seth not to screw things up," she informed me as we washed our hands. "He said even if Uncle Seth is famous, him getting a woman like you defies belief."

I laughed and smoothed down the skirt of my dress. "I don't know about that. I don't think your dad gives your uncle enough credit."

Brandy gave me a sage look, worthy of someone much older. "Uncle Seth spent last Valentine's Day at a library."

We returned to the lobby and spoke a bit more before Terry declared they needed to rescue the babysitter who'd been left with their other four daughters. Andrea touched my arm as they prepared to leave.

"You're coming to Seth's birthday party, aren't you?"

I looked at all of them in surprise. "When is it?"

"Thanksgiving. They fall on the same day every once in a while."

"It's a good ploy to get turkey *and* presents," remarked Terry. He was shorter and more clean-shaven than Seth but otherwise bore a fair resemblance to his older brother.

"I didn't even know it was coming up." I shot Seth an accusing look.

"I forgot." For anyone else, that would probably have been a lie, but I believed him.

"So you'll be there?" Andrea again gave me the impression they were desperate to foster Seth's love life. I could have probably negotiated a stipend for showing up.

"With bells on."

Seth and I went back to his place this time. I shape-shifted into my favorite pajamas—flannel pants and a cami—and crawled into bed with him. His bed was bigger than mine and had a feather duvet, as well as a teddy bear named Damocles who wore a University of Chicago T-shirt.

Still a little wound up, we talked in the dark about Emerald City for a while, then moved on to books in general. We had a vast array of familiar literature in our repertoire, and we jumped around authors and genres. We both admired Toni Morrison and Tennessee Williams. Neither of us could get through *Anna Karenina*. Seth hated Jane Austen, whom I adored. As we debated back and forth, I was relieved to be reminded we truly did have a lot in common. Sex was not the only thing between us, even if it was the only thing that *stood* between us.

At some point in the literary discussion, I began to drift off. The long day had worn me out, and sleep felt luxurious. Seth seemed tired too. He and I drew close, lying on our sides, legs touching.

Random thoughts whispered in my head as unconsciousness tugged at me. How Aubrey was doing. Whether Paige's baby would be a boy or a girl. If Bastien was any closer to bedding Dana. How in the world Doug's band had become so amazing so quickly.

I opened my eyes a couple hours later, uncertain what had woken me. One of those weird, unseen things that suddenly break you out of sleep, I guessed. Quiet darkness still enveloped us with no sign of morning in sight. A little moonlight filtered inside, casting funny shadows around the desk and other bedroom furniture. Unlike my place in Queen Anne, car traffic here dropped off at night, so I heard only the sound of breathing and electrical humming.

Then I noticed that Seth and I had moved our bodies even nearer than before. Our legs wrapped around each other pretzel-style, our arms kept us close together. His scent flooded my nose. As my eyes adjusted, I noticed his were open as well. Intense pools of darkness. He was watching me.

Still a little sleepy, I moved my hand up to his neck, twining my fingers in his hair, drawing my face closer to his. His hand rested on the small of my back where the tank top rose away from my flannel pajama bottoms. He touched the skin there just as he had at the concert, his hand sliding toward my side, tracing the curve of my hip before running toward my thigh. The fingers that beat such a steady tattoo on computer keys were as delicate as feathers on me.

My eyes never left his as we touched each other, and I swore I could hear my heart thundering in my ears. Then, despite some screaming voice in the back of my foggy brain, I pushed my mouth toward his and kissed him. Our lips were tentative at first, as though surprised they had gotten this far. We tasted each other, slowly and gently. His hand on the back of my thigh slid upward, and something about shy Seth Mortensen stroking my ass sent a thrill through me. A soft exhalation lodged in my throat, and as my tongue explored past his lips, seeking more, he suddenly pushed me onto my back with an urgency that I think astonished both of us. His other hand slid up under my shirt and cupped the bottom of a breast, and through his boxers, I could tell that more than just his hands and lips wanted this to progress.

Then, ever so slightly, I felt something else. A slight tingling. Angel-fine tendrils of prickly bliss slowly snaking through me, wrapping around me. Exhilarating. Better than any intoxicant I'd ever experienced. Pure life, pure energy.

It was delicious and tantalizing, another dimension of the physical pleasure we stood on the brink of. The fact that it was Seth's was even more alluring. It had his unique essence written all over it. I wanted to dive into it, close my eyes and forget all about being responsible while that sweetness filled me.

But I couldn't. My resolve was weakening by the second, true, but I was still holding on.

Barely.

I broke the kiss reluctantly, trying to muster my strength and move away from him. At the first sign of my struggle, he immediately let me go.

"I-I'm sorry," I said, sitting up and putting my face in my hands. I rubbed my eyes as though waking from a dream, which in a manner of speaking, I was. "We can't. It . . . it started . . ."

"Just from kissing."

It was a statement, his voice coming out husky with desire and sleepiness . . . and regret. He knew better than most how lethal a passionate kiss could be; I'd almost killed him the last time. Of course, that had been an exceptional situation, and my near-death state had sucked away much more than a deep kiss normally would.

"Just from kissing," I repeated bleakly. It didn't take intercourse for one person to give themselves up to another. There were no loopholes in this game.

Tense silence crept in around us until Seth sat up as well and shifted his body away from mine. I could hear genuine pain and guilt when he spoke again. "I'm sorry about that. I don't know . . . meant to have better control. But I just sort of woke up . . . and I was half-asleep . . . and then . . ."

"I know," I whispered into the darkness. "I know. And I'm sorry too."

More silence.

"I guess," he finally said, "I should go sleep on the couch . . ."

I closed my eyes, feeling terrible but knowing he was right. We'd been playing with fire by fooling around with this chaste-sleeping thing. It was a wonder something bad hadn't happened sooner. The more it sunk in, the more I realized how much damage I could have caused. Hell, how much damage had I caused already by taking those few drops of life from him? A week off his lifespan? A few days? Even one minute would have been too much.

Bitterness—at the world, not him—dripped from my voice when I spoke. "No. I'll take the couch. We're at your place."

"Whatever. Leave me some remnant of chivalry."

I didn't say anything, and we sat once more in awkward silence. A hundred questions hung in the air between us, but neither of us could broach them. Both our faults. When an emotional situation turned uncomfortable, I had a tendency to run from it or pretend it wasn't happening. And while Seth wouldn't exactly run away, he wouldn't initiate the dialogue needed to explore something like this. So we continued sitting there.

At last, he stood up. "I'm sorry. Sorry for what I did."

He blamed himself, which was typical of him but not fair, especially since I had technically touched him first. I should have said something then, told him it wasn't all his fault. But the words stuck on my tongue, held up by my own confused feelings. After a few more moments, he left for the living room.

I lay back down, Damocles in my arms, but slept badly the rest of the night. When morning came, Seth and I ate breakfast in more tense silence—he'd finally made my pancakes—broken only occasionally by stiff small talk. We then went to the bookstore together, parting ways quickly. I hardly saw him the rest of the day.

Bastien was in the city for some reason or another that night, so he picked me up later and drove me over to his place for the ridiculous heist at Dana's. When I saw the post-sex energy wreathing him, I knew what had brought him downtown.

"Don't you get tired of getting laid every day?" I asked him, wishing I could have gotten laid last night.

"I'm going to pretend you didn't actually just ask that, Fleur." He then proceeded to ramble on about his various Dana sightings in the last few days, how chummy they were getting, how it could only be a matter of time before the inevitable.

When I didn't really respond, he cut me a sidelong glance. "What's the matter with you? You look miserable."

I sighed. "I kissed Seth last night."

"And?"

"And what?"

"What else happened?"

"Well . . . nothing. I mean, a little groping here and there, but that's it."

"So?"

"So, I shouldn't have done it."

A dismissive look crossed his face. "A kiss is nothing. It's not like you gave him a blow job or anything."

"Good lord, you're crass."

"Don't act like I offended your delicate sensibilities. And you know what I'm talking about."

"Doesn't matter. I was weak. I got some of his energy from that."

"Fleur, I love you as much as I've ever managed to love anybody, but this whole thing is absurd. You're never going to be happy until you've fucked this guy, so just get it over with. It'll take away the whole forbidden attraction and allow both of you to get on with your lives."

"'Get on with our lives?' What's that supposed to mean?" I asked sharply.

"I mean half the reason you guys are so infatuated with each other is because you can't have each other. It's not love, but it is a normal human reaction, a catalyst for physical attraction." He paused and considered. "Your maniacal obsession with his books might also be a factor."

"That's not true. None of that's true at all. Well, I mean, those books are good enough to be the basis of a religion, but that's not the same thing. That's not why I . . ."

Love him? Hell. I still didn't know if I did or not. I wasn't even sure what love was after all this time.

Bastien shook his head, not believing me but not wanting to argue either. "Fine. Keep going with this. I still think you should fuck him, though. Even if it doesn't make you both realize you're better off apart, it'll at least remove one source of tension between you and maybe let you attempt some sort of normal dysfunctional relationship."

I stared bleakly into space. "I can't. Not even one night. It'd take years off his life. I couldn't live with myself."

"Bah. Only a handful of years at most. What's that? Besides, men have done stupider things for sex—with women they don't even really like. If he really does love you, he might think it's a fair trade."

I shuddered. I didn't think it was fair at all, but he was right about the silly things men would do for sex. I'd seen and initiated plenty of them.

We finally gave up both sides of the argument when we pulled into his driveway. The clock was ticking, and we had to start this operation. Bastien had watched Dana and Bill drive off earlier, and their teenage son had gone down the street to stay at a friend's house. Shifting to be invisible to mortal eyes, Bastien and I crept out the back of his house and scaled the fence into Dana's yard. It sort of made me feel like I was in a spy movie; I half wished we could crawl under some motion-detecting lasers.

"They have a security system," I whispered to Bastien as I watched him pick the back door's lock. More useful skills gleaned from long centuries. "Being invisible isn't going to deactivate it."

"No problem. I've done some invisible reconnaissance. I know the code."

Sure enough, he punched it into the console once we were in the house, and the readout's red light turned green.

We started in the Dailey office, as that seemed like the most logical place to stash paperwork. Dana had a meticulous sense of organization that creeped me out, and we had to make sure we left everything the way we found it.

Unfortunately, most of the stuff was completely useless. Memos. Efficient—and honest—budget reports. Invoices. Press releases. She had a lot of pictures too, which were at least more fun to look at than the papers. Most of them showed family or CPFV events. A number of the shots had Jody in them, which saddened me. I recalled the other woman's sly wit and passion for art. Why would someone with any sort of intelligence want to get involved in all this?

"I didn't realize how active Jody was in this group," I remarked to Bastien. "She wasn't so bad. Dana's corrupted her."

"Dana's a persuasive woman. Hey, did you know Jody's last name is Daniels? And her husband's name is Jack?"

We giggled over that and continued searching a while longer before finally abandoning the office. We then ransacked—neatly, of course—any other cupboards or drawers we could find on the main floor. Nothing.

"Maybe there are secret panels behind paintings," suggested Bastien.

"Or maybe the pool-boy thing was a fraud, Dana's honest with her business dealings, and there's really nothing else to get on her except that she's a prejudiced bitch."

He rolled his eyes. "One place left. The true sanctuary. The bedroom."

I grimaced. Going into someone's bedroom freaked me out. The ultimate violation of privacy. But Bastien charged on, still confident this wild goose chase would yield results.

Fortunately, the bedroom had the neat, sterile look of a hotel, not the warm and sensual air of one's most intimate space. It made searching easier, like I was breaking into a vacant room. We sifted through drawers and closets, again finding little to go on.

"Eek!" I suddenly cried, staring into an open drawer. Bastien flew to me.

"What? What is it?"

I held up what had to be the most wholesome pair of granny panties I'd ever seen. They were like great-granny panties. They were even white. You would have thought she could at least go out on a limb and get them in blue or green or something.

Bastien elbowed me for my overreaction. "How can you even act surprised after hearing her rants about modest clothing?"

"Modest is one thing, but Jesus . . . how high do these things go? Up to her neck?"

"Put them back. We've got to—"

Click.

We'd both heard. I shot Bastien a panicked look and shoved the underwear back in the drawer.

"I thought you said—"

His tone was grim. "I know, I know."

Someone had just entered the house.

Chapter 7

We stood rooted in the bedroom, frozen, both of us too terrified to blink. Downstairs, the door shut and footsteps could be clearly heard on the hardwood floor. A low murmur of voices drifted up, the words inaudible.

"What are we going to do?" I whispered. Invisible we might be, but I still didn't want to slink through the house with others around. It would also make leaving inconspicuously a problem.

Bastien frowned, apparently trying to discern the words below. "Those are all male voices. Not Dana. Come on."

He grabbed my arm, and we crept out into the hallway where we could hear more clearly.

"You sure they aren't coming home?" asked an anxious voice.

"Yup. They'll be out 'til, like, midnight."

"Cool."

Bastien grinned at me. "Reese," he breathed.

Reese. The son. The son who was supposed to be down the street at a friend's house. That was better than Dana, but still disconcerting. I shot Bastien a questioning look. *What's he doing here?* I mouthed.

Bastien shrugged by way of answer and gestured for me to follow him the rest of the way downstairs. Reese and his friend obliviously made enough noise to cover any of our movements.

I hadn't really seen Reese yet and was curious. I'd expected a clean-cut, dutiful altar-boy type, but he seemed perfectly average—in that sullen, T-shirt wearing sort of way. He had Dana's black hair and blue eyes, paired with some of Bill's unfortunate facial features. His friend had long hair and wore a beat-up army coat with jeans.

"Where should we do it?" asked the friend.

Reese glanced around. "Outside. Otherwise they'll smell it later."

"Okay. But roll it in here."

They huddled around the kitchen table. Reese produced a tin of rolling papers and a plastic Baggie with enough marijuana in it to keep a family of five stoned for a week.

The friend skillfully rolled an enormous joint, and the boys took it outside, going out the same door we'd come in. Bastien and I exchanged glances, both of us barely holding back hysterical laughter. We walked into the still-dark living room and stood at the window, watching the boys outside. They left all the outdoor lights off, not wanting to attract neighborly attention. The joint made a pinpoint of orange light in the blackness as they passed it back and forth.

"Oh my God," I gasped. "This just justified the whole break-in."

Bastien's expression was speculative. "Maybe we can use this against her."

I turned on him. "What? Come on. He's just a kid. No need to drag him down with her. Besides, if I had his parents, I'd want to be high too."

Bastien looked momentarily uncertain, finally yielding with a small nod. "Okay. You're right. So. You want to finish the bedroom and then head out? I doubt they're going to notice much going on around them."

We went back upstairs, still hoping for some incriminating photo or piece of paper. No such luck.

We left Reese and his friend alone, using the front door to make our getaway. Once we were safely back at Bastien's, we settled into the immaculate living room, defeated.

"Well. That was pointless," I said.

"Not entirely." Bastien reached into his pocket and tossed over Reese's plastic bag.

I caught it and straightened up in my chair. "Jesus H. Christ! You swiped that poor kid's pot?"

"He shouldn't have left it out like that."

I held it up. It was half-full. "There's a special hell for people like you."

"Yeah, I own a condo there. Besides, it's for his own good. Pot's a gateway drug, you know."

"I can't believe this. You don't think they're going to notice this is missing?"

"Nah. By the time they come back in, they'll be so far gone they won't remember where they left it. They'll spend the next few days accusing each other of losing it."

I shook my head. "I know I've said it before, but this really is a new low. I . . . I'm so shocked now, I don't even know what to do."

"*I* do."

An hour later, we were both on the floor, giggling endlessly, though I wasn't entirely sure what about. Bastien passed the joint to me, and I took a hit off it, sighing happily. I handed it back.

"I'm not saying Monique wasn't a bitch," he was explaining, "but you have to admit, she knew how to get things done."

I leaned against the back of the couch, letting my head roll around on the cushions. "Yeah, but . . . she was . . . you know, sloppy. Like, no creativity whatsoever. Being in the business isn't just about sex. It's about . . . pride . . . pride in your work."

He inhaled and passed the joint back. "Oh, she had pride in her work, believe me. Used to ride me like a horse." He paused a moment, then started laughing. "She totally did me proud."

I sat back up. "What, you slept with her?"

"Sure, why not?"

I poked him with my foot. "You fucking slut."

"Look who's calling the cauldron black."

"*Kettle*. It's a kettle. Get your metaphors right."

"That wasn't a metaphor. It was a, you know . . ." He stared off into space, blinking. "One of those things that's symbolic of another thing. But isn't the same thing. Just like it."

"You mean a metaphor?"

"No! It's like a story . . . like . . . a proverb! That's it."

"I'm pretty sure that wasn't a proverb. Maybe it was an analogy."

"I don't think so."

"Look, I know these things. I work in a—oh!"

"Oh what?"

"How am I going to get home?"

"You're leaving? Or is that an analogy?"

"I'm not leaving yet . . . but you drove me . . . you can't drive me back."

"Sure I can. I feel fine."

"You wish. I haven't smoked that much."

I rummaged through my purse, found my cell phone, and dialed the first number in it. Beside me, Bastien muttered about analogies while staring entranced at the smoke swirling off the joint.

"Hello?" answered Seth. We hadn't really spoken since our awkward morning.

"Hey, it's me."

"Hey."

"So . . . I, uh . . . need a favor."

"What is it?" When I didn't say anything right away, he asked, "You still there? You okay?"

"Yeah . . ." I started laughing uncontrollably. "I am *so* okay."

"Um, all right. What do you need?"

It took me a moment to remember. "A ride."

"A ride?"

"Yeah. A ride."

Bastien made a rude gesture at the mention of "a ride," and I kicked him again. I gave the address to a clearly confused Seth and then disconnected.

"Idiot!" I yelled at Bastien, even though I thought the whole situation was hilarious, as did he. I went in for a tackle. "What were you—"

The doorbell rang. Our eyes went wide as we froze midgrapple, panic flooding us like two kids who had just been busted hardcore.

"Shit," I said.

"Damn. That author drives fast."

"It's not him, you dork. Don't move. They'll go away."

He lumbered to his feet. "No . . . I gotta see who it is . . . maybe it's Jack Daniels . . . could use a drink . . ."

"Don't do it!" I begged, suddenly terrified for no reason I could identify.

He turned invisible and strolled over to the door. Half a second later, he came tearing back. "It's Dana! She's back early." He ran his hand frantically over Mitch's neat, blonde hair. "What's she want? What's she doing here?"

"Maybe she wants Reese's pot back."

"This is my chance! She's here alone. She wants me. Quick." He yanked my arm and dragged me to the stairs. I cried out in surprise. "Get out of sight. Throw that away."

"I'm not throwing this away! Besides, you don't think she'll notice that your whole fucking house smells like this? Jesus. Your pupils are the size of her granny panties. Virtuous or not, she isn't stupid."

"Just go! Hurry! Don't come down."

Grumbling, I went upstairs while Bastien scurried to the door. Turning invisible, I sat cross-legged at the top of the stairs and kept smoking. Below, I heard him greet Dana.

"Well, hello," he bellowed. "Sorry if I kept you waiting . . .

I was . . ." He trailed off stupidly, and I shook my head. Sloppy, sloppy. He would have never been at a loss for words sober, but then, his sober self would have immediately noticed the foolishness afoot. "I was . . . um, busy. Upstairs."

"I see," replied Dana. Her tone was once again set to cool and formal. I decided Bastien had imagined the warm and friendly rapport he kept claiming they had when alone. "Well, I apologize for disturbing you, but when I dropped off the cookies earlier, I think I may have lost an earring."

I straightened up. Cookies? He hadn't mentioned that. Maybe he was making progress after all. Cookies. I wondered what kind she'd brought. Peanut butter? Chocolate chip? Oh. Maybe even white chocolate macadamia.

He and Dana commenced a search for the earring, coming up empty. The whole time, Bastien tried to act like he wasn't stoned, but Dana couldn't have been fooled. Not with those cyborg eyes of hers. Hell, I didn't even need to see it. The audio track alone was entertaining enough.

Meanwhile, I couldn't stop thinking about those goddamned cookies. They sounded good. Really good. Suddenly, I wanted them more than I'd ever wanted anything in my life.

"Well," I heard Dana say, "I must have lost it somewhere else. Thanks for looking."

"Sorry I couldn't help you."

"It's all right." She allowed an elegantly crafted pause. "Isn't that Tabitha's purse over there? Is she here?"

Oh, shit. I had a feeling Bastien was thinking the same thing.

"Uh, well, yeah . . . but . . . um, she's upstairs lying down," he faltered. "Has a headache."

"Oh, that's too bad. Did she take anything for it?"

"Um, yeah, she did."

I looked at the joint. Had I ever.

Bastien and Dana started talking about something else, and I decided then that I *had* to get those cookies. I was starving. The lovebirds sounded like they had moved to the living room, so I could sneak invisibly down the stairs and raid the kitchen without them knowing. Standing up, I put the joint out in the upstairs bathroom and moved on to my covert descent. Pot doesn't usually mess with motor control the way alcohol can, but it can certainly distract you from ordinary things. Like watching where you're going.

About three steps down, my foot slipped out from under me.

I uttered a sailor-worthy expletive and slid painfully down the rest of the way, landing hard on my butt at the bottom, my legs twisting into unnatural positions underneath me. I had barely enough sense to snap back to a visible Tabitha, lest Bastien and Dana think a clumsy ghost had just fallen down. A moment later, they came running.

"What happened?" exclaimed Bastien. He sounded more upset about the interruption than my immediate health.

"I . . . I tripped . . ."

Looking down, I tried moving my left ankle to a more comfortable position. I winced. It hurt like hell, but at least it moved.

"Well," he said crisply, "so long as you're okay. I'm sure you'll want to go and—"

"Okay?" Dana gave him an incredulous look. "We need to get her to the couch so she can straighten that out."

"Oh no," I protested, seeing Bastien's murderous expression. "I . . . I'm fine . . . really . . ."

But there was no arguing with Dana. She supported me under one arm, and he took the other. I hobbled over to the couch, putting my weight only on the right foot. Once I was stretched out, she pushed my jeans up over my calf and felt the ankle with cautious, expert precision, carefully examining each inch. I appreciated her solicitous concern and apparent first-aid know-how, but the thought of this wretched woman touching my leg repulsed me. Besides, what I really wanted were those cookies. Fuck my ankle.

"It doesn't feel broken," she finally decided. "Probably just a sprain, lucky for you. We should ice it."

When Bastien neither did nor offered anything useful, she went into the kitchen. I could hear her opening drawers and the freezer.

"Do you hate me or something?" he hissed once we were alone.

"This wasn't my fault," I countered. "I think you've got a defective stair."

"Defective my ass. The only thing that's defective is your sense of timing. Do you know how close I was to scoring?"

"Close? *Close?* Not to use a cliché, but hell was closer to freezing over than you were to scoring. I don't think she really goes for the babbling, high kind of guy."

"I wasn't babbling. And there's no way she knows I'm high."

"Oh, come on. If you were any higher, you'd—"

I shut my mouth as Dana returned with the ice pack. She knelt by my feet and carefully set the pack on the injured ankle. I grimaced at the sudden change of temperature, but the shocking cold did numb the throbbing.

Still concerned, she surveyed the rest of my lower leg with those sharp eyes. Again, she felt around the ankle area, her hands gently touching here and there. She frowned. "I could be wrong about how serious it is. You should keep icing it and take ibuprofen. If it doesn't get better in a couple days, go see your doctor."

"Thanks," I said, looking away. Honestly, what I found most disconcerting now was how sincerely concerned she seemed. Maybe we'd misjudged her all along. Nah.

"Well," breezed Bastien, "if Tabby Cat's okay, maybe we should go to the kitchen and have some coffee—"

"Do you know how it happened?" Dana asked me, ignoring him.

"Oh . . . just a misstep I think . . . or maybe the stair is defective."

"I doubt there's anything wrong with the stairs," said Bastien. "Tabitha's always been clumsy, that's all. It's legendary in our family."

Dana, oblivious to me glaring at the incubus over the slam to my gracefulness, glanced over at my shoes sitting near the door. They were strappy and black, with three-inch heels.

"Are those what you've been wearing?" She fixed me with a stern, motherly look. "I know how strong societal pressure can be in making you think you need to fit a certain mold. But walking around in shoes like that all day will do serious damage to your feet. Not only that, they send a message that you have no shame when it comes to—"

The doorbell rang then. None of us moved at first, and then Bastien rose, looking amazed that this night could get any worse.

Dana dropped her wardrobe lecture and switched to a medical one. "You really need to be careful with this. Too much stress will agitate it."

Bastien returned a moment later with an utterly puzzled Seth, whom I suspected had no idea who had just let him in. Indeed, his bewilderment grew as he scanned Dana and me, no doubt wondering if he had the right house.

"Hi Seth," I said pointedly, in too loud of a voice, "thanks for coming to pick me up."

He continued to stare, and then the faintest gleam of understanding showed in his eyes. He'd seen me shape-shift clothes often, but this was the first time he'd ever seen me in another body.

Dana looked around expectantly.

"Oh," I said, my mind still running a little slow from the pot. "This is, um, Seth. Seth, Dana."

"Hello," she said, rising smoothly and shaking his hand. "Nice to meet you."

"Um, yeah. You too." I had a feeling he would bolt if given half a chance.

"Seth is Tabitha's boyfriend," explained Bastien. "I imagine they'll want to be on their way now."

"I'd heard you were single. How long have you two been dating?" she asked, steering us toward casual conversation.

Neither of us answered. "A couple months," I said at last, wondering if my virtue was once again being assessed.

She smiled. "How nice."

I started feeling those creepy vibes again, and suddenly I did want to leave. I tried to sit up, and she rushed to my side. "Someone grab her other arm."

When Bastien didn't move, Seth was finally spurred into action. He supported my other side and helped me stand. It was clear, however, that touching me in this body unnerved him, and he tried to manage it while staying as far away from me as possible. Consequently, all of his movements seemed awkward and unnatural, and no doubt Dana thought we were even weirder than before.

She and Seth helped me to the car, Bastien following with a pout. When I was situated in the passenger seat, Dana offered a few parting words of instruction to both Seth and me on how to care for the ankle.

"Thanks for the help," I told her.

"Happy to. Just try to be more careful from now on." She glanced at her watch. "Well. I should probably go home myself."

"Do you have to?" asked Bastien stupidly. "Er, I mean, no need to feel rushed . . ."

"Thank you, but no. Bill will wonder what happened to me."

I saw her walk back to her house as Seth pulled out. I also saw the look on Bastien's face. The morning after was not going to be pretty.

We were almost in the city when Seth finally spoke. "Can you . . . uh . . . you know . . . change? This is really weird."

"Huh?" I had been staring bleary-eyed out the window, intrigued by the blur of city lights. "Oh. Yeah."

A moment later, I was the Georgina Kincaid he knew.

"Thanks. So, uh . . . I don't suppose I really want to know what was going on back there . . ."

"Nope." I craned my head to look in the backseat. "You really don't."

"What are you doing?"

"You don't have any cookies back there do you?"

"Uh . . . no. I'm all out."

I sighed and sank into my seat. "I am *starving*. I don't think I can hold on much longer. You sure you don't have any other food?"

The ghost of a smile curled his lips. "Nope. Sorry. You want to stop somewhere?"

"Yes!"

He pulled into a Taco Bell drive-thru, looking surprised when I gave him my order. When it came up, he wordlessly handed me my bag of four tacos, two bean burritos, and a tostada. I dove into them before he'd even accelerated away.

When we got back to my place, he didn't give me the chance to limp in. He scooped me up effortlessly, almost like O'Neill might have in one of his novels. If not for me being stoned and clinging to a taco, it would have been terribly romantic.

"You think I'm a freak, don't you?" I asked, once I was situated in bed and he sat on its edge. Seth had tended me once before, after a night of heavy drinking. I felt so irresponsible compared to him.

"Well, the tostada was kind of excessive, but I've seen freakier."

"No . . . you know. I mean . . ." I hesitated. "Well, you may not realize this, but I've sort of been smoking . . . some stuff."

"Yeah. I kind of picked up on that."

"Oh. Well. Sorry." I bit into one of the burritos savagely.

"Why are you apologizing?"

"Because . . . well, you don't do this."

"Do what?"

"Smoke pot. Or drink. Geez, you even avoid caffeine. Don't you think I'm like, I don't know . . . corrupt?"

"Corrupt?" He laughed. "Hardly. Anyway, you don't think I've ever done any of that?"

The idea was just shocking enough to give me pause. I put my gluttony on hold. "Well . . . I don't know. I just figured, well, no. Either that, or you had some tragic history . . . like you got drunk and hit a mailbox or took off all your clothes in public and now avoid all such vices."

"That would be tragic. But rest easy, I indulged in plenty of 'vices' in college. That's why it took me six years to graduate. Well, that and changing my major a few times. In the end, I just decided to abstain altogether. Didn't like myself otherwise. Sobriety's better for writing, and I say too many stupid things when I'm drunk or high."

"Yeah," I said uneasily, trying to remember what I'd said tonight. It was kind of a haze. "So you don't think I'm like . . . I don't know, a shameless lush?"

"Nope. So long as you don't do yourself harm." He eyed the ankle suspiciously. "It doesn't matter to me. Honestly, half the reason I like you is because you're so . . . I don't know. You like life." He looked away from my eyes, amused as his thoughts spun, considering. "You're fearless. Bold. Not afraid to enjoy yourself. You just go out there and do what you want. I like the whirlwind you exist in. I envy it. It's funny, really." He smiled. "I used to think I wanted someone exactly like me, but now I think I'd be bored to death with another version of myself. I'm surprised I don't bore you sometimes."

I gaped. "Are you kidding? You're the most interesting person I know. Aside from Hugh maybe. But then, he installs breast implants and buys souls. That's a hard combination to beat. But he's not nearly as cute."

Seth's smile increased, and he squeezed my hand. Silence fell between us again, but this time it was kind of cozy.

"Thanks for rescuing me," I said slowly, "and for . . . well . . . I mean, I'm sorry about last night. Sorry I shut down."

His face sobered. "No, I'm sorry. I shouldn't have—"

"No," I said firmly. "Don't blame yourself. It was me too. My fault too. And really, I was the one who started it. I should have just talked to you about it then. Especially after you made me pancakes this morning. You know, those suddenly sound really good again." I looked at him meaningfully.

"We shouldn't have done what we did . . . in bed . . . but, at least we did manage to stop. That's worth something."

I nodded, crumpling up the Taco Bell bag and tossing it across the room into my wastebasket. Score.

He studied me, eyes warm and affectionate. He sighed and turned pensive again. There apparently was more seriousness to come. "I'd like to try sleeping together again, but I suppose . . . we should take a break from that."

I mirrored his sigh. "Yeah. I suppose." Remembering something, I cocked my head and gave him a sharp look. "Hey, hypothetically—and I'm not offering this, so don't get any ideas—would you, like, give up part of your life to sleep with me? Er, but I mean . . . not actually *sleep* . . ."

He laughed out loud, the laughter underscored with a wry edge. "Thetis, I'd give up part of my life to do any number of things with you."

My interest flared. "Like what?"

"Well . . . isn't it obvious?"

I leaned toward him. Maybe I was still high and suffering from weed-induced horniness—and hey, in another reality, shouldn't we have been entitled to make-up sex?—but I suddenly and desperately wanted to hear him articulate what he wanted to do to me. "Tell me."

He shook his head. "I can't. You know how I am." His eyes narrowed intently. "I could maybe . . . I could maybe write it for you, though."

"Really? Not in published story form this time?"

"Yes, not in published story form."

"I'd like that."

I must have looked expectant because he laughed. "Not tonight, Thetis. Not tonight. I think we both need some sleep."

I was disappointed but could see the wisdom here. Having more time would ensure some good writing, I guessed. Furthermore, it was hard to be too sad when the tension from last night's mishap appeared to be gone. Our rapport and affection had returned, and watching him, I felt my feelings for him practically increase by the second. We chatted a bit more, and then he kissed me lightly on the mouth and rose. I wistfully watched him go, wishing he were staying.

Drifting off to sleep, I finally contented myself by thinking about all the things *I* wanted to do to him. It was a long list, and I was out before even getting through a fraction of it.

Chapter 8

"Georgina?"

I looked up from a baffling return Tammi had asked me to help her with. A customer without a receipt was attempting a refund on a stack of books with dog-eared pages and broken spines, claiming all of them were duplicates someone had just given him for his birthday.

"Just a sec," I told her. "I've got to finish this."

"Okay," Beth said. "I just thought you should check out Casey."

"Casey?"

"Yeah. She's up in the café."

That snagged my attention. I finished up with the customer, telling him nicely that we couldn't accept books in this condition. Maybe if the alleged other books were in better shape, he could bring those in. He pouted and argued a bit before finally skulking off. I rolled my eyes once he was gone. One thing that never changed among humans: there were always those who wanted to get something for nothing. It was what kept hell in business.

I found Casey sitting in the café, drinking a glass of water. There were dark circles under her eyes, and she didn't display her usual care in makeup and hairstyling. She stared bleakly at the table, eyes dull and glazed over.

"Hey," I said gently, pulling up a chair across from her. "How's it going?"

After a moment's delay, she looked up, not really focusing on me. "Okay."

"You sure? You don't look so okay."

"Dunno." Her tone was flat, distracted. "I just had a late night, that's all. Sorry. Sorry I came in like this."

"No problem. I've had my share of crazy nights." The thing was, Casey didn't exactly look hungover. I mean, she definitely looked like she was recovering from something . . . but I couldn't put my finger on it. It was weird. "What'd you get into? A party?"

"Yeah. Doug's band had another one."

"Really." News to me. "Must have been pretty good."

"Dunno."

"What do you mean? You were there."

Her brow furrowed, confusion glinting in her brown eyes. "I don't . . . really remember. Stupid, huh? I must have really been trashed. I remember . . . being with Alec. Then we left. We went somewhere."

"You don't know?"

She looked upset and closed her eyes. "There was this big house, and . . . I don't know. I just . . . I just can't remember. I'm sorry, Georgina. I shouldn't have come in today, okay? Sorry."

"It's okay. So you have no idea what you did with him? Nothing at all?"

She shook her head. I shouldn't have kept pushing for details of an employee's personal life, but something here bothered me. It was more than my bias against Alec too. I remembered him pushing alcohol on women, his invitation to go somewhere "more intense." Casey's inability to remember what had happened with him smacked of date-rape drugs.

"Did Alec give you anything?"

For the first time in this conversation, her dull expression sharpened and looked alert. "I . . . no. No."

But she was lying. I could tell. Why? Fear of him? Embarrassment? I couldn't bring myself to question her anymore. She looked too miserable. I told her she should go home and get some rest; she didn't need much convincing.

I took her place at the registers, silently fuming at that jerk Alec. My anger was furthered by the fact that I could do nothing. Casey's life wasn't really my business, and without her admitting to anything, Alec stood blameless.

With Casey now gone, Paige out sick again, and Warren golfing in Florida, I felt relieved when Doug showed up. He looked as energetic as ever, so I hoped he could counter my plunging mood.

"I heard you had a party."

"Yup." He grinned, working the register next to mine. "I tried calling you, but you weren't home."

"Had a party of my own. Hey, did you notice anything weird with Casey and Alec last night?"

"Weird how? I mean, they seemed to be hitting it off."

"Nothing else?"

"Nope. Not that I saw. Why? Are you interested? He's a little young for you, but if you're into that, I can give you his phone number."

"Hardly."

"Whoa," he suddenly exclaimed. "Check this action out."

He picked up one of the books his customer was paying for. It was a romance novel, emblazoned with a big chested man holding an equally big chested woman. Her neck was arched back, her lips open in a moan. And her dress was falling off.

"Bet there's some good shit in here. Nothing like some throbbing members and private time to get you off, eh?"

He winked at the customer, who turned crimson and didn't say anything. She handed over some cash and hurried away as fast as she could.

Aghast, I ignored the customers standing there and grabbed Doug's arm, jerking him away from the counter.

"What the hell was that?" I asked in a low, angry whisper.

He laughed loudly. "Oh come on, Kincaid. I was just having a little fun. Those romance novels always crack me up."

"You do *not* comment on customer purchases. Furthermore, you certainly don't swear in front of them."

"Basic training. I know all this."

"Yeah? Then act like it."

We stood there, both of us shocked at my tone. I didn't think I'd ever talked to Doug in such a reprimanding way. Certainly not here. We were both assistant managers, partners in crime. Our entire working relationship was one of lightheartedness and messing around.

"Fine," he said after a moment. "Whatever."

We went back to the registers, both of us pointedly ignoring the other. We worked without incident a while longer until I heard him say, "Man, this has to be rough. Hope it all works out."

Looking over, I saw his customer buying a book about STDs. Doug returned my gaze with a challenging look. I finished my own purchase and then put up a "register closed" sign. Finding Andy at the information desk, I told him to ask Doug to swap spots.

"Don't tell him I told you to."

Doug seemed safer helping customers find books, yet no matter where I was in the store, I could hear him. He spoke and laughed too loudly. Whenever I caught sight of him, he was always in motion—like he couldn't stay still. Once, he was—literally—juggling books for a customer. Another time, I saw him actually skipping as he led a customer over to the cooking section. I frowned, unsure what to do. His lively nature had been fun this last week, but he was pushing it now, and I wasn't entirely sure what my role should be in all of this.

"That redheaded girl said you're the manager here," a middle-aged woman suddenly said, approaching me as I rearranged a display.

"I'm an assistant manager," I told her. "What can I help you with?"

She pointed to the information desk. "That man was so rude to me. He helped me find some books, and then . . . he said . . ."

She couldn't finish, oscillating between anger and distress. I looked at what she held. Books on clinical depression. Lovely. At least it wasn't called *Going Postal in an Insensitive Bookstore*. I took a deep breath to steady myself and apologized profusely, promising I'd deal with it. I then walked her over to the head of the check-out line and told Andy to ring her books up for free. Warren never approved of that, but I didn't care at the moment.

I waited for Doug to finish with his customer and then pulled him aside once more. "We need to talk in the office."

He gave me a lopsided grin. Studying him, I saw his eyes glittering with a distracted fervor. "What for? Let's talk here. I've got customers to help, you know. Can't let this god-damned place go unattended."

I blanched at this, still forcing calm. We had a line of about four customers listening.

"No. Let's go in the back."

He rolled his eyes and threw a friendly arm around me. "Christ, you're uptight. What's this about?"

"You know what it's about," I returned, wiggling out from under the arm. "You're out of line today."

His smile fell. "No, *you're* out of line. What's with the attitude anyway? You can't talk to me like this."

He was still too loud. More people were stopping. "I can talk to you like this when you're acting like a jerk. You're upsetting customers. You're doing stuff that's completely inappropriate, and you know it."

"'Inappropriate?' Jesus Fucking Christ, Kincaid! You sound like Paige now. I'm having *fun*. Remember that? Remember when you and I used to do that around here back before you got this stick up your ass?"

We had a bona fide audience now. Customers and staff alike. Dead silence, save for the faint sounds of Vivaldi playing through the store's sound system.

"I mean," he continued, thriving on the attention, "where do you get off acting like this? Who put you in charge? You and I are the same rank, remember? It's like you get ten seconds of fame in Mortensen's story, and now you think you can put on airs. Why don't you go find him? Maybe if you got laid again, you'd stop being such a bitch."

"Doug," I said, astonished at how firm and strong my voice was. It was like someone else was using my body to confront him, and I only watched. "You need to go home. Now. If you don't leave, I'll have you removed."

Of course, I had no clue how I was going to pull that off. As it was, I felt almost terrified to be facing off against him like this. My heart raced. We were standing close, thrusting our wills at one another, and he had half a head's height on me and a bigger build. I didn't really fear violence from him, but the physical intimidation was as scary as the psychological. Still, I held my ground, keeping my expression commanding and decisive.

At last, he backed down, breaking eye contact. He shrugged and gave his goofy grin to those watching, like they were in on some joke with him. "Sure. Whatever you want. I don't care. I could use a day off anyway."

He looked around again, face smug and defiant, like he'd won. After another survey of the crowd, he laughed and stalked out.

Nobody spoke or breathed after that. I drew myself up, like none of this had bothered me either. I strode purposefully away, saying to Beth as I passed: "Will you cover the desk now?"

I went upstairs to the café and had the barista make me a mocha. I took it with shaking hands and turned around to find Seth standing there. He wore a Ratt shirt today.

"Thetis," he said softly.

I walked over to one of the windows, and he followed. Outside, cars and people moved throughout Queen Anne. I watched them without seeing them. Seth moved behind me, his presence steady and reassuring. Waiting to catch me, even though I refused to fall just yet. This, I realized, was why I chose to stay with him, sexual mishaps or no.

"I suppose you witnessed all that."

"Yeah," he said. "You handled it well."

"I didn't want to handle it at all."

"Someone had to." He touched my arm gently. "You can be pretty fierce sometimes."

I shook my head, still numb. "I don't want to be fierce either."

"Georgina. Look at me."

I turned and looked. Those lovely eyes were soft and full of love, yet underscored with strength.

"You did the right thing." He rested his hands on my arms, thumbs stroking the bare skin. "*You did the right thing.*"

"He's my friend."

"That doesn't matter."

"What's wrong with him, Seth? What's gotten into him?"

"Isn't it obvious?"

"Not to me."

He smiled ruefully. "The same thing that made you eat a bag of Taco Bell food last night."

"What? Pot doesn't do that. Make him behave like he did, I mean. Not the Taco Bell thing."

"No," he agreed. "Pot won't do that, but he was obviously on something."

I turned back to my view, thinking. I recalled Doug's nonstop vigor, that feverish look in his eyes. Yes, it made sense, and it was saddening. I'd never known him to mess around with anything much harder than alcohol and marijuana. Yet . . . there was more to his exuberance lately. A drug couldn't make you good at Tetris or churn out an album's worth of songs in under a month.

"I don't know what it could be then. I've tried almost everything once," I admitted sheepishly. Immortality allowed experimentation without the dangerous consequences mortals faced. "But I haven't made enough of a study to really ID anything. What do you think? Some kind of amphetamine?"

"I don't really know either."

I rubbed my temples, sensing a nasty headache coming on. I wanted nothing more just then than to go home and veg on the couch with Seth on one side, Aubrey on the other, and a plate of brownies on my lap. It wasn't going to happen.

"I've got to get back down there. We're short two people now. I'm going to be here until closing again."

"You want me to come over after work? I'm supposed to paint at Terry's, but I can bail on it."

I assured Seth he didn't need to change his plans for me and then returned downstairs. Functionality had resumed as though nothing out of the ordinary had happened. The only thing noteworthy was the way the other staff watched me now. Not with mockery or amusement, but something else. If I hadn't known better, I would have said my respect rating had just shot up.

I got home after work, drained. Weak with exhaustion, mental and physical. When I absorbed life from victims, it was usually to sustain my immortal existence and shapeshifting. But life was full of other things that required energy. Breaking and entering. Working two twelve-hours shifts in a row. Staying virtuous around the man of your dreams. Reprimanding one of your best friends and discovering he was probably addicted to something nasty.

The need for vitality itched within me, making me irritable and anxious despite my worn-out feeling. For me, that energy-longing translated into lust, a sudden need to be touched and consumed by someone I could consume in return.

I called Bastien.

"What is it now?" he asked sarcastically. "I suppose you're just going to cut to the chase and call Dana. That way you can get it over with and tell her how her neighbor has a plan to seduce her and bring down her organization. Maybe while you're at it, you can mention the break-in and get me arrested. You could even key my car if you wanted. It would be a perfect ending to my already ruined career."

"Oh shut up," I snapped, not having the patience for this. Apparently I still had some fury left in me from earlier. "First, you were not going to bed Dana last night, so get that out of your system. Second, you probably deterred her by answering the door in the first place, as stoned as you were. Third, if you'd really wanted to endear yourself to her, you would have shown more concern for me rather than coming off as an uncaring asshole."

"How *is* your ankle?" he asked reluctantly.

"Fine. You know how it goes." A sprain was barely a day's concern for an immortal. "Good enough to go dancing on."

"Dancing?"

"Yes. I want you to take me out. Now. I just had the worst day ever."

"Sorry."

"Sorry? Are you turning me down? Since when have you been such a grudge-holder?"

"It's not just that . . . well, okay, maybe a little. But Bill invited me over to watch a football game."

"You hate football."

"Yeah, but I might see Dana. Sorry, Fleur. You're on your own tonight."

Annoyed, I hung up and dialed the next best dancer I knew.

"Cody," I said, "we're going clubbing."

"Okay," he returned agreeably, "but I'll have to bring Hugh and Peter."

"Ack. They dance almost as badly as Seth."

"Yeah. But I promised I'd hang out with them tonight. Unless you want to come over here? We're playing D&D right now. Do you know how many hit points a succubus has?"

"All right, all right. Bring them along."

I hung up. It didn't really matter who came anyway. I mostly just wanted people to go out with. Companionship gave the outing some semblance of normality, though it wasn't like I needed any of them for what I was going to do.

"Jesus, woman," breathed Hugh when I answered my door an hour later. "You're kind of screwing with my sisterly feelings for you."

I had on a pleated black skirt that covered less than half my thighs. My top was off the shoulder with three-quarter sleeves, and it stopped just above my belly button, leaving my midriff bare. It was made of clinging, stretchy black lace that looked opaque in dim lighting and showed everything— and I do mean everything—in full light.

The only decision left was what body to go out in. I didn't like to do succubus work in my usual shape—the one that worked at Emerald City and slept with Seth. I wanted an anonymous face, one that could forget and be forgotten. Staring at my bathroom mirror, I considered a number of features and ethnicities. Finally, I opted for a pretty Latina look, sultry with long dark hair.

We went to the same club Bastien and I had danced at before. It played varying genres of music, but all of it was fast and heavy. It thrummed in the blood. Hugh immediately parked himself at the bar, looking exactly like the creepy guy who ogled younger women that he was. Peter seemed torn between joining him and hitting the floor. He was homebody enough to want to stay with Hugh, but I knew places like this were fertile hunting grounds for vampires and succubi alike. Reluctantly, the frumpy vampire bought a drink and then made his way to the dancers, looking hopelessly out of place. I knew he'd survive, though; he'd been doing what he did almost as long as I had.

I walked up to the bar and ordered a shot of Rumple Minze, which I downed immediately. It was funny—part of me thought that I could scorn Doug for getting mixed up with some drug when I turned so readily to alcohol to ease my own tension.

"Dance with me," I told Cody, grabbing his hand.

He looked good tonight, wearing a button-up shirt untucked and loose. It had a neat printed pattern on it, one of those that only confident guys with real fashion sense could actually wear. With his agile dancing and golden blond looks, he made a good partner.

"What am I, your warm-up?" he asked me a few songs later.

I laughed. We were dancing awfully close, and I had been moving my body more provocatively than I normally would with a friend. Unconscious motion. My succubus hunger surfacing.

"Does it bother you?"

"Nope. Well, other than giving me that weird incest feeling Hugh was talking about. But I don't think you're going to get what you need off me."

"True," I said scanning the crowd. The place was packed with mortals, all warm and energetic and burning with life in a way my friends and I did not. Again, the itch of longing seized me. I wanted to touch them all and knew I'd have to break from Cody soon.

"What's got you all fired up anyway? We don't usually see you like this."

That was true. Mostly he and the others just heard me bitching and moaning about my infernal job and how I hated seducing nice guys. "Need to burn off some Seth lust. That, and I got majorly run down today," I explained, proceeding to tell him the rest.

Cody felt as sad as I did about Doug, whom he knew and liked. The young vampire agreed that Doug's erratic behavior sounded amphetamine based, and he threw out a few suggestions for me. I made a mental note to look them up later.

Cody and I finally split up, each to take care of our own business. I started working the room, much as I had the other night, only this time my motivation was legitimate. I had my pick of partners and no end of free drinks. Each time I got someone to buy me one, Hugh—still at the bar—would shake his head with wry amusement.

In about two hours, I had my mark. He was young and muscular, made extra gorgeous by sexy Mediterranean features. Italian descent, I suspected. He was also sweet and shy, clearly astonished that I kept dancing with him. His friends, watching from afar, apparently felt the same way.

We had moved to a crowded part of the dance floor, jam-packed with other sweating, frenzied bodies. I rubbed mine against his in a more intimate way than the crowd quite required, my hands sliding over his body as we swayed. When our lips brushed against each other's, he pulled back.

He told me then—awkwardly and reluctantly—that he had a girlfriend. That didn't come as a surprise to me. We stopped dancing, getting jostled by the crowd, and I feigned modest embarrassment for my boldness while pretending not to notice how he hadn't seemed to want to make the girlfriend admission.

"Er, wait," he said as I started to turn and leave. Hesitation hung heavy in his voice. The voice of someone trying to rationalize something he knew he shouldn't be doing . . . but wanted to anyway. True consternation churned on his face. "I mean, we can still . . . we can still . . . keep dancing. Can't we?"

Five dances later, I'd sweet-talked—and bribed—one of the waiters into letting us into a storage room in the club's basement. It was dark and small and filled with extra tables, but it sufficed for what we needed. I could still hear the music from above, though none of the song's specifics. The whole building vibrated with the beat. My guy still appeared nervous, but alcohol and opportunity were clearly winning out over his better judgment. I didn't tell him my name. I didn't ask for his.

I pulled him to me, and we kissed—the kind of hard, furious kissing that makes your lips feel swollen afterward. His hands started on my hips and then moved upward, peeling the lace shirt up as they went, exposing my breasts. His hands fondled them wonderingly, feeling their shape and size, making my nipples harden and stand out. He leaned down and put his lips to one, sucking hard. When I felt his teeth bite gently, I grunted in approval and shifted my hands down to loosen his belt.

He straightened back up, and this time I was the one who went down—literally. On my knees, I tugged on his boxers and released the erection that had been straining at the fabric.

I ran my tongue along its tip, tasting the few salty drops that had already seeped out. Then, without further hesitation, I took the whole thing into my mouth, letting my tongue roll over it as my lips moved back and forth along the length of the shaft. He groaned and laced his fingers across the back of my neck, trying to push more of him inside. The first tendrils of his energy began flowing into me, sweet and delicious. He was a good one, full of strength. I sucked harder, teasing him for a couple more minutes, then broke away and stood up. The look on his face when I stopped became almost comically desperate. Like he couldn't believe I had just done that to him. Like I had just gone and hit his shins with a baseball bat.

I licked my lips and smiled. "You want more? You're going to have to come and get it."

This was the clincher. If I was going to go to the trouble of bagging a guy with a strong life force, I might as well hit my quota with Jerome and do some corrupting as well. A guy with a serious girlfriend might feel guilty about fooling around with another woman, but he'd feel guiltier still if he was the one who took serious steps toward initiating it. It was too easy to say *she made me do it*. My part was done; he had to take over now.

This guy might not have realized my ulterior motives here,

but he seemed to sense the gravity of the situation. He stood on the edge now, the edge of a decision that could affect his eternal soul. Did he or didn't he? Did he give in to his lust and betray a woman he cared about? Did he take a chance with me he might never get again? Or did he reject me and walk away? Did he stay faithful?

My smile grew, slow and languid, as he debated. I paced around the room like I had all the time in the world, like I didn't care what he decided to do. The click of my heels sounded loudly on the hard floor. I turned away from him, trying to make out some old framed picture on the wall. It was mostly a dark blur in the dim lighting.

Then, I felt him behind me. His hands slid from my waist down to my hips, then lower to cradle my ass. He pushed up what little of the skirt there was and pulled down the strappy black thong I had underneath. Slowly, his hands traced every curve, feeling and exploring. One hand moved around the outside of my leg toward the front, between my thighs. The movement forced him to move closer to me, and I could feel him—still hard, still ready—press against my flesh.

The exploring hand pushed farther between my thighs, and his breath was hard and hot on my neck. His fingers brushed the small, neatly trimmed patch of hair between my legs, then moved lower, dancing at the edges of my lips, teasing them. A small, urgent moan left my mouth, and I ground against him, hoping to get a response.

He slid his fingers in a smooth rhythm, stoking my already raging desire. A minute later, those urgent fingers moved into me, probing and exploring. I was wet and slippery, but it still caught me by surprise, and I exclaimed loudly. He wrapped his other arm around my waist, pulling me even closer, and continued driving those fingers in and out. His life poured into me again. A purely physical burning welled inside of me too, growing stronger each time he moved in. But before that feeling could reach completion, he pulled his fingers out and left them out. My turn to feel unfulfilled. Gripping my shoulders, he turned me around, and I braced myself to be shoved on top of the table or up against the wall.

To my astonishment, he pushed me onto my knees instead, his breathing frantic now, his eyes burning with hunger and lust. "Your mouth," he gasped out. "I want your mouth again."

Unexpected—and perhaps a little disappointing—but it all worked the same for me. Before I could even act, he thrust himself back between my lips. A surprised sound lodged in my throat, and it seemed to turn him on even more. I no longer had to worry about who was taking the initiative here; it was all him. His hands held my head and neck in place as he pumped away, pushing into me over and over.

The life-force transfer started in earnest, his energy flooding into me with his thoughts and feelings. *Finally, finally, finally,* he thought, aching desire crackling through him. Feeling his mind and soul, I realized then he might not have been so easy a tag as I originally thought.

He loved his girlfriend. Loved her passionately. But she didn't like oral sex, and one of the biggest fantasies of this guy's life was to—bluntly—fuck her face. Had I started foreplay in some other way tonight, he might very well have been strong enough to decline. But I had given him the one thing he couldn't refuse. It overpowered the guilt lurking in the back of his mind.

I'll never get this chance again. Allison doesn't have to know.

I knew that rationalization well. It was just about the oldest in the book.

He thrust more urgently, that long shaft filling my mouth as his eyes watched me eagerly, and unintelligible, primal noises sounded in his throat. And for me, who had been denied an orgasm, pleasure was building in a different way. Life-force transfer doesn't occur at the point of a physical contact or even orgasm. It's bigger than that, more holistic. Soul to soul. His energy washed over me now in waves, and it was pure ecstasy as I rode that ocean higher and higher. My body burned with it, nearly to the breaking point. Before that crest crashed over, before our connection broke, I caught one more thought from him, plain and simple: *mouth or face?*

Ah, men.

He chose mouth, moaning loudly as he came. Warm, bitter liquid flooded over my tongue as his body spasmed and his nails dug into my neck and scalp. I waited until he finished, then swallowed because I knew it was what he wanted me to do. It was what every guy wanted. And really, it was the least I could do for him, because with his orgasm came a climax of my own.

The full force of his energy hit me like a bolt of lightning at the same time he felt its loss. I broke from him, gasping at the feel of that power, swimming in that bliss, invigorated and alive. He, however, stiffened and paled, suddenly weak and confused at losing something he hadn't even known he had. He groped blindly for support and caught the edge of a table as his legs gave out underneath him. The table saved him from completely falling over, and I caught his other arm, balancing him. Carefully, I eased him down so he could sit and lean his body against a chair.

His eyes struggled to stay open as the shock of his energy loss pulled him toward unconsciousness. Another cardinal succubus rule: the stronger the guy, the stronger his loss would be. "Oh my God . . . what's wrong with me?"

Pushing aside whatever kindly feelings or sympathy I might have, reminding myself he'd—eventually—recover, I stared down at him coolly and rearranged my clothes. "I think you drank too much." I leaned over and tugged up his pants. "I'll go get help."

He started to protest, but I was already out the door. I strode back to the dance floor, haloed in his energy. I felt like a goddess entering a temple of worshippers, and many sets of eyes seemed to regard me as exactly that. A few quick searches, and I found his friends from earlier. I told them he'd passed out downstairs and left them to deal with it.

"This one's on me," I heard Hugh say when I walked back up to the bar. My post-sex glamour would be especially obvious to him.

I ordered a shot of Jägermeister and chased it with another shot of Goldschlager. Nothing like funny-named liquor to top off an evening.

"Does it make you feel better?" the imp asked. He inclined his head toward the two empty glasses.

"No," I said. "But sometimes it helps me not remember as much."

I went home after that and cooked myself in a long, hot shower, trying to wash away the feel of sex. My buzz soon yielded to my second headache of the day and a slightly nauseous feeling. I had just settled down on the couch for mindless TV watching, back in my normal shape, when Seth showed up.

"I wanted to see how you were doing," he explained, sitting down next to me.

"Better," I told him uneasily. "Sort of. I went out with the gang."

"Ah. Sounds fun." He didn't sound entirely sincere. I think "the gang" still kind of weirded him out a little.

He leaned his head on the couch and stared at me for a long time, not saying anything.

I laughed in spite of myself. "What?"

"I don't know," he said, face serious. He reminded me of a child staring at the tree on Christmas morning. "It's weird. It's just you're so . . . so beautiful tonight. I mean, you're always pretty, of course, but tonight, I don't know—I can't take my eyes off of you. I want to . . ." He didn't give voice to the urge.

"Must be the wet hair and pajamas," I said lightly. "Always a turn-on."

But I knew what was bedazzling him. The guy from the club. Or rather, that guy's stolen life. Humans couldn't resist it. Immortals couldn't resist it. Racking my brain, I realized Seth had never seen me so soon after a fix. He'd seen me the same day sometimes—and also commented on my attractiveness then—but this was the first time he'd received its full effect. It made me feel guilty to see him looking at me like this.

His hand reached for mine, and I tried not to flinch as he took it. Even after the shower, I felt dirty and cheap. I didn't want him to touch me after what I'd done, even if it had been in a different body. I didn't deserve such love.

Seth sighed, still enchanted. His long fingers traced warm, whirling patterns on my skin. I felt my breathing grow heavier. "I wish I could put your beauty into words. But I'm not that good of a writer. Guess I need some work."

I stood up hastily and tugged at his hand. "Now you're just being silly. I think you're the one that needs to go home and rest."

He blinked. "Oh. So no more, uh, attempts at sleeping?"

I hesitated. I wanted to do it again but still didn't trust myself. Or Seth actually, not with the way he kept watching me with such rapt admiration, that heat burning in his eyes. One would have thought a backroom fling might have sated my lust for the night, but I wanted Seth just as much as ever. Of course, in retrospect, maybe that wasn't a surprise after all. Said fling hadn't exactly addressed *my* physical needs.

"No," I told Seth. "Not yet. Too soon."

He looked like being separated from me would hurt him physically, but he finally conceded when I let him kiss my cheek. It was long and lingering, more sensuous than one would expect, making me inhale and then exhale a long, shuddering breath. I wouldn't return the gesture, however. Not with these lips. He waxed on about my beauty a few more times before finally leaving, and I went to bed shortly thereafter.

Lying there, I told myself over and over that I had done the right thing at the club. I had done what I needed to do to keep myself strong and capable. After all, Seth had said he loved my "whirlwind." Sex was the means of keeping it strong. *I had done the right thing.* And I had done the right thing with Doug too. Everything I'd done today had been for the best.

And yet . . . if that was true, then why did I feel so terrible about it all?

Chapter 9

"Nice glow," Bastien told me when he answered the door the following afternoon.

"Yeah. Tell me about it."

I traipsed into his house wearing the Tabitha body, and pulled up a stool at his kitchen counter. He handed me a Mountain Dew from the refrigerator.

"Why so glum? Couldn't have been all that bad."

"It was okay. In that sleazy, backroom sort of way. Seth came over afterward and couldn't stop telling me how pretty I was."

"Of course he did." Bastien was sporting a glow of his own today. "How could he help it? He's a weak mortal, just like they all are."

I ignored the jibe and took down half the can in one gulp. "On the topic of 'weak mortals,' how'd your football game go?"

"Ridiculously boring. Bill must have fantastic speech writers because his conversation is on the same level as that cupboard's over there. But, on the bright side, I did talk to Dana several times, and I think I repaired the damage you did."

"Ye gods, will you get over this? I didn't do anything. You have no one to blame for that but yourself."

"Hey, I didn't fall down the stairs. Anyway, I took your

advice and played sympathetic brother. She really seemed to go for it. Except . . ."

"Except what?"

He frowned, blue eyes perplexed. "She seems to like me well enough. She asks about my job, she asks about you. But something's weird. I just don't feel like . . ."

"Like she's going to throw herself at you any time soon? Huh. I never would have guessed."

His expression hardened, doubts banished. "It's just a matter of time, that's all. Like that convent in Brussels. Remember how well that turned out?"

I grinned. "Just a matter of time. Sure. So what are your plans today?"

"Nothing. I'll probably go out later, but now I'm just sort of hanging around. Mitch is supposed to be at work, after all."

"Well, let's sneak you out and go see a movie or something."

Frankly, I was eager to do something semi-fun. I had finally made it to my day off, and it hadn't come a moment too soon. The only thing that bothered me was not knowing what had happened at the bookstore when—or rather if—Doug came in this morning. If Warren or Paige had been around, they might have banned him for a while. But I certainly didn't have that power, and I hated to lose the coverage anyway. I'd finally resorted to calling Janice, telling her to ring my cell immediately if there were any repeat problems. I hadn't heard anything so far.

Bastien allowed himself grudging interest in a movie. "Anything good playing?"

The doorbell rang before we could check.

"Geez, Bas. It's like Grand Central Station whenever I'm here."

"Probably a Jehovah's Witness," he decided, checking out the door invisibly. "Huh. It's Jody. Wonder what she wants."

I supposed Dana visiting would have been more serendipi-
tous, but I found Jody's presence a relief. "Well, let her go.
You're supposed to be at work."

He nudged me. "You answer."

"Me?"

"Sure. Make up some reason to be here. She's chummy
with Dana. You can do some reconnaissance."

"Oh, for goodness—"

The doorbell rang again, and Bastien looked at me plead-
ingly. I had a good opinion of Jody, but I didn't like him mixing me up in his affairs. Grumbling, I went to the door.
Maybe she was just dropping off more baked goods or something, I thought. Her face burst into a grin upon seeing me.

"I was hoping it was you! I thought I recognized the Passat."

I smiled back at her. "Good memory. Did you need Mitch?
He's at work."

"No, not really. I just saw the car and wanted to say hi.
Are you hanging out here?"

"Uh, yeah. It's my day off, and I promised him I'd . . . do
some yard work."

Bastien, hovering invisibly nearby, got a kick out of that.

"It's a great day for it," she agreed. I supposed it was, in
that crisply sunny sort of way that sometimes shows up in
winter. At least we had no rain today. "What were you going
to do? It looks like the lawn service took care of most of the
leaves."

That it had. I tried to think of something superfluous that
suburbanites wouldn't have already underpaid someone else
to do. "I was going to plant some flowers."

"Oh!" She clasped her hands together, brown eyes alight.
"That's a great idea. Do you want some help?"

"Uh . . ."

Beside me, Bastien nearly had a seizure. He nodded his
head vigorously and mouthed the word *reconnaissance*.

Yard work was the last thing I wanted to do on my day off,

but now I'd gone and boxed myself in. "Sure. I don't really know what to do anyway." That had to be the understatement of the year.

"Let me grab my coat, and we'll go to my favorite nursery," she squealed. "This is going to be fun."

She dashed back to her house, and I glared at Bastien. "I hate you."

"Don't I know it." He clapped me on the back. "I'm sure you have a green thumb somewhere, Fleur. If not, you can shape-shift one."

"You owe me. Big time."

Jody drove us to some gardening place that looked like a maze of greenery to me. Actually, greenery wasn't quite the right word. Many of the trees and plants had lost leaves, turning brown and yellow as winter deepened. A maze of vegetation, I guess.

"They're still alive," she told me, assessing plants with an expert eye. "Although, this isn't exactly the best time to do plantings. Still, we should be able to manage something since the ground isn't too hard yet."

I grimaced. "Sounds dirty."

She laughed. "How'd you get slated for this?"

"My brother doesn't . . . always think things through. And he's pretty persuasive when he wants to be." And annoying. And pushy.

"I can see that. He's pretty cute too. Bet he gets women to do anything he wants."

"You have no idea."

This made her smile again. "Well, hang in there. Once you get started with this kind of stuff, you get into it. And it's not that dirty. You want dirty, I'll tell you about Guatemala someday."

"When were you in Guatemala?" Whoa. Somehow I managed her circle picking places like Malibu and Paris for vacations.

"When I was in the Peace Corps."

"You were in the Peace Corps?"

"Yup. When I was younger."

I stared after her as she continued checking out the selection. Jody had been in the Peace Corps and worked as an art teacher. She was clearly talented creatively. She was smart and had a good personality. How the hell had she gotten mixed up with Dana?

We ended up buying several plants she called Christmas Roses, plus some bulbs she warned might or might not come up in the spring. Once back at Bastien's, we bundled up in coats and gloves and set to digging in his front yard. I saw him peek out the window and wave at me at one point; I stuck my tongue out at him when Jody wasn't looking.

Jody was only too happy to tell me about her past. I'd ask the occasional clarifying question, and she'd then go on for a while more. I listened, commenting occasionally, and—as much as I hated to admit it—found the afternoon passing pleasantly. She had been right: garden work wasn't so bad once you started. Inevitably, her chatter turned to the CPFV, and she both surprised and relieved me by admitting some discontent.

"I mean," she was saying, "I stand by them. Absolutely. It's just sometimes, I wish we were doing things in different ways."

I looked up, happy to take a break from hacking at the hard ground. "What kinds of things?"

She pursed her cute lips together. "I guess . . . like . . . we spend a lot of time telling people what to do and what not to do, you know? Like we're trying to help them lead better lives, and I think that's good. After all, Dana says an ounce of prevention is worth a pound of cure."

Ugh. Cliché anyone?

"But I also wish we were doing something for those that need help now. Do you know how many families in this area don't have enough to eat? It'd be great if we could work with local food banks to do something about that—especially with the holidays coming up. Or like . . . we do a lot to help teens make smart choices, but I visited some shelters for girls that are already in trouble. They've run away. They're pregnant. Dana says they're lost causes, but . . ."

"You don't think so?" I asked gently.

She had stopped digging too and stared absentmindedly at the bulb she held. "I don't think anyone's beyond help. But Dana . . . I mean, she's so smart. She knows more than me about this stuff. I trust what she says."

"Nothing wrong with questioning."

"Yeah, I suppose. It's just, well, she's been a good friend to me." Her eyes focused on something not here, something far away and long ago. "A couple years ago, Jack and I had some, you know, problems. I mean, it happens right? No relationship's perfect."

"No," I agreed grimly.

"Anyway, she helped me work through that. I feel sort of . . ."

"Obligated?"

Jody fumbled. "I-I don't know. I guess so. Sometimes, she's hard to know . . . like she can surprise you with things you never saw coming. Other times . . ." She shook her head and gave a nervous laugh. "I don't know what I'm saying. She's wonderful. The most amazing person I've ever met. She does so much good."

She changed the subject abruptly after that, and I let her. We moved on to happier topics, and I found myself laughing along with her and enjoying her company. At one point, I ran into Bastien's kitchen and made us hot chocolate. We drank it outside as we finished the last of our plants, finally sitting back and admiring our handiwork. Despite my initial misgivings, I kind of liked accomplishing something so tangible.

"Look," said Jody. "Dana just came home."

Sure enough, Dana's Explorer pulled in next door, and a moment later, the woman herself strolled over. She graced us with one of those ice-bitch smiles.

"This looks cozy."

Jody's earlier bubbly nature seemed somewhat diminished. "Tabitha needed some gardening help, so I came over."

"Wasn't that nice of you."

Dana gave the other woman a look I couldn't interpret, save that disapproval and possibly anger underscored it. Although I had been arguing to the contrary with Bastien, I got the feeling I might truly have pissed off Dana more than I'd suspected, creating the bad impression he kept accusing me of. It looked like Dana may even have voiced her opinions of me to Jody.

I watched Jody's face pass through a range of emotions. I felt pretty confident there was more iron in there than her surface showed, and for a half a second she looked as though she might lash out in defiance. Then, after a moment's eye contact, she looked away, backing down.

Perhaps I should have simpered just then and tried to weasel into Dana's good graces, but mostly I felt angry at what I perceived as her chastisement. She had no right to do that Jody.

"It was incredibly nice," I said sharply. "Jody's one of those rare, honestly good people in the world. Not just one who pretends to be. But of course you already know that."

Jody blushed furiously, and the edges of Dana's smile twitched a little. "Yes. Yes, she is. How's your ankle doing?"

"Good as new."

"Glad to hear it."

We all waited in awkward silence. I decided I would wait out Dana this time, no matter how scary that stare. She, of course, was a master of waiting, so it wasn't a surprise when Jody was the one who cracked. Honestly, I couldn't blame her.

"Well. Jack should be home soon. I should get going."

I stood up with her and helped her gather the tools. We all exchanged a few more stiff remarks, then parted ways.

"What happened? What happened?" exclaimed Bastien when I came back inside. "I saw Dana out there."

"Nothing new. Jody's a saint; Dana's a bitch. I hope you hurry up and get this done with."

"Damn it, I'm trying! I don't suppose you found out anything useful?"

"Not really . . . although, I think Jody knows something about Dana. Something juicy enough even for you. She wouldn't tell me exactly what."

The incubus clung to this piece of information like a dog with a bone. "You've got to find out what! Call her up tomorrow. Take her to lunch."

"Jesus, Bastien. I like her, but I'm not doing your work for you. This is *your* show, remember? Besides, I do have a life, you know."

He scowled. "That's up for debate."

"Why are you so worked up about this Dana thing anyway? I mean, I'd love to see her fall, but the way you're acting . . . I don't know. It's totally pushing you over the edge."

"Why shouldn't I be worked up? Just because you don't play the soul game anymore doesn't mean the rest of us don't have an eye on our careers."

I knew Bastien too well not to suspect there was some other reason we were fighting all the time. "And that's all it is, huh? Just good old-fashioned American work ethic?"

"Yes," he said stiffly. "There's nothing wrong with that."

We locked matching Hunter gazes, and I tried to let him know with my eyes that I knew there was more than he was telling me. He stared stonily back, refusing to open up. At last, I shook my head, not wanting to be drawn into any more fighting.

"Mind if I use your hot tub?" I asked instead.

He gestured toward the back patio. "Sure. Have the run of the house. Use me and go."

"You're being childish."

Not answering, he went off to watch TV.

I let myself out through the patio and flipped open the hot

tub's lid. Hot steam poured out, and I sighed with pleasure. It felt downright decadent after being out in the cold all day. Glancing around, I took in the vine-covered privacy trellises. There were three of them with a person-sized gap between each one. Dusk was rapidly giving way to darkness, and I felt pretty obscured from the neighbors.

I stripped off my clothes and tentatively put a foot in the tub. Hot. Very hot. I yanked it out, then waited a minute before trying again. Slowly, I eased the rest of me in, bit by bit. When I was finally submerged from the neck down, I exhaled happily and leaned my head back against the edge. Fantastic. I kicked on the bubbles and closed my eyes. Suddenly, I found myself able to forget it all. Doug. The guy from the club. Dana. Seth.

Well, maybe not Seth entirely. But I could forget the bad things, at least.

When my hair had curled from the steam and sweat was rolling down my forehead, I stood up and sat on the tub's edge, letting the air dry me off. A lot of people don't understand outdoor hot tubs, but I preferred them to indoor ones. Nothing can match that temperature change.

Once cooled, I sat back in the water, ready to repeat the process. I could have done this all night and been perfectly happy.

I'd only been back in the water a few minutes when I heard a twig snap from somewhere nearby. It was like a bad-horror-movie cliché, but terrifying nonetheless. I shot out of the water, splashing everywhere, scrambling over the side as I heard a rustle of leaves and brush.

"Bastien!" I yelled, running back into the house.

He tore into the room, face pale and alarmed. "What's the matter?"

I backed away from the patio, pointing. "There's someone out there."

Nothing could really hurt me, of course, but being immortal does not relieve a person of instinctual fear and caution.

There'd be time to feel embarrassed about girly behavior later.

His eyes cut to the patio, and he moved outdoors without any hesitation to look around. My knight. I waited in the kitchen, dripping water onto the wood floor, my heart still thumping. He returned a few minutes later and shook his head.

"There's nothing out there. You imagined it."

"No. It was there. I heard it."

"Then it was an animal." He suddenly smirked. "Or maybe Reese getting a thrill."

When I didn't laugh at the joke, he approached and pulled me to him, unconcerned about getting his clothes wet. My body trembled against his.

"It's all right," he murmured. "You're okay. You're safe."

He pulled off his blazer and wrapped it around me. It was too big, but it felt wonderful. I huddled against him, still too fazed to shape-shift some more substantial clothing on.

"Come on, Fleur. You know I'm here. You know I won't let anything happen to you."

The animosity we'd built from our fight went away, and suddenly we were back to normal again. He took me upstairs to his bedroom, still keeping his arm around me. I shape-shifted dry as we walked and turned back into my Georgina self. Changing into his usual shape as well, he pulled me down to the bed with him so my head rested on his chest.

A lot of immortals don't understand the way incubi and succubi relate to each other. We tend to touch a lot, in ways that are small but still intimate by most standards. I'd been accused many times of being sexually involved with Bastien—or someone else—over the years. Yet the truth was that in all of our time together, he and I had never actually had anything romantic happen. We were close, physically and emotionally, but that came from friendship, nothing more.

Because honestly, when you spent most of your existence giving complete strangers access to your body, it seemed stupid not to enjoy physical bonding with those you actually cared about. And again, by physical bonding, I just meant small things, not even those that resulted in orgasm or a PG rating. Petting. Stroking. Massaging. Kissing here and there. They were all signs of closeness. We needed them, I think, to keep ourselves sane with the way we lived. And there was a certain comfort to knowing that in doing this, the other person got exactly the same thing in return. I could not have had such an equitable emotional relationship if I'd sought a similar physical exchange with, say, Hugh or the vampires. It would have meant something different to them.

Which was why I could lay there in Bastien's bed, half naked, with my body twisted around his. We laughed under the blankets, reminiscing about past times when we had to sleep in similar—but less comfortable—ways. Ship cabins. Narrow boardinghouse beds. Campsites along country roads. Then too, we'd huddled together for warmth and security.

I ended up spending the whole night with him. He held me the entire time in as gentlemanly a way as Seth might have. But with Bastien, I didn't toss and turn with worry all night over what damage one careless touch might do. It was the best night of sleep I'd had in weeks.

When I returned home the next day, I called Seth and asked him if he'd been at the bookstore yesterday. He verified that he had and that Doug had behaved himself.

"He was kind of goofy and chipper but nothing like that day."

"Good. I hope that's the end of it."

There was an awkward pause, and then Seth asked, too casually: "Were you out again last night? I called you pretty late and didn't get an answer."

"Oh, yeah. I stayed at Bastien's all night."

"Oh."

Silence.

"It's not what you think," I hastily assured him. "We just slept. Perfectly platonic. Just like . . ."

"You and me?"

Silence.

"Nothing happened. He's like a brother to me. Honest. He's the last person you should be jealous of."

"I'm not jealous. Not exactly. But if you say it's nothing, then it's nothing. I didn't mean to sound like I was accusing you of lying. I know you wouldn't do that."

I thought about oral sex at the dance club and my bare skin pressed against Bastien's. I might not lie, but I didn't always tell Seth the whole truth either.

A few days later, Seth and I went to another Nocturnal Admission concert. Doug and I had worked together all week in a civil manner, if not exactly a friendly one. Seth picked me up at my place and again could only stare in wonder at my appearance. I'd gone out hunting with Bastien last night—against my better judgment—and had taken another victim. The glamour hadn't quite diminished yet, and I would have looked hot even in a burlap bag. So, I suppose wearing the kind of dress I did was just outright mean. It was a little slip of a dress in gray cotton jersey, with a ribbon threaded around it that tied just under my breasts. The thin-strapped, V-necked top showed lots of cleavage; the skirt hung soft and drapey to just above my knee. It was like a winter sundress.

Seth put his arms around me and nuzzled my neck. "You never fail to surprise me. I always think I know what to expect with you. Then I actually see you, and . . ."

He couldn't finish, but his eyes did it for him. They slid up and down my body, making my insides melt. *Throw me on the bed and take me,* I begged silently. Out loud I said, "We should get going."

At the concert, Nocturnal Admission performed as spectacularly as last time. Their following had increased, and people packed every square inch of the place. I had trouble seeing the stage but could hear every golden note.

Fortunately, I got to see plenty of Doug later. The venue had let him use the place for another wild, post-concert party. Adoring women—and several men—clung flirtatiously to him and the other band members. Doug hugged me when he saw me, arranged for someone to make me a decent drink, and acted as though nothing had happened between us. I guessed I was glad to set aside the hard feelings, but now that I knew what to blame his behavior on, his bright and wild demeanor unnerved me.

Casey showed up at one point, still looking a bit gaunt, but obviously on the mend. From across the room, I watched her tentatively approach Alec. He'd been talking to Wyatt the guitar player and turned to give her an obviously forced and fake smile. I couldn't hear the conversation, but the message came through loud and clear. She wanted to talk to him, to get his attention in some way, and he was blatantly snubbing her. I could see him shaking his head as she spoke, an almost desperate look on her face. Finally, he simply walked away, leaving her staring and upset.

"I want to go over there and punch him," I told Seth.

"No, you don't. It's their business, not yours."

I turned on him. "Damn it, Seth! How can you always be so placid and nonconfrontational? Don't you stand up for anything?"

He regarded me coolly. If he was surprised or offended by my outburst, he didn't show it. "I stand up for plenty of things. I just know when to pick my battles, that's all. So should you."

"You realize he slept with her and then turned around and dropped her cold. He may have even used sinister ways to do it."

"Believe me, I'm not condoning that, but Casey's got to be the one to say something. Otherwise, it's just you making accusations and starting a scene."

I scowled, half agreeing with him but still wishing I could help. Looking around, I couldn't see her anymore, which was probably just as well. With any luck, she'd gone home and would swear off the company of men for a while. Seth left for the bathroom, and almost the moment he was gone, Alec sidled up.

"Hey, Georgina. You look hot."

"Thanks," I said. I angled my body away, hoping he'd get the signal I wasn't interested. He was lucky I didn't just turn around and deck him.

"You're, like, the best-looking woman in here tonight."

Whether that was actually true or not, I knew the life-force surplus made me the most attractive. There was a difference. Eyeing Alec, I suddenly toyed with the idea of returning his flirtation and sleeping with him. I rather liked the idea of seeing him sprawled out unconscious and sick somewhere. Nah. On second thought, considering he was such a sleazebag, I probably wouldn't steal enough energy to do much more than wind him.

"You drinking those vodka gambits again?" he asked, still pushing the act.

"Gimlets," I corrected.

"Well, the bar can make anything if you want something different. And there's weed everywhere. I think I saw Corey with acid too."

This guy just couldn't stop trying to fuck women over. He didn't care how he did it. Seth showed up just then, and I turned to him with a dazzling smile.

"Nice talking to you Alec," I said breezily, taking Seth's arm. "See you around."

"What was that about?" asked Seth, once we were out of earshot.

"That asshole was trying to pick me up again. Right after turning away Casey. God, I hate him. He was trying the usual stuff too. Trying to push more drinks on me. Telling me how hot I was."

Seth leaned his face toward mine. "You are hot."

"Stop that. You're giving me funny ideas."

He continued holding me close. I really needed to wait two days before seeing him after a fix. "Ever wonder how far I could kiss you on the lips?" he asked.

"What do you mean?"

"Well, I can somewhat substantially kiss your cheek and neck, right? Your lips though . . . well, those have to be quick, brushing kind of kisses. Too much intensity and tongue with your mouth is right out. So, I figure there must be a middle ground."

"Have you been drinking?"

"Just thinking, that's all."

The rapture from my glow was reflected in his face. Forgetting about anyone we knew seeing us, I let him lean his mouth toward my own. Ever so gently, his lips touched mine. Not a family-type slip of a kiss, nor a saliva-exchanging deep kiss either. It was like a caress. His lips slowly stroked my lips, his tongue just barely tracing the contours of my mouth. Electricity ran from my head to my toes and tried to run back up again, but it got delayed between my legs. Seth stepped away.

"Anything bad happen?"

"No," I breathed. "But I think we need to conduct several repeat experiments, just to make sure."

Suddenly, from across the room, we heard whoops and cheers, followed by a terrific crashing sound and gasps of alarm. Without conscious communication, Seth and I moved as one to see what had happened.

Doug lay in a heap on the floor in front of the stage, laughing hysterically. "What's going on?" I asked Corey.

His eyes were heavily dilated, and I remembered Alec saying the bass player had acid. "It's a new Olympic sport. Stage-table High Jumps."

Following his gaze, I saw a table set up on the stage. About fifteen feet away, on the floor by Doug, was an overturned table. I looked back and forth. "Did he try to jump from that table to that one?"

Corey cackled. "Sure did. Shit. He almost made it. Caught the edge on his way down."

"He could have broken his leg," muttered Seth in disgust. "Or worse."

Doug seemed to be okay. Some solicitous women in tight shirts were helping him stand. He caught my eye and laughed harder.

"Don't look so panicked, Kincaid. I'm fine . . . but if you want to make sure, you can come kiss me too and make it all better."

He winked at Seth, and others laughed with him, without knowing why. I was soon forgotten as more adoring people swarmed in. Seth and I retreated.

"What was he thinking?" I fretted. "I mean, he's always doing crazy acrobatic stuff on stage, but he had to have known he couldn't make that."

"If he's not thinking straight, there's no telling what he believes. Drugs'll do that. Give you a sense of invincibility."

I reminded myself to look up those drug names Cody had suggested. I didn't know if it'd do any good, but it'd at least make me think I was doing something.

"Hey," I exclaimed, pulling Seth to an abrupt stop. "It's him again."

"Who?"

"That guy talking to Alec. The weird gothic, male-model-type guy."

Seth followed my gesture. Way on the other side of the place, near the bar, Alec and the man I'd seen at the earlier concert were having a heated argument. The GQ-poet guy looked stern and cold tonight, dampening his otherwise suave and polished looks. Alec had a pleading look. The drummer gesticulated frantically, his face desperate and frightened. The other man shook his head sternly, face unyielding. He waved a hand toward the crowd and then said something to Alec. Alec's face paled, and he once more turned into a pitiful supplicant. The other man shook his head yet again, then strode off.

He didn't approach us exactly, but he had to move in our direction to reach the exit. He was still a good fifty feet away and separated by walls of people when an odd, prickly feeling touched my skin. It was strange and discordant, yet sleek at the same time. It was almost like what I'd felt around Doug and the band, except that had been unidentifiable. This was clearly a person's signature. It was linked to that man, pulsing with sentience. I choked out a strangled sound and quickly stepped back out of range. Pulling Seth with me, I threw my arms around him and kissed his neck.

As I did, I watched out of the corner of my eye as the strange man froze and jerked his head around, looking out over the crowd. He had felt me too. His eyes passed over us several times, but we drew no especial focus. We were just another couple getting hot and heavy. I tensed, waiting for him to come closer and try to sense me again. Without knowing why, I didn't want him to find me. He scanned a bit longer before giving up and continuing his retreat.

When he had left, I relaxed and leaned into Seth.

"What . . . ?"

"That man that was talking to Alec," I said, still in shock. "He's an immortal."

Seth's eyebrows rose. "Really? What kind? Angel? Demon?"

"None of the above. He's not one of mine."

"What do you mean not one of yours?"

"Not all immortals are part of the heaven and hell system. There are a lot of other creatures walking the world: nymphs, orisha, oni . . ."

"You do realize you've just thrust me into a theological quandary likely to keep me awake at night for years," he joked. When I didn't answer, he turned serious. "Okay. So what kind was he?"

I shook my head. "That's the thing. I don't know. I don't know what he was exactly."

Chapter 10

Jerome didn't seem very happy to hear from me the next morning.

"Do you have any idea what time it is, Georgie?" he growled into the phone.

"Why are you whining? You don't even need to sleep."

"Make this fast."

I told him about my experience at the concert and my inability to ID the mystery immortal. "He wasn't one of us. Er, I mean, you know ... not part of our ... pantheon," I finished lamely.

"'Pantheon?' I've never heard it put quite like that—outside of an introductory mythology class, of course."

"So?"

"So what?"

"So isn't that weird? I've met hundreds of different immortals and never felt one like this. He didn't feel ... normal. I mean, he did feel like an immortal, but it was just weird."

"Well, hard as it is to believe, there are still a lot of things out there you haven't experienced—despite your *vast* age."

"Yeah, yeah, I know I'm an infant, all right? But doesn't this worry you at all?"

He yawned. "Not in the least. Something angelic or demonic would, but some random demigod or satyr? Hardly. They're not part of the game. Well, they're all part of *the* Game. What I mean is, they're not part of our game. They don't have to get permission to be here. As long as they don't interfere with our business, I don't really care. They do their own thing. We'll just catalog them and move on."

"Catalog? You've got a record then?"

"Well, I don't, of course. That's one of Grace and Mei's things."

No surprise there. Jerome wasn't really big on . . . well, work. Grace and Mei were subordinate demonesses who did a lot of the dirty jobs he didn't want to. I hardly ever saw them.

"I'll have to page them," I murmured, mind spinning.

"You know, I suppose it goes without saying that there are a hundred other more useful projects you could be channeling your energy into. Like, say, helping your incubus friend. From what I hear, he's stuck high and dry out in the suburbs. Emphasis on the *high*."

"Hey," I said, defensive of Bastien's honor, "he's just taking his time. You can't rush quality work. Besides, he learned everything he knows from me."

"Somehow that doesn't reassure me." Jerome disconnected.

I hunted down Grace and Mei's number. I waited for the tone, punched in my call-back number, and hung up. A minute later, a Fourth of July worthy shower of sparks appeared in my living room and the two demonesses stood before me.

For having chosen two very different bodies, the pair looked remarkably alike. Grace was slim in an all-business, non-nubile sort of way, enhanced by the designer black skirt and jacket she wore. She had pale blond hair cut bluntly at chin length, brown-black eyes, and skin that never saw the sun. The only true color on her was the fire engine red lipstick she wore.

Mei dressed exactly the same, down to the red lipstick. Her hair, also chin-length, was a deep blue-black. Despite the softer lines, higher cheekbones, and delicate almond shape of her dark eyes, she radiated no more warmth or friendliness than her counterpart.

The two always stuck together, and I assumed they must be friends. Sort of. I had no doubt they'd claw each other's eyes out—or Jerome's, for that matter—if an opportunity for power or promotion was on the line.

"Georgina," said Mei.

"Long time no see," said Grace.

Both watched me expectantly. Aubrey watched them from the back of my couch, her hair on end and tail poofed out.

"Hey guys," I replied uneasily. "Thanks for coming over so fast. Slow day?"

They both stared at me.

"Um, so, okay. Jerome said you keep records of immortals who pass in and out of the city. Immortals who are outside of our . . ."

"Game?" suggested Grace.

"Pantheon?" suggested Mei.

"Yeah. Sure. So . . . do you?"

"Who are you looking for?" asked Mei.

"What kind of immortal?" asked Grace.

"That's the problem."

I told them everything I knew about him, which mostly included appearance and other encounters when I'd felt that weird sensation. Describing his signature was harder. I couldn't exactly say he felt like an incubus or an angel or a nymph or an oni. I hadn't run across his type before.

The demonesses processed this information, glanced at each other, and then shook their heads.

"He doesn't sound familiar," said Grace.

"But we can double-check the records," said Mei.

"Thanks," I told them. "I'd really appreciate it."

They nodded curtly and turned as if to leave. Mei suddenly glanced back at me.

"You should hang out with us sometime," she said unexpectedly. "Cleo's in Capitol Hill has great specials on Ladies Night."

"There are so few of us girls around here," added Grace. "We need to stick together."

They smiled and disappeared. I shivered. Going to a bar with those two sounded only marginally more appealing than stamping with Dana's CPFV friends.

Speaking of which, I decided to visit Bastien later that afternoon. I hadn't heard from him in a few days.

"Do you have any idea how much I don't care about your mortal friends?" he snapped when I told him about the whole bizarre situation surrounding Doug, Alec, and the mystery man. "I have real problems here. I'm dying. I'm getting nowhere with Dana. I keep seeing her, she's nice, and that's it! It's like she only wants—"

"To be friends?"

He stopped pacing around his kitchen and cut me an arch look. "Women are never just friends with me." He leaned against the counter and closed his eyes. "I just can't think what else to do. If I don't act fast, one of our superiors is going to find out how bad things are."

I decided not to mention Jerome's "high and dry" comment just then.

"Well, jeez, take a break and do something fun. Peter's having another poker game. Come over and play with us. I'm going to bring Seth."

"I thought you said this was going to be fun."

"Hey! Who was that a dig at? Peter or Seth?"

"Pick one, Fleur. Although, admittedly, Peter does make a pretty decent soufflé. What can the author do?"

"I wish you'd stop picking on Seth. You don't even know him."

Bastien shrugged. "Sorry. You just make it so easy."

"You're jealous."

"Hardly," he snorted. "I've had my share of mortal infatuations, thank you. So have you, if memory serves. And you've also had a number of immortal boyfriends you seemed to have liked reasonably well. None of them ever gave you as much grief as this guy."

"Seth's different. I can't explain it. Being with him just feels so . . . right. I feel like I've known him forever."

"Fleur, I've known you forever. You've only known this guy for a couple months."

We had gotten involved pretty quickly, and it did bug me sometimes, but I truly believed in the strength and depth of my feelings for Seth. They were neither superficial nor transient—I hoped.

He had once told me there was no one else in the world for him but me. When I'd pointed out that was a bold statement in light of how long we'd known each other, he'd simply said, "Sometimes you just know."

It was remarkably similar to what my husband, Kyriakos, had told me when we'd first met, back in my long-ago, dust-covered days as a mortal. I'd been fifteen at the time, and my father had sent me down to the docks of our town with a message for Kyriakos' father. Sending me alone was a bit unorthodox, but my father hadn't thought much about it since he was only a short distance away at the market. Nonetheless, I found it a frightening walk.

Sweaty, dirty men worked ceaselessly, unloading and loading in the hot sun while the turquoise Mediterranean shimmered beyond them. I got directions from a short, bald man who leered up at me when he finished.

"You're a tall girl," he observed. "Bet that might bother some men, but not me. You're just the right height as far as I'm concerned."

He laughed, and some of his companions laughed too. The

man's face came up right to the height of my chest. I hurried past them with lowered eyes, honing in on the indicated ship. Relief flooded me when I found Kyriakos checking lines and talking to some of the workers. I'd never spoken to him, but I knew who his father was and knew he was trustworthy. He looked up at my approach and smiled.

"You're Marthanes' daughter, right? Letha?"

I nodded. "I'm supposed to tell your father that the shipment can be ready this evening if he wants it early."

"I'll let him know. He's not here."

"All right." We stood there awkwardly for a moment. I could sense him studying me out of the corner of his eye while pretending to study the workers. He looked like he wanted to say something, but when nothing came, I made motions to go. "Well, thanks. I should get back."

"Wait, Letha." He reached out a hand to stop me from turning, then shyly pulled back before actually touching me. "You . . . didn't walk here by yourself, did you?"

"My father said it wasn't that far. And that I wasn't in much danger of attracting interest."

Kyriakos made a harsh sound in his throat. "Your father's a fool. Let me walk you back." He hesitated. "But don't tell your father I called him a fool."

He exchanged a few curt words with one of his men and then set out back to town with me. He was older than me, his face tanned from sun and sea. His hair was black and messy, about chin-length, and he stood almost—but not quite—as tall as I did.

"I saw you at that wedding a few days ago," he said after a long stretch of silence. "You were dancing with some other girls. You know . . . you're really good."

The compliment surprised me. "I think the wine helped."

"No. The wine helped the other girls—or hindered, maybe. I'm not sure." He glanced over at me, and I nearly stumbled at the intensity in his dark eyes. "But you . . . dancing lives inside of you. The music spoke to you, and you understood it."

"You were playing a flute," I recalled, trying not to blush at the regard in his voice.

"Yes." He sounded happy that I remembered. Silence fell again. We were almost to the market; the sounds of people and commerce drifted down to us. Kyriakos clearly wanted us to keep talking. "So . . . I heard your sister got married last spring."

"Yes."

"What about you?"

I eyed him. "I didn't get married last spring."

A smile turned up the edges of his lips. "What about next spring?"

"Are you offering?"

"Just checking. I heard my father say . . ."

I stopped walking near the edge of the market, so I could look him in the eye again. People and animals moved around us, and across a walkway I could see my father talking to a fruit vendor.

"Look," I said brusquely, "I heard my father say it too—how they're thinking about making a marriage between our families. It'd create good trade deals. But if you're trolling for that, you should talk to your father about one of my sisters, not me."

"What? Don't you want to get married?" His smile faltered. "Or is someone else lined up for you?"

I stared incredulously. "No, of course not. You just don't want to marry me, that's all."

"I don't?"

"No. You want one of my sisters."

"I do?"

"Yes. They're shorter, prettier, nicer—and softer spoken."

"Can they dance?"

I considered. "No. They're terrible."

His shy smile returned. "Then I want you."

"You're crazy. You don't know what you're talking about. You don't know anything about me." Of course, in those days, most people knew little about their betrothed. What I found remarkable was his conviction that we were compatible.

"It doesn't matter. I can just tell that you're the one. Can't you feel it?"

I met his eyes and felt a shiver go through me, like I'd stumbled into something bigger and more powerful than both of us. For just a moment, I allowed myself to consider that this man from a highly respected family might legitimately be interested in me. It was a heady feeling, and not just from the honor involved. It was from the way he looked at me and spoke to me, like I was both worthy and an equal. Something built between us, drawing me to him, and it confused me.

"You don't know anything about me," I repeated quietly, my mouth feeling dry.

His tentative smile grew bolder. "I know plenty. I know that you dance and that you're smart—too smart, according to my father. And I know that your family is banned from Lais' bakery because you called her daughter a—"

"That wasn't my fault," I interjected quickly. Across the way, my father caught sight of us. I held up a hand of greeting, and he impatiently gestured me over. "My father wants me."

Kyriakos cast an uncertain look over there and hastily turned back. If I was known for a sharp tongue, my father was reputed to be worse, and however love struck and brazen, Kyriakos apparently wasn't quite up to facing him yet. "I'll have my father talk to yours."

The earlier joking was gone; Kyriakos was all seriousness now. But there was more than just that. His eyes were looking at me in a way I'd never been looked at before. I felt hot, then cold, and then hot again. A tingle played along my flesh. I couldn't take my eyes away from his.

"This isn't about trade deals," I whispered.

"No. This is about you and me. You're the one."

I stared, uncharacteristically short on words. My shock now came more from that crazy feeling swirling inside of me, not from the preposterous nature of his proposal—one he shouldn't have even brought up without the involvement of our families. Later I'd learn what a leap this whole conversation had been for him. He was not given to long speeches or bold behavior. He said little, as a general rule, more content to express himself through his eyes and his music, and later . . . after we were married, his lovemaking.

"Look," he said, suddenly growing nervous as he misinterpreted my silence and expression, "I've saved. We can get a nice house. You won't have to live with so many people anymore. I'll be gone a lot, but you can probably run things and make deals better than me anyway. Not being able to buy bread will be problematic, but we might be able to afford a servant, or you can learn to—"

"Shut up," I said.

He stared. "What?"

"Just shut up. You're wasting time. Go tell your father to talk to mine. And," I added wryly, "I know how to make bread."

He caught his breath. "You're sure?"

"About the bread? Yes, I'm sure."

A slow smile bloomed across his face, spreading up into his eyes, making them smolder. I felt my pulse quicken and smiled back. Nothing else needed to be said. My father yelled again, and I ran off to join him.

Pondering this memory and what was now happening with Seth, I stared dazedly out the front window and caught sight of Jody checking the mail.

"Hey," I told Bastien. "I want to go say hi to her."

I ran outside and waved, making her break out into one of her big, beautiful smiles. To my surprise, she even hugged me.

"Ooh! I'm so glad to see you. How have you been?"

We exchanged a few pleasantries, and then she grabbed my arm excitedly. "Are you busy today? You want to go to the mall?"

To my surprise, that actually sounded like fun. More fun than listening to Bastien bitch and moan. "Sure."

"Great. I'll go tell Dana."

Chapter 11

When I went inside to relay this to Bastien a few minutes later, he took Dana's presence on the proposed shopping trip much better than I had.

"That's fantastic! More time for—"

"So help me, if you say 'reconnaissance,' I'm going to smack you. I'm only in this for the clothes."

"Fair enough. But this is a golden opportunity, and you know it. You can feel her out. Put in a good word for me, maybe. Something. Anything. I *need* this. But," he added, "don't do it at the cost of being . . . detrimental."

"Give me some credit here, all right? I understand the situation's gravity. I'll help you."

His roguish smile lit up his face, or rather, Mitch's face, which was kind of weird. "While you're at it, maybe you can brush up on your female bonding."

"What's that supposed to mean?"

"Do a count of all your closest friends someday. I don't think you like female competition."

I made a face at him just as Jody and Dana showed up. They took me to some astonishing shopping nexus a couple of miles away. I couldn't believe that much retail space could be crammed indoors. We had a few enclosed shopping centers in Seattle, but nothing like this.

Browsing stores with Dana was about as horrible as I

could have imagined. She eyed scantily dressed teenagers askance and spoke to a black saleswoman like an underling. Still, despite my distaste, I remembered my duty and attempted friendliness. Over and over, I tried to bolster Bastien's reputation.

"He's so into what your group's doing. He'd like to get more involved. Maybe you could come talk to him about it sometime."

Fortunately for "Mitch," these comments did elicit a warm response from her. Yes, she'd be happy to give Mitch some one-on-one time. Anything for the cause. How nice that he cared. Truly, he was a smart and compassionate man. Blah, blah, blah. She always enjoyed spending time with him.

Yet, despite this fleeting progress, her demeanor remained stiff, and her attention always shifted back to me. She peppered me with all sorts of questions, as if she were specifically probing for some key piece of information. She wanted to know what I did for a living. How close Bastien and I were. Where my "relationship" with Seth was going. What my take on the CPFV was. What my values—race, sexual orientation, etc.—were. I felt like I was being grilled, but she pushed on in that honeyed voice of hers. Despite her aloofness, she always managed to sound friendly and nonthreatening. I could see why she so enthralled her fans.

This isn't just curiosity, I realized. *She doesn't trust me.* Dana knew something was going on with Bastien and me, and now she was trying to figure it out. That was probably why he wasn't really getting anywhere; she was on to him. True, she probably didn't suspect a covert plan featuring an incubus, but I'm sure she had her share of more mundane enemies. She was on guard for such things, hence her skepticism about our cover stories. Bastien had no idea what he'd gotten us into.

So, I worked hard to maintain our innocence, answering her queries as best I could. My usual charm still wasn't working on her here, but I performed better than in previous en-counters—except for the questions about Seth. The reality with him was weird enough without having to live another version of it via Tabitha Hunter, and I found myself stutter-ing and blushing when she brought him up.

When Dana left us at the Christian Dior counter of Nord-strom to go look for slips, I nearly sagged in relief.

"What about this one?" Jody held out a tester of pale pink lip gloss that would look great on Tabitha, less so on Georgina.

I opened it and studied the color. "Too light. Besides, it'd probably come off with one sip of something."

She gave me a mischievous grin. "Or in other activities."

I rewarded her with a look of mock astonishment. It wasn't hard to do; she was full of surprises, it seemed. Fun ones. "Why, Jody. Here I thought you were a respectable married woman."

"Are you kidding? Marriage only makes you less re-spectable. Gives you a lot of time to invent new things."

Grinning back, I swapped the pink lip gloss for a red one. "Better not let Dana hear you talking like that. I got the third degree about my boyfriend, as it is."

Jody's mirth dimmed a bit, though she held her smile. "It may feel like the third degree, but she's just curious about you, that's all."

"Yeah, I guess. No other reason, I suppose." Best not to mention my theory that Dana suspected Bastien and me of duplicity.

To my surprise, Jody looked back down at the eye shadow display, pointedly avoiding my eyes. I was reminded of that day in the yard when I'd had the sense she wanted to tell me something about Dana. Something bad.

"Jody," I murmured, setting down the lip gloss, "what is it? What's wrong?"

She shook her head. "Nothing. Forget about it."

Dana returned just then, and the moment was gone.

"They don't have what I need. Let's check Victoria's Secret."

I perked up. That was the best thing I'd heard all day, aside from another possible insight from Jody. We entered what had to be one of my top five favorite stores. We split up, Jody going to pajamas and Dana looking for some slip that would undoubtedly match that god-awful underwear of hers.

As for me, I promptly sought out risqué lingerie sets—once I'd ascertained the other two women were occupied. No way was I having a repeat of the swimsuit incident. Unfortunately, the store had a more outstanding selection than usual, and what I'd intended to be a mere browse turned into a full-fledged mission when I found a few sets I simply *had* to try on.

Dana and Jody were still deeply engrossed with their own wares, so I inconspicuously slipped into the dressing-room line, hoping to be in and out before either of them could investigate what sweet, innocent Tabitha was into. I had just made it to the head of the line when both of them squeezed in next to me.

"What a crowd," Jody said. "Mind if we just share your room? They're huge here."

I felt the blood drain from my face as I tried to think up some reason to decline. An idea for a contagious, flesh-eating disease was forming in my mind when the sales associate ushered us into a room that was indeed more than big enough to hold the three of us.

Dana only had two skirt slips to try on, and she pulled off her slacks with unconcerned efficiency. I winced upon seeing the granny panties again. Meanwhile, Jody tried on a set of cute flannel pajamas.

When I made no moves of any kind, Dana asked me if I was all right. Swallowing, I slowly began removing my clothing. She watched with narrowed eyes. The first bra and panty set I tried on was made of ivory lace decorated with black bows. The second consisted of deep magenta satin and was cut so racily it was barely a few scraps of fabric. When I got to the third one—sheer black mesh decorated with embroidered pink flowers—I wanted to die.

Jody and Dana had finished and were waiting for me. Jody's face was pleasant and casual. Dana maintained a look of neutrality, but still radiated disapproval. Great. I could feel myself blushing furiously. Bastien would kill me if he found out I'd not only damaged the wholesome image, I'd completely destroyed it.

While Dana stayed stone-faced, Jody cocked her head at me curiously. "I think you have the wrong bra size, Tabitha. They all look too big."

Of course they were too big. Tabitha Hunter didn't wear a 34C. Georgina Kincaid did. I'd intended to shape-shift to my preferred body when I was alone in here.

"Oh," I said stupidly, feeling like the whore Dana thought I was. Make that a dumb whore. "Well. I lost some weight recently."

I tried on the last one—red with glittering silver flowers—and even in the wrong size, it was stunning.

"That looks great," Jody said, echoing my thoughts. "I wish I was brave enough to wear something like that."

Dana studied me thoroughly. "That bra offers no support whatsoever. It has no purpose."

"She doesn't need the support. Besides, that's the point. It doesn't have to be functional. She just wants to be pretty."

"Pretty for who? And why? She isn't married."

"So what? It's none of our business."

Dana glared daggers at the other woman. "None of our business? Humanity is our business." She must have read Dickens recently.

Icy silence filled our little room. I felt invisible, regardless of the fact that I was half naked. "Hey guys? Maybe we should go. I'll just take this off."

"No," said Jody sternly, eyes locked with Dana's in a battle of wills. "It's beautiful, Tabitha. You have nothing to be ashamed of."

"She is beautiful," concurred Dana smoothly, "but that outfit would be better suited to a married woman." Her tone suggested that even that was questionable.

I was on the verge of just leaving the room as is, but seeing Jody defy Dana like that kindled something warm and fuzzy inside of me. Bastien would kill me, but I couldn't keep myself from joining the fight.

"You know," I remarked to Dana, making sure she noticed my blatant examination of my backside, "if that's the case, then maybe you should try this one on. It's just your color. Kind of Christmasy too. I'd love to see it on you. And I bet Bill would really dig it."

Dana just stared at me, biting her lip again as she held my challenging gaze. She looked like she might snap back but instead simply pursed those lips together in a hard, straight line. Without another word, she left the dressing room, door banging loudly behind her.

Jody stood there uncertainly for a moment. "It looks great," she reiterated before following Dana out.

By myself, I decided I might as well use the alone time to shape-shift and try on the lingerie in the body they'd been intended for. As expected, they looked pretty hot, so I bought them all. I figured I deserved to salvage something from this disaster.

"So how'd it go?" asked Bastien when Jody and Dana dropped me off at his place later on.

"Fine," I said, having already stuffed the illicit purchases in my car, lest they raise questions from him. "Just fine. Well . . . sort of."

I told him about Dana's interrogation and my theory that she might suspect us of something insidious, even if it wasn't what we actually planned. His face grew grimmer and grimmer as I spoke, and I knew he thought I had a point. When I finished, I leaned my head against his shoulder, hating to see him so miserable.

"Hey, don't worry. We'll get through this. I mean, look on the bright side: Dana and I did *a lot* of bonding today. I think we had a real . . . breakthrough."

I knew doubts still plagued him, but he had cheered up by the time we—no longer as Mitch and Tabitha—arrived back in Seattle later that day. We picked up Seth on the way to Peter's apartment, promptly ensuring that neither man spoke to me for the rest of the car ride.

Once again, Jerome chose not to grace us with his presence, but everyone else had turned out for more good food and poker: Peter, Cody, Hugh, and Carter. Carter seemed quietly intrigued by Seth's presence while the others greeted him like a long-lost brother. Considering how often he came up in conversation among us, I think the other immortals regarded him as one of our inner circle already.

He stuck close to me for most of the night, but turned out to be a pretty damned good poker player. I think his quiet, placid nature fooled others into forgetting he was there. Amusingly, he seemed pretty pleased about his winnings too, albeit in a mild, Seth sort of way. It made me happy to see this side of him, happier still to know he was enjoying himself with my friends.

I didn't really know what side of me he saw that night. My friends sure didn't pull any punches when it came to teasing me about my various idiosyncrasies, and Bastien seemed to think it was Memory Lane Night. He kept telling all sorts of stories from my past, trying to lure me into inside jokes no one else knew about. I stayed away from that path as much as possible without offending him. My priority was still making things work with Seth, and as I held his hand all night and only gave polite smiles to Bastien, I think it became clear to the incubus where my loyalties lay. He didn't seem too thrilled.

Halfway through the game, I received a joint call from Mei and Grace.

"Hello, Georgina," said Grace.

"It's us," said Mei.

"Did you find out anything?"

"No matches," Mei told me.

"Oh." So much for that avenue.

"But that may not mean much," said Grace. "We always miss some."

"And it doesn't really matter," said Mei. "They're not a problem if they don't meddle in our affairs."

"And most don't?" I had run into countless immortals over the years, from all sorts of cultures and powers, but I had not paid much attention to how they operated with each other in a political sense. I had always been content to worry about my job and my job alone, safe in the knowledge that the authorities I answered to wielded enough power to deal with anyone else.

"Most don't," the demonesses agreed in unison.

The poker players regarded me curiously when I hung up.

"Who was that?" asked Peter.

"Grace and Mei."

Hugh made a face. "Ack. The crazy-bitch-dyke twins."

"Hey, that's uncalled for. They've been very helpful."

"Yeah? Well, just wait," he warned. "Next thing you know, they'll be wanting to cut your hair and dress you in black too."

Cody smiled at my outrage. "Why do I get the feeling there's another illicit Georgina investigation afoot?"

"It's not so illicit."

"Illicit enough," remarked Bastien with a yawn. "You and your mortals."

He pocketed the money he had left, downed his bourbon, and thanked Peter again for another fabulous evening.

"Leaving so soon?" I asked.

"Off to find fairer company. No offense to you, Fleur." He

leaned down to me and brushed a kiss over my lips that lingered a breath too long for friendship. "Good night."

His departure spurred a new round of the Bastien Fan Club as they all speculated what sexual escapade he was about to embark on now.

"How does he do it?" asked Peter.

"I wish I was that good," added Cody.

"Hey," I complained, "pursuing women isn't any harder than men. Sometimes it's easier."

"That guy's amazing." Hugh acted like I hadn't even spoken. "Going after a new one tonight when he's still sporting a glow that can't even be a day old. I wish I got lucky that often."

Seth didn't like to speak much with this group—or any group for that matter—but like my other friends, he was in awe of the incubus. Hugh's comment especially piqued his interest.

"What do you mean by 'glow?' Like an afterglow?"

Hugh grinned at him. "Sort of . . . you must know what I'm talking about. The post-sex thing? The glamour?"

"Whose deal is it?" I asked sharply, not liking the conversation's new direction.

Seth turned thoughtful. "Well, then it is like an afterglow. I mean, everyone sort of has something like that after sex."

"Yes, but it's different for an incubus or a succubus," explained Peter professorially. Unless I was mistaken, he was starting to pick up a British accent. Too much exposure to Bastien. "In their case, it's more of a literal glow—to other immortals at least. When they've had sex, they take that person's life. Life force is alluring. To an immortal, a just-laid incubus or succubus will almost—"

"Glitter," suggested Cody. "Or sparkle. And yet . . . not. It's kind of hard to explain. Hasn't Georgina told you all this?"

"Not *this*," said Seth. "So I . . . er, mortals don't see it?"

"Are we playing or not?" I asked impatiently, raising my voice. Carter caught my eye.

"Not like we do," continued Peter. "But they—you—feel it. Or maybe 'sense' is a better word. It pulls you in. It's very attractive."

I sunk lower into my seat, trying to decide if anyone would notice if I suddenly turned invisible. I might as well have been since no one was listening to my protests anyway.

"You must have noticed it," pointed out Hugh, taking a swig of whiskey. "There must be days when you see Georgina and practically can't control yourself because of how hot she is. You can only stare. Of course, it's probably hard to tell the difference since she's always so hot, huh?"

Everyone except Carter, Seth, and I laughed. I knew the imp had meant that last part as a compliment, but I wanted to throw my gimlet glass at him nonetheless. The hilarity soon died down, and we returned to cards. But the damage was done. Seth and I hardly spoke for the rest of the night, not that anyone—save Carter, I suspected—even noticed.

When Seth and I left, I knew something bad was coming. I dropped him off at his place, and he invited me inside to eat Rocky Road ice cream. He was a big ice cream fan. I should have just turned around and left, but Rocky Road has supernatural powers. Plus, I remembered what Seth and I had discussed after the recent make-out session in bed—how we had to communicate about issues, rather than ignore them. I still believed that to be true, but theory and practice were two completely different things.

He made up two bowls for us, and we ate the ice cream in silence for a while. When he finished, Seth played with his spoon, not looking at me.

"So," he asked, "is it true?"

"Is what true?" Like I didn't know.

"Come on, don't make me spell it out," he said gently. "I just want to hear your version, that's all."

I opened my mouth to speak, to find some way to neutralize all this, but my tongue felt thick and useless. No coherent words formed.

"Is it true?" repeated Seth. When I still didn't answer, he continued, "When I see you sometimes . . . when I see you—like that one night—and can barely even breathe because you are so beautiful . . . so beautiful that I can do nothing but act like an idiot, does that mean that you've just . . . slept with someone? But, of course, I don't actually mean, um, 'sleep' . . ."

Damn, this communication thing really did suck.

Chapter 12

"Thetis," he said after several more moments of silence, "talk to me here."

I looked up sharply. "What do you want me to say? You already know the answer. They wouldn't lie. Well, actually, they lie all the time but not about something like that."

He nodded and set the bowl and spoon on the coffee table. Slouching back on the couch, he didn't look at me, instead staring off across the room in thought. I could guess what was going through his mind. He knew what I was and what I did. But it was one thing to have a superficial knowledge of it and another to suddenly know there was tangible evidence each time I had sex. He would recognize the glow now and know that I had just come from someone else's bed, that not so long ago I'd been in someone else's arms doing the most intimate things two people could do. Things I couldn't do with him.

"I'm sorry," I said, not knowing what else I could say.

"For what?"

"For . . . this. For doing what I do."

"Why? It *is* what you do. It's what you have to do, right? There's no need to apologize for your own . . . uh, nature."

"So . . . what? You're okay with that? Knowing what I'm doing with other guys? Or rather, when I'm doing it?"

"'Okay' is a funny word, but yeah, I guess. What I'm not okay with is . . ." He paused, as always considering his words before speaking. "What I'm not okay with is you being afraid to tell me about this. You must have seen how . . . entranced . . . I was. But you never brought it up or explained it to me."

"What was I supposed to say? 'Thanks for noticing how pretty I am. It's because I just went down on some stranger in a sleazy club.'"

Seth flinched, and I immediately regretted my example.

"Maybe . . . maybe it could be phrased a bit more, uh, tactfully than that, but yeah. I guess essentially that's what you could tell me."

I poked at the melted remains of my ice cream. "It's not that easy, and you know it. It's got to be hard enough for you to accept that I'm sleeping around on you, so to speak, without real evidence to confirm each time it happens."

"Why don't you let *me* decide what I can or can't accept."

He didn't sound angry exactly, but I'd never heard him so sharp and assertive. The arrogant part of me didn't like being spoken to like that, but I knew he was justified in the comment. And, I had to admit, that confidence was kind of a turn-on. Alpha males. Yum.

"I know what you are," he continued, "and I know what you do. I had to acknowledge that from the beginning of the relationship. It bothers me, yeah, but that doesn't mean I can't go on with the knowledge." He laid his hand over mine, his fingertips absentmindedly stroking my skin. "But you can't be afraid to tell me the truth. Not ever. Even if it's ugly. What we have isn't about sex—like that wasn't already perfectly obvious. But if we don't have honesty either, then there's nothing left."

I forced my eyes up to him and smiled. "How can you be so young and so wise at the same time?"

"I'm not that wise," he said, pulling me to him so I leaned

against his shoulder. He didn't challenge the "young" comment. Looking at our ages objectively, one could practically accuse me of cradle robbing.

I sighed and snuggled into him. "It means nothing, you know. All that stuff I do. I don't even remember their names."

"I know. You've told me. Although . . ."

"What?"

"Sometimes that's not exactly comforting. Sex isn't supposed to be about 'nothing.' I don't really like the idea of you being with guys you don't want to be with. Even if you're technically my girlfriend . . . I'd rather you at least liked what was going on."

"Well . . . in the ultimate heat of it, I sort of do like it. The energy I get from sex . . . well, you can't really understand it. But it . . . it's literally what I live for. So even if I don't want to be with someone before and after the deed, there's still that one moment, no matter how brief, when I want them." I tried to give him a reassuring smile. "Besides, don't feel too bad for me. Things are a lot better than they used to be. I have more of a choice about who I'm with now, which makes a big difference. It's not like I just take whoever comes along."

"What do you mean you have a choice *now*? Haven't you always?"

I laughed uneasily. "Oh, come on, Seth. You know women didn't start getting any real rights until about a century ago. Men haven't always been kind or considerate in their relations with the fair sex—especially those in the lower classes."

He stared at me, shocked, and pulled back a little. I loved how expressive those eyes were, even if their current emotion wasn't exactly positive. "You're talking about . . . it . . . it sounds an awful lot like rape."

I shrugged, immediately realizing we needed to steer out of these waters. "It's hard to rape a succubus. In the ultimate climax, the succubus is the conqueror—especially if the guy ends up blacking out."

"You aren't really answering my question."

"And you aren't really asking it."

We lapsed into silence. A moment later Seth took me back into a tight embrace, burying his face in my shoulder this time.

"Hey, now. Don't let it bother you. Don't judge the past by the standards of today. It won't work. They're incompatible."

"I don't like the idea of you doing things you don't want to do," he said gruffly. "I wish I could do something . . . wish I could, I don't know, protect you."

"You can't," I whispered, kissing the crown of his head. "You can't, and you have to accept that."

We went to bed together after that, the first time since the kissing incident. Seth held me tightly all night, even in his sleep, clinging as though I might slip away if he let go.

Again, I marveled at his understanding. And again, I questioned whether I was in love yet. How would I know? What was love anyway? I ticked off a list as my hands held tightly to his back. Affection. Connection. Understanding. Acceptance. All these things he gave me. Those were parts of love. All these things he offered freely, no matter how terrible each new discovery about me was. I wondered whether I returned as much as I received. Did I have any right to be in this relationship? Somehow I doubted it, yet it made me want him all the more.

When we drove to the bookstore the next morning, he held my hand with a thrilling possessiveness. He didn't let go until we actually cleared the bookstore's door.

"Did Doug come in today?" I asked Beth after I'd made a sweep of the store.

"Yeah. He was here earlier. I think he's in your office."

I walked to the back. The office was dark. When I turned on the light, I found him hunched in a corner, his body curled up in a tight ball. I immediately dropped down beside him.

"What's wrong?"

After several seconds, he lifted his eyes up to mine. They were dark and troubled. "Nothing."

To contradict him seemed both obvious and pointless. "What can I do to help?"

He laughed bitterly, a terrible sound. "Don't you get it, Kincaid? Nothing helps, that's the problem. There's no point to any of this. You know that as well as I do."

"Do I?"

He gave me a cynical smile. "You're one of the most depressed people I know. Even when you're smiling and flirting and all of that. I know you hate this life. This world. I know you think it's all stupid."

"Not true. There's good in the bad. There's always hope. What's gotten into you?"

"Just reality, that's all. Just woke up and realized how stupid it all is. Dunno why I even bother."

I touched his arm. "Hey, you're kind of freaking me out here. Did you get any sleep? Do you need something to eat?"

He leaned back against the wall, face still bleak and full of snide humor. "Kincaid, I need so many fucking things, it's not even funny. But you know what? We don't get them. That's how it is. What's that saying? Life is brutish and short?"

"Er . . . close enough."

I sat there with him for a long time, listening to him go on. His words were an outpouring of bitter anger and black despair. A frightening combination. I'd never heard him like this. Not upbeat Doug, always ready with a joke. Doug, the guy who never took anything seriously. His bleak face reminded me of Casey's when I'd found her in the café, but she hadn't been this down.

As the clock ticked, I wondered what I should do. He certainly couldn't work today, yet I feared sending him home. Who knew what he might do in this mood? Previously, I would never have worried about him hurting himself, but all bets seemed to be off now.

"I want you to stay here," I finally said, standing up and straightening the kinks out of my legs. "I've got to get back out there, but I'm going to check on you later, okay? Promise you'll find me if you need me. We'll eat lunch later on. I'll get us some falafels from that place you like."

He only gave me a twisted half-smile, face stormy and mocking. I left, taking the letter opener with me.

His mood didn't change as the day wore on; even the falafels did no good. Once more, I wondered desperately what I should do. He had no family in the city I could call. I knew the hospitals had psych emergency services; should I contact one of them?

Shortly after lunch, Alec showed up. He avoided Casey's pleading eyes and gave me a smile that tried too hard. "Hey Georgina, is Doug around?"

I hesitated. I didn't like Alec, but he was sort of Doug's friend. Maybe that would help. I led the drummer to the back. When Doug saw him, he leapt up with an astounding burst of energy, his face both desperate and rapt.

"Jesus Christ, man! Where have you been?"

"Sorry," said Alec. "I got held up."

They huddled together, then looked uneasily over at me. Sensing I was unwanted, I backed out of the office but not before I saw Alec reaching into his coat and Doug looking very eager.

It was Alec, I realized. Alec was feeding Doug whatever drug he was addicted to. The realization made me want to go in there and throttle him, wipe that stupid grin off his face. Yet, when the two emerged a half hour later, the change in Doug was so marked that I couldn't bring myself to act.

A swagger had returned to his step, the normal cheery grin back on his face. Janice passed by, and he made some playful remark that caused her to laugh. Seeing me, he pranced up and saluted.

"Ready for duty, boss. What do you have for me?"

"I . . ." I stared stupidly, which only made him smile more.

"Rein it in, Kincaid," he said with mock severity. "I know that as a good groupie, you're ready to take me anytime, anywhere. But, as literary professionals, we've got to control our passion until after hours."

I was still staring. "Um . . . why don't you, uh, grab a register?"

He saluted again and clicked his heels together, military style. "Can do." He turned to Alec. "I'll see you at the rehearsal tonight?"

"Yup."

Doug flashed both of us a grin, then sauntered off.

I stood there alone with Alec. He waited expectantly, like I was supposed to say something. The words "fuck off" seemed appropriate, but I changed my mind. I smiled at him. It was a slow, sweeping smile that started with my lips and then shone in my eyes, the kind of smile that said I'd just noticed something I'd never seen before. Something I suddenly liked—and wanted.

Alec's own smile faltered. I think hitting on me had become so automatic, he didn't expect a response anymore. He swallowed and then turned his own grin back on.

"A rehearsal, huh?" I said. "You guys got another show coming up?"

"Next weekend. You going to come?"

"I'll try. Are you going to have another party after?"

"Probably. Wyatt's having one tomorrow if you wanna go to that."

"Are you going to be there?" I asked silkily, catching his eye meaningfully.

"You bet."

"Then I'll be there." I turned to go, still giving him the hypnotic smile. "See you then."

As soon I was out of his sight, my smile lapsed into a grimace. Ack. I hadn't thought it was possible to loathe that guy anymore, but I'd been proven wrong once again. Still, flirting with him, I'd realized, might be the best way to figure out what was going on with Doug. I felt pretty sure Alec had tried to push whatever he had on Casey. If I appeared to fall prey to his so-called charm too, he might let me share in the goods.

Doug, as I soon discovered, certainly wasn't going to provide any help in the matter.

"You've got something," I teased later when he and I ran into each other in the fantasy books. I gave him the lethal smile.

He returned it. "Magnetism? Sex appeal? Intelligence? Babe, I've got it all."

I stepped forward and pulled playfully on his shirt, looking up into his face. "That's not what I mean. You've got something good, something you aren't sharing."

He stayed close to me and tugged on a lock of my hair in return. "Don't know what you're talking about."

"The hell you don't. Do you know how many hours I've been working for you and Paige lately? Good lord. It's driving me crazy. Grey Goose only goes so far. If you've got some stash, you need to spread the love."

"Hey, I'll spread as much love as you want. Name the time and place."

"I thought we were friends." I pushed lightly on his chest and stepped back with a pout. "You're holding out on me. No way could you have perked up so quickly. Not after how you were this morning. You took something."

"Bah, mood swing. You're a woman; you understand. Just woke up grumpy, that's all. A little falafel and some Kincaid charm, and now I'm good to go. Great even." He took a step back toward me, apparently hoping I'd renew the flirtation. Heat burned in his eyes, something a little darker and more intense than our typical bantering called for. "In fact, I'm downright unstoppable now. A god, babe. Come on back to the office, and I'll show you."

I walked away, giving him a taunting look over my shoulder, still playing it light. "Not my religion, babe."

He laughed as I left him. We'd been flirting for years, and I knew he'd probably take no offense at my teasing or baiting.

I, on the other hand, was pissed. Bad enough this shit of Alec's could push Doug into over-the-top exuberance and inappropriate behavior at work. Dragging him into the pits of despair, however, was an entirely different matter. I was going to find out what was going on and put an end to it—even if it meant cozying up to that sleaze, Alec.

Remembering one of the other complications in my life right now, I called Bastien later that night for a status check.

"Don't even ask, Fleur. The clouds of failure are gathering."

"What the hell is it with you depressed guys today? Why do I have to be everyone's goddamned cheering-up committee?"

I ordered him to drive to Queen Anne immediately. When he arrived, he was still whining. "Dana's being really nice to me," he conceded, "but nothing intimate. She can't ever come over alone either. She's always got Jody with her or some other CPFV freak. My odds are probably better at getting her sidekicks into bed as a group than ever nailing her. They're all trying to get me to join their cult. I suppose making the gesture can't hurt, but I think I'll see more of her if I pretend to be a hesitant convert. You know, she also asks about you a lot."

"Like what?"

"Random stuff. Last time she wanted to know how the clothes you bought were working out. What's that about?"

"Not a clue," I lied.

It was ironic, really, because just then Bastien noticed the Victoria's Secret bag still sitting on my counter. My privacy apparently not a concern, he emptied it out and looked through the lingerie with approval.

"You want to try something on?" I asked wryly, noting his scrutiny.

"You always did have good taste." He held up the black mesh bra and peered at me through it, as though imagining how it would look on. "Although I still don't know why you buy this stuff. Just shape-shift it."

"I have a respect for 'intellectual property.' Whoever designed this deserves their pay."

"Even if it was constructed by third-world labor?"

I made a face. "Come on, let's get out of here."

"Where to?"

"A piano bar."

Surprise put his malaise on hold. "Are those still around?"

"Yup. There's actually a couple of them in Seattle."

In fact, one was even nearby, less than a fifteen-minute walk away. As we went, however, Bastien wouldn't stop worrying about the Dana thing. It drove me crazy. I hated her too, believe me, but I couldn't figure out what was making this such a maniacal obsession for him.

Fortunately, the piano bar was just wacky enough to distract him—as I'd hoped it would be. We ate yummy bar food and drank froofy drinks like Midori martinis and Sex on the Beach. Meanwhile, dueling pianists sang everything from Eminem to Barry Manilow. As the evening passed, getting a request played cost more and more money. However, the patrons grew drunker and drunker, so they didn't mind putting the cash down.

Knowing this in advance, I had brought a stack of bills, and Bastien and I took great amusement in seeing just how well the piano players could keep up with our increasingly older and more obscure requests. Bastien and I sang along beautifully. Shape-shifting, in addition to so many other benefits, could modify one's voice and vocal cords. The piano players had an astounding knowledge of our requests, and we were so impressed—and drunk—by the end of the night that we gave them a hefty tip.

Before we could leave, however, Bastien made me wait to hear one more request. "I slapped a fifty down with it," he said. "They've got to play it soon. I picked it just for you."

"If it's 'Superfreak,' I walk," I warned.

He laughed. "You'll know it when you hear it. It reminded me of you and your writer."

Sure enough, I immediately knew which song his silly sense of humor had led him to. The smile cracking his face was sort of a giveaway too. Pulling half of me onto his lap, he sang along loudly with Fiona Apple's lyrics:

> *"I've been a bad, bad girl*
> *I've been careless*
> *With a delicate man*
> *And it's a sad, sad world*
> *When a girl will break a boy*
> *Just because she can."*

"You're truly a creature of hell," I told him, trying to wiggle away. "You know that, don't you?"

"I just tell it like it is." He held onto me and kept singing.

> *"Heaven help me*
> *For the way I am*
> *Save me from*
> *These evil deeds*
> *Before I get them done . . ."*

When we finally left the bar, both of us laughing and humming, we passed a group of girls even more drunk than us. A few of them gave Bastien open looks of invitation, and I glanced at him expectantly. He shook his head.

"Too easy. Besides, I'd rather go home with you. So to speak."

He walked me back toward my apartment, holding my arm as he had once done when social mores dictated it for anyone of good breeding. The pavement was slick from earlier rain, and a moist chill hung in the air. Not far away, the Space Needle gleamed watchfully above the nearby build-

ings; it would have Christmas lights on it soon. Bastien tightened his hold on my arm and turned his gaze absentmindedly
toward the cloudy sky for a while before looking over at me.

"Fleur, do you want to know why I'm so gung-ho about
this Dana business?"

I willed myself to sober up, suspecting something big was
about to come. "You mean other than your righteous fury at
her?"

He smiled gently and looked down at the pavement, watching our feet. "I'm in trouble. Big trouble." He sighed. "You
ever heard of a demon named Barton?"

"No. Should I have?"

"Maybe. He works in Chicago. Very high up. Very powerful. He's one of those who expects 'favors' from his staff."

I nodded in understanding. It was one of the occupational
hazards succubi and incubi faced, and probably something
else Seth would be happier not knowing about. As workers
in the sex industry, so to speak, our demonic supervisors often
thought we wouldn't mind one more "customer." Many saw
it as our duty. Whatever his other failings, Jerome at least had
never demanded anything of that nature from me.

"So . . . anyway, Barton has this succubus named Alessan-
dra. Relatively new. You know, a century or so. Beautiful.
She has as good an eye for exquisite physical detail as you.
And she's bright. Wicked sense of humor. Outgoing."

I stared at him in astonishment. "Are you in love, Bastien?"

"No, but I was—am—very attracted to her. Hard not to
be. We got to know each other, and well, one thing sort of led
to another . . ."

"As it often does with you."

"Yes," he admitted ruefully. "But let me tell you, it was
amazing. That woman . . . wow."

"So how are you in trouble?"

"Well, the thing is, Barton's kind of possessive about his
people. He expected Alessandra's body to be exclusively for
his use—mortal business aside, of course."

"And he found out?"

"Yes. He turned unbelievably jealous." Contempt filled Bastien's voice. "Stupid emotion for our kind. Of course, demon or no, I suppose he might have had reason to feel insecure knowing his girlfriend had been with a sex-master like myself. I mean, once you go Bastien . . ."

"Keep telling the story, ego-master. What happened?"

"Well . . . to say he was pissed off would be an understatement. Honestly, I don't think I'd be enjoying your lovely company today if Janelle hadn't done some serious intervening." Janelle was Bastien's archdemoness in Detroit. "But mostly she just protected me from physical torture. Everything else is a mess. My career is in shambles. Barton has powerful friends, and Janelle's made it clear she's not going to cover my ass anymore."

We had reached my building and stood outside it now. He ran a hand through his dark curls, face suddenly weary. "I'm on everyone's shit list all of a sudden. Plans are already in motion to transfer me somewhere else, and I know it's going to be horrific. Like Guam. Or Omaha. That's why I need this Dana thing. A big hit like this—a public humiliation for the other side. It'll put me on top again. They won't be able to punish me, not if I've got a takedown like that on my record."

I started to understand his obsession with the radio host. "But the takedown isn't exactly taking."

"I don't know what else to do. I've tried all the old tricks, all the textbook moves plus a few exclusive Bastien moves. None of it's working."

I reached out to him. "You might have to accept that she's got a strong will, Bas. It happens."

"I know." He sounded so miserable, it broke my heart.

"Hey, come on. Don't give up the fight yet. I taught you everything you know, remember? We'll find a way out of this. We'll get that wench wet yet."

He laughed and brushed a finger against my cheek. "You always make me feel better when I'm around you, you know that? It's one of the wonderful things about you. That and—if the rumors are true—your mouth."

"The rumors are true, and I'm going to help you with this, you'll see. Besides, nothing else works on her, there's always hard liquor, right?"

"Ah yes, the old standby." He hugged me tightly and kissed each cheek. "Good night, my sweet. Thanks for a lovely evening."

I kissed him back. "Anytime."

I had my hand on the door handle when I thought of something.

"Hey, Bastien?"

He turned from where he'd been walking away down the sidewalk. "Yes?"

"Why'd you do it?"

"Do what?"

"Alessandra. You must have known how Barton felt about her, right?"

"I did."

"So why risk it?"

He looked at me like he could scarcely believe I had to ask. "Because I could. Because she was beautiful and wonderful and I wanted her."

I knew better than to argue with that. It was textbook incubus logic. Smiling, I went inside.

Chapter 13

Min, Doug's saxophonist, rummaged through the array of liquor bottles on Wyatt's counter. "I don't think he has any," he finally said. "Can you make a gimlet without lime juice?"

"Um, no," I replied. "That kind of defeats the whole purpose."

"Oh. Okay. Well, then, you just want a shot or something?" He held up a bottle of—God help me—Skyy vodka.

"I think I'll pass." I surveyed the humming, thumping party around me. Tons of people had showed up as usual; I doubted the band even knew half of them. The wages of fame, I guessed. Also as usual, there were drugs and drinks aplenty for those who wanted such things—as long as one's vices didn't stray to lime juice, apparently. I turned back to Min. "You seen Alec tonight?"

"Nope. Said he'd be here. I hope he shows soon."

Min shifted restlessly, and I wondered just how many people Alec was stringing along. The whole band, after all, had displayed that crazy, uncaring behavior.

I'd spent most of the day planning for tonight, trying to figure out what it would take to get information and possibly the drug itself from Alec. Finally, as the party drew nearer, I accepted that I was overthinking the matter. Alec was hardly a criminal mastermind. If I wanted something from him, it was a safe bet that the removal of clothing and an orifice would suffice.

With that in mind, I'd dressed for the part in another little dress. Like the one I'd worn to the last concert, this too had a V-neck, straps, and short skirt. Unlike that one—which had been cotton and more like a sundress—this one was silk and looked kind of like a nightgown. Its rich, emerald green mirrored the green flecks in my eyes. I'd made sure of that, enhancing the color in both.

"Finally," I muttered to myself, catching sight of Alec's blue-streaked hair across the crowd. He saw me, and I waved, making him grin smugly at my acknowledgment.

"Hey," he said, looking me over. "Wow."

"About time you showed," berated Min, handing over a beer. They greeted each other with some kind of weird, shoulder-punching guy thing. Then Min held up a bottle of Tropical Soiree Key Lime Schnapps. "Hey, look what I found. Will this work?"

"Sure. Whatever," I said. I wanted to start working Alec, putting him at ease. If it involved some unholy drink concoction, then I'd have to take that risk.

Min handed me a plastic cup filled with bright green liquid, and Alec and I wandered off to mingle.

"You're letting Min experiment on you?" he asked, pointing at the cup.

Inspiration hit. "He's been experimenting on me all night." I laughed, a bit too loudly and held on to his arm. Alec didn't need to know this was my first drink. "But none of the other stuff he made looked this bad."

He smiled and casually placed his arm around my waist. "Have I told you how great you look?"

"Yeah, I kind of got the message," I told him. Sniffing the cup, I detected nothing but sugar. Tentatively, I brought the cup to my lips and tasted. Bleh. It was like Kool-Aid and mouthwash. Fortunately, I don't have much of a gag reflex, so I managed to swallow without choking.

Alec flattered me a little more, and then I steered him toward the one topic guaranteed to captivate him: himself. It worked. Within a few minutes, I discovered that subject area was even more limited than I'd suspected. He only wanted to talk about the band.

"So yeah, we figure we should start expanding out of Seattle and hit some of the other big cities in the area. You know, like Portland and Vancouver. If we can start getting a following in the Northwest, we can hit the rest of the west coast, you know? And Corey's dad knows this guy who knows someone at a record company, and he's going to send him the review that was in the *Seattle Times* . . ."

I let him go on, nodding my head and saying "uh-huh" a lot. I should point out that I really was interested in Nocturnal Admission's success. I believed in them and their talent. Just not tonight. Other things demanded my attention.

"You know," he suddenly said out of nowhere, "I didn't think you really liked me."

Yeah. Good observation.

I smiled. "Sorry about that. There are so many jerks out there that I come off a little bitchy at first, until I know a guy. But the rest of the band swears by you, and I trust them. Besides"—I leaned closer, lowering my voice to a sultry purr— "I know you now, and I definitely like you now."

To my astonishment, Alec broke away from me. How unexpected was that? Weirder still was that I saw interest in his eyes but *only* his eyes. The rest of him was plainly distressed about something. My surprise must have been reflected in my expression, because a moment later, he laughed like nothing had happened and returned the hand to my waist.

"I wouldn't really trust the guys on much, but hey, if they've convinced you, whatever."

I turned the smile back on, pretending I hadn't noticed the weird reaction. We started talking again, and I continued to let him dictate the parameters of our conversation. When he brought up skateboarding and the benefits of one board brand over another, I decided Doug didn't appreciate the extent of my love for him.

Slightly bored, I leaned into Alec and drank from the cup without thinking about it. "Son of a bitch!" I swore, tasting that mess again.

"What?"

"This." I set the cup down on a rickety coffee table, sloshing the green liquid. "It's terrible." I realized this was my opening. "God, I've had such a fucked-up week." I turned so that I stood even closer, resting a hand on his back, sliding it down to his waist. "I'm glad you had this party. You guys must need to get a little crazy too to handle all the stuff you've been doing."

He seemed happy about my proximity but didn't move his hand from my waist. "We know when to work, and we know when to play." He spoke with a ridiculous swagger, again attempting to project a wisdom he was too young to have.

I grinned at him. "I like to play too."

Like before, the look in his eyes said he did want to play—especially if we played doctor. But his body language didn't match it. He was holding himself back for some reason, which didn't fit with my image of him as a womanizing drug lord.

But he kept smiling, even if the rest of him was stiff. "How do you like to play?"

"Not with that." I pointed at the jettisoned cup and looked back up at him with doe eyes, both innocent and provocative. I tried to recall the stupid expression he'd used at the first party. "You maybe got anything . . . harder?"

A pleased and—unless I was mistaken—relieved smile danced on his face. "Maybe I do."

I punched him lightly, then snaked my arm around his neck. "I know you do. I saw you give it to Doug. You guys are in on something good, and you won't share. Whereas me . . . well, I always share . . ."

He still didn't take the physical bait or go for my over-the-top vixen lines, but the rest had piqued his interest. "I've got something," he said, glancing around carefully. "Let's go talk in the bedroom."

Ah. Now we were getting somewhere. I followed him back to Wyatt's small messy bedroom which miraculously wasn't occupied yet. I sat on the unmade bed, crossing my legs, keeping my body language as open and relaxed as possible.

"Are we going to play now?"

He answered with a question of his own: "You sure you can handle the hard stuff?"

I arched an eyebrow. "Baby, I can take it as hard as you can give it."

Reaching into his coat pocket, he sat down on the bed beside me and held up a tiny plastic bag, much smaller than the bag Reese kept his pot in. In the poor lighting, I could discern tiny glittering crystals. Almost like red sugar.

"This," he said in a low voice, "is what you've been waiting for your whole life. This is the stuff that's going to change your world. Make you who you were born to be."

I was rendered speechless, but not from his melodramatic prologue. It was the crystals. This close to them, I . . . well, felt them. They had an aura, almost the same way an immortal has a signature. Only this wasn't exactly a pleasant aura. The crystals felt strange to me. They sent little shockwaves into the air. They made my skin crawl.

And weirdest of all, I'd felt them before. Once with Doug, once with the band.

I hoped Alec would interpret my frown as cute confusion. "What is that?"

A sly smile spread over his face. "A magic potion, Georgina."

I smiled back, not having to feign puzzlement. "I don't believe in magic."

"Oh, you will after this." He pressed the bag into my palm, and I squelched a sharp cry. I didn't like touching the crystals. "Go grab something to drink and put them in it. Mix it all up and then drink—preferably as fast as you can. You'll get the effects sooner."

"What'll they do?"

"Something good. Something you'll like." He ran his hand through the strands of my hair. "Man, I can't wait to see how you react to them."

How I reacted? I didn't like the sound of that. Maybe I wasn't getting the same thing as Doug after all. Maybe I was getting the date-rape drug. Of course, with as inviting as I was trying to be, he had to realize those kinds of extremes weren't necessary. I pushed the unease out of my head. "What do I owe you for these?"

The smoke in my voice clearly told him how I'd like him to extract payment.

"Nothing. It's a gift."

"Nothing?" I trailed my hand across his leg. Believe me, I really didn't want to sleep with this guy, but I wanted to stay in his good graces to figure out what the hell this stuff was. And yeah, okay, I sort of wanted to see him suffer from the energy loss. "Are you sure?"

I slid my body closer to his, gently pushing him back on the bed. His eyes widened as I lay down next to him, brushing my lips over his neck. Turning his face toward mine, I moved my lips closer to his, lightly kissing the area just by his mouth.

"Are you really sure?" I asked, voice lower.

His breathing grew heavy, and he stroked my side, tracing the shape of my hip and moving down to my bare leg. Looking half-terrified, he moistened his lips in anticipation. My tongue snaked up to them, dancing around their edges before gently probing inside. He stifled a moan and then pushed me aside.

"No . . . I . . . no. No." He sat up, shaking. "Not yet."

I sat up as well, moving in one fluid and graceful motion. Tossing my hair over one shoulder, I gave him a languid smile. "Come on, I want to."

"I can't . . . but maybe, well maybe later we can work something out."

Both longing and reluctance showed in his expression, which I found relieving. Nice to know my charms were still working and he wasn't all business after all. Maybe this was just a first-one's-free type of deal, and he'd be more thorough in his demands later. Fine by me. It wasn't the end of the world if I didn't sleep with him, and hopefully we wouldn't even need the second batch.

"Here." Having seized control of himself, Alec held out his beer to me.

"Huh?"

"Go ahead and try them. You can mix them in this."

I looked down at the sparkling red granules. They almost had a light of their own. That weird sensation pulsed out at me, grating my immortal senses. No way was I going to ingest the contents of this bag. I shook my head.

"I can't right now. I've got to go to another party. I promised a friend. I'll try them later, okay?"

He didn't look happy about that. "I wanted you to try it now."

"What's wrong with later?"

"Nothing I guess . . . just, look, don't let anyone else know, okay? I don't have a lot of this stuff. If word gets out, everyone'll want some. Right now I'm only letting special people try it."

"Am I special?" I teased.

Alec gave me a long, searching look, blatantly studying my face and the way the silk fit me. Again, the appreciation and attraction shone in his eyes, but he held himself back from my smile of invitation. "Very special."

I managed to extract myself from the party shortly thereafter but not before Alec had warned me again to keep the crystals to myself. He also urged me to let him know how I liked them.

"The second dose is even better," he promised.

Finally escaping, I breathed a sigh of relief, alone in the cool night air. As I walked to my car, I shoved the crystals into my purse, still creeped out by how they felt. They were supernatural; that much was obvious. I knew I had to get them to someone who could identify them. That, however, would have to wait a little longer since I was already past when I'd said I'd call Seth. Happily, I discovered I could no longer sense the packet once it was encased in the fabric. That was something, at least.

"Where are you at?" I asked Seth when he answered his cell phone.

"Terry and Andrea's. You want to come over?"

Spending the evening with his family sounded refreshingly ordinary after the sleaze and debauchery of Alec and that party. In fact, compared to everything else weird in my life at the moment, it sounded downright wonderful.

Identical blonde faces greeted me at the door when I arrived, both sets of lips forming a perfect 'o' when they saw me.

A moment later, Brandy appeared behind her little twin sisters. "Oh, Georgina, that dress is so pretty."

She pushed Morgan and McKenna out of the way, both still starstruck. I stepped inside the Mortensen home and found complete chaos. Sheets of clear plastic lay everywhere. Masking tape covered the wall trim. Most of the furniture had been pushed out of the living room, shoved into a pile in the hallway beyond. Those items remaining were wrapped in thick cocoons of more plastic sheeting. Paint buckets, trays, and brushes littered most of the free space, and everything—the people included—was splattered with yellow paint.

"Georgina!" squealed eight-year old Kendall, tearing toward me. Her mother, walking into the room, leapt out and tackled her daughter.

"Don't touch her!" Andrea exclaimed, tumbling to the ground. "Not in that dress."

I laughed, wanting to sweep up each one of the girls in an enormous hug, the dress be damned.

"Seth," chastised Terry, standing on top of a ladder, "why didn't you tell her this was a war zone?" The Mortensen Brothers always entertained me. Despite being younger, Terry always seemed exasperated by Seth's scattered behavior and often had to prod him into reality.

Seth sat cross-legged on the floor with Kayla, youngest of the Mortensen daughters, on his lap. Like everyone else, he had paint all over him—including his *Writers Do It at Their Desks* shirt. Looking as serene as a Buddhist monk, he flashed me one of his distracted smiles. "Because it's always a war zone over here."

"Well, get her out of here and take her somewhere nice," Terry said. "No need to drag her down into this."

This immediately triggered cries of outrage from the girls.

"I don't mind staying," I told them. "I'd like to help."

Andrea rose from her tackle, one arm still around Kendall. "We're going to have to cover you up then. Come on, let's see if I've got anything that'll fit."

She released Kendall. The little girl took a step toward me but didn't touch anything. "You look like one of the ladies in the Victoria's Secret catalog."

"My favorite reading material," I told her solemnly.

"Daddy's too."

Her mother groaned and led me to her bedroom, forcing us to squeeze through the furniture packed hallway. Being in Terry and Andrea's bedroom was a lot different than being in Dana's. It was messier for one thing, with an unmade bed and piles of laundry on the floor. The color scheme and decorating were a lot less coordinated too, suggesting it had all been pieced together over the years, not preplanned with a designer's cold eye. Pictures of the girls at various ages covered the walls and dressers, and free surfaces held odd pieces of jewelry, books, and change. And yet, despite that clutter, the whole room felt filled with love, like the people who occupied it were happy and cared about each other. It made the place warm and cozy, not sterile and sharp as Dana's had been. It made me feel good to be in here, jealous that I had nothing like it with another person, and almost intrusive to be in such an intimate setting. It was like eavesdropping.

"Ah, here we are," murmured Andrea, rummaging through drawers. She handed me some clothes. I slipped out of the dress and tried them on. While she had a fantastic body for having birthed five daughters, Andrea was still taller and bigger than me, so the clothes hung loose and long. Changing her mind, she handed me denim overalls instead of the jeans. They had to be rolled up at the cuffs, but the straps kept them on me. I tied my hair in a ponytail and was ready to go.

Seth laughed when he saw me.

"Hey," I said, poking him with my foot, "be nice."

"I think this is the first time I've ever seen you look anything less than . . ." He paused, playing with word choice. "Well-planned."

"Why, you silver-tongued romantic devil. That *is* the look I usually go for. Other women go for sexy or chic or beautiful. But me? Well-planned all the way."

"You know what I mean. Besides, unplanned isn't a bad look for you. Not bad at all."

His voice sounded deliciously low and dangerous, and something ignited between us as we held each other's eyes.

"You guys can flirt on your own time," said Terry briskly, handing me a roller and tray of paint. "Right now, you work for us. Think you can do this part of the wall?"

"Sure." I glanced over at Seth, whose main job still seemed to be restraining Kayla. "Why aren't you painting?"

"Because he isn't allowed to," answered Brandy, painting deftly around a doorway.

"Uncle Seth's a libation," explained Kendall.

"Liability," corrected her mother. She grinned at me. "The odds say you *have* to be a better painter than him. Correction: the laws of the universe say you have to be."

"Of course she is. She's good at everything." Seth watched me apply a smooth, even coat. "See?"

Painting with the Mortensens made for an utterly normal and utterly enjoyable evening. They were so funny and nice that it was hard not to love them. Working side by side, I could almost pretend I was really one of them. Like this could be my own family. They included me in everything and spoke as though Seth and I were a done deal, assuming I would be with them not only for Thanksgiving but also for Christmas and an assortment of other get-togethers.

The simple, casually extended affection made me feel happy inside, and sad too. I would never be able to quite fit in with any mortal family, even if this wacky relationship with Seth did ever stabilize.

I pushed aside a plastic-covered box and got a peek inside. Moving the sheet further, I smiled down at a framed picture of Terry and Andrea's wedding party—including a much younger Seth.

"Look at you," I teased. "You used to shave."

He rubbed the stubble on his lower face. "I still shave."

"So this is the infamous occasion Seth almost missed?"

"Yup," said Terry, a rueful tone in his voice. "Apparently finishing *A Talented Heat* was more important than witnessing my nuptials."

"Oh," I said neutrally, "that's a really good one." I wasn't sure if it was missing-a-wedding good, but it was still one of my favorites. It might have been worth the sacrifice. "Who's the other guy beside you?"

"Our other brother. Ian."

"Another Mortensen? You guys are abundant."

"Tell me about it," said Terry. "Ian's the black sheep."

"I thought I was the black sheep," said Seth, sounding almost hurt.

"No. You're the unfocused artistic one. I'm the responsible one. Ian's the wild, hedonistic one."

"What's hedonistic?" asked Kendall.

Her father considered. "It means you run up a lot of credit card bills you can't pay, change jobs a lot, and have a lot of . . . lady friends."

Brandy rolled her eyes. "Good euphemism, Dad."

Only in the Mortensen family, I decided delightedly, would a fourteen-year old use a word like "euphemism."

Andrea walked over to the portrait and admired her younger self. In the picture, she wore a long-sleeved lace dress that left her shoulders bare.

"Ah, those were the days," she sighed. "Back before pregnancy ruined my body."

"Well, that wasn't *entirely* before pregnancy," observed her husband in an undertone. She shot him a dangerous look. Brandy groaned.

Seth tried to hide a smile and changed the subject. "That church had horrible carpet. Burgundy shag." He shook his head. "I think I'm going to get married outdoors."

"Oh my God," said Terry with mock horror, "I can't believe you just acknowledged you might get married. I thought you were married to your writing."

"Hey, I've never had a problem with polygamy."

Kendall's eyes widened. "What's polygamy?"

Later, when we'd finished the living room, Seth and I offered to start cleaning up while Terry and Andrea put the brood to bed. The girls resisted, clinging to Seth and me, wanting us to talk and come back tomorrow.

"My nieces think you're a rock star," he observed as we

washed brushes in the kitchen. "I think they like you better than me."

"I'm not the one they had to tear Kayla from. Hey, does she ever talk?"

"Sometimes. Usually when there's bait involved—like candy or small objects she might choke on."

We washed the brushes in silence until I brought up the topic that had been on my mind ever since he'd mentioned it.

"An outdoor wedding, huh?"

The notion of Seth getting married held a perverse fascination for me. Fascinating because I was female and attracted to such things. Perverse because I knew I wouldn't be the bride at such an event. Succubus logistics obviously made that impossible. Then, of course, there was the fact that my mortal marriage had not gone so well. In addition to me cheating and pushing my husband into a debilitating depression, it had later resulted in me selling my soul and joining the ranks of hell. That didn't make for a good matrimonial track record.

Seth cut me a look, eyes amused. "Yup."

"I didn't know guys ever thought about that kind of stuff."

"Sometimes we do."

"You got any other details worked out? Or just the outside lovefest part?"

He pondered this as we returned to the living room. He wore the intense expression that seized him when he was trying to write a certain line or think of something clever to say. "I want a good buffet," he said. "Not one of those cheap ones with cold cuts. And no bows on the chairs or anything like that. Man, I *hate* those."

"Wow. I guess you've got it all figured out." I began pulling masking tape off the trim while he knelt down to gather more brushes.

He continued on, still considering. "And I want my bride to wear open-toed shoes."

"Why open-toed?"

He looked up with astonishment. "Because toes are sexy."

I looked down at my own bare feet. They were small and cute, each toenail painted a pale lavender. Andrea hadn't had any shoes my size.

I gave him a sly smile. "Like these toes?"

He looked away and returned to his work.

Forgetting my masking tape, I strolled over to him, trying not to laugh. "Why Seth Mortensen, do you have a fetish?"

"It's not a fetish," he replied evenly. "Just an appreciation."

This time I did laugh. "Oh yeah?" I moved my foot out to tickle his arm, wiggling the toes. "You appreciate these toes?"

"I appreciate everything about you—even how mean you are."

I crouched beside him and slung an arm around him. "To think, all this time I've been prancing around you in low-cut shirts and no underwear, in awe of your stalwart resistance, when really it was my toes—"

"No underwear?" he interrupted. "Wait. Are you wearing any now?"

"My lips are sealed. You'll have to find out the old-fashioned way. I'm not going to talk."

"Oh," he said in a warning voice, "we have ways of making you talk."

"Like what?"

In one surprisingly quick motion, Seth sprang up and rolled me onto my back. One arm pinned me and the other held a paintbrush over me, wet with paint.

"Hey!" I cried. "That's not sexy. That's not even cool." Actually, being pinned to the floor by him was about as sexy as it got.

He stabbed it toward me playfully, never actually making contact, but I flinched anyway. "What's the problem?" he teased. "You can just shape-shift it away."

"Oh! You're a twisted bastard."

His lips quirked into a wicked smile, and he dabbed the

brush at my cheek, leaving a small streak of paint. A second later, he added a matching mark on the other cheek.

"Ready for battle," he declared.

I yelped in dismay, then used his momentary satisfaction to break free and reverse the situation, rolling him over. Now I hovered on top of him, one hand on his chest, the other on his arm.

"I'm learning more about you every day," I observed, leaning my face toward his. My hair had come undone from its haphazard ponytail and now hung down, almost creating a curtain around him. "You've got a real dark side."

"Is that a problem?"

"Actually I kind of like it."

I lowered my mouth and gave him what we had now dubbed a "stealth kiss"—the kind of semi-deep kiss perfected at the concert that just pushed the envelope of succubus absorption.

I pulled up a moment later, my lips still tingling from where we'd touched. He shifted one hand to the small of my back while his other tangled itself up in my hair. A lazy and contented smile played on his face. "You want to go grab something to eat after this?"

"What do you have in mind?"

"Anything. So long as the company stays this good."

I smiled and leaned down to kiss him again, only this time I had trouble keeping the kiss as stealthy as it should have been. When I should have broken away, I kissed him a little harder instead, letting my tongue probe more boldly into his mouth. Surprisingly, what abruptly stopped this indiscretion was not the twinge of energy transfer, but Seth himself.

"Thetis," he warned, pushing me away—not harshly, but not gently either.

I stared, my better judgment suddenly scrambled. I wanted to kiss him again. And again. To hell with the succubus thing.

And it wasn't just because of the chemistry or the physical roughhousing, the comments about my toes and lack of underwear. It was about everything tonight. Pretending I was part of his family. Talking about weddings that could never happen. I was suddenly overcome with emotion. Joy and delight over the way just being around him felt. Knowing he loved me for both my inner and outer selves. A warm contentment that his presence naturally brought on. And, of course, the dark emotions were there too. Anger that our relationship could never be complete. Despair that he was not immortal. Jealousy that I could never be his bride. What had Jerome said? That being with me denied Seth all the normal things in life? Kissing him was a base, anxious reaction to all these emotions I couldn't otherwise deal with.

"Thetis," he repeated, studying my face and whatever crazy expression was on it. "Come on. You're stronger than this."

He sounded sad and sympathetic, yet stern and parental too. His words snapped me out of my emotional vortex, suddenly making me feel, well, inadequate compared to him.

Terry walked back into the living room, looking rightfully startled to see me on top of his brother. "Do you guys need to go to bed too?"

Seth and I exchanged bitter, amused smiles. "If only," I said.

Once everything was cleaned up, Seth and I left to find a very late dinner. We stayed quiet, neither of us bringing up what had happened earlier. I think he knew I was taking it harder than he had and wanted to say something to cheer me up. But nothing apparently came to mind, so silence reigned until we returned to Terry's house to get our respective cars.

"Georgina," he said suddenly, hesitantly, as we stood by my car. "I have to know something."

I looked at him wearily, not liking the seriousness in his voice. I really didn't want to deal with any more weighty issues tonight. I sighed. "What?"

He studied me a moment, apparently assessing my emotional state. "So . . . *are* you wearing any underwear now?"

I blinked in astonishment, taken aback. Then I saw how hard he fought to keep a straight expression. It was too funny. Seth was trying to make me feel better, very much in a goofy way I might have attempted. The tight coil of frustration inside of me unwound.

"Yes," I told him with a smile.

"Oh," he said, looking relieved to see me relax but disappointed by the answer.

"But you know what the real beauty of shape-shafting is?"

"What?"

"I'm not anymore."

Chapter 14

I wasn't prepared for Dana to answer Bastien's door the next day.

Oh my God, I thought. *He finally slept with her.*

The truth turned out to be far less exciting. Bastien—as Mitch—was covered up to his elbows in flour, his hands busily kneading a medium-sized lump of dough.

"Hey Tabby Cat," he said upon seeing me and my startled expression. "Dana's teaching me to bake bread."

"Wow," I said. Really, there was no other way to respond to a statement like that.

I had personally seen Bastien make bread in far more primitive conditions, but he apparently believed the old teacher-student routine was going to pave the way to Dana's bed for him now. It did have its merits, of course. Human nature liked showing superiority in areas of expertise, and a teaching relationship provided lots of alone time together. I suspected that even with that tactic, Dana might still be out of reach, but hey, maybe it was worth a shot. The fact that she actually made time for this struck me as odd. I figured she'd be too busy bombing abortion clinics and handing out school uniforms.

Speaking of alone time, I worried that I'd blundered into some meaningful opportunity for the incubus. I met his eyes.

"I can come back later if it's a bad time," I told him.

"No, no. Dana's got to go to a meeting soon. You can keep me company once this baby's in the oven."

His tone was genuine. He'd probably already exhausted efforts to get her to stay.

Uneasy in her presence, I sat on one of the stools by the counter and sipped the white-chocolate mocha I'd picked up on my way over. Dana sat down beside me. I resisted the urge to move away. Glancing at his kitchen table, I saw stacks of CPFV pamphlets and brochures.

"Why the interest in cooking?" I asked blandly when no one said anything.

"A bachelor can't live on fast food and frozen dinners forever, huh?" He turned up the dial on his smile. "And hey, I'm always open to new experiences. Next time she's going to teach me to make crème brûlée."

I grunted. "You learn to make crème brûlée, and I might have to move in."

Dana turned to me, elegantly crossing her legs, showing that oh-so-wholesome slip obtained during the infamous shopping trip. I'd given up on slips a while ago. They just delayed the main event. "I could show you too."

Hell no. I'd gotten roped into yard work by pursuing a similar vein of conversation with Jody. No more domestic vices for me. Besides, I knew Bastien wouldn't welcome my presence.

"Thanks, but I'll just leave it to Mitch. He's the brilliant one in this family anyway."

Bastien gave the bread a final pat. "Okay, now what?"

"Now we put it in the pan."

She walked over to show him. As she did, he leaned in extra close, supposedly to get a better look. He even reached out his hand to brush hers, following her motions as they transferred the bread. Perhaps it would have been polite to look away, but there was nothing overtly romantic going on, and besides, I felt a professional interest in the matter. His technique was good, I had to admit. Very subtle. Nothing that could be misconstrued as more than a polite accident. Yet, I saw Dana—just as subtly—stiffen and step away once the bread was in its pan.

"Now you just let it rise," she said, in a somewhat cooler tone. "Then it goes in the oven."

Interesting. She hadn't liked Bastien's proximity. That didn't bode well for him. I didn't think he noticed, however.

I would have expected her to leave, but she sat down next to me again. I could never think of anything interesting to say around her; she unnerved me too much. So I let the two of them talk, answering only when spoken to and otherwise letting Bastien run the show. He positively glowed. Dana tried to draw me in a number of times, again asking me things about my life I really didn't want to answer.

When she finally rose to go, she commented, "I'm off to a board meeting to plan our upcoming rally against gay marriage. You two should join us when it happens."

"Absolutely," said Bastien, who probably would have agreed to an anti-incubus rally at this point.

She glanced over at me. My tongue suddenly felt thick, words again eluding me.

"Are you for gay marriage?" she asked with surprise. "I thought when we talked about this at the mall, you had implied you were more in favor of helping them see the error of their ways."

Christ. Had we discussed this on the mall trip? I couldn't remember. The only thing I recalled clearly was the lingerie debacle.

I wanted to argue right then that I didn't think homosexuality was a "choice" for all people, nor did I believe there should be laws about who people loved. Fortunately, my control switch was fully operational. That, combined with Bastien's heavy gaze, made me redirect my answer and evade the question. "I'd love to go to the rally," I said flatly. "It'll depend on my schedule."

She smiled thinly, made a few parting remarks, and then left.

I exhaled. "Sorry about that, Bas. I nearly choked up on you."

"Not a problem. You recovered. Besides, I think things are turning around. I thought of it the last time she and Jody were over. This cooking thing is going to be what does it." He peered into the oven at his now-baking bread before sitting at the kitchen table happily. "Can't you see it? We'll be like, I don't know, baking a cake together, and I'll say, 'Why Dana, you have chocolate frosting on your cheek.' Then she'll say, 'Will you get it off for me?' Then I will, only I'll lick it off—"

"Okay, just stop now, please. I get the picture. I really don't want to hear about you two rolling around in cake batter."

"You'll have to once it's on the evening news."

I smiled, relieved to see him so cheered up after our last encounter. I couldn't bring myself to tell him I didn't think the cooking lessons were making Dana quite as hot and heavy as he would have liked. If we were going to save Bastien from demonic wrath, I believed we needed a better understanding of what—if anything—turned that woman on. And I had the distasteful feeling that I would be a better agent for that particular piece of reconnaissance than he would be. One more thing to add to my list.

"So what's new with you?"

"Oh, the usual. Another awkward physical encounter with Seth. Not nearly as big a deal as the last one, but still."

Bastien shrugged. "Alas for mortal weakness."

Dana left my mind as my own personal relations came to the forefront. "That's the thing. Everyone's been going on and on about how he wouldn't be able to handle our relationship, but it's not his weakness that's the problem. It's me. I'm the faulty piece here. Seth's done exactly what he's supposed to. He handles every horrible thing I tell him about myself, and he never does anything to cross the sexual line. His one moment of weakness was when *I* initiated things. He's perfect."

"Nobody's perfect, Fleur. If there's anything I feel certain of in this world, it's that. Even the angels themselves are imperfect."

I thought about Carter's chain-smoking and penchant for hard liquor. "That's for damned sure. But Seth comes pretty close. At least as mortals go. Whereas me . . . I don't know. I feel so useless in our relationship."

He stood up and drew me to him. "What is this, your day to feel melodramatic and depressed? Look. No way are you useless—not if you've been with him this long. He's in it for more than sex. He's in it for *you*. For that delightful wit and charm that manages to cheer even grumpy bastards like me up. What I can't figure out is what the hell you're getting out of it."

"Plenty," I said, thinking of Seth's humor and intelligence, his serious and steady nature. "And I suppose he's happy with what he's got, but he must still, you know, feel unfulfilled. He's a man, right? I see him looking at me sometimes, and I know what he's thinking . . . what he wants." I thought about my toe-teasing. "I don't think I really make it easy on him either. I flirt without thinking about it. I wish I could give him, I don't know, something. Something nonlethal to reward his amazing celibate strength—and overall amazingness with everything that's happened so far."

"Nonlethal's going to be hard for you. You're the ultimate look-don't-touch girl."

My slumping head shot up. "That's it."

"What's it?"

"Looking without touching. You're going to help me." I felt my natural optimism and vigor seizing me as I flashed the incubus a saucy grin. "You're going to be my photographer."

His eyebrows rose, but I think he already knew where I was going with this. "And pray tell, what will I be photographing, my dear?"

"Me. In a bevy of alluring poses and skimpy underwear. Or nothing at all. We'll do a whole spread."

His smile twitched at the word *spread*. "And you think this will help him? All it'll do is drive him into the bathroom alone for ten hours."

"Hey, he can do whatever he wants with them, but it's a great idea. It'll be a treat. A safe way of having me without having me." I poked the incubus in the arm. "You'll help, won't you? You're the only person I trust to take these."

"Of course I'll help you. Why'd you even ask?"

I sighed happily, like a great load had been taken off of me. "Of course, even if this is good for Seth, it doesn't solve the problem of me being a weak-willed strumpet. I'll still be thinking about him all the time. Still wondering what it'd be like to touch—*really* touch—him. Still breaking down with him in moments of weakness." I sighed again, this time with frustration. "There's no helping me, I guess. Pictures of him won't do it."

"Hey," said Bastien, touching my chin. "Smile again. You'll figure out something. And if not, I promise you I will. The brother you never had, remember? We're here for each other, *n'est-ce pas?*"

I smiled and leaned my head against his chest. "*Oui.*"

We stayed like that for a few pleasant minutes until I remembered far less sentimental issues. I sat up.

"Oh, hey, you have got to check something out."

I picked up my purse and pulled out the bag of crystals Alec had given me. Bastien recoiled when I held them out to him.

"What the hell are those?"

"That's the million-dollar question. These are what's causing my friend at the bookstore to act so weird."

Regaining his composure, he leaned in to look closer but

wouldn't touch the bag. "They're strange," he said slowly. "They give off something . . ."

"Like an immortal signature," I agreed. "But I've never felt an inanimate object that did this. It's not the same as an enchantment."

"It doesn't feel bad exactly . . . just not right."

"I asked Seth about it. Mortals don't feel anything, only us. Ever come across anything like this?"

"No, but then I'm the novice next to you, right?"

I slid the crystals back into my purse, to the relief of both of us, and then explained what Alec had said about mixing them in liquid.

"Curiouser and curiouser," mused Bastien. "Not like any drug I know, but it's not giving off any legitimate potion vibes either. If you want to know what this is, Fleur, you're going to have to break out the big guns."

I knew he was right. We hung out together a while longer, moving on to less weird subjects. The bread smelled so good cooking that there was no way I could leave until I'd tried a piece. Upon tasting it, I decided that whatever her other faults, Dana knew what she was doing with food. I ended up getting away with a good half loaf of the bread and then drove back downtown to find the "big guns."

I got a lucky break, and Jerome actually answered his cell phone and gave me his location. Even if he hadn't, it would have been on my list of places to try. The Cellar was an old, dark pub in Pioneer Square, Seattle's historic district. You had to take a flight of stairs down to get to the Cellar, and I always had the feeling the place wouldn't survive the Northwest's next big earthquake. The Cellar was one of Jerome and Carter's favorite haunts.

I found them both there in their usual corner. The place was dark, as always, and was starting to pick up a little with happy-hour traffic. Angel and demon watched me enter with their typically amused expressions, both having sensed me before I cleared the door. Jerome always gave the impression over the phone that I was taking up his time, but neither seemed particularly busy now. I ordered a gimlet at the bar, smiling at the two guys who made conversation while I waited, and then moved on to join the dynamic duo.

"A working lunch?" I asked, inclining my head at the empty shot glasses in front of them. The two practically sat side by side, so the only other chair was across from them, like I was at an interview.

Carter picked up one of the empty glasses and offered me a mock toast. I clinked my glass with his. "Don't question the divine workings of the universe, Daughter of Lilith."

"The Lord's work is never done," added Jerome solemnly.

They both seemed a little loopy, but I wasn't fooled. Higher immortals like angels and demons could control their levels of intoxication. The other lesser immortals and I had said a number of stupid things in front of them when we thought either Jerome or Carter had been wasted. Their eyes held a shrewd scrutiny even now that told me they were both curious about why I'd sought out my supervisor in the middle of the day.

"Been to see the incubus?" Jerome asked a moment later.

I nodded. "He thinks he's making progress."

"*Thinks?*" asked the demon, raising one eyebrow. I wondered if John Cusack could actually do that. "Is there a doubt?"

"I didn't say that."

"But you also didn't say that he *is* making progress."

"A slip of the tongue. I misspoke."

"You don't misspeak often, Georgie. And I've come to actually believe you do know something about seduction after all. And maybe even human nature."

"Something?"

Carter laughed at my incredulous tone.

"So," continued Jerome, "in your expert opinion, is your friend going to be able to do this or not?"

I was about to say "of course," but knew Carter would

recognize the lie. Hell, even Jerome probably would. "I don't know. She's hard to read. Very strange woman." I pursed my lips, thinking. "If anyone is capable of seducing her, though, it'll be him. With my help." I hesitated before adding, "You know about the Barton thing, don't you?"

"Of course. Very foolish on Bastien's part."

"I guess." I didn't want to slam one of my best friends in this company. "But it's not like our side is really known for impulse control. And it seems kind of stupid for Barton to get so worked up over a woman who sleeps around all the time anyway. What's one more person, immortal or not?"

"Because the immortal meant something," said Carter seriously. "You of all people should recognize the nuances here. What would Seth think if you slept with me?"

"Are you offering?" I turned to Jerome, feigning excitement. "I get to retire if I bag an angel, right? Full pension and everything?"

"Depends on the angel," yawned Jerome.

Carter kept his complacent smile, unfazed by jokes about his celibacy or immortal standing. "You know what I mean. There's a difference between business and choice."

I nodded. I did know what he meant, and he was right—being with Seth made me especially cognizant of the subtleties.

"You know, I didn't come here to discuss this," I told them. Both had the tendency to steer me off topic into subjects I didn't want to explore.

"Well, do enlighten us then," said the archdemon indulgently. "I'm dying to know what would draw you away from suburban conspiracy and mortal intrigue in the middle of the day."

"Actually, it involves mortal intrigue."

I gave them a debriefing on the Doug situation. Jerome maintained his perpetual look of disinterest. Carter almost did, but snide or not, he was still an angel, and I saw compassion flicker in his eyes as I spoke. He couldn't help it.

"So, I finally managed to get Alec to give me the stuff, and now I need to know what it is. You two seemed like my best shots at identification."

Jerome's disinterest turned to astonishment. "This is what we've been reduced to? Drug identification? Do we look like the DEA?"

Carter stretched lazily. "Remember the good old days when succubi used to want our help defending them from nephilim and other lethal creatures? This is a sign of the times, I tell you."

I let them have a good laugh at my expense, forcing myself to stay calm and not say something that would get me into trouble.

"Are you guys done?" I asked a minute later. "Because I'd really like to get moving on this."

"Are you going to share some of it with us if we can tell you what it is?" asked Jerome.

Rolling my eyes, I reached into my purse. With a flourish, I tossed the little bag out onto the table so it slid across the surface and came to rest just in front of both of them.

Their smiles disappeared.

They stared at the bag for a moment and then—in almost perfect synchronization—looked at each other and back to me.

When Carter spoke, he was amused, but grimly amused. "Maybe I shouldn't have been so quick to rule out supernatural monsters after all."

"How," exclaimed Jerome, nostrils flaring, "do you always manage to get yourself mixed up in the middle of this shit?"

I looked back and forth between the two of them. "What? What is it?"

"This, Georgina," announced Carter, tapping the bag with his finger, "is the Food of the Gods."

Chapter 15

A dozen snappy comebacks rose to my lips, but the intense looks on both their faces made me think better of it. Instead, I opted for the obvious next question.

"What do you mean?"

The edge of Carter's lips turned into a half-grin. "My goodness. I thought you'd be up on your lore. Greek mythology especially."

"Well, ambrosia . . . is called the Food of the Gods," I offered slowly. I had grown up in a Greco-Roman society, but that didn't mean I was an expert on all the stories. I'd only been exposed to some in my youth. It wasn't until later scholars started compiling tales from all over the Greek world that I learned just how vast the mythology was.

"Yes," said Carter, nodding at me as one would a child reciting a lesson. Jerome remained tight-lipped, a stormy expression on his face. "What else do you know?"

"Ambrosia was what gave the gods their immortality," I continued. "Although I always thought it was some kind of drink . . ." I stopped myself. The crystals weren't liquid at the moment, but they were meant to be consumed that way. A further alarming thought hit me. "Are you saying this Greek stuff will make Doug and the others immortal?"

I'm downright unstoppable now. A god, babe.

"Not exactly," said Carter. "And I suppose I should point out that ambrosia isn't just found in the Greek stories. It appears in almost every culture's legends in one form or another. In King Arthur's world, it was said to have filled the Holy Grail. It gave new perceptions and enlightenment to its drinkers, and promised to heal the land. Some have also suggested the flames that appeared over the apostles' heads at the feast of Pentecost were not flames at all, but rather visions they saw after drinking ambrosia. It made the apostles vivid and charismatic and let them communicate with people of all cultures and languages."

"I know a number of devout Christians—my good friend Dana included—who would find that offensive."

Jerome couldn't stay silent anymore, despite how disgruntled this topic appeared to make him. "Imagine her reaction if she knew that some people have speculated the Eucharist has little to do with the blood of Christ and more to do with a lost ambrosia ceremony. Said people argue those who participate today are only mimicking the ancient experience, equating the Holy Spirit with the high from ambrosia."

"That would upset a lot of people," I agreed. All three of us knew that many of the rites and beliefs that had been passed down to today were bastardizations of the originals. Some, not all.

Carter continued on pleasantly, like he was in an auditorium giving a lecture. "Ancient Hindu culture called ambrosia *soma* and even personified it as a god of the same name. His presence was as intoxicating as the drink itself and muddled the senses of those around him."

"Soma was also the feel-good drug in *Brave New World*," I recalled. "I didn't realize how widespread this was."

He nodded. "And these stories are only the tip of the iceberg. A lot more where they came from."

I enjoyed the information. Getting any sort of meaningful explanation from these two was usually like driving through downtown Seattle in rush hour: slow, painful, and fraught with collisions. And yet, forthcoming or not, they weren't exactly giving me what I needed.

"Yeah, but you guys are real careful to say things like 'some people believe' or 'they say.' Which is it? What's really going on? Are any of those stories true?"

Carter's gray eyes twinkled. "Ah, I can't spoil the mysteries. Humans spend their lives trying to discern the truth of divinity. Even a succubus can't be in on all the secrets."

I gave him an exasperated look. *This* was more like their typical behavior. "Okay, forget the myths. Can you tell me what's up with this stuff, then? Does it make people immortal?"

Angel and demon looked at each other. "No," they both said in unison.

"But it makes you feel like you are," said Carter.

I thought about Doug's reckless behavior, his overwhelming confidence about everything from performing his music to stage-diving. He had no fear, no concern that anything might be less than perfect.

"So it's like a stimulant or any other mood-altering drug, then," I said. "It makes you feel good."

The angel shook his head. "No. It's a lot more than that. Ambrosia works by . . ." He grasped for the words. "I guess the best way to put it is that it amplifies your best abilities. It draws out what you're good at, what shines in you. And then it cranks up the volume on that to, well, godly levels, I guess."

"Yes, of course," I breathed.

That was why the band had suddenly shot off so successfully and rapidly. They were talented already. The ambrosia hadn't given anything new; they'd just had their natural abilities increased tenfold. A hundredfold. And Casey . . . mathematically talented Casey had been able to do calculations in seconds that would have required a pen and paper for most people. Even Doug's Tetris skills showed signs of ambrosia enhancement.

I can't wait to see how you react to them, Alec had said. Indeed, how would I react? What good abilities in me would get amplified? What abilities did I have? The obvious joke was that I'd be able to really rock some guy's world in bed. I didn't like that answer, however, partially because I believed I already could rock a guy's world pretty hard-core without the help of creepy crystals, thank you very much. Plus, I hated to think that's all I was. There had to be more to me than just sexual prowess.

"Everyone who was on it crashed," I reminded Carter. "Doug, Casey. And when they crashed . . . they *really* crashed."

"It does that," he agreed. "One might argue that the withdrawal brings out your worst traits . . . or possibly turns your good ones bad. More often than not, it just makes a person depressed . . . and lacking. It's hard to go back to being ordinary."

That would explain Doug's bleak outlook the other day. I realized too he'd been having a withdrawal reaction on the day I kicked him out of the store. The lack of ambrosia had turned his normally sarcastic tongue and playful behavior into something dark and twisted. And yet . . .

"It must be nice to feel like a god. I guess I can understand wanting that."

"Well," said Jerome, speaking up at last, "as we all know, you can't get something for nothing."

Carter nodded. "At a basic level, it's an addictive substance, and everything addictive has a cost—mainly that it enslaves you and makes you feel horrible when you don't have it. But, the other truth is that humans are not meant to be perfect. That's what humanity is: a series of successes and failures, a testing of one's own nature and aptitude. Neither the body nor the soul can sustain such a state. Eventually it consumes a person."

I pointed at the crystals. "What would have happened if I'd taken them?"

"Isn't it obvious?" asked Jerome, his tone suggesting the same sexual possibilities I'd wondered about earlier.

Carter gave me a straight answer. "Similar superficial effects. Enhance your good qualities. Immortals wouldn't fall prey to the addictiveness so quickly; they can sustain it for quite a while since in some ways, they already feel like gods. But in the long run, the consequences are still the same. You can't function at such high levels. Now, the ambrosia couldn't destroy your body, of course, but it'd still cause other serious problems if you took it for a long time."

"It'd probably just make you go insane," explained Jerome helpfully. "Until the end of time."

"That's horrible," I said.

"Don't worry, Georgie. If it happens to you, we'll put you down first."

Ignoring him, I looked over at the crystals, suddenly feeling more repulsed by them than I had before. This time, my reaction had nothing to do with the creepy aura.

"The real question, of course," said the archdemon more seriously, "is where the hell did you get these?"

"I told you. From Alec."

The two higher immortals exchanged glances once more.

"Tell us about this guy again," ordered Jerome. "Everything you know."

I did. When I finished, they looked at each other once more, having a mental conversation I was not privy to. God, they were annoying.

"Alec's not the one," said Carter finally.

"The one who . . . ?"

"The one who this is coming from," explained Jerome.

"Well, I got it from him . . ."

"Doesn't matter, Georgie. Some twenty-year-old blue-haired punk is not the source here. He's getting it from some-

one else. He's a peon in the chain. Besides, you never felt anything off him, did you? Something like the crystals but not
quite like them?"

"No, but . . ." But I *had* felt something from another person. Someone who spent time with Alec. The last card in my
head flipped over. "I know who it is. It's him. That guy."

"Of course," said Carter dryly. "I knew it was that guy. It's
always *that guy*."

"Hold on, and I'll explain." I turned to Jerome. "Remember that funny immortal I told you about? The really romantically dressed good-looking one? He's got to be the one.
Alec's supplier. I've seen them talking together and even saw
Alec sort of having a breakdown with him." I added a little
more background for Carter's benefit, explaining how *GQ*
Poet Guy and I had sensed each other.

Jerome and Carter considered this in silence. At last, the
demon said, "Yes, that sounds like him."

Nobody said anything for a while after that. I was dying to
ask who "he" was exactly, but recognized that angel and
demon would take their own time on this.

"So what are we going to do?" Carter asked a few minutes
later.

Jerome cut him a narrow-eyed glance. "Why do we have
to do anything?"

"Because it's the right thing to do."

"I don't know where you've been since the beginning of
the universe, but the 'right thing' isn't really on my list of pri-
orities."

"He's poisoning mortals."

Jerome crossed his arms over his chest. "I don't care."

"He's doing it in your territory. Right under your nose."

"Stop trying to bait me. He's not involved with us. He can
do whatever the fuck he wants to mortals."

Once again, I was dying to jump in but restrained myself.
Listening to Carter and Jerome argue always unsettled me.
Mostly, it just didn't happen that much. Usually they stood

together in an exasperating wall of solidarity, good and evil notwithstanding. And, of course, watching them argue always made you wonder if something terrible might happen if tempers got out of control. Tables tipping over. Glasses exploding. The Four Horsemen showing up.

Nonetheless, I felt confident Carter wouldn't let this matter go unattended. He would win. As I had noted earlier, I didn't know if I could trust him, but I did respect him—and his powers of persuasion.

"It's a power play," warned Carter. "He shouldn't even be trying it. His time is past; we're the ones who control the game now. Doing this insults us—especially you, since you guys are the ones who actually draw territorial lines. It's an unannounced challenge."

This, I saw, had an effect on the demon. He recognized Carter's attempts to draw him in, but it was working nonetheless. Pride wasn't one of the Seven Deadly Sins for nothing. Jerome, as a faithful servant of hell, couldn't help but be susceptible. I'd seen his pride come into play before; he didn't like others messing with his reputation. And while the demon naturally had many weaknesses, I'd say it was this more than anything else that would make him take action.

"We can't intervene," he said flatly. "You know that. Even if we are in control, we'd start an outright war. I for one don't want to deal with the repercussions of that."

"Agreed," murmured the angel, lapsing into silence again.

I looked back and forth between their faces, waiting for one of them to offer a brilliant plan. A brilliant plan which involved the angel and demon fighting in awesome, smiting glory to destroy Alec and his bastardly supplier friend.

"Georgina could do it," said Carter suddenly.

"What?" I squeaked. That wasn't how the fantasy went. They turned their eyes on me.

Dark outrage flashed in Jerome's eyes, then it faded as quickly as it had arrived. "Hmm. Perhaps."

"What are you guys talking about? I'm not doing any smiting."

"It wouldn't exactly be smiting," said Carter, face promptly sobering. "But it could be dangerous if not done the right way."

"Why do I have to do it?"

"Because you, Georgie, are a lesser power than we are. You are less subject to scrutiny and ramifications than us. It's the difference between a country declaring war and a small rebel faction striking out."

"Great," I said, sinking back in my chair. "I'm a faction."

Carter was smiling again. "Don't you want to help Doug?"

A moment passed. "You know I do."

"I meant it when I said it'd be dangerous, but if we're careful, you'll come out okay."

I thought about Doug's black despair and reckless behavior. The thought of this ambrosia "destroying" him clinched it for me. "Yeah, okay. I'll do it. Whatever it is. Dangerous or not." I paused. "Um, what is it?"

Neither answered.

"Oh come on! You can't expect me to do this and not know what it is."

"It'll take some prep work," Carter told me, apparently enjoying my consternation. But there was another expression on his face too . . . pride, I thought. The good kind of pride, like when you thought someone was doing the right thing. Not the bad kind of pride that made you do rash things. "As soon as it's in place, we'll let you know. I'll come find you."

I made a face. "You'll understand if I don't really find that a satisfying answer."

"And you'll understand," retorted Jerome, "that it's the best one you're going to get."

Carter was a bit nicer. "What you can do in the meantime, however, is try to get access to the supplier. He's the one you'll ultimately have to deal with. Keep schmoozing with Alec. Do what you've got to do."

I nodded. Schmoozing I could do in my sleep. I felt relieved to be back in familiar waters.

After leaving them, I put the ambrosia assignment on hold and went over to Seth's to play Scrabble, in keeping with a prearranged date. I'd vowed I wouldn't cheat this time, but I supposed that would depend on how desperate the game became. When I arrived, however, I found Seth in no condition to play.

He sat at the desk in his bedroom, brow adorably furrowed as he stared at his computer screen, apparently willing it do something for him through mental determination alone. His condo had an office, I knew, but unpacked boxes currently filled it, making this room the combination office-bedroom. All his essentials in one place. If it had had an attached bathroom, he would have probably never emerged.

"Can you give me . . . like . . . another hour?" he asked absently when he realized I had walked in, not looking at me. "I've just got to finish this chapter."

It was a moot request. Even if I hadn't been willing to give him another hour, he still would have kept writing. Mountains moved more easily than Seth in the middle of a story line. Happily accommodating, I kissed his cheek and wandered off to the office to find something to read. Sifting through those boxes made it difficult, however. By the time I had several of them emptied, I decided I might as well just go the whole way and do the job right.

I unpacked all of the boxes—even the ones in his living room. I didn't know how many books that left me with, but it was a lot. My bookstore instincts made me sort them into categories, and that alone was time-consuming. Looking up at one point, I realized almost three hours had passed. I stood up, stretched, and returned to the bedroom.

"Hey," I said. "We're way past your hour."

He kept typing.

I slipped my foot out of its sandal, shape-shifted the toenail color to burgundy and ran it up his leg. He jumped.

"Hey!"

"Hey yourself. Sorry to interrupt, but you need food, or you're going to pass out on your keyboard."

"Wouldn't be the first time," he said. His eyes strayed, threatening to return to the computer, so I poked him again with my foot. He arched an eyebrow, then grabbed my foot, nearly making me fall over as he pulled me onto his lap. "You know, your toes aren't that compelling. It's not like I want to have sex with them or anything weird like that. I just think they're pretty. So don't think you can have your way on everything now."

I wiggled out of his grasp. "Say whatever you want. I've got new leverage with you. So, look, can you tear yourself away long enough to go get food?"

It turned out he couldn't, toes or not. Disappointed, I ended up ordering pizza. We ate together and talked, but both of us were in our own worlds. He was with his characters in places I couldn't follow, and I was thinking about the ambrosia. Suddenly, I started laughing.

"What?" he asked, startled.

I told him about the ambrosia and what it did. The news obviously astonished him, but Seth had had some time now to accept the many unseen, supernatural things occurring in the world. I ended my story by saying Carter and Jerome were going to do something about it. I did not mention I would be taking on a large and possibly dangerous role too. There I was, holding back again, but it seemed pointless to get him worried when I had no concrete details yet.

"So, anyway, I was laughing because I was trying to imagine what you'd be like on ambrosia," I told him.

"Why is that funny? Maybe I could churn out a book a week."

"Yeah, but I'd never see you again. You'd never bathe or cut your hair. It'd grow down to your waist—so would your beard—and you'd be sitting here in the dark, hunched over, wasting away in your Punky Brewster T-shirt."

"That's not funny. That's how I plan to spend my retirement. Besides, if I were going to wear the same shirt for the next fifty years, it'd be my Flash Gordon one." His features shifted to a frown as he chewed. "The entire concept of Doug's problem being 'magically' induced . . ." He shook his head. "It's crazy. And scary. Will they really be able to help him?"

"They will if they can. Carter especially."

"You always put a lot of faith in him. Seems ironic, given the circumstances."

I supposed it was, and again, it was kind of new for me. I guess I was just starting to realize that although I might be on Jerome's side, it was Carter who was on *my* side lately. I smiled for Seth.

"Well. If you can't put faith in an angel, who can you put faith in?"

The muse called to him after dinner, and I let him go, unable to stand against her. I wondered if it would be possible for Seth to date someone who didn't love his books. Few women would be able to handle the competition. And yeah, sometimes it was hard for me to handle the competition too. It was hard enough that Seth wasn't into the livelier things I liked to do, like dancing. But also being denied the low-key things poked at me on occasion.

Knowing his neglect was for the greater good, I returned to my book sorting, which allowed half of my brain to churn over the Alec problem and how I was going to get to *GQ* Poet Guy. Getting a hold of Doug in the evening was never easy, but I'd see him at work tomorrow. He'd offered Alec's number to me once; hopefully he'd be as obliging this time.

I finished my cataloging and shelving job around two in the morning. All the books had homes on either the office or living room shelves, and all the books were indexed by genre and author in a way Emerald City might have lauded. The office now had room for the desk.

In the bedroom, Seth still typed in the dark, lit by the glow of his monitor. I kissed his cheek once more and fell asleep in his bed, exhausted.

I awoke hours later to someone kissing my cheek. "Hey," I murmured drowsily, trying to pull Seth into bed with me. "You're giving me funny ideas."

He leaned over me and planted a kiss on my nose. Morning sunlight lit up the coppery highlights in his messy hair and perpetual five o'clock shadow. He regarded me fondly, those luscious lips smiling.

"You put my books away. All of them."

"I had to. Good grief. If anyone at Emerald City found out I was letting that slide, they'd fire me."

He curled up beside me and put an arm over me. "You're pretty good to me, Thetis, considering what an idiot I am sometimes."

"Stop making fun of my favorite author, or I'll have to deck you."

"I mean it. I've lost girlfriends for less than what I did last night."

"You weren't that bad. I've seen you worse." I sat up a little. "Hey, how many girlfriends have you had anyway?"

Laugh lines appeared around his eyes, making him even cuter. "It was all research for the books, I swear."

It was ironic, I realized, that I kept ending up with artistic types. A very long time ago, I'd been married to a man I swore loved his music more than me sometimes. I had loved him for that musical passion and hated it at the same time. Similar scenarios with other mortals had repeated over the centuries. Remembering my thoughts from last night, I worried that Seth might bring out the old green-eyed monster again.

"How'd the chapter turn out?" I asked, mussing his hair further.

"Good. Great even." He gave me a sweet, bemused look. "I don't suppose . . . I don't suppose you'd ever want to read the manuscripts as I work on them, would you? See how the process works?"

I froze, realizing just what a precious gift he was offering me. Seth had told me once he never let anyone read the early drafts. He didn't want feedback that might influence his own creative flow. It wasn't until he had a complete manuscript and he felt the books were nigh-perfect that he finally allowed his publishing posse to take a look. That he would offer this to me both thrilled and touched me.

"No," I said softly, smiling. "But thank you. I don't want to interrupt your normal cycle. But maybe . . . maybe when you've got a fairly polished draft ready to send off, I'll take a look then."

He nodded, returning my smile. Something passed between us then that had nothing to do with manuscripts or book sorting but was fired by both of them nonetheless.

"Here," he said, standing up. Turning to a nearby chair, he picked up a tray I hadn't even noticed. "Since you fed me last night."

I looked down as he set the tray across my lap. Pancakes—with smiley faces—drowning in maple syrup. Good strong coffee. Even a little vase with two stems of purple irises. Seth had a thing for purple flowers. I touched one of the velvety soft petals.

"You didn't get these from your kitchen. You must have gotten up pretty early to go out."

He shook his head, looking sheepish. "I never went to bed."

I therefore wasn't surprised when Seth lay down beside me while I ate and promptly fell asleep. I finished the exquisite breakfast, did the dishes, and left for work, leaving him a note that promised I'd call later.

At the bookstore, I was getting so used to Paige and Warren's absence, it was like they didn't even work there anymore. I found Doug when he arrived, and as hoped, he did indeed give me Alec's number—though not without a few jokes at my expense.

I called Alec on my lunch, unsure if he'd be home. He was there and sounded overjoyed to hear from me. Yes, yes, of course he could get more. He was *so* glad I'd liked it. Giving me the address of a coffee shop he'd be at, he told me to stop by right after work.

I showed up there five minutes after my shift ended. The coffee shop was perfectly ordinary, nothing dark or sinister. Hardly the stereotypical rendezvous for a drug transaction. I spotted Alec sitting at a table in the back, but someone was with him. Not wanting to interrupt, I stood in line to order a mocha.

Alec's companion was a young man, younger than him even. Eighteen, if I had to guess. And he was beautiful. He had swept his thick, dark-blond hair into a short ponytail at the nape of his neck, and his face was all clean, strong lines. When he smiled at some comment of Alec's, perfect white teeth showed against the tanned skin. I expected to see this guy in an Abercrombie & Fitch ad soon.

Or maybe not, since he too was apparently wasting his life away. Alec reached into his pocket and gave the guy one of the telltale bags. Happiness and relief shone on the golden boy's face, making him look—if possible—even more attractive. He left. Angrily gripping my drink, I took his chair and forced a cheerful attitude.

"Hey," said Alec in greeting, clearly in a good mood. "You have no idea how glad I am to see you. You look hot, as always."

"Thanks. How's it going?"

"Awesome, now." He grinned broadly. "Fabulous day." He leaned toward me. "So? What did you think?"

I set my cup down heavily and acquired some little-girl wonder. "You were right . . . it was amazing. It was like I was . . ." I decided a lack of words was better than trying to describe something I hadn't experienced. He was only too happy to help fill in the blanks.

"Better than ever? Who you were meant to be?"

"Yes," I said breathlessly. "You—you've got to give me more."

"Can do." His hand reached into the magic pocket. One of the lethal bags appeared, and that ugly feeling snaked down my spine. He held the crystals teasingly out of my reach. "You know, they get better the more you do it. You up for that?"

I stared at the bag longingly, then up at him. "Don't you have more than this? I mean, I want that one . . . but it's not going to be enough. I need a lot of this."

"Slow down. You don't want to take more than one bag."

"I know that, but this is good for what, a day or two?"

His eyes glinted. "Big plans already, huh? Most people don't get quite so fired up this fast."

I chewed on my lower lip, not wanting to raise any alarms. Assessing my self-inventory, I tried to think of something nonsexual the ambrosia would have affected. Alec's earlier visitor gave me the answer.

"It's weird. I know this guy at a modeling agency, and he always gives me the runaround. But I saw him yesterday when I took this . . . and it was like, I don't know. He couldn't get enough of me. He wants me to come back for some major shoots." I gripped Alec's arm. "I don't get how this could be doing it . . . maybe it's coincidence. I don't know. But I want more. I think I need it to make this gig work out. You've got to help me. Or take me to wherever you get this. I'll pay. I'll do anything."

His face told me I had said exactly the right thing.

"It's not coincidence," he told me smugly. "And I'll get you more."

I exhaled with palpable relief. "Promise? Like a big supply?"

"I promise. Here, take this one."

"What do I owe you?"

"Nothing."

"Come on! They can't all be free." My hold on his hand changed to something softer and more suggestive. "I told you before . . . I'm happy to pay . . . however you want . . ."

He sighed, regarding me wistfully as he briefly ran his fingers over my hand and then pulled away. "I know. You want a big batch of it? That you'll have to pay for. I'll take you to the guy who gets it for me, and you can pay him."

"What'll it cost? How much am I going to need?"

Something unreadable flashed in his eyes. "You've already got exactly what you need. Can you meet me tomorrow night?"

I hesitated. Carter had said we needed some prep time before I faced the supplier, time in which I had been told to arrange the meeting with him. This was too soon.

"I'm busy," I told him, trying to put heavy regret into my words. "What about the next night?"

He didn't seem happy about that, just as he hadn't liked the delay in me drinking my first batch. But where his urgency had been underscored with an eager curiosity last time, he now displayed an almost panicked anxiety. I wondered just how demanding his master was. "Sooner would be better. You aren't going to be able to go that long anyway, not if you want it this bad already."

I stayed firm. "I don't have a choice."

He agreed after a little more wheedling, and we set a time and place to meet in two days. As I stood up, he warned me, "Call me sooner if you can't hold out, okay? Here's my cell."

"Okay, thanks."

"Hey," he called as I started to walk away. "Good luck with the shoot."

For a minute, I didn't remember what he was talking

about. Then I recalled my alleged modeling gig. I smiled and thanked him, chuckling to myself as I left. In all of the lies I'd just told him, there had been a kernel of truth.

I did have a photo shoot. Tonight was the night Bastien and I were going to take the pictures for Seth.

Chapter 16

I rang Bastien's doorbell for the third time and then glared peevishly at the house. Where the hell was he? I was a little earlier than our agreed meeting time but not significantly. I gave the door a petulant kick as I imagined Bastien "held up" in the arms of some panting housewife.

"He's not here," said a cool voice nearby. I looked over and saw Dana standing there, a small leashed dog by her feet. It looked like the product of a tragic accident at the cotton-ball factory.

"Nice dog," I said.

"My sister's. I'm taking care of him for a few days. You want to walk with us?"

No, but I had promised myself the other day that I would pick Dana's brain to figure out how I might aid Bastien, and this seemed as good an opportunity as any. Besides, he'd kill me if he knew I'd passed up a chance for "reconnaissance."

I fell into step beside Dana and the fluff ball, congratulating myself for the hundredth time on being smart enough to choose cats over dogs. Tutu—yes, that was his name—pranced along daintily, small tongue hanging out. His beady black eyes peered everywhere as he trotted merrily, but otherwise seemed oblivious to the wet sidewalk dirtying his tiny white feet.

"How's your rally going?" I asked after we'd exhausted dog topics.

"Excellent. I'm surprised you haven't heard about it in the news. We're getting a lot of press."

"Haven't paid that much attention to the news."

She told me the date and time. "Think you can make it?"

"I think I'm working that day," I said automatically.

Dana gave me a knowing look. "Tabitha, I get the impression you're not entirely settled on that issue."

You think? I looked away, again fighting the mental battle of speaking my mind versus causing trouble for Bastien. I finally opted for something that sounded vaguely like the truth.

"I just think . . . there's a lot of different ways to look at it, that's all."

"It's okay to be unsure, you know."

That was astonishing, coming from her. "Is it?"

"Of course. That's why groups like the CPFV exist. To help you see the truth of an issue."

I repressed a snort. I'd thought for a moment she might startle me with a display of open-mindedness. I let the silence collect again.

"So," she began after a moment, "what do you believe then?"

"Er, on what? Homosexuality? Or homosexual marriage?"

"Either."

My opinion was simply that people wanted who they wanted, end of story. There was no regulating love or saying it was wrong. But Dana's views on that were religiously based, and I of all people knew better than to argue the right or wrong of faith.

"I'm just not sure people choose who they're attracted to," I explained, not exactly attacking her question head-on. "So, I guess, it seems weird to me to talk about 'helping' or 'changing' people who can't really do anything about their natures, regardless of whether that nature is right or wrong."

"So you think homosexuality is inborn?" That sweet voice couldn't entirely hide her scornful surprise.

"For some people. I think there are those who engage in . . . uh, same-sex activities for the fun of it, but for others, it's biological."

I had a feeling Dana wouldn't describe same-sex activities as fun, but I still felt better at having voiced my opinions.

"You express yourself very well," she admitted. "Even if I don't necessarily agree with you."

I laughed out loud, and she looked at me strangely. "No, I didn't think you would."

We grew quiet again, and I remembered I was supposed to be sounding her out on what she found romantic for Bastien.

"I wish I could choose who I was attracted to," I said out of the blue, bringing up personal matters in a manner that was out of character for both Tabitha Hunter and Georgina Kincaid.

Dana seemed appropriately startled. "Things aren't going so well with your boyfriend? What was his name? Sven?"

"Seth," I corrected, feeling only a little bad at dragging him into the cover story. Things with Seth were actually beautiful at the moment, but for the sake of appearances, I kept lying. "He's okay, I guess, and I like him . . . but he's not very, you know, romantic."

"Ah," she said neutrally.

"Am I crazy? Is that too much to ask? Maybe I should focus on other things."

"What do you consider romantic?"

"I don't know. Little touches and flourishes here and there. Gestures to show how important you are, how much the other person cares about you." Irises, smiley-face pancakes. "What do you think it is?"

She shrugged. We were rounding the corner back to Bastien's

now. "I've come to see romance as not quite so important anymore," she admitted. "Neither Bill nor I have time for it."

"Oh."

"That's not a bad thing. I'd say, more important than superficial flourishes is being able to connect with someone. To talk openly with them and share yourself. To know they're feeling what you're feeling."

"Oh," I said again, surprised. Her comments almost made sense. In some ways, they were a variation of Seth's views on honesty in a relationship. Biting my lip, I plunged on. "And what about . . . you know, attraction and sex appeal?"

She gave me a sidelong glance. "What about it?"

I shrugged. "I don't always feel it around him." Liar, liar, pants on fire. "Do I have the wrong ideas about it? What do you think is sexy?"

Her answer took a long time in coming. "I don't know."

Bastien stood by his front door as we approached. He waved a hand in greeting. "Hello, ladies." He looked pleasantly astonished to see us together—and getting along.

Dana thanked me for the company and returned to her own home after refusing Bastien's automatic invitation to come inside and stay a while. Once she was gone and we were in the car headed to my photo shoot, I gave him the scoop on our talk.

"She doesn't know what's sexy?" he exclaimed. "She's practically begging for me to ravage her. Hmph. And Bill's not romantic. Well, no surprise there. You think she was lying about saying it wasn't important? Sort of a defense mechanism?"

"I don't know. Possibly. But even if she does miss romance, I think too many over-the-top gestures would throw up a flag. She isn't stupid. Profound conversation might be the way to go."

"Then the cooking thing is a good idea. Lots of talking there."

"I guess." I didn't tell him that I had doubts about the efficacy of that method. Honestly, I wasn't sure what he could do anymore.

We'd decided to pull out all the stops for my pictures. He drove us downtown to the Hotel Andra, one of the nicest local spreads, despite its plain exterior. Through some charm I didn't know about, he'd even managed to book us the hotel's one-of-a-kind Monarch Suite on practically no notice. It had more room than we could possibly need, but its true selling point—for me—was an utterly sumptuous, utterly sexy bed. Enclosed in its own romantically lit alcove, it had a deep, royal purple spread and a headboard of gleaming, black wood. The whole effect was dark and sensuous. We shape-shifted out of Mitch and Tabitha upon clearing the door.

"This bed alone," declared Bastien, "will sell these pictures. Well, that and your naked flesh. But really, it's a tough call."

He raided the mini-bar and made us improvised Grand Marnier martinis, which I gulped down with surprising eagerness. Suddenly, facing these pictures seemed a lot more daunting than I'd originally believed.

"Nothing to it," he said, sensing my nervousness. "Put on something sexy and sprawl on the bed."

I hadn't brought anything in particular to wear, for once willingly opting for shape-shifting. I started with a basic black nightgown. Super short, super low-cut. It seemed like a safe bet. Bastien positioned me on the bed, lying back in a sort of languid pose. He mussed my hair and requested a lazy pout.

"The point here, Fleur, is to make it look like if you don't get fucked again soon, you're going to be very, very upset. Men go for that."

My apprehension melted away as Bastien took over, directing my postures and expressions, snapping away with his digital camera. We ran the gamut. Some shots I did completely naked, hiding nothing. For others, we found the suggestion of nudity could almost be more provocative. The way the slipped strap of a chemise could nearly reveal a breast. The way a sheer bra and panty set could cover and yet not cover.

Nor did we give all of them the just-got-fucked look. In some, I was very elegant, unbelievably perfect in every possible way, not a strand of hair out of place. In others, however, we played up the messy, wild look—"unplanned," as Seth would say. We also didn't limit ourselves to the bed, as gorgeous as it was. I posed by windows, by a sofa, by the bathtub, in the bathtub. Both of us, as was requisite for our jobs, had pretty good imaginations for what was sexy and alluring. Nonetheless, we had brought along a few lingerie catalogs and adult magazines for inspiration. We would take breaks to plan, both of us frowning and giving each new pose serious thought.

All in all, it was an exhausting endeavor, but Bastien's energy never flagged as he guided me through it all with a professional ease. And honestly, after a certain point, I didn't need his coaching. I knew I was sexy, and it was easy to play that up, especially knowing that Seth would view all of this.

When the incubus had filled up the memory card, we finally called it quits. Sprawling on the bed beside me, he called room service and ordered us some professional martinis, since we'd run out of Grand Marnier. They arrived, and we luxuriated in a well-deserved rest, sipping our drinks.

"Thanks Bas," I told him, touching his arm. "You're a good friend."

"Easy to be one when the subject matter is so nice to look at. You're going to have a bitch of a time getting these printed, though. Take them to a store, and you won't get them back."

I'd already thought of that. "Hugh has a snazzy, state-of-the-art printer. I'll do it there." I considered. "Although, he might keep a few too."

"I wouldn't blame him." Bastien set his drink down and rolled over to regard me affectionately, face almost serious for a change. "You're a beautiful woman, Fleur, and that means something when you can perfectly control your appearance. It's not your physical side—as nice as it is. It's something in here." He tapped my breastbone. "Something warm and sensual and lovely that shines out. I'd know you in any body, in any place."

I curled up against him, happy. "I'm glad you're here. Even if it's because of the Barton and Dana mess. We're going to fix that for you, you know. I promise. I'm not letting them ship you off somewhere horrible."

A faint, playful smile curled his lips. Affection shone in his dark eyes, affection that was no doubt mirrored in my face. Suddenly, he leaned over and kissed me.

Whoa.

It wasn't a friendly kiss either, not the kind we so regularly planted on each other's lips in a careless way. This was a deep kiss, an erotic kiss. His lips felt like velvet, his tongue slowly sliding over mine. I was so floored by what was happening that for a moment I couldn't do anything except sink into that kiss and let it send shockwaves through my body.

My senses returned to me, and I broke away, sitting up. "What the hell are you doing?"

He sat up as well, as surprised by my reaction as I had been by what triggered it. "What do you mean?"

"You kissed me. I mean, *really* kissed me."

He grinned, sensual and provocative. I shivered. When incubi targeted you with that charm, it was bewildering, even for a succubus.

"What's wrong with it? You mean more to me than anyone else in the world. This is a natural step for us. We should have been doing it a long time ago."

I shook my head, backing away. "I like the way we've always been."

"Only because you haven't tried anything else. Look, I'm

not asking you to run off into the sunset here. We're friends. I know that, and I like that. But you've said it yourself—sleeping with people you don't care about is wearying."

"Yeah, but . . . I don't think this is necessarily the answer."

"Then what is the answer?" he demanded. "Sleeping—or rather not sleeping—with a mortal you do care about?"

I climbed out of bed. "That was harsh. And it's unrelated. I don't want us to be anything more than friends, Bastien. Sex'll mess things up."

He stayed on the bed, watching me pace. "Sex will fix a lot of things. It's about time we got some satisfaction that wasn't all business. It'll be therapeutic for both of us. We need it."

I turned away, staring out the window without seeing. "*I* don't need it."

"Don't you?"

Only the voice that asked me that wasn't Bastien's. It was Seth's.

I spun around, eyes wide. "Stop that! Change back right now!"

Bastien—as Seth—lay back easily against the pillows. He wore jeans and a Whitesnake T-shirt, just as Seth might have. His hair was unkempt. He'd even perfected that cute, distracted smile.

"What's the problem, Thetis?"

I stormed up to the bed, wanting to give him the full force of my fury even as I longed to run away. "This isn't funny! *Change back now.*"

Sitting up again, he slid to the edge of the bed. "Come on, how have you not seen this coming? This is the perfect solution to all your problems."

"No, it's not. It's really not."

He stood up and walked toward me, not touching me but coming close enough to make my heart race. I stood rooted, unable to move.

"Of course it is. If you ever want to get Seth out of your system, this is the way to do it. You spend all this time pining for him, wondering what it'd be like to touch him and be with him. Well, this is your chance. This is the only safe way, your chance to do everything you want without hurting him. Do this now, and you could save yourself a lot of grief in the future."

I shook my head, as my mouth apparently couldn't move now either. Too many conflicting feelings. The entire scene was unreal. Mindblowing. I was still shocked by Bastien's audacity in doing it in the first place. I knew he was rash and bold, but this was crossing the line, even for him. On the other hand, Bastien had mimicked Seth down to the last detail, and seeing him had the effect it always did on me. Everything was the same. Cute and flawless. More intoxicating still was the truth of Bastien's offer. I really could do what I wanted here. It was wrong on so many levels, but I couldn't deny the pull. The perfect temptation.

"I won't cheat on Seth."

"What's cheating between you guys? You do it all the time."

"Then I'm not going to be one of your conquests," I snapped.

"Fine." He shape-shifted the shirt away so I saw only lovely, bare chest now. He drew my hands forward, resting them on his skin. I discovered it was almost entirely smooth; there were just a few soft and silky golden hairs. "You do the conquering."

"I'm not doing any conquering."

"All right. Then take your hands away."

I stared at where my hands lay on his chest. On Seth's chest. He was warm. My hands matched him almost perfectly. We both had light, barely tanned, golden skin. *Take your hands away.* That's all I had to do. I just had to move my hands, step away, and leave this ridiculous game behind. I was only a hair's breadth from normality . . . yet I couldn't seem to move away. I knew it wasn't Seth, but the illusion was so powerful, I could easily imagine that this was exactly how it would feel to touch him.

Without thinking, I ran my fingers down his chest, down to his stomach. Seth was no bodybuilder, but he was lean and trim from swimming and running. I had seen him in boxers before; the strong muscles were firm and exactly where they should be. Again, a perfect illusion. My hands had brushed this same part of Seth in bed before, but I never allowed myself to sensually explore him, the way I could now. I moved my fingers further, tracing the lines and contours.

For his part, he didn't say or do anything. But whenever I looked up, those brown eyes were on me, brimming with heat. They made my body respond with a heat of its own. Would Seth look at me the same way if we were together like this? Somehow, I expected the answer would be yes. I knew Seth viewed sex as a serious matter, despite his characters' casual attitudes. He would treat such an encounter seriously. Also—although I had no proof—I thought Seth would be just as cautious as Bastien was being now, letting me take the lead. Nothing aggressive.

My hands slid farther, down to the edge of his jeans where blue flannel boxers barely peeped out. I ran my fingers under the edge, arousing myself further with this dangerous game. Being this close to hitherto forbidden territory was heady. My scouting fingers started to tremble. Never, never would I have let things reach this point with Seth. Not with both of us pressed together. Not with both of us in so little clothing. My common sense would have long since kicked in before something dangerous might happen. But Bastien was right: nothing dangerous could happen tonight.

At least not physically.

I looked back up. His own breath had quickened. The space between us sizzled. He was so like Seth, I realized. So very much like him. It would be so easy. Easy to pretend.

I leaned up and kissed him, again tasting those soft lips,

pushing my tongue past them so I could fully savor him. His hands moved around my back, touching silk and bare skin. I was in the same outfit I wore for the last picture: another chemise, this time with a revealing top of ivory lace and a rose-pink silk skirt. I pushed into that kiss, letting it burn me. He kept his hands carefully neutral the whole time, not taking liberties, instead letting me dictate the terms.

Reaching around, I grabbed a hold of his hands and moved them over me. I wanted to know what it was like to have him—Seth—touching me. I moved them down to my backside, then over to the sides of my thighs, urging him to push the chemise up. He did, letting silk gather up in his fingers as it slid up, up over my breasts and then over my head. I exhaled as those hands traveled up my body, every part of my skin electric and alive as I stood completely naked now.

"Lay down," I said, surprised at the rough note in my voice.

He obliged, and I crawled onto the bed after him, straddling his hips with my legs so I leaned over him, letting my hair brush his chest as it had that night at Terry and Andrea's.

Seth. I had Seth. And I could do anything I wanted.

I kissed him again, harder than I had before, as if my mouth realized this could stop at any moment and had to get as much as it could right now. Pulling back slightly, I placed his hands back on me. "Don't stop touching me."

I returned to his lips, crushing his in return, letting my teeth nibble that soft flesh. All the while his hands roved over me as I'd commanded, coming to rest under my breasts so that he could cup them and stroke them. His fingers trailed to the nipples, which were already standing erect, brushing them lightly at first and then squeezing with greater intensity. I cried out, my own savage urges stoked, and I moved my lips to his neck. My mouth worked fiercely against that tender skin, pressing and biting, as though by leaving a mark I could somehow brand Seth as mine forever.

Breaking away at last, I raised myself up slightly on my knees and moved his hand between my legs. He stroked me without being told to, letting his fingers slide over my clitoris, building up the mounting, scorching sensation in my lower body. His fingers moved easily, aided by my own wetness. Greater and greater that swelling ecstasy grew until it was almost agony, but I stopped him before I peaked and could find release.

Frantically, I tore at his jeans and boxers, getting them off as fast as I could. I sighed shakily, looking at that long, perfect hardness as though it could keep me alive when nothing else could. I moved myself back down and ground myself against him, rubbing myself against that hardness, letting it finish the job his fingers had started. I came almost instantly, having been already on the edge, and before those spasms could even begin fading, I slid him inside of me, letting him fill me up entirely until it seemed there was nothing left of me in my own body, only him.

He was still letting me take charge here, but he wasn't unaffected. His breath came heavy and hard now, his own lips parting slightly with desire, eyes begging me to do more.

As for me . . . I was losing myself. I didn't care about anything else but him inside me, as close as I'd ever been able to get to Seth. It still seemed like something had to give, something had to stop us. But it didn't. I became more than a conqueror. I was a ravager, taking what I wanted with no thought of the consequences.

I rode on top of him, bringing myself down hard each time, willing him to pierce right through me. My hands held him down as I thrust, not that he was trying to get away. My breasts shook as our bodies moved together, the nipples still hard and sensitive. I heard the slap of skin on skin each time I moved down, forming a rhythm with our ragged breathing.

I was drowning in Seth, in his sweat and in his touch. I was liquid and golden, merged into him. My body ached, unable to get enough of him, and I moved harder still. I knew exactly which angle I needed to make myself come, and I didn't even try to hold back the waves and waves of pulsing bliss that racked my body. Small crackles of energy passed between us occasionally—not the usual absorption that occurred with a victim, but the inevitable sharing that happened between an incubus and succubus, two creatures whose bodies were made to collect the power of life.

I needed to consume Seth, take as much of him as I could. I had no other purpose. Time passed. My body took its pleasure greedily and often. I said his name over and over, sometimes whispering it, sometimes screaming it, until finally exhausted, I couldn't move anymore. I stopped, nearly collapsing against him.

Barely able to work my lungs anymore, I struggled to get the air I needed. He was still inside me, still ready, but I had nearly rubbed myself raw. My throat was dry and painful. Sweat formed a slick coating on me, and I hung over him panting and desperate, an animal who had just sated her hunger with no concern for who lay beneath.

He watched me intently, running a careful hand over my damp cheek. Then, at some unspoken signal between us, he flipped me over onto my back to at last finish himself off. Gripping my ankles and putting them over his shoulders, he knelt before me and pushed back inside. A soft whimper passed over my lips. I was jelly now, unable to do anything but lay there and let him have his way with me. My arms spread out carelessly over my head, fingers brushing the black headboard, and I closed my eyes, just letting myself feel Seth taking me now. I was weak and spent, but it still felt wonderful. I opened my eyes and watched him working hard against my body, at last able to give in to his own pleasure. He'd held back for so long for my benefit, waiting until I had satiated my lust. Now he was the greedy one, ravaging me in the way he wanted. At last, he climaxed with a small groan, closing his eyes briefly, holding himself against me as he came into me.

When he finished, he slumped forward and pulled out, lying beside me.

We stayed like that for several moments, and then he pulled me roughly to him so we spooned, the back of my body pressed against the front of him. Both of us still breathed in heavy, torn gasps as our hearts gradually slowed. I let my cheek rest against his arm. I still shook all over from sex with Seth, with the feel of Seth inside of me and the way he had broken my body with that devastating ecstasy.

Then, as one hand tightened on me and his other ran gently over my hair, I noticed something. He didn't smell right.

I don't mean to imply that he smelled bad. He didn't. He just didn't smell like Seth. The sweat wasn't the same. There was no fleeting smell of apple, leather, and musk, no unique Seth scent. He smelled like Bastien. He *was* Bastien, I reminded myself sternly, and with that, the illusion shattered, the spell broke. I wasn't with Seth, no matter how perfect the shape. I was with my friend the incubus.

"Change back," I whispered.

"What?"

"Change back to yourself."

He didn't ask why, and a moment later, I rested in Bastien's arms. It wasn't Seth, I realized with a dull and terrible emptiness, but it was the truth. We said no more after that, staying in bed together for the rest of the night. Sleep never came for me, however. I lay awake the whole time, staring off into the shadows.

Chapter 17

"Should I put up Lorelei Biljan's posters now? Or wait until after E. J. Putnam's gone?"

I looked up from the invoices on my desk. I'd just reread the same line of numbers about five times without comprehending any of it, and I was having only a little better luck parsing Tammi's question.

I rubbed my eyes. "Why . . . would we wait?"

She shrugged. "Dunno. Just seems kind of rude to be advertising one author during another one's signing."

My mind moved slowly, probably because only 5 percent of it was actually here at the bookstore. The rest of my brainpower attempted to muddle through the disaster that was my life.

"Um . . . no, it doesn't matter. Put them both up. They're only a week apart, and we want Biljan to get a fair shot at publicity too. Besides, I don't think authors really get worked up over competition like that. They're pretty low-key."

Tammi ran a hand through her short red hair. "I don't know. They're famous *and* artistic. Seems like that's a bad combination. Temperamental and stuff. Not all writers can be like Seth. In fact, I bet when he gets angry enough about something, he could really let someone have it."

"Anything else?" I asked, a sharp note of dismissal in my voice. "Otherwise, just put up all the posters, okay?"

She gave me a startled look and left the office. When the door closed, I put my head down on the desk and groaned. Tammi, in her blissful adolescent naiveté, had no idea how close to home she had hit. Like her, I too believed Seth could display a lot of anger if given enough cause.

Like, say, his girlfriend cheating on him.

True, Bastien had been right in saying Seth and I had loose definitions of "cheating," but even I knew what did and did not qualify. There was no gray area here. No mutability. I had fucked up hard-core.

I'd known it too, lying there in that unholy union with Bastien. After my sleepless night, I'd left him around dawn and took a cab back to Queen Anne, my body still aching. I hadn't wanted to talk to him. He'd slept so heavily, he hadn't heard me leave. No guilt weighed him down.

But me? My cup of guilt was runnething over. Not only that, I still had to make the next decision in this mess: to tell or not to tell? That was what had really bothered me all day at work. The past was over; I could only worry about it for so long. My attention now focused on how to proceed with the future.

Fortunately, Seth had worked from home today, which helped a little. He and I eventually had plans to meet up in the evening, but until that happened, I still had time to come up with something. Anything. Yet when I walked home at the end of my shift, I was no closer to an answer than I had been at the beginning of the day.

Miserable, I pulled up a chair at my kitchen table and sat down with pen and paper. Aubrey jumped up on the table's flat surface and lay down to watch me, half of her sprawling on the page. I slid her off and made the following list:

DON'T TELL SETH
Pros: status quo resumes, he won't be upset
Cons: my own gnawing guilt, totally blowing the honesty thing

I considered the list for a moment, surprised that neither the pro nor con side had more items. It was just that simple. Moving farther down the paper, I wrote up the reciprocal list.

TELL SETH

Pros: right thing to do
Cons: admitting I'm an idiot, painfully emotional blowout, inevitable breakup, a literal eternity of heart-wrenching sorrow and regret

I held the pen and looked back and forth between both lists.

"This isn't really clearing things up, Aubrey." In an effort to relieve my frustration, I hurled the pen somewhere into my living room. She watched it sail off with interest and then darted off to confirm the kill.

"What do you need to tell Seth?"

"Jesus!" I yelled, practically jumping ten feet in the air. Carter had appeared out of nowhere and now stood beside the table, looking casual and laconic. He wore a black T-shirt over a gray thermal shirt and the same jeans I swear he'd had on for the last couple decades. "Don't do that, okay? Knocking isn't a lost art."

"Sorry." He pulled a chair out and straddled it, so his long arms draped lazily over the back. Flipping his stringy blond hair out of the way, he gestured toward my list. "Didn't mean to interrupt."

"You're not," I muttered, crumpling up the paper. I tossed that into the living room too, so Aubrey could have more to hunt.

"Anything you want to talk about?" he offered.

I hesitated. Of all the people I knew, only Carter had been a steadfast believer in Seth and me having a serious relationship. He was the only one who hadn't treated it as a joke. In some ways, that might have made him a good confidante, yet it also disqualified him. I could not confess to the one person who had believed in me just how seriously I had messed things up in a weak moment.

"No," I said brusquely. "But I assume *you* have something to talk about."

He eyed me a moment, like he might push me on what I clearly held back, but then he let the matter go. "I have something for you."

He extended a balled fist. When he opened it, I found a small pouch lying on his palm. I picked it up and stroked the material. I had no idea what it was, but the cloth's smooth texture felt like a flower petal. I started to open it.

"Don't," he warned. His commanding tone instantly made me stop. "You'll break the spell."

"What spell?"

"The one that masks what's inside the pouch. And the one that masks your immortal signature."

I nodded with understanding. I might not know what to do with my own love life, but immortal conspiracies I could follow. "To hide me and this from Alec's supplier."

The angel nodded in return.

I held up the pouch and waggled it at him. "So do I get to know what's in there?"

"It's a . . ." He paused, not from a reluctance to tell me but to search for the right word. "It's a dart, I guess. Or maybe . . . like, an arrowhead. But that sounds weird. Nah, let's call it a dart. It's only about an inch long. A dart that looks like a small wooden arrowhead."

"Um. Okay. Got it. And what do I do with this darting arrowhead thing?"

"You pierce the other immortal's heart with it."

"Whoa. Like . . . staking a vampire?"

"Uh, not entirely. You'll sort of have to see when the time comes. The key is to move fast. As soon as you open the pouch, he'll know what you are and what's in there. You don't want to give him time to react because it won't be pretty if he does. Act fast, and don't second-guess yourself."

"How is a small piece of wood going to solve all our problems?"

"It's special wood," he replied with a grin.

"Oh, yeah, that explains everything."

"Are you close to meeting him?"

"Terribly close, actually. I probably could have met him yesterday if I'd wanted. Alec was very keen on introducing us."

Carter frowned, turning this over in his mind. "Hmm. Odd."

"Should I be worried?"

"No more worried than you already should be at the thought of attacking an immortal."

"But I'll be fine if I just act fast and don't overthink it, huh?"

"Right. I imagine that's pretty common for you anyway."

"Anything else I should know?"

"Well . . . let's see. Yeah. One thing. Don't actually do it until there's provocation."

"What?" I stared. "Being a bastard who pushes addictive substances that destroy mortals isn't provocation enough?"

"Oddly, no. You have to be threatened in some way."

Annoyed, I tossed the pouch onto the table. This was so typical of Carter and Jerome. A bizarrely complex scheme with ridiculous nuances and loopholes. "Threatened? How can he threaten me? He can't unless . . . wait, he's not an immortal who could kill me, is he?"

"No, of course not. But he could make things very . . . uncomfortable for you. Anyway, there's a lot of ways to threaten a person. If he hurts you . . . or you feel vulnerable . . . like he could abuse his power over you, then that'll work. He's a stronger immortal than you. Preying on you—especially when you belong to Jerome, so to speak—is a big no-no. You would be justified in protecting yourself. But, if you attack wantonly, you'll get in trouble from the powers that be for targeting other immortals. You'll also get us in trouble for arming you."

"This sounds kind of like entrapment."

"That's an ugly word. Let's just keep it in terms of self-defense."

"So, you think things are going to get rough enough that I'll actually need self-defense?"

He hesitated. "I don't know. I just don't know."

"Yeah, but then, if this guy's perfectly nice and just sells me a stash of ambrosia, I can't do anything? We've wasted the trip?"

"Like I said, I don't know. Really. But honestly . . . if they're making it this easy to find him, I have to think something weird is going on. Just be careful, okay?" His face was all seriousness now. "You're smart. You can pull this off."

"And I don't suppose, at any point in this, you're going to tell me who this guy actually is?"

"I believe ignorance is bliss."

I threw my hands up, not knowing what else to say. Carter traded a few more jokes with me and then rose to go. Hesitating, he gave me a curious look.

"You sure you don't want to talk? You've obviously got something bugging you."

"I do. But I've got to deal with it on my own."

"Fair enough. See ya." An eyeblink later, the angel disappeared.

Seth showed up about an hour later, a little blue paint smudged on his face. "Terry and Andrea are painting the kitchen now."

I smiled at him, swallowing all the churning emotions within me. "How can you get so messy when you don't even do the painting?"

I found a washcloth and dabbed at his face in a fruitless effort to clean him up. Standing so close, I suddenly had a flashback to last night. His hands stroking my breasts. Feeling him inside of me, filling me up. Our bodies moving together. His lips parting slightly when he came.

"It won't come off," I said abruptly, jerking away.

"Oh. Okay."

I stayed moody and silent for the rest of the night, stiff and distant at any sort of touching. Seth picked up on the vibe right away and let me have my space. We walked a few blocks down the street to a theater that only showed Oscar nominees and artsy, independent films. We saw one of the latter, and I have to admit, it did take my mind off my love life, if only for two hours.

Sitting at an Italian restaurant afterward, I let him draw me into a discussion of the film's merits. It amazed me that my mouth could keep up with the conversation while the rest of me was in an entirely different world.

Over and over, I replayed what had happened last night—and not just the sex part. I analyzed everything, the events that had led up to it. Why had I done it? What had made me give in? Had it really been an altruistic attempt to fix Seth and me by removing the temptation? Had it been an aching desire to take comfort in Bastien? Or, most likely, had it been something selfish on my part? A burning desire to touch what I wasn't supposed to have—not because it might help our relationship, but because I just wanted to do it. I had wanted that pleasure. I had craved his body and simply gave in to the hedonism I longed for. I was a creature of hell, after all. I had observed before that we weren't exactly known for our self-control.

Yet none of that changed the fact that it had happened. It had happened, and I had to do something about it. Or . . . did I?

Seth sat across from me, looking happy and content as we talked. Ignorance really is bliss sometimes. I thought back to the lists. If he never found out, the truth couldn't hurt him. We could go on as we had. The only problem would be that I knew the truth. I had to live with this betrayal, not only of our physical relationship but also of our attempts at honesty and openness. One more entry on the list of dark and nasty secrets I already kept.

"You with me, Thetis?" he asked suddenly.

"Huh?"

He gave me a small, sweet smile and moved his hand over to hold mine. I squeezed it back. "You look like you're miles away."

I gave him a half-smile in return. Apparently I wasn't as subtle as I thought. I looked at him, studying those beloved features, and shook my head. I couldn't do it. I couldn't tell him. Not yet.

"Just tired," I lied.

We shared a dish of gelato and then returned to my apartment. We had just set up the Scrabble board when I felt immortal signatures approaching.

I groaned, not wanting to deal with this. "Hail, hail, the gang's all here."

Seth looked puzzled until we heard the knock at the door. I opened it, letting in Hugh, Peter, Cody, and Bastien.

"You are alive," said Peter cheerfully, smothering me in a hug. "We tried calling you tonight."

"And I've been trying to get a hold of you all day," added Bastien pointedly.

I was perfectly aware that he had called me many times. I had purposely not answered my phone.

"Sorry," I said to all of them.

"Hey, Seth," said Cody, clapping the writer on the back. The vampire and the rest of the immortals spread themselves out around my living room like they lived there. I gave their giggling and careless behavior a withering glance.

"You guys been barhopping?"

"Yup," said Hugh with pride. "You—both of you—could have joined us."

"Fortunately, the night is still young," declared Bastien. He strolled around the living room, arching an appalled eyebrow at the Scrabble board. "When you didn't answer, we decided to come issue an invitation in person."

"We're going to go shoot pool," explained Cody happily. "Over at that place in Belltown. You guys should come along." He gave Seth a conspiratorial grin. "Georgina's a wicked pool player."

"Thetis is good at everything," Seth murmured automatically. I could tell by his body language he wasn't comfortable with a bunch of drunken immortals in the room. I also knew he didn't want to go out.

"Sorry, guys," I told them. "We've already been out. We're staying in."

This earned snide remarks and groans of disapproval.

"Oh come on," begged Hugh, trying to get Aubrey's attention with a cat toy on a string. She didn't fall for it and hissed at him instead. "We always get better service when you go with us."

"Besides," said Bastien nastily. "It doesn't look you're doing anything else exciting. You should be grateful we came along. We're giving you something. *Something you couldn't otherwise get.*"

I remained calm, but I think the others picked up on the sudden tension in the air. "Sorry," I repeated. "We're staying in. You guys can hang out for a little bit, but then I've got to kick you out. We're doing our own thing."

"I wasn't aware you guys *did* anything at all," muttered Bastien in a voice only I heard. Maybe the vampires too, with their superhuman hearing.

"You got anything to drink?" asked Peter, gently nudging me toward being a good hostess.

I was still locked in a battle of wills and eye contact with the incubus. "Yeah, I just bought a six-pack of Smirnoff Ice."

"Oh," said Cody. "Score."

He and Hugh raided my refrigerator, passing out bottles of prissy malted beverage to everyone except Seth and me. We abstained. Lounging around, conversation on silly topics

soon ensued, although Bastien, Seth, and I did not participate. Seth stayed quiet because he always stayed quiet in such
settings. Bastien and I stayed quiet because we were pissed
off at each other.

I excused myself for the restroom and found Bastien waiting outside the door for me when I finished.

"Alcohol runs right through you, huh?" I asked, pushing
past him.

He blocked my way, backing me up against the wall.

"What the hell's wrong with you?" he demanded in a low
voice.

"Nothing. Let me go."

"Bullshit. I left you like a hundred messages. You're avoiding me."

"So? It's my prerogative. Just like that song."

He snorted. "Let me guess. You're having some sort of
melodramatic moral crisis over what happened last night.
That's so typical of you lately."

"Don't talk to me about last night. You shouldn't have
done what you did."

"*I* shouldn't have? My God, Fleur, don't act like you're the
victim here. Nobody forced you. You more than consented.
In fact, I daresay you enjoyed it."

"It was a mistake."

"And so avoiding me is going to fix it? Don't delude yourself. It wasn't a mistake. It was good for you. I helped you. I
gave you something you would have never gotten otherwise.
You'll remember it for the rest of your life."

"Gee," I said, dripping sarcasm. "How kind of you. Because that's really all there was to it, wasn't there? You only
did it to help me. Nothing more. You certainly didn't do it
just because you could. Because I was 'beautiful and I was
wonderful and you wanted me.' "

"Listen to me—"

"No. You listen to me. If I want to avoid you, let me avoid
you. Don't show up at my house drunk and try to force your

way into a dialogue. It makes you more of an asshole than you'd be otherwise. I don't want to talk to you. Not anytime soon. Maybe not ever."

"Forever's a long time." He leaned closer, one hand on my arm. "Don't you think you're overreacting to one fuck? Besides, you can't cut me off. You've got to help me with Dana."

"No," I declared icily. "I do not. You're on your own with that. And if you get sent to Guam, then it's your own fucking fault. Maybe it'll give you some time to think about your relations with women outside of business."

"Damn it—"

"Georgina?"

We both turned and saw Seth standing in the hallway. Bastien and I were close—too close—but not romantically close. Anyone with half a brain could tell we were locked in a dispute. Our postures radiated it, as did our expressions. The grip Bastien held on my arm was not friendly.

"Are you okay?" Seth asked carefully. His words came out low and measured, but I saw something unfamiliar in his expression. Not anger, but something else kindling in his eyes. He had told me once he chose his battles carefully, and I wondered then what he would do if he thought the incubus was a real threat to me.

"We're fine," I said. I broke from Bastien's grasp, and he didn't fight it.

"Yes," he agreed with a cold smile. "We're fine."

He walked past me but stopped when he was even with Seth.

"You should be flattered," Bastien told him. "Most women invoke God during sex, but Fleur yells your name. One would have thought you were a deity, considering how many times she paid homage to you last night."

He continued on to the living room, and I didn't even stick around to see Seth's reaction. I stormed after Bastien.

"Get out," I told him. I looked over at the other immortals. "All of you, *get out now.*"

Peter, Cody, and Hugh stared at me in astonishment. I'd kicked them out a number of times, but none of them had ever heard me use this voice on them. Consequently, they heeded it. They scrambled out the door in under a minute, Bastien shooting me a dark glance as he left.

When they were gone, I took a deep breath and turned to Seth. Anger and despair boiled inside of me.

"Let me guess. You want to know what he meant."

His face was unreadable. "Honestly, I don't know." He suddenly sounded tired. "I don't know if I want to."

"Yeah, well, I'll tell you anyway."

The words tore at me while coming out, but I really didn't want to hold onto the secret anymore. Not only because Bastien had given it away but also because I knew I wasn't going to be able to stand having it fester inside of me. It hurt too much. Talking to the incubus had made me realize that.

So while I didn't mention the pictures, I told Seth everything else. Everything.

When I finished, he didn't say anything. He stared at some nonexistent spot in the air, face blank once more. After a couple of minutes of aching silence, he finally turned back to me.

"So. How was I?"

Chapter 18

"That's not funny," I said.

"Seems like a reasonable question."

I looked at him and then wrapped my arms around myself. "Is that all you're going to say?"

"I . . . I don't really know what else to say."

"This is the part where you yell at me."

His eyebrows rose. "Oh, I see. I didn't know this was already scripted out."

"That's not what . . . look. I slept with someone else. And not just slept. I didn't have to do it . . . not the way I have to with humans. You get that, right?"

"Yes," he said, still dead calm.

"And I wasn't drunk or anything. Tipsy maybe, but still in control of my senses."

"Yes."

"So aren't you mad?"

"Stunned is the dominant emotion at the moment. Finding out someone impersonated you is almost more troubling than the sex part."

"He didn't impersonate you, per se . . . I mean, I knew it was him."

"I know. But it's still weird."

When he fell silent again, I could only stare with incredulity. He caught my look and retuned it.

"What do you want?" This time he did sound annoyed, almost angry. "Do you want me to be mad? Will that like . . . punish you or something? Is that what you want?"

I said nothing and realized that was exactly what I wanted. I had read a book once where a guy accidentally killed a girl while driving drunk. His powerful family had managed to keep him out of jail, and he'd hated it. He'd wanted the cleansing catharsis of real punishment, of paying for his crimes. Right now, I needed the same thing.

"I deserve it," I told Seth.

His voice was cold. "Well, I'm not going to give it to you right now. You can't dictate what I feel. Sorry."

My mouth started to drop open, unsure what to do with this turn of events. The ringing of my cell phone interrupted my rumination. I glanced at my purse, then let the phone go to voice mail. A moment later, it rang again.

"You should answer it," Seth told me.

I didn't want to talk to anyone. I wanted to crawl into a hole. But I got the phone and read the display. No one I recognized. Sometimes that was Jerome. If I didn't answer, the demon was likely to teleport on over, and that was quite possibly the only thing that could make this scenario worse.

"I'm sorry," I said softly to Seth, just before I answered. I didn't know if I was apologizing for the interruption or what I'd done with Bastien. "Hello?"

"Hey, Georgina. This is Wyatt."

It took me a moment. From Doug's band. "Hey, how's it going?"

"Bad. I didn't know who else to call. I'm at the hospital with Doug."

My heart stopped. "Oh my God. What happened?"

"He, uh, took some pills."

"What kind of pills?"

"Not sure. But he took a whole bottle of them."

Wyatt's news spurred Seth and me to action. It was funny how tragedy could override anger. Whatever unresolved issues ensnared us, we put them on hold as I drove us downtown.

Wyatt had briefly told the rest of the story as I'd left my apartment at a run. Alec hadn't come through with his latest shipment. Doug had crashed again, plunging into that frightening darkness I'd observed before. Wyatt didn't entirely know what had triggered the overdose. He blamed everything from a suicidal urge to a desperate attempt at recapturing the high through other means. The emergency room had pumped his stomach, and the doctor said he was okay for now, but he hadn't yet regained consciousness. Wyatt had called me because Doug had no family here, and no one knew how to contact the ones who lived out of town.

Corey and Min were there when we arrived. They elaborated a bit more for us and said there was no change in Doug's condition. Seth stayed silent, but I could tell he was as concerned as I was.

I asked if I could see Doug, and a nurse told me I could. I entered the room alone and found him asleep, hooked up to tubes and a bleeping machine. I had watched medical technology change over the years, from leeches to defibrillators, but that didn't mean I felt comfortable with any of it. Machines that kept people alive rubbed me the wrong way. They weren't natural, even if they did good.

"Oh, Doug," I murmured, sitting at his bedside. His skin was pale, his hand cold and clammy. The bleeping machine registered a steady heartbeat, so that was something. None of the other readouts meant anything to me.

I watched him, feeling helpless. Mortals, I thought, were fragile things, and there was nothing I could do about that.

Many, many years ago, Bastien and I had worked at a dance hall in Paris. Dancers in those days were almost always prostitutes too, but I hadn't minded. The opportunity had provided me with both succubus energy and monetary income. Bastien had been a bouncer and ostensibly my lover.

This allowed him to sing my praises, bolstering my reputation and sending me a large clientele.

"There's a young man who shows up every night," the incubus told me one day. "He has 'virgin' stamped all over him, but he's rich too. I've talked to him a few times. He doesn't like the idea of paying for sex, but he's completely obsessed with you."

The news pleased me, and when Bastien pointed out the gentleman, I made a lot of eye contact with him throughout the performance. Sure enough, a manservant of his discretely solicited me on behalf of his employer afterward, and I hurried to prepare myself backstage.

"Josephine," called a voice beside me. I turned and saw another dancer, an especial friend of mine named Dominique.

"Hey," I told her, grinning. "I have a nice prospect I've got to get to." Her grim face made me pause. "What's wrong?"

Dominique was small and blond, with an almost waifish appearance that made her look like she wasn't getting enough to eat. That wasn't a surprise, however. None of us in that profession ever got enough to eat.

"Josephine . . ." she murmured, blue eyes wide. "I need your help. I think . . . I think I'm pregnant."

I stopped in my tracks. "Are you sure?"

"Pretty sure. I . . . I don't know what to do. I need this job. You know I do."

I nodded. From the wings, Jean—the man who took cuts from our liaisons—yelled at me to hurry up and meet my young man. I gave Dominique a quick hug.

"I have to go do this. I'll find you later, okay? We'll figure something out."

But I never really got a later. The young man, Etienne, proved to be adorable. He was much younger than my apparent age, and engaged to be married. He was torn on the issue of sex. Part of him felt he needed to be pure for his bride; the other part wanted to be experienced on his wedding night. That was the part that won out, the part that brought him to my bed and gave me the succubus bonus of both a moral corruption and an energy yield.

He resented me for both my lifestyle and my hold over him, but that didn't stop him from coming back every day for the next few weeks.

"I hate you for this," he told me one day after we'd been together. He lay back against the sheets, in a sweaty, post-coital repose. I stood near the bed, putting my clothes on while he watched. "Marry me."

I laughed out loud, tossing my hair—then honey blond and curly—over one shoulder.

He flushed angrily. He had dark eyes and hair and a perennially brooding look. "Is that funny?"

"Only because you hate me in one breath and love me in the other." I smiled as I laced up my undergarments. "I suppose there are a lot of marriages like that."

"Not everything's a joke," he said.

"Maybe not," I agreed. "But this comes pretty close."

"Are you turning me down?"

I pulled my dress over my head. "Of course I am. You have no idea what you're asking. It's ridiculous."

"You treat me like I'm a child sometimes," he declared, sitting up straighter. "You're not that much older than me. You have no right to act so wise . . . especially since you're a . . ."

I grinned at him. "A whore?" He had the grace to look embarrassed. "And that, sweeting, is the problem. Never mind your family's scandalized reaction. Even if we managed to pull it off, you'd never get over that. You'd spend the rest of our marriage—which would probably be short-lived—obsessing about all the men I'd been with. Wondering if one of them had been better. Wondering if I'd done something with them that you thought was new and novel with you."

Angry, he stood up and pulled on his pants. "I would have thought you'd be grateful."

"Flattered," I said coldly, "but nothing more."

That wasn't entirely true. The truth was, despite his youthful certainty and mood swings, I liked Etienne. A lot. Something about him appealed to me. Maybe it was because all that emotionality and pride came from an artistic nature. He painted as a hobby. There it was again, my unfortunate obsession with creative men. Luckily, at that time in my life, I had enough sense to avoid deep entanglements with humans.

"I wish you could choose who you love," he said bitterly. "Because I wouldn't choose you, you know. But, here we are. I can't stop thinking about you. I feel like there's some pull to you I can't fight."

"I'm sorry," I said gently, surprised at the small ache in my heart. "Wait until you're married. Your wife will make you forget all about me."

"No. She doesn't even compare."

"Plain?" Egotistical of me, perhaps, but I heard it a lot.

"Boring," he replied.

Then I'd heard a scream, a bloodcurdling, horror-filled scream. I forgot all about Etienne and tore out of the small, dank room. Down the hall I ran until I found a congregation of people and the source of distress.

It was Dominique. She sprawled over a narrow pallet, lying in blood. "My God," I gasped, kneeling beside her. "What happened?"

But I already knew. I didn't need the forthcoming explanation from the other dancers. I had neglected her pleas for help a couple weeks ago, caught up in my own whirlwind romance. So she had sought her own solution, as so many lower-class women often did. Unfortunately, there were no machines or sanitizing in those days. An abortion was a dangerous, often deadly, business.

"Oh God," I said again. I had never lost the need to appeal to my creator, despite my theoretical renouncement.

I clutched her hand, not knowing what to do. A half-dressed Etienne appeared in the crowd. I looked up at him desperately.

"You have to go get a doctor. Please."

Whatever injured pride he harbored over my rejection, he couldn't refuse me in that moment. I saw him make motions to leave, but Bastien grabbed his arm. "No, it doesn't matter." To me he said: "She's gone, Fleur."

I looked at Dominique's young face. Her skin was pale, eyes blank and glazed over as they stared at nothing. I knew I should close them, but suddenly I didn't want to touch her. I dropped her hand, slowly backing up, staring in horror.

It was by no means the first time I'd seen a dead body, but something struck me about it then I'd never really considered with such shocking clarity. One moment she was here, the next she wasn't. Oh, the difference one heartbeat could make.

The stink of mortality hung in the air, painting the awful truth about humans. How short their lives were. And fragile. They were like paper dolls among us, turning to ash in the blink of an eye. How many had I seen come and go in over a millennium? How many had I seen pass from infancy to a gray-haired death? The stink of mortality. It threatened to overwhelm the room. How could no one else sense it? I hated it . . . and I feared it. Feeling suffocated, I backed up further.

Both Bastien and Etienne reached for me in some fumbling attempt at comfort, but I wanted none of it. Dominique, barely out of childhood, had just bled her life away in front of me. What fragile things humans were. I had to get out of there before I became sick. I turned from those who would console me and ran away.

"What fragile things humans are," I murmured to Doug.

The feeling that welled up within me now as I sat beside him was not sorrow or despair. It was anger. White-hot anger. Humans were fragile, but some of them were still in my care. And whether that was foolish or not on my part, I could not shirk my duty. Doug was one of my humans. And someone had nearly cut his time short.

I stood up, gave his hand a last squeeze, and strode out of the room. From the shocked glances Corey, Min, and Wyatt gave me, I must have looked terrifying. I hit the pause button on my righteous fury when I noticed something. "Where's Seth?"

"He said he had to go," said Corey. "He left you this."

He handed me a scrap of paper with Seth's scrawled writing.

Thetis, I'll talk to you later.

I stared at it, suddenly feeling nothing. I went numb. My mind would not allow me to focus on Seth just then. I crumpled the paper up, said good-bye to the band, and left the hospital. When I reached the lobby, I took out my cell phone and dialed.

"Alec? This is Georgina."

"Hey, Georgina!" I heard the anxious note in his voice. Almost desperate.

"You were right," I began, hoping I sounded anxious too. "You were right. I need more. Now. Tonight. Can you do it?"

"Yes," he said. There was palpable relief in his voice. "Absolutely I can do it."

We set up a meeting spot immediately. It couldn't be too soon for me. I'd been on an emotional roller coaster in the last twenty-four hours, and I was about to take it out on Alec. I couldn't wait. The fact that he seemed so eager for it was icing on the cake.

"Oh, hey, Georgina?" he asked, just before we disconnected.

"Yeah?"

His voice sounded strange; I couldn't decipher the emotion. "You have no idea how glad I am you called."

Chapter 19

The dealer's house sat away from the road, just like all sinister houses should, I suppose. My biased perceptions aside, there was actually little else about the house that was all that creepy. It was big and expensive-looking, spreading out lazily on beautifully manicured lawns, visible to me even at night. In a region where yards were at a premium, that much land signified a great deal of money. Unlike Bastien's place, this house had no similarly well-to-do neighbors. This house was in a class of its own; it could not be part of a mere suburban neighborhood.

"Where are we?" I asked, because it seemed like the kind of naïve, starry-eyed question I should be asking. Alec had met me downtown and then driven me out to this place in his own car. We were about twenty minutes outside the city.

"This is where the guy lives," he told me happily. His mood improved as we got closer to the house. "He'll hook you up."

The car followed the long, sinuous driveway and came to a stop by the garage. In an oddly chivalrous way, he opened the car door for me and gestured that I follow him inside. Glancing back at his beat-up Ford Topaz, I couldn't help thinking that being an immortal drug lord's lackey should pay better.

Alec led us through a side door in the house, and even I was taken aback at what I found inside. The first word that came to mind was *lush*. And not the drunk kind either. I meant in the opulent sense, the kind of lush you sink your teeth into. The walls, floor, and ceilings consisted of gleaming dark hardwood, almost like we were inside a lodge—say, a lodge that cost seven figures. Beams of that beautiful wood crisscrossed the open, cathedral ceiling. Jewel-toned oil paintings in gilt frames hung on the walls, and I had enough of a sense for the value of art to recognize they had not come from Bed Bath & Beyond.

We crossed out of the foyer and found more of the same in a large living room. Its focal point was an enormous fireplace whose brick façade stretched to the ceiling. A multicolored stained-glass landscape hung above the fireplace's opening, and flames from the roaring fire—along with several strategically placed candles—cast the only light in the room. Nothing electrical.

In that dim, flickering lighting, I sensed the man before I saw him. The same unfamiliar immortal signature from the concert carried to me, coupled with something else. This close to him, I noticed how much he felt like the crystals. Or rather, how much the crystals felt like him, as if they were pale, fractured versions of the masterpiece. The whole vibe from him felt weird but not quite as discordant as the crystals themselves had.

"Alec," said a creamy voice, "who is your lovely friend?"

The man unfolded from the couch, standing in one fluid motion. I now saw the same features as before: flawless tanned skin, long black hair, high cheekbones. He also wore the same hot Victorian couture, complete with another of those gorgeous silk shirts that billowed around his arms and showed smooth skin through the V-neck.

"This is Georgina," said Alec, voice quaking with nervousness and excitement. "Just like I said."

The man glided to us and took my hand in both of his. "Georgina. A beautiful name for a beautiful woman." He drew my hand to his lips—which were full and pink—and kissed my skin. He held my hand a moment, letting his dark eyes bore into mine, and then he slowly straightened up and released me. "My name is Sol."

I turned off all my impulses to make snappy jokes and/or maul this guy, instead opting for stunned innocence mingled with a little fear. "H-hello." I swallowed nervously and looked down at my feet.

"You've done well," Sol told Alec. "Very well."

I didn't have to see Alec to tell he was practically melting with relief. "So . . . does that mean . . . I can, you know . . . ?"

"Yes, yes." Unless I was mistaken, a slight note of irritation underscored that pleasant voice. "Afterward. Go upstairs now. I'll summon you when I'm ready."

Alec started to leave, and I grabbed his sleeve, still playing frightened maiden. "Wait—where are you going?"

He smiled at me. "I'll be right back. It's okay. You wanted more, right? Sol's going to get it for you."

I must have truly looked terrified because he squeezed my arm reassuringly. "It's okay. Really."

I bit my lip and gave him a hesitant nod. His eyes held mine for a moment, and something very like regret flickered across them. Then he left.

"Come sit with me," intoned Sol, taking my hand again.

He led me to a sumptuous couch by the fire. Warmth from that orange glow spilled over me, and the flames were reflected in his dark eyes. I sat down gingerly, scooting back because the cushions were so big. We sat there quietly.

He smiled expectantly, and I gave him a faltering smile back. "Alec said you could give me more . . . you know . . . of that stuff."

"You enjoyed it then?"

"Yes. Oh yes. It made me feel . . ."

"Immortal?"

"Y-yes, that's it. Please. I need more. I can pay you . . . whatever you want."

He waved a hand carelessly. "We'll discuss such mundane

matters later. For now, let's see if we can't satiate your hunger." He leaned over to a small table and lifted up two goblets. Goblets. How quaint. "This should tide you over until we can arrange a larger batch."

I took the cup from him. It felt heavy, like gold. Nothing but the best if you were going to drink the food of the gods, I thought. They held a dark red liquid. If the crystals felt like a weak approximation of Sol, the aura radiating off of this cup felt like mega-Sol. It was intense and strong, making the vibe from the crystals seem like a total nonevent. Maybe that was what happened when ambrosia liquefied.

I realized then he'd been waiting for me while I pondered. "Drink up."

I hesitated, not having to feign apprehension this time. Drink up? What should I do? If I didn't drink, my cover might be blown, and I still hadn't had "provocation" to smite this bastard or whatever one did to someone with a dart-arrowhead-thing. Carter and Jerome had said ambrosia wouldn't hurt an immortal; they'd even said an immortal could resist its nasty effects to a certain extent, much longer than humans. That didn't necessarily make me feel better, though. I preferred to be in my normal range of skills to deal with this, but it looked like I didn't have that luxury. I couldn't delay any longer.

Smiling shyly, I brought the cup to my lips and drank. He did the same. Who could tell? Maybe personality amplification would help me out here. Maybe I had a secret Amazonian alter ego lurking within me who was dying to jump out via the ambrosia and bludgeon this guy with a goblet.

Once Sol started drinking, he didn't stop. He tipped the cup back until he'd consumed it all. I followed suit. The stuff really didn't taste so bad. In fact, it tasted sweet, almost sickeningly so. Weirdest of all was its consistency. Thick. Almost viscous.

"There," he said, taking my empty cup. "You'll feel better soon, and then we can talk reasonably." He shifted into a more comfortable position, long legs stretched out and re-laxed. He had a slim build and delicate features. His narrow fingers wound one of his black curls around it. "Tell me about yourself, Georgina. What do you do?"

"I, uh, work in a bookstore."

"Ah, you're a reader then."

"I try to be."

He inclined his head toward a wall covered in books. "I'm a reader myself. There's no greater pursuit than improving one's mind."

He started talking to me about some of his favorite books, and I smiled and commented as appropriate. As we talked, I began to feel . . . well, for lack of a more descriptive term, good. Really good. Almost like I was buzzed from an excellent liqueur. My limbs tingled a little, and a warm sense of euphoria burned through me. I heard myself laughing at one of his jokes. I almost sounded genuine.

"You're very beautiful," he suddenly said, and I wondered when he'd moved so close to me. I had to blink to stay focused. The room spun slightly, and my hands and feet kept delaying in obeying my orders. Sol reached out and touched my cheek, trailing those graceful fingers down my neck. "Your beauty is a gift."

I tried to move, mainly to see if I could actually manage it, not to avoid his touch. Honestly, his touch was pleasant—extremely pleasant. It made my pulse pick up a little. I could, I soon discovered, still move. I was just a little sluggish.

"Shhh," he crooned, placing a restraining hand on my wrist. "Don't be afraid. Everything will be all right."

"W-what are you doing?"

He had an arm around my waist now and was moving his mouth toward the spot where my neck met my shoulder. His lips, when they touched flesh, were warm and full of promise. I trembled a little under that kiss and tried to figure out what was going on here.

The short answer, obviously, was that something had gone

wrong. I felt dizzy and disoriented enough to be at a frat party over at U.W. On top of that, this immortal—this strange immortal I barely knew—suddenly seemed more alluring than I'd imagined possible. Hadn't I come here to kick his ass? Why was I making out with him? Was this what ambrosia did to me? Were these my core traits—the power to get buzzed and take pleasure in sex? To become even easier than I already was?

His hands moved down and unbuttoned my shirt so they could slide down and cup my breasts, which were just barely covered by the black mesh bra I'd bought with Dana. He kissed me directly now, his mouth pressing against mine. As his tongue delicately slipped between my lips, I tasted a sweetness akin to the ambrosia.

Bottom line: it needs to be self-defense.

So Carter had said, but suddenly I didn't really need much defending—unless it was from myself. My own hands were moving without my conscious knowledge to unfasten his pants, and our bodies were becoming entwined together on the soft cushions.

Self-defense. Self-defense. Why self-defense? What was I forgetting here?

Ah, of course. The dart.

I pushed through the red haze muddling my senses, forcing clarity. The dart. The dart would stop Sol somehow, stop him from continuing to spread the poison of ambrosia. It would stop him from hurting people . . . like Doug.

I battled through my disorientation and pulled my mouth away from Sol's, attempting to squirm the rest of the way out of his grasp. I won a little room but not much. He was still close.

"No . . ." I gasped out. "Don't do this. Stop."

Sol, regarding me with surprised amusement, shushed me. "You don't know what you're saying."

"I do. Stop."

I wriggled one arm free, one arm that then snaked to the

pocket containing Carter's pouch. I needed the other arm free too, but Sol was holding it. Looking down, I suddenly saw that his wrist was bleeding. How had that happened? I hadn't caused it.

"Georgina, you are about to be honored above all mortal women. Lay back. Stop struggling. No harm will come to you. You will enjoy this night, I promise."

He moved his mouth back to mine, and again that blazing euphoria swelled within me. A traitorous moan of pleasure caught in my throat. Taking this as submission, Sol's grip on my restrained arm lessened, and I shifted it away just enough that both of my hands now touched the pouch. Yet, it was a hard battle. My motor control still wasn't all it should be. Kissing him, in that moment, seemed much more important than some silly pouch. My mind didn't want to focus on any-thing else.

But I forced it to. Through sheer strength of will, I pushed the physical pleasure out of my head and instead replayed every consequence of the ambrosia I'd seen: Casey's devasta-tion, Doug's wild swings from darkly frenetic exuberance to even darker depression, and finally his limp body in the hos-pital.

Mortals are fragile things.

Very fragile. And Sol played with them as if they were nothing. The smoldering coal of my anger began to burn again.

He's a stronger immortal than you. Preying on you—espe-cially when you belong to Jerome, so to speak—is a big no-no. You would be justified in protecting yourself.

Again, I pulled my mouth away. "Stop," I said again more firmly. "I want you to stop. Stop doing this."

"I'm not going to stop," Sol snapped. Anger marred his honeyed tone. His breath was heavy, and his chest heaved with exertion. He—or I—had removed his shirt, and I had a perfect view of that unprotected skin. "I'm not going to stop, and believe me, once I start, you won't want me to stop either."

My fingers moved to open the pouch; the other hand slowly readied itself to reach inside. The ambrosia in my system dulled my reflexes, but I kept battling through it and sized up where in his chest his heart would be.

"I've asked you three times to stop. Once should have been enough. No means no."

"No means nothing from someone like you." He laughed a little, still not taking me seriously. "What's wrong with you? I thought you wanted to be immortal."

My hand was inside the pouch, pulling the dart out. Sol and I both felt its power at the same time, just as he realized what I was. His eyes widened, but I didn't give him time to react. I didn't think or falter. Just as Carter had ordered, I simply took action—well, with a cheesy punch line, of course.

"Been there, done that," I said, slamming the dart into his heart. For half a beat, Sol froze, unable to believe this was happening.

And that's when things got messy.

Chapter 20

Striking Sol with that tiny piece of wood was like dropping a nuclear warhead into the room. The blast threw me off the couch, and I hit the floor with a jarring, painful thud. Small objects flew into the walls. Art tumbled to the ground. The windows in the room blew out in a sparkling shower of shards. And it was raining inside. Blood and glitter fell down around me in red, gleaming streaks.

Mine wasn't the only true nature to be revealed. In the instant before Sol had exploded, I had felt him. *Really* felt him. Yes, he was part of a different system than mine, but he was no minor immortal player looking to stir up a little trouble. He was a god. A bona fide, honest to goodness god. Now, I should point out that gods come and go in the world based on belief. Godly power is directly proportional to the faith of their believers. So, those whose names no one remembers often walk around literally as bums, no different from humans save for their immortality. Sol, however, had had a fair amount of power. Not like Krishna power or God with a capital G power, but a lot. Certainly more than me.

Holy shit. I had just destroyed a god.

I straightened up from my fetal curl and looked around. Everything was still except for a light wind blowing in though the now-open windows. My skin and clothing were spattered with sticky scarlet blood, like I'd been at the wrong

end of a paintbrush at the Mortensens'. My heart rate refused to slow.

A moment later, I heard the pounding of footsteps on the
stairs. Alec burst into the room, drawn by the noise and the
shaking. He looked around, his lower jaw practically dropping to the floor as he came to a screeching stop.

My intoxication had not passed with Sol's destruction.
That fucking ambrosia was still in my system, and it was actually getting worse. Still, my anger at Alec was such that I
again overcame my befuddled senses and reflexes, and with a
speed that came as a surprise even to me, I sprang at him and
knocked him to the ground. A moment's shape-shifting, and
my short and slim frame suddenly held considerably more
muscle and strength than its appearance suggested. I straddled Alec with my legs and arms, and panic blazed on his
face when he realized he couldn't budge an inch from my
grip. I hit him hard across the face. My coordination might
have been off, but it didn't take much to apply brute force.

"Who the hell was he? Sol?"

"I don't know!"

I hit him again.

"Honest, I don't. I don't know," blathered Alec. "He was
just this guy . . . he found me and made me a deal."

"What was the deal? Why'd you bring me to him?"

He swallowed, blinking back tears. "Sex. He wanted sex.
Lots of lovers all the time. Didn't matter if they were guys or
girls, just as long as they were good-looking. I wasn't supposed to touch them. I just hooked them up with the potion
until they wanted to meet Sol. Then he, you know . . ."

"Fucked them and dumped them," I finished angrily. I
thought about Casey and the Abercrombie model guy in the
coffee shop. I recalled Alec's desire to get me on the ambrosia
but his reluctance to touch me, no matter how much he
wanted to. I was meant for Sol. "So that wasn't ambros—er,
potion in my cup tonight. That really was some date-rape
drug."

"I don't know," Alec whimpered. "Come on, let me go."

I tightened my grip and shook him. It took a moment since my fingers had a little trouble keeping hold. I had to work to maintain the fierceness of my face and voice. "What'd he give you? Did he pay you or something?"

"No. He just . . . he just gave me more of the potion. All I wanted, so long as I kept the people coming."

"And you gave it to the band," I realized.

"Yeah. It was the only way . . . the only way we could get big. It's all I've ever wanted. To land a record deal and get famous. This was the only way."

"No," I said. "It was just the fastest way."

"Look, what'd you do to Sol? What are you going to do to me?"

"What am I going to do?" I yelled, my anger rising through the drug. I shook him, knocking his head against the floor. "I should kill you too! Do you know what you've done to all these people? To the band? Doug's in the hospital right now because of you."

His eyes went wide. "I didn't know that. Honest. I didn't want to hurt him . . . I-I just couldn't get the stuff on time. Not until I delivered you."

He spoke of me and the other victims like we were commodities. I wanted to pick him up and throw him out the window. I could do it too. Humans were indeed fragile things, and while my succubus shape-shifting didn't have the power to maintain this uber-strong shape all night, I could hold it long enough to do some major damage.

Despite my normal abhorrence of violence, I have to admit that throwing people around a room is actually more satisfying than you'd think. After Dominique had died, I tracked down the corrupt doctor who had botched her abortion. I had changed from Josephine and wore the shape of an apish, seven-foot-tall man with bulging muscles. Storming into the doctor's small, sinister office, I didn't waste any time. I grabbed him as if he weighed nothing and tossed him against the wall, knocking down shelves of curiosities and so-called medical implements. It felt fantastic.

Striding over, I picked him up by the front of his shirt and punched him hard in the side of the head, ten times harder than I'd hit Alec. The doctor staggered and fell but still had enough life to scramble backwards, crab-style, in an effort to get away.

"Who are you?" he cried.

"You killed a girl tonight," I told him, moving menacingly. "A blond dancer."

His eyes bulged. "It happens. I told her. She knew the risks."

I knelt down so that we were at eye level. "You cut her open and took her money. You didn't care what happened to her."

"Look, if you want the money back—"

"I want *her* back. Can you do that?"

He only stared, shaking with fear. I stared back at him, shaking with my own power. I had the ability to kill him. To throw him again or snap his neck or choke the breath from him. It was terrible and wrong, but seized by my own rage, I couldn't control myself. Honestly, it's fortunate in the long run that most incubi and succubi have mild personalities more bent on pleasure than on pain. With the ability to take on any shape, we can be pretty deadly to mortals if we're pissed off enough. They can't really stand against us. This doctor sure as hell couldn't.

But another immortal could.

"Josephine," murmured Bastien's voice behind me. Then: "Fleur."

When I still didn't respond or loosen my grip, Bastien said, "Letha."

My birth name penetrated the bloodlust pulsing through me.

"Let him go. He isn't worth your time."

"And Dominique isn't worth avenging?" I demanded, my eyes never leaving the wretched human before me.

"Dominique is dead. Her soul is in the next world. Killing this man won't change that."

"It'll make me feel better."

"Maybe," conceded Bastien. "But it isn't your place to mete out punishment to mortals. That's reserved for higher powers."

"I am a higher power."

The incubus rested a gentle hand on my shoulder. I flinched. "We play a different role. We don't kill mortals."

"You and I have both killed before, Bas."

"In defense. Protecting a village from raiders isn't the same as cold-blooded murder. You may be damned, but you aren't this far gone."

I released my hold on the doctor and leaned back on my knees. He stayed frozen. "I loved Dominique," I whispered.

"I know. That's the problem with mortals. They're easy to love and quick to perish. Better for all of us to keep our distance."

I didn't touch the doctor, but I didn't move either. Bastien gave me a gentle tug, still quietly reasonable.

"Come on, let's go. Leave him. You don't have the right to end his life."

I let Bastien lead me out. Once in the dark alley flanking the doctor's office, I shape-shifted back to my more natural-feeling Josephine form.

"I want to leave Paris," I told him bleakly. "I want to go somewhere where there is no death."

He put an arm around me, and I leaned into his soothing presence. "No such place exists, Fleur."

In Sol's house, I still bore down on Alec, again empowered with the ability to crush his life if I chose. But Bastien's words echoed within me, and I realized with an ache how much I regretted my current hostility with the incubus. Regardless, he was still correct after all these years. Revenge killings were not my right. It was unfair for an immortal to take advantage of a much weaker mortal. I would be no better than Sol. And looking at Alec underneath me, I realized just how terribly young he was. Not much older than Dominique.

And anyway, my strength and coherence were failing by the second. I leaned in menacingly to Alec.

"G-get out," I mumbled through numbed lips. "I want you to get out. Out of Seattle. Don't ever contact Doug or anyone else from the band again. If I find out you're still in the city tomorrow night . . ." I struggled for an appropriate threat. My mental processes were grinding to a halt. "You, um, won't like it. Do you understand?"

My bluff worked; he was clearly terrified. I climbed off him and sat crouched because I couldn't stand. He scrambled up, gave me a last terrified look, and tore out of the room.

As soon as the door closed, I passed out.

Chapter 21

I woke up the next morning with the worst hangover of my life, and that's saying something.

It was actually the cold air that woke me, blowing in through the shattered windows and whipping the curtains around. Seattle had mild winters, but it was still November. I shape-shifted on a heavy sweater and then noticed that Sol's blood had not disappeared from my skin during last night's transformation, the blood had dried to fine, glittering red crystals on me and everything else. I picked up his discarded silk shirt and discovered it did a pretty good job at wiping them off.

The previous night was a blur, and I had trouble remembering the fine details. I supposed I could blame whatever mystery liquid I'd drank for that. Looking around at the wreckage brought a lot of the events back to me, and the rest I pieced together. Not wanting to linger in this place, I found my cell phone and called for a cab.

As I rode back into Seattle, I decided I wanted nothing more than to go home and sleep some more. My shift didn't start until later; Doug was opening. Wait. No, he wasn't. Doug was in a hospital bed. Sighing, I directed the driver to take me to the bookstore.

Three voice-mail messages waited for me when I arrived in the office. One was from the author we had doing a signing that night, E. J. Putnam. All was in order with his flight; he expected to be here as scheduled. The second message was Beth calling in sick. Jesus. Couldn't anyone stay healthy anymore? That put us down two people now. Warren wrapped up the messages, saying he'd be back from Florida later today and would stop in tonight. I decided to be mad at him out of sheer principle. I'd spent the last week dealing with chaos; he'd been golfing in eighty degree weather.

I got the store running and then staked out a register. Short-staffing will keep a person busy, at least. It gave me little time to reflect on last night's events. Or Doug. Or the fact that Seth hadn't come in today. Or my fight with Bastien.

"Are you Georgina?"

I looked up into the face of a pretty Japanese-American woman. Her face and build just barely crossed over into plumpness, and she wore her black hair in a high ponytail. Something about her smile seemed familiar.

"I'm Maddie Sato," she explained, extending a hand. "Doug's sister."

I shook her hand, astonished. "I didn't know Doug had a sister."

Her smile quirked a little. "Lots of them, actually. We're kind of spread out around the country. We all sort of do our own thing."

"So you came to . . . see Doug?" I hesitated to bring up such a delicate subject, but why else would she be here?

She nodded. "I've been with him this morning. He's doing great and said to tell you hello."

That was the best news I could have received. "He woke up."

"Yes. He's grumpy and punchy but otherwise fine. He said he has some CDs in your office he wants. He asked if I could pick them up."

"Sure, I'll show you," I said, leading her toward the back. Wow. Doug's sister. "How'd you find out about Doug?"

"Seth Mortensen called me."

I stumbled and nearly walked into a display of gardening books. "How do you know Seth?"

"I write for *Womanspeak* magazine. Seth had some questions about a feminist organization that he needed answered for his book, and Doug gave him my e-mail address about a month ago. So, we've been in touch a couple times. When Doug . . . got sick, Seth tracked down my number in Salem and called last night."

Part of me felt a little jealous that Seth had an e-mail correspondence with her that I hadn't known about, but I immediately quashed such feelings. What he'd done had been terribly considerate. And typical of him. Quietly efficient and kind. I led Maddie into the office and found the CDs in a drawer.

"Did you drive up last night or this morning?"

She shook her head. "Actually Seth picked me up."

"I . . . what? In Salem? That's, like, four hours away."

"I know. It was really nice. I don't have a car, so he drove right down after he called, got me in the middle of the night, and then brought me to Doug."

My God. Seth had made an eight-hour round-trip last night. No wonder he wasn't here; he'd gone home to crash. That also meant he hadn't necessarily taken off from the hospital to get away from me. He'd done it to help Doug. A pleasant flutter spread through me at this, half of it relief, half of it a response to still more evidence of Seth's continuing decency and consideration of others.

Maddie left me her cell phone number and promised to send my good wishes to Doug. As she was leaving my office, Janice entered it.

"Hey Georgina, Lorelei Biljan's here."

"Oh, okay. Wait." I did a double take. "You mean E. J. Putnam."

"No. It's definitely Lorelei. E. J.'s a guy."

"I know that," I said. "But her signing's a week from

today. Putnam's is today. I had a message about it and everything."

"I don't know. I just know she's here."

A horrible sinking feeling built up in me. I followed Janice out and shook hands with a small, solidly built middle-aged woman. I'd seen Lorelei Biljan's pictures in her books. Everything was the same from her brown pixie haircut to her characteristic black clothing.

"I'm going to see some sights today but wanted to check in first," she told me.

"Oh. Okay. Great." I smiled thinly, willing myself to keep breathing.

We chatted a little bit more, and as soon as she was gone, I tore back to Paige's office and ransacked her desk. Sure enough, her schedules showed both authors coming in today. On the master staff calendar, however, she'd put them on separate days. Our own in-store posters also had them on separate days, but checking newspaper ads, I saw them again scheduled for the same day. Our website declared both appeared today, which meant we'd have fans of both here tonight.

Good grief. This was like some bad, clichéd sitcom. We had two dates for the dance.

I sat at Paige's desk and rubbed my temples. How had this happened? How had perfect, efficient Paige messed up? I quickly answered my own questions: because she had other things on her mind. She had an increasingly complicated pregnancy on her hands, one that had kept her out for almost three weeks now. A distraction like that would let anyone make mistakes. Unfortunately, I had to deal with them.

Andy stuck his head inside. "Oh, hey, there you are. Bruce said to ask you if any of us can help in the café. They're short. And Seth just called the store's main line. Said to tell you he can't do the thing tomorrow."

"Seth called?" I asked stupidly. So he wasn't asleep. And

the "thing" tomorrow had been a date to see a local Celtic band play at a pub. But he was cancelling. The noble reasons I had attributed to him for keeping away from me suddenly seemed less altruistic. "Okay. Thanks."

I stared into space. My world was falling apart around me. I wasn't speaking to the two men I cared about the most. I was in charge of a bookstore that didn't have enough people to run it. Two authors were coming tonight, each expecting to have center stage to promote their books. We didn't have room for that. And to top it all off, I felt like shit. The residual effects of that drug had left me with a wicked headache, and I hadn't gotten nearly enough sleep. Killing a god will really wear you out.

I had too much to do and not enough energy or willpower to do it. Let alone the means. I needed a miracle. Divine intervention. And as feasible as that might seem in my line of work, it probably wasn't going to happen. Unless . . .

Divine intervention?

I found my purse and pulled out one of the packets of ambrosia. Those weird crystals pulsed out at me as I stared at them. What would happen? Nocturnal Admission had risen to stardom in a short time on these. Could I survive one hellish day at work? Would these give me the stamina and know-how to get through it? Or would I just turn into a slobbering sex kitten? I no longer believed Sol had given these to me last night. That had indeed been a date-rape drug. But these . . . these might be able to offer me some sort of inspiration to get out of this mess.

Of course, there was the whole dangerous addiction and withdrawal problem. But this was my first time. Even mortals had to go through a couple doses before things got nasty, and Carter had said it would take even longer for me to hit the downside. I was probably safe, so long as I didn't get too into whatever it was I was about to become.

Maybe it was the fatigue, but I didn't hesitate further.

Don't overthink it, just act. I ordered a white-chocolate mocha from the café and dumped the crystals in once I was back in my office. "Bottoms up," I muttered, just before knocking it all back.

When I'd finished, I rested my head on the desk and waited for something to happen. Anything. Mostly I still felt sleepy. I yawned. When did this stuff kick in? How would I know? And good grief, what would I do if this turned into a disaster too? What if it made my day worse? I mean, not that it could get worse. I had two authors booked for tonight. The jealousy Tammi had once joked about could very well occur. Two was a bad number. Two led to rivalry. Add more, and it becomes a friendly group matter, not a one-on-one competition for space and spotlight. I'd been to big events where lots of authors spoke and read. Sometimes they sat on a panel and answered questions together about writing, inspiration, and publishing. Getting those perspectives was neat. It was a cool opportunity for fans of all the writers, and then later, said fans could have books signed by multiple authors. Those events were big deals. They took a lot of planning and a lot of advertising, not to mention a lot of staff.

I sat up a couple minutes later, realizing I'd long since jolted to alertness. I didn't have time to note when that had happened or what it meant. I had too many things to do. My mind raced. In a flash, I was out on the main floor, hunting down Andy. I handed him a staff roster.

"I need you to call every person who's not working today—except for the sick ones. See if they'll come in. Preferably for the rest of the day. If not, we'll take what we can get. Then ask everyone here who's not closing if they can close. Tell them they'll get time-and-a-half."

Andy stared as though he'd never seen me before, but I didn't give him time to question me. I went back to my office, paged Maria, and called Maddie Sato while I waited. When Maddie answered, I explained to her what I hoped she could do for me. She sounded surprised by my request, but she agreed nonetheless. She also promised to make another phone call for me that I wasn't too keen on making myself.

Maria appeared just as Maddie and I hung up. Maria worked part-time and was shy and quiet. She preferred to avoid the registers if she could, being much happier lost in the shelves. She was also an amazing artist.

I handed her a piece of poster board from our supply cabinet. "I need you to make a poster for tonight's event."

"The signing?" she asked. "Er, signings?" Everyone had heard about the double booking by now.

"Not just a signing. It's a literary extravaganza. It's . . ." I came up with and then promptly rejected several possibilities. "It's the Emerald Lit Fest." Boring, but straightforward. Sometimes that was better than a gimmick.

"Yes. The first annual one. And put on here that these authors will be there." I handed her a list I'd already made up. "Mention that they'll autograph books. And that we'll have drawings for prizes." I thought some more, making it up as I went along. The ideas just leapt off my tongue. "And that 10 percent of all sales will be donated to the Puget Sound's Literacy Project."

"Wow," she said. "I didn't know all this was going on."

"Yeah," I agreed briskly. "Me either. Draw it, type it, cut and paste, whatever. Just do it. I need it in twenty minutes. And it needs to look good."

She blinked and then immediately set to work. While she did, I made phone calls. Print ads were a no-go, but almost everyone had a website. I called the big papers and the small artsy ones. I also called the local writers' groups and convinced them to e-mail their members. Finally, I called radio stations. They were less willing to do anything on short notice, but they were my best bet at immediate advertising. I could have the DJs mention us without a formal commercial. That took a bit of finagling, but we had an account with most of them already that guaranteed payment, and the charitable angle was hard to resist. Okay, *I* was hard to resist. Even over the phone, I could hear myself wooing and persuading with an unholy skill. Maria stopped working at one point to stare at me with an almost hypnotized look. Shaking her head, she returned to her poster.

Andy popped in with the annotated roster. We hadn't roped in quite as many as I would have liked, but we'd definitely increased our numbers. And most of the current staff was staying.

Maria finished her poster just then, and it did look good. I drove to the print shop that usually handled our business and turned the poster over to them.

"No," the manager told me flatly, making my manic flurry of activity come to a screeching halt. "I can't do all that in under an hour. Three hours maybe."

"Hour and a half?" I cajoled. "It's for charity. An emergency situation just came up."

She frowned. "An emergency literacy situation?"

"Literacy is always an emergency. Do you know how many children in the Puget Sound area struggle with reading due to lack of resources and education?"

Fortunately, being in the book business, I knew all the grim stats. By the time I was done with her, that battle-axe was nearly in tears. She'd do my order, she promised, and she'd do it in my original hour.

While those were being printed, I traveled over to Foster's Books. Locally owned, that store wasn't as big as Emerald City, but it had the same sort of reputation as a local landmark. Technically, we were rivals.

Garrett Foster, the owner, looked up when I entered. "Looking for a job?"

"I've got one for you," I told him sweetly, leaning on his counter. "I need you to get in touch with Abel Warshawski for me."

Abel Warshawski was a reclusive local author who wrote wildly popular books about the Pacific Northwest. He and

Garrett were longtime friends, so Abel only did appearances at Foster's.

Garrett arched a grizzled eyebrow. "Abel only comes here. You know that."

"I do. Which is why I didn't ask for his number."

I laid into Garrett then about how half of Emerald City's staff were in dire health. I talked about charity and literacy statistics. I pointed out that we weren't technically rivals anyway, since he was in Capitol Hill and I was in Queen Anne. Besides, the book industry was like a family. We all had the same goals.

"My God, woman," he murmured when I finished. I didn't think I'd taken a breath during my entire spiel. "Are you sure you don't want a new job?"

"I just want Abel for the night."

He bit his lip. "Think we could get Mortensen over here for a signing some time?"

"Hmm." I considered this. Bartering was in my blood. "That depends. You guys close a few hours earlier than us, right? Think we could get a few of you to help us out tonight? Paid, of course."

"You've got some balls," he muttered. He stared at me, still thinking, but I knew I had him. He couldn't resist. "Okay, but only if we get Mortensen during a hot time— around his next release."

"Done." I didn't like sharing Seth, but lots of big authors made multiple Seattle appearances when a new book came out. I hoped Seth didn't mind being whored out. Oh, well. That was for later.

Before I left, I bought all of Foster's *American Mystery* and *Womanspeak* magazines. He hesitated a moment as he rang them up. "Hey . . ." He looked me over. "I don't suppose you read that story Mortensen wrote . . ."

"Well," I said with a breezy smile, no longer caring about my doppelganger, Genevieve, "let's just say he's not the first man I've given some 'inspiration' to."

As a parting gift, I also gave Garrett one of our advertisements since I'd had the print shop make me a few to take with me before starting the big order.

He stared at the poster incredulously. "You already put Abel on it! Before you even talked to me!"

I left him gaping and went to pick up my posters. I returned to the bookstore and distributed them among three of the staff, arming each with a list of places to hang them. I sent them off and then managed the bookstore end of things, which mostly involved moving a lot of furniture and assigning employee duties for tonight.

When six o'clock rolled around, it really was like a miracle had occurred. Signings normally occurred in the second floor café. That spot still made up the heart of the show, but I'd had the rest of the second floor cleared out. That meant a lot of shelves and displays got crammed together while the speakers were on, but it didn't matter so much. Most of the people there wanted to hear the authors, not browse books quite yet.

And what people we had. E. J. Putnam and Lorelei Biljan had each drawn in their respective science fiction and literary fiction crowds. That was big enough, but my advertising had drawn in even more. We were packed. We needed every inch of space rearranging the furniture had allowed. I couldn't remember ever having this many people in the store.

Putnam and Biljan had been a little shaken—and initially unhappy—to find themselves in the midst of the Emerald Lit Fest rather than an ordinary signing. I passed off the confusion as a miscommunication with their people and thanked them for helping the charity. I also reminded them this was a good opportunity to show off for people who normally read other genres, and it wasn't even like either writer was slighted . . . too much. Each of them got to read a ten-minute excerpt and then field fifteen minutes of questions. It was a bit expedited for a signing, yes, but it worked and gave us time to then have a Q&A session with our *full* panel of authors, consisting of the two headliners plus Seth, Maddie, and Abel. Prize-drawings occurred throughout it all, and I emceed everything myself, not even knowing what I said half the time.

"I can't believe you gave Seth second-billing to Putnam and Biljan," Andy remarked softly to me during the panel. Only those two authors had been given exclusive spotlight. "He's bigger than both of them put together."

"He's also extremely good-natured," I murmured back. Now that I had a momentary breather, I couldn't stop drinking Seth in. I felt like I hadn't seen his whimsical smile and brown eyes in ages. In fact, I hadn't *ever* seen that particular Captain and Tennille shirt he wore. I wanted to run up to him but held back. Maddie had been the one to ask him to participate, on my behalf. It was one of the things I'd asked her to do this morning.

When all the speaking was done, I had the staff more or less move everything back. We left the café cleared out and set up a table for each of the authors to do signings. Even Maddie, who was fairly obscure, had some takers. *Womanspeak* had sort of a cult reputation, and I think she'd gained a few fans during the panel.

Passing by Seth as he spoke to a fan, I caught his eye and paused. A moment of awkwardness hung between us that even my ambrosia-induced mania could not overcome. We had too much unresolved business between us yet.

"Thank you," I said simply. "Thank you for doing this."

"Well," he said after a moment. "You know me. I haven't missed an Emerald Lit Fest yet. I'm not about to start now."

The store was nowhere near emptying when closing came, so we let them stay, especially since we were doing a hell of a business. It was around then that Warren showed up.

He stood next to me and joined me in a survey of the crowd around us. "Why," he said after a moment, "do I feel like a parent who has just returned home and found his teens throwing a party?"

"Paige double-booked Biljan and Putnam. This seemed like the logical solution."

"And when did you discover the double-booking?"

"This morning."

"This morning," he repeated. "So, instead of, say, moving furniture on the first floor and simply having two concurrent signings, you decided—with less than a day's notice—to have a star-studded, massively advertised soiree with more people than this store can hold?"

I blinked. Wow. That really would have been a simpler solution. "It's a 'fest,' actually. Not a soiree. And don't forget it's for charity."

Warren jerked his head toward me. "We're donating this to charity?"

"Only 10 percent," I assured him. "But there's actually a woman here from the Literacy Project who was so impressed that she wants to talk about us getting involved in a much bigger fundraiser with them. It probably won't be until next year—in the spring, of course. We wouldn't want to conflict with the next Emerald Lit Fest."

"The next one?"

"Well, yeah. It's a tradition now." I'd been riding the high from all of this pretty steadily all night. I was still so high, in fact, I probably could have arranged and implemented the second Emerald Lit Fest for tomorrow morning. Something suddenly occurred to me. "Hey, am I in trouble?"

He rubbed his eyes. "Georgina, you are . . ." He shook his head. "Beyond words. And not in trouble. Definitely not. We won't do this much business on Black Friday." He gave me one of his nicer smiles, reminiscent of our more intimate days. "Why don't you go home now? You need it. Your pupils are really big."

"Are you throwing me out? Are you sure I'm not in trouble?"

"You're not in trouble. But I've heard about how much overtime you've been putting in, as well as . . . other things.

Paige is going to be here next week, and we'll sit down and talk then." He suddenly did a double take. "Is that Garrett Foster working one of our registers?"

I walked home reluctantly. It wasn't easy abandoning one's brainchild. I still felt high and giddy, like pure adrenaline ran in my veins. I couldn't just go home. I needed to do something. Plan something. Anything active. A few guys glanced at me as we passed each other, and I smiled provocatively at them, nearly making one run into a garbage can. Maybe there were other ways of being active tonight.

My cell phone rang, and I answered without thinking. It was Bastien.

"Damn it. I forgot I was supposed to be screening my calls. I'm still not speaking to you."

"Don't hang up. I have to talk to you."

"No, I told you—"

"Fleur, I'm leaving."

I heard a strained, weary tone to his voice. He wasn't talking about going out for the night. My euphoric glow dimmed a little. "You're leaving Seattle."

"Yes."

"Why?"

"Because it isn't going to work with Dana. We both know it."

I stood in front of my building now and stared at it blankly, waiting for some ambrosia inspiration to give me the insight that would help Bastien finally woo Dana. Nothing happened, so I did the only thing I could.

"I'll be right over."

I found his door unlocked when I arrived and walked inside. "Mitch" stood in the kitchen with his back to me, hands resting on the island, entire posture slumped. I walked up to him and wrapped my arms around his waist, resting my head against his back.

"I'm sorry," I whispered.

"Me too."

"The cooking thing didn't pan out?" I almost laughed at my own pun. God, this ambrosia was great.

"No. Although, I can make a lovely crème brûlée now. I have some in the refrigerator if you want to try it." He sighed. "But no, it wasn't working. And you knew that, didn't you?" He turned around so that we faced each other.

I looked away. "Yeah. But I didn't want to . . . I dunno. I hoped, I guess. Hoped it would work out."

We stood there in silence for a while. No matter how angry I was at him, I hated seeing him like this. Devastated. Defeated.

"Fleur, I want to apologize about that night—"

"No, it's not all your—"

"Just listen to me first," he admonished. "There's something I have to tell you. Something about Seth."

And then, just like every other time I visited, the doorbell rang. The incubus waved an annoyed hand.

"Leave it."

"It could be her."

"I don't care. I don't want to see her."

Maybe he was pessimistic, but I'd eaten the Food of the Gods. I felt like I could do anything. I *knew* I could do anything. My confidence and cleverness knew no bounds. I had created a new tradition at Emerald City in a matter of hours. Surely I could still find some last glimmer of hope for Bastien if I had a chance to speak to Dana face-to-face.

"There still might be a way," I told him as I walked to the door. "Go invisible if you want. I want to talk to her."

"If it's even her," he called after me.

But it was her.

"Tabitha." She smiled. "I thought I saw you come in."

I returned her smile with my own. A dazzling one. I wasn't going to be shy and idiotic around her anymore. I should never have been that way under normal conditions, let alone now, when I was at my finest.

"I'm so glad you could stop by," I told her, warmth oozing

out of every pore. I beckoned her in as though I lived there. As much as she saw me over there, I might as well have. "Please, come inside. Let me get you something to drink."

For the first time, I saw Dana off guard. I was not the Tabitha she knew, and she didn't know how to handle it.

Bastien stood in the kitchen, invisible, arms crossed defiantly over his chest. I winked at him and then turned back to Dana.

"Mitch is out for a while, if you wanted to see him."

"Oh. That's fine. I can, um, stay for a little while . . . I guess."

She seemed unnerved by my control of the situation. I poured us both iced tea, and we sat down at the table. I led us into conversation about our days, telling her about an awesome charity event I'd been to at a downtown bookstore. Dana recovered some of her composure and returned to her smooth and controlled self. Her bigoted nature aside, the woman could manage a decent conversation, and we clicked. Too bad she didn't channel her intelligence into more useful areas, I thought.

As we talked about assorted things, the solution to the whole Dana situation struck me—it was so obvious. I don't know if it was the ambrosia or not, but I couldn't believe how blind we'd all been. How had none of us figured out the problem with her? What kind of seduction experts were we? Bastien was right. Dana was a lost cause.

For him.

"Dana," I interrupted in a most un-Tabitha way, "I'm really glad you came over tonight because there's something I've needed to ask you."

She choked on her tea. "Yes?"

I propped my elbows on the table, resting my chin in my hands so I could have solid eye contact. "You said a little while ago that you and Bill had lost the romance and that you didn't care. But you know what? I don't believe that. I think you miss it. I think you crave it. But not with him."

Dana's face went pale, eyes wide. Bastien, standing nearby,

wore a similar look. I didn't care. We had nothing to lose at this point.

"Am I right?" I leaned closer. "There is something missing, isn't there? And you were lying about not knowing what's sexy. You know. You know what turns you on, and you want it. You want it so bad, you can taste it."

I swear, you could have heard a pin drop in the room. Dana worked forcibly to control her breathing, staring and staring at me as though I might vanish if she blinked.

"Yes," she finally croaked. "You've been right about a lot of things. Like how we can't choose who we want. And yes . . . I think we both know what I'm talking about, Tabitha." Some of her old confidence began to return. "At first, I wasn't sure. You were so hard to read. But then, after I saw how awkward things were with you and your boyfriend—how you never wanted to talk about him and said you weren't attracted to him—I knew for sure. That little lingerie show you put on for me cinched it. You were amazing. I couldn't stop thinking about it. I'd already seen you naked in the hot tub, and that had been agonizing enough. I had to see you naked again. And then, as I talked to you more, I realized you were intelligent too. Just like tonight." She took a deep, quaking breath and reached out her hand to cover mine, fingers slowly dancing along my skin. "You're right. I do want something. So bad I can taste it. I know it's wrong, and I know it's immoral, but I can't help myself. I can't help who I want. Can't help wanting you."

No wonder Bastien hadn't been able to close the deal. Dana had wanted me. Probably from the moment I stepped out of the pool in that skimpy bathing suit. Staring at her, I thought about all the horrible things her group did. I also thought about Bastien being tortured by some demon. In some cases, being immortal wasn't always a blessing. Now, I could save him from that fate and send a little payback to the CPFV.

I smiled back at Dana, letting my body language speak for me as the tension mounted. I admit, I was a little surprised that all of my previous encounters had been read as advances on her, but well, whatever. The invisible incubus had run out of the room somewhere around "I had to see you naked again." He returned now, wielding the video camera. Seeing my calculated silence, he waved the camera at me frantically, glee all over his face.

I held the power now to change everything. The power to achieve what Bastien had been fighting for. To save him and humiliate the CPFV. If I could just pull this off. The ambrosia had proved today that my strongest talents lay in improvisation and planning, the ability to multitask and solve problems. That was great. It made me feel better about myself than I had in a while. It was probably what had led me to realize the truth about Dana too. But what about my earlier musings about the ambrosia? In regard to sex? Was my sexual prowess still a key part of me? Had the ambrosia enhanced that too? Could I rock some man—or woman—in bed? Looking at Dana and her now-obvious lust, I knew the answer. I gave a sultry laugh and jauntily brushed my hair out of my face.

I could and would rock her world. I was a team player, after all. For both teams.

Squeezing her hand, I moved toward her.

"I feel exactly the same way."

Chapter 22

The waiter brought me another gimlet just as I finished my last one. Good man, I thought. He deserved an ample tip.

Four days after the Emerald Lit Fest, I sat in the Cellar with Jerome, Carter, Hugh, Peter, Cody, and Bastien. The usual suspects. It was the first time I'd seen any of them in days. I'd been keeping a low profile, essentially only leaving my home to go to work and back.

I hadn't seen or heard from Seth in that time either.

None of us spoke. We just sat there in the dark, nursing drinks. Other people in the pub moved around and laughed, but we were a corner of silence. I could have sliced and diced the awkward tension among us. Finally, unable to take it anymore, I sighed.

"All right," I snapped. "You can stop pretending. I know you've all seen the video."

It was like letting the air out of a balloon. An opening of the floodgates.

Hugh spoke first, admiration shining in his eyes. "Jesus Christ, that was the absolute best thing I've ever seen."

"I've seen it, like, ten times," added Peter. "And it doesn't get old."

Cody's delighted look spoke for itself.

I took down half of my drink in one gulp. "Sometimes I look around, and I can't believe this is my life."

Bastien had done an Oscar-worthy job of capturing my romantic escapade with Dana on film. She had never noticed the disembodied camera floating around; only the incubus had actually been invisible. Of course, Dana had been too preoccupied to really notice much. I'd made sure of that, and while I felt a certain amount of glee over my powers of pleasure and distraction, my post-ambrosia self still didn't like having that prowess put on display any more than I'd liked Seth's story being linked to me. At least no one knew who Tabitha Hunter was.

"Fleur, I swear you did things I didn't even know about," teased Bastien.

"Oh, be quiet," I told him, knowing he lied. "This whole thing is embarrassing enough. I can't believe you had it all over the Internet in a matter of hours."

He shrugged. "Good news is hard to keep to yourself."

Jerome's eyes gleamed with subdued satisfaction. "No need to be embarrassed. What you did is laurel-worthy, Georgie. You'll be Succubus of the Year now."

"Great," I said. "Maybe that comes with coupons that haven't expired."

"Joke all you want," continued the demon, "but you've caused havoc in a powerful religious group. That is definitely worth celebrating."

So much so that Bastien was probably off the hook. True, he hadn't been in the spotlight, but I'd made sure that Jerome played up his role in the official written report. I think the demon knew I'd gone a little overboard in crediting Bastien for his assistance in this caper, but he hadn't dwelt on the technicalities. Regardless of what the paperwork said, the diabolical community knew it was Jerome's succubus in the extremely popular video. My boss's reputation had gone through the roof.

As for the CPFV . . . well, yes, it was most definitely in chaos. Dana had resigned as soon as the scandal went public. Suddenly missing their strong leader, the group had collapsed into confusion, flailing about with no clear direction. Poor Bill. In addition to the embarrassment of a philandering wife, he now had to do damage control and still maintain his strong stance on family values for the sake of his political career. Reelections were next year; no one knew how he'd fare.

I had mixed feelings about the whole matter. Sure, I hated the CPFV's horrible actions and was glad to see them go down. But Dana, despite her many flaws, had cared about Tabitha. It might not have been love, but the emotions were genuine. She'd opened herself up to me, and I'd made a mockery of it. Even if she managed to wade out of this mess, she'd probably never accept her sexual inclinations again. She'd bury them, continuing a campaign of homosexual intolerance. That bothered me, for the sake of both her personal and her political lives.

"And when not taking down conservative bitches," noted Hugh, "she destroys gods in her free time. Did you really beat up that kid too? You're, like, a size four."

"Don't forget about the Emerald Lit Fest." Cody grinned mischievously. "Man, I can't believe I missed that."

"Is there anything you don't do, Georgina?" marveled Peter. "You haven't been learning to cook soufflés behind my back, have you?"

I rolled my eyes and turned to the greater immortals, ignoring my friends' over-the-top praise. "Are you finally going to tell me the whole story on Sol, or whoever he was? You guys have been terribly laissez-faire about me killing a god."

"You know most of the details," Carter told me.

"And you didn't technically kill him," added Jerome.

I started. "I didn't? But . . . he exploded. There was blood everywhere. That seems kind of, I don't know, final."

"You destroyed his human manifestation," explained the

angel in an almost bored way. "The body he used to walk the mortal world. Sol—or Soma as he's accurately called—still very much exists."

"Soma's another name for ambrosia . . ." I began slowly.

"Yes," Carter agreed. "In Hindu spirituality, the god Soma is the divine embodiment of the drug. It runs in his veins and is then distributed to mortals."

I remembered his bleeding wrist and how his blood had dried. "His blood forms the crystals that make the ambrosia. That's what everyone was drinking. That's what I drank!" I shuddered.

"You also drank it in its pure form," noted Jerome, watching for my reaction, "straight from the source."

"Oh Lord," I realized. "The goblet. I thought it was some sort of date-rape drug."

"In some ways it was," Carter told me gently. "His blood, in its crystal form, serves as a self-enhancement that can be tolerated by mortals—and immortals—because it's diluted. In its concentrated form, it's too much to handle. It's disorienting. It goes beyond amplification of skills. It overloads the system, making you feel insanely good and susceptible to physical touch and strong emotion."

Hence my reaction to his advances—and subsequent attack on Alec. Of course, I was still so mad at the former drummer that I half believed my actions wouldn't have been any different sans ambrosia.

"That's so disgusting," I muttered. "I drank blood. Gross."

Cody and Peter exchanged glances. They grinned.

"What was the deal with that dart thing?" asked Hugh. "The thing she impaled him with."

"Mistletoe. It guards the gateway between worlds. The Norse always said it grew on the Tree of Life—the tree that holds the world."

I frowned. "So, if he's just lost his physical body, then he's not really gone."

"He's never gone," said Carter. "The Food of the Gods is

always around—or at least some concept of it. Mortals always have and will continue to believe and pray for some magical cure-all that will change their lives. That's why he still has so much power, despite most not knowing who he is. People don't always have to know what they're worshipping or believing in to still grant it power."

"But, when he pops back down to this plane next time, he'll probably hole up somewhere else," said Jerome more practically. "If Carter or I had done anything, it would have been an open declaration of war. Innocent Georgie's desperate defense sent a charming get-the-fuck-out message that didn't get any of us in trouble. It only required a small report." He made a face; the demon hated paperwork.

I sighed. "Okay then. One last question. Why the sex? Why go to all that trouble to get Alex to procure victims?"

"Who doesn't want sex?" asked Hugh.

"The stories do resound with his lechery, actually," said Carter. "One myth even talks about him carrying off some god's wife because he just wanted her that badly. When you're a being of euphoria and ultimate physical prowess, I guess sex sort of goes with it. So I've heard, anyway."

I scowled. "And he was too lazy to even get the victims himself. What a bastard."

"He's a god," said Carter, as though there were nothing more to add.

I turned to the angel, thinking about what he'd said. "You've been a veritable wealth of knowledge today. But doesn't it bother anyone else that we're openly discussing and accepting, what, three different spiritual systems here? Hindu and Norse—plus ours. Which I always thought was the true one, by the way."

Jerome looked genuinely delighted. "Come now, you've rubbed shoulders with immortals from all sorts of 'spiritual systems' since the beginning of your succubus existence."

"Yeah, I know . . . but I never thought about the logistics too hard. I thought we were all disparate—remember? They do their thing, we do ours? Now you're mixing it up like . . . like . . . we're all doing the same thing."

"Yeah," said Cody. "Which one's right?"

Angel and demon shared smirks.

" *'What is truth?' Pilate asked.*" Carter just couldn't stay away from his quotes. His eyes held barely contained laughter.

I sighed again, knowing we'd get no better answer from either of them.

As our evening get-together wound down, Bastien unhappily declared he had to leave for Detroit. He made his farewells to the others, and then I walked him out.

We stood outside the pub, wrapped in our own thoughts as locals and tourists alike moved through Pioneer Square. Finally, at the same time, we spoke.

"Fleur—"

"Bastien—"

"No, let me go first," he said adamantly. I nodded for him to go on. "What I did at the hotel wasn't right. I shouldn't have led you into that—especially when you told me right off not to. And what I said to Seth at your place . . . that was unforgivable. Yeah, I was pretty sloshed, but that's no excuse. Not by a long shot."

I shook my head. "God knows I've done a lot of stupid things while drunk. And people, for that matter. But don't beat yourself up too bad—at least not over what happened . . . uh, between us. You were right. I wasn't a victim; I went along with that. I made my own choices, choices that I have to deal with."

"It doesn't matter. You shouldn't forgive me. Especially after you saved me on the Dana thing. You figured out what I'd been too blind to see. No, I'm definitely beyond forgiveness."

"Maybe. But I'm going to forgive you anyway." I gave him a playful punch. "And you can't stop me."

"Only a fool would stand in your way," he said gallantly. "But I still don't think I deserve it."

"Bas, I've seen people come and go for over a thousand years. Hell, I've seen civilizations come and go. I don't have many constants in my life. None of us do. I don't want to write off one of the best ones I've got."

He opened his arms for me, and I rested my head against his chest, sad that he'd be going away again. We stood like that for a long time, and then he broke away so that he could look at me.

"Confession time: I didn't have sex with you for altruism. You were right about that. And I didn't do it just because I could either. I did it because I wanted you. Because I wanted to be closer to you." He touched my cheek and winked. "You're worth ten Alessandras. You would be worth going to Guam for."

"What about Omaha?"

"No one's worth going to Omaha for."

I laughed. "You're going to miss your flight."

"Yeah." He hugged me again, then hesitated before speaking. "There's one more thing you need to know. The day after my, uh, idiotic drunken outburst, Seth came to see me."

"What?" I racked my brain. That would have been during the time I was preparing for the Fest. "Why?"

"He wanted to know what happened. Between us. All the details."

"What'd you tell him?"

"The truth."

I stared off at nothing.

"That guy's crazy about you," Bastien said after a moment's silence. "Love like that . . . well, hell itself has trouble standing against love like that, I think. I don't know if a succubus and a human can really make things work, but if it can happen, he'll be the one it happens with." He hesitated. "I think, no, I *know* I was a little jealous of that . . . both that he had your love and you had someone who loved you like that." He gave me a bittersweet smile. "Anyway. Good luck. I'm always here if you need me."

"Thank you," I said, hugging him again. "Keep in touch. Maybe we'll get assigned together again some day."

The roguish look, long absent during our solemn conversation, flashed to his face. "Oh, the trouble we could cause. The world isn't ready for us again."

He pressed a soft, sweet kiss against my lips, and then he was gone. A minute later, I felt Carter's presence behind me.

"Parting is such sweet sorrow."

"That it is," I agreed sadly. "But that's life, mortal or immortal."

"How's your high-wire act with Seth going?"

I turned to him, almost having forgotten that reference. "Bad."

"Did you look down?"

"Worse than that. I fell off. I fell off and hit bottom."

The angel regarded me with his steady gaze. "Then you'd better get back on."

I choked on a bitter laugh. "Is that possible?"

"Sure," he said. "As long as the wire hasn't snapped, you can always climb back on."

I left him and walked a few blocks to catch a bus back to Queen Anne. While I was waiting, I blinked and did a double take as Jody walked by. I hadn't talked to her in ages. After the Dana scandal, Mitch and Tabitha Hunter had dropped off the face of the Earth.

I left the bus stop and ducked into a dark doorway à la Superman. A moment later, I hurried to catch up with her as Tabitha.

"Jody!"

She stopped and turned around. Her brown eyes widened when she recognized me.

"Tabitha," she said uncertainly, waiting for me to get to her. "It's good to see you."

"You too. How are things?"

"Okay." We stood there awkwardly. "How are you? I mean, after everything . . ." Her cheeks crimsoned.

"You don't have to avoid the topic. I can deal with it," I told her gently. "It happened. Nothing to be done about it now."

She looked down at her feet, clearly troubled. "I've been wanting to tell you something. It wasn't . . . it wasn't just you, you know." She looked back up, embarrassed. "She sort of, you know, approached me too, and we did some things . . . things I didn't really want to do. But I couldn't say no either. Not to her. It was a rough time in my life . . ."

So. I wasn't Dana's first taste of forbidden fruit. The notion that she had forced Jody appalled me, more so than Dana throwing herself into rallies that denied her own nature. Suddenly, I didn't feel so sorry for her anymore.

"Then she got what she deserved," I declared icily.

"Maybe," said Jody, still looking upset. "It's been a disaster for their family. I feel the worst for Reese. And then there's the CPFV . . . they're a disaster too."

"Maybe it's for the best," I said neutrally.

She gave me a sad half-smile. "I know you don't believe in them, but they do have potential to do good. I'm actually on my way to a meeting right now. We're going to decide the fate of the group. I don't think we'll disband . . . but I don't know what direction we'll go in either. There are some people who think just like Dana. They're not a majority, but they're loud. Louder than people like me."

I remembered our gardening conversation. "And you still want some of the things you talked to me about? Helping those who need help now?"

"Yes. I wish I could walk right in there and speak up. If I could get enough people's attention, I think we could really go in a new direction. A better direction that might actually affect change instead of just censuring and calling people names."

"Then you should do exactly that."

"I can't. I don't have the skill to talk to people like that. I'm not that brave."

"You have the passion."

"Yeah, but is that enough if I can't get it out?"

Suddenly, I had to fight a giddy smile from taking over my face. "I've got something for you," I told her, reaching into my purse. "Here. Take this."

I handed her the last packet of ambrosia. It was dangerous, perhaps, to give it to a mortal, but one dose wouldn't hit her too badly, and she'd never be able to get more. Besides, taking the temptation away from me was probably for the best.

"What is this?"

"It's a, um, herbal supplement. Like an energy blend. Haven't you seen those?"

She frowned. "Like ginseng or kava or whatever?"

"Yeah. I mean, it won't change your life, of course, but it always sort of gives me a kick. You just mix it in a drink and go from there."

"Well, I was about to buy coffee . . ."

"That's perfect. And it can't hurt or anything." Smiling, I squeezed her arm. "Do it for me, so I'll feel like I've given you a good-luck charm."

"Okay. Sure. I'll take it as soon as I get the coffee." She glanced at her watch. "I've got to take off now if I want to be on time. You take care of yourself, okay?"

"I will. Thanks. Good luck tonight."

To my surprise, she gave me a quick hug and then disappeared into the crowd of pedestrians. As I rode the bus home, I found I felt better about myself than I had in days. I'd sort of wanted to save the ambrosia for next year's Emerald Lit Fest, but I supposed I wouldn't need it so long as I actually allowed myself two days instead of one. After all, a little leeway never hurt.

Chapter 23

The CPFV meeting didn't get nearly as much press as a hot lesbian affair did, but it still drew a reporter from the *Seattle Times*, as well as some other media attention.

Jody had delivered the speech of a lifetime at the meeting. She'd outlined a fully detailed vision for the CPFV, one that involved dropping the group's current attack on homosexuality. Her plan encouraged outreach to those in need, the same teen mothers and runaways she'd spoken to me about before. Since the CPFV had a national presence, she also wanted the chapters to address local needs in order to have a more meaningful impact and foster a sense of community. Her presentation had been brilliantly thought out and inspiring. The meeting had ended with cheers and applause, as well as a vote that made her the organization's new head. I suspected that, post-ambrosia, she might be a little terrified by what she'd wrought. After all the creative and interesting things she'd done in her life so far, though, I felt confident she could manage. Plus, I had a feeling she'd be happier being involved in some meaningful vocation again after her days in the doldrums as a housebound wife.

It occurred to me also that although we might be hellish superstars for our Dana-related actions, Bastien and I hadn't really helped the greater diabolical cause in the end. Really, Dana had been spreading evil and intolerance. Ousting her for Jody had actually brought more good into the world than before. I hoped Jerome never made that connection. He was pretty pleased with me at the moment.

The CPFV article was a few days old now, but I kept it on my desk at work because it made me happy during what had otherwise been an unsettling week. Seth hadn't shown at the store at all.

"Did you see that on the Internet?" Doug asked me, noticing the paper.

I gave him a blank look. "Why would I watch something like that?"

"Because it's hot. You're totally missing out."

He sat on the edge of the desk and played with a pen, flipping it in the air. Neither of us were doing the work we should have been. It was just like old times.

"How are you feeling?" I asked.

"Pretty good, I guess." He knew that I knew about the ambrosia, but he wasn't aware of my role in what had happened. All he knew was that Alec was gone. "The band's sort of plateaued now. I guess that had to happen. Not having a drummer really doesn't help either."

"Well, you'll fix that, won't you?"

"Yeah. Just a pain. Gotta have auditions." He stopped playing with the pen and sighed. "We were so close, Kincaid. A little bit farther, and we'd have made it."

"You still will. It'll just take longer. Everything you guys did—that was still you."

"Yeah," he said, not sounding convinced.

"Besides, I'm still your groupie. That's got to count for something, right?"

His easy grin returned. "You bet it does. I think Maddie might be joining your ranks. She won't get out of my apartment."

I laughed. "Doesn't she have to go back to her job?"

"*Womanspeak* is run out of Berkeley. She was already

telecommuting, so she's just doing more of the same. She says she wants to keep an eye on me."

"That's sweet."

"Dude." Doug gave me a droll look. "I'm trying to be a rock star, and my sister lives with me. That's not sweet."

"Working hard as always, I see," a smooth voice said.

We both looked up from our banter. "Paige!" I exclaimed delightedly. I would have hugged her, but we'd never exactly had a touchy-feely relationship.

Our long-absent manager stood in the doorway. She almost looked casual in loose black slacks and an empire-cut pink maternity blouse. Her stomach had grown even more in the last month, and seeing it made a little fuzzy spot tickle in my chest. I'd been unable to conceive a child while mortal and could not now as an immortal. That knowledge still stung on a personal level, but I never held it against those I knew. I loved pregnant women and babies. I was happy for Paige, happier to see her back and looking well.

A smile played on her glossed lips as she took in the two of us. "Georgina, could you come to Warren's office? We want to talk to you. It won't take long."

"Sure," I said standing up. Doug quietly hummed the *Jaws* theme.

Paige, Warren, and I sat down in his office with the door closed. I didn't really think I was in trouble, but being with them like this felt kind of intimidating. Especially since both seemed to be watching me expectantly.

"So," began Paige, "we've been looking over all the accounts of what happened while we were gone. We've talked to some people too." She paused purposefully. "You've been busy."

I smiled, relaxing. "It's always busy here. If I wanted a slow store, I'd go down to Foster's."

Warren laughed. "I heard he offered you a job."

"Yeah, but don't worry. I'm not going anywhere."

"That's good," Paige said crisply, "because I understand we now have some sort of annual event you've got to plan. Lorelei Biljan sent me e-mail asking to be invited back to next year's Emerald Lit Gala."

"Fest," I corrected. "It's a fest."

"Whatever. The point is, what you did was remarkable . . . if a little unorthodox. To pull that together so quickly and then turn over such amazing sales stats." She shook her head. "It was superhuman."

I squirmed at the adjective. "It needed to be done."

"And you did it. Just like you've been doing a number of other remarkable things around here. Things that we're very impressed with."

"Hey, now," I said, suddenly uncomfortable with the way they both watched me, "don't think that was an ordinary day. It was kind of an exception. I can't do that kind of stuff all the time. I was just having a good day, that's all."

"You've had a lot of good days, Georgina," Warren spoke up. "You haven't had a full staff here in weeks. You've come in on your days off. You've run this place when no one else was around to do it. You've handled crisis after crisis—and not just the Fest thing. I'm talking about the whole situation with Doug too."

I sat up straighter. "What are you going to do? You aren't going to fire him, are you? Because it wasn't all him . . . I mean, there were extenuating circumstances. He's better now. He's the best employee you've got."

"We've spoken to him," said Paige calmly. "And he'll stay on for now, although he understands he'll sort of be on probation."

Relief coursed through me. "Good. That's really good."

"I'm glad you think so because you'll be the one who's supervising him."

"I—what?" My train of thought derailed horrifically, and I looked back and forth between their faces, waiting for the punch line.

"This pregnancy is proving more difficult than expected,

as you've probably guessed. The baby's healthy, and I'm still on track for a normal delivery, but I need to eliminate certain risk factors. One of them, unfortunately, is working."

I stared. Paige had hired me. She couldn't leave. "What are you saying?"

"I'm saying that I can't keep working here."

"But . . . after the baby . . . you could come back, right?"

"I don't know, but I'm not going to put the store on hold while I figure that out. I'm resigning, and we want you to take my place."

"As manager," added Warren, like that wasn't perfectly obvious.

"I . . . I don't know what to say."

"You'd get a salary increase, of course," she said. "And then we'd hire someone to fill your old position. You'd take over all of my duties."

I nodded. I knew what her duties were—especially since I'd done them for the last few weeks. They involved more paperwork than sociability, but certainly Paige had worked the floor plenty and interacted with others. The job still involved people, but in a different way. I'd have no peers and no one above me save Warren. It could potentially put a damper on how much I hung out with the staff after work—particularly my goofing off with Doug. The position would entail a whole new set of complications and difficulties.

On the other hand, I'd have a lot more freedom and power. Paige planned all of our signings and promotional events, much as I had the Fest. It had been fun. I could do that all the time now. I could experiment with new things. That had appeal—a lot of it. And really, the challenging aspect of it also had its appeal. It would be new and different. I'd lived for centuries, and I knew the dangers of a static lifestyle. I had enough experience and education to take on very prestigious occupations—and I had done so in the past. This time around, I'd chosen a more laid-back job; was I ready to move on now?

My decision was made, but when I saw how anxious my silence had made them, I couldn't resist a little teasing. "Would I get my own office?"

They nodded as one, still tense, thinking that was what held me back.

"Oh. Okay. Sold."

I went home that night heady with the knowledge of my new job. I would miss Paige, but the more I thought about it, the more excited I grew about being store manager. Celebration was definitely in order, so I called Hugh and the vampires, and we went out on the town. I had fun with them, but honestly, I wished I could celebrate with someone else.

The late night of drinking made me sleep in considerably the next morning. I awoke to Aubrey sprawled across my neck, dangerously close to cutting off my air, in a position only a cat could find comfortable. My clock read noon, and I lay there, warm in the blankets and wondering what I was going to do with myself. The store wasn't open. It was Thanksgiving.

My phone rang. I rolled over and grappled for it, just barely avoiding getting Aubrey's claws in my jugular.

I stared at Seth's name on the caller ID as if it had magical powers. Taking a deep breath, I answered.

"Happy birthday," I said, trying to sound cheerful and not utterly petrified.

There was a pause and then a small, surprised chuckle. I hadn't known what to expect when he and I finally resumed contact after last week's drama, but his laughter hadn't been a contender. Unless it was bitter laughter while my heart bled onto the floor and I begged for forgiveness.

"Thanks," he said, his voice sobering a little. "But, uh, I don't believe you."

"Believe me what?"

"That you want me to have a happy birthday."

"I just said I did."

There was a long silence. My anxiety grew with every passing second.

"If you wanted me to have a happy birthday, you'd come over to my party."

"Your party," I repeated flatly.

"Yeah, remember? Andrea invited you?"

I remembered. I'd been thinking about it every day this week.

"I didn't think I was still invited." I hesitated, heart aching. "I didn't think you'd want me there."

"Well, I do. So hurry up. You're late."

We hung up, and I just sat there. Seth had called at last. And he wanted to see me. Now. What was going to happen? What should I do? I looked at Aubrey and sighed.

"Guess I should have kept that last pack of ambrosia, huh?"

Chapter 24

Seth had chided me for being late, but with five daughters, the Mortensens were always running late. So no one, except Seth, really paid much attention to my tardiness.

Likewise, with so much chaos, no one really noticed that he and I didn't talk much. The girls spoke more than enough for all of us, and I took some comfort in their presence. As always, they couldn't get enough of me, crawling all over me and tugging at my sleeve to make sure they had my undivided attention. I enjoyed it all in a bittersweet sort of way. Convinced Seth and I were on the verge of a break-up, I mostly kept thinking that this would be the last time I would hang out with this wonderful family.

Andrea provided us with an equally distracting birthday/Thanksgiving meal. Terry and Seth had helped her, it turned out, but I still marveled that they had pulled it off while still managing the little ones. I said as much to Andrea.

"Parenthood makes you the ultimate multitasker," she informed me. "You'll see what I mean when you have kids."

I smiled back politely, not bothering to tell her there'd be no kids for me.

"Besides," Terry said with a grin, "we understand you're already sort of a superwoman. Seth was telling us about some crazy shindig you threw together at the bookstore?"

"Uncle Seth said it was cool," added Brandy.

"It was a fest," I corrected, glancing at Seth in surprise. I couldn't figure out at all what his feelings were for me. He'd invited me over and had apparently been singing my praises. None of that jibed with the fallout I expected from the Bastien incident, nor his initial stunned reaction to it.

Seth opened presents after dinner, the bulk of which were books and more contributions to his wacky T-shirt collection.

"Where's your present?" Kendall asked me.

"I left it at home."

We all hung out and talked after that, my apprehension mounting as I wondered where this evening would lead. When the party finally disbanded, Seth asked me if I wanted to go somewhere.

I took a deep breath. It was now or never. "Let's go to my place."

Once back there, we stationed ourselves on my couch—at a proper distance—and talked about everything except our relationship. I told him about my new position and got his congratulations. He told me about some interesting fan comments he'd received at the signing. When this had gone on for nearly thirty minutes, I couldn't take it any more.

"Seth, what's going on?" I demanded. "With us."

He leaned his head back against the couch. "I wondered when we'd get to this. Can't avoid it any longer, huh?"

"Well, yeah. This is a big deal. This isn't like a dispute over where to go for dinner . . . this is us. Our future. I mean, I . . . you know. You know what I did."

"I do." He studied my ceiling for a moment, then turned his amber brown eyes on me. In that moment, I almost understood why he always seemed to be staring somewhere else. When he turned his eyes directly on you, it was a hard and powerful thing. They were electric. "Aren't I allowed to forgive you?"

"Er . . . no. Well, I don't know."

This conversation echoed the one I'd had with Bastien earlier. He had said the same thing, and after weighing everything, I'd decided it wasn't worth being mad at him. Was it so easy to forgive the ones you loved?

"I won't lie, Thetis, it hurt. It still does. But, in some ways . . . well, it's only one step away from what you normally do."

"A big step."

He laughed. "Whose side are you on? Are you trying to turn me against you?"

"I'm just trying to make sure you stand up for yourself."

"You're always worried about that. Don't worry. I'm not a complete doormat."

"I didn't mean that. I just . . . I don't know. I'm not very good at this dating thing."

"I know that. Neither am I. I've done plenty of stupid things in my past relationships. I deserve a few karmic turnabouts. Of course, that doesn't mean I want this to become an ongoing thing, but one mistake . . . one mistake I can forgive. If I haven't had much practice dating, you've got to be even worse after, what, how many years of casual, uh, flings?"

"A lot," I replied vaguely. For some reason, I was reluctant to tell Seth my age.

He picked up on that, his eyes narrowing ruefully. "And right there. That's another thing. Almost worse than what happened. You're doing it again."

"Doing what?"

"You don't tell me things. Things about you. It's like you're afraid to show me who you are. But like I said, that's what love is. You open yourself up. I want to know you. I want to know everything about you. Sometimes I feel like no matter how strongly I feel about you . . . I still don't know you at all."

"I'm not very good at that part either," I said softly.

Seth pulled me into an embrace, crushing me against him. There was a fierceness in that motion, an unflinching sense of possession that stirred my blood. "You're my world right now, Georgina, but I can't go on with this . . . not if there's no honesty."

His tone was gentle and loving, but I heard the warning between the lines. I'd had my fuckup. The next time, I would not get such amnesty.

This terrified me a little, yet I was proud of him and realized I had a lot more to learn about him too. He had every right to be laying down the law. He was not a doormat. I regretted my mistakes, and while I was glad to be forgiven this time, I didn't want Seth to waste his life on me if I couldn't ever treat him right.

My young French lover, Etienne, had never recovered. I'd learned years later that he'd broken his engagement, staying forever single. He'd thrown himself into his painting, earning a small following. Several portraits of me—as a blond Josephine—still hung in private European collections.

Etienne had not been able to get me out of his system, and it had made a mess of him. I wanted things to work with Seth so badly. I wanted us to be together and be happy for as long as we could manage it. But if we couldn't, I didn't want him to waste his life on me as that young painter had.

"I love you," I murmured into Seth's shoulder, astonished when the words just slipped out. And I realized then just how much I meant them. He inhaled deeply and held me even tighter, and I felt the love pouring off of him, even with no spoken declaration. "I'm pretty sure I don't deserve you."

"Oh, my Thetis, you deserve a lot of things. And honestly"—he shifted around and studied me—"as much as it hurts . . . I'm sort of glad that you, you know, had that chance with Bastien."

I frowned. "That chance to be with a copy of you?"

"Well, no. That's still kind of weird. I mean the chance to have sex and, well, enjoy it. Every time I think about what you do on a regular basis . . ." He closed his eyes a moment. "I just envision you being raped over and over. And I hate it. It makes me sick. I'm glad you were with someone you cared about . . . even if it wasn't me. You deserve to have good sex for a change."

"You do too," I said, overwhelmed by Seth's nonstop self-lessness. "And you know . . . if you ever wanted to find someone and just, well, have sex for the fun of it . . . well, you could. You know, just to fulfill the physical need. I wouldn't mind." I didn't think I would, at least. I uneasily re-called my slight jealousy over his correspondence with Mad-die.

He looked at me seriously. "I don't have sex just to fulfill a need. Not if I can help it. Sex may not be a requisite part of love, but it is an expression of love. It should at least be with someone you care about."

The answer didn't surprise me. In fact, it suddenly re-minded me of something. "Hey, I've got something for you."

Despite our dire romantic status, I had nonetheless chosen twenty of the best pictures Bastien had taken of me and had Hugh print them this week. I hadn't known until now that I'd actually be able to give them to Seth. I found them in my bedroom, bound with a pink ribbon.

"Your birthday present." I started to hand the pictures over.

"Wait," he said. He opened up the messenger bag he car-ried his laptop around in. A moment later, he offered me sev-eral sheets of paper. I gave him the pictures. We sat in silence, each of us studying our respective offerings.

For half a second, I thought he was sharing a manuscript after all. A few lines into it, I realized it was addressed to me. It was the writing he'd promised me a while back. The de-tailed exposition of all the things he wished we could do.

Reading it, I sort of lost track of the world around me. What he'd written was exquisite. Some of it was like poetry. A beautifully crafted ode to my beauty and my body and my personality that made my heart swell. Other parts were brazenly explicit. Hot and steamy. They made O'Neill and

Genevieve's elevator look like a kindergarten classroom. I could feel the blood rushing to my cheeks as I read.

When I finished, I looked up at him breathlessly. He was watching me, as the pictures had taken less time to peruse.

"I take it all back," he told me, holding up one of the shots. It showed me sitting crosswise in a chair, naked. My legs draped over the edge lazily, showing a nice view of my pink painted toenails. A hardbound copy of one of Seth's books sat on my lap. "Sex might be a requisite part of love after all."

I glanced down at the manifesto. "Yeah. It just might be."

We sat there a moment, then burst out laughing. He rubbed his eyes. "Thetis," he said wearily, "what are we going to do with ourselves?"

"I don't know. Do the pictures just make things worse?"

"No. They're wonderful. Thank you. They're a good way of having you . . . even if I can't have the real thing."

An idea slowly coalesced in my mind. The pictures just involved looking. Looking was safe. And one didn't just have to look at a two-dimensional image. "Maybe . . . maybe you can have the real thing." He gave me a quizzical look, and I hastily amended: "In a hands-off way. Come on."

"This seems dangerous," he said when I led him to the bedroom.

Sunset was filling the room with mood lighting. I pointed to a chair in the corner. "Sit there."

I moved to the opposite corner, hoping it was enough space.

"What are you— Oh." He bit off his words, swallowing. "*Oh.*"

I slid my hands slowly up over my hips and breasts, over to the top button of my blouse. Slowly, deliberately, I unfastened the button. Then, just as carefully, I moved down to the next button. And the next. Then I unbound my hair, letting it fall messily over my shoulders.

A striptease is all about letting go of self-consciousness. And it's about pacing too, I supposed. Admittedly, doing a show in front of Seth, whom I loved, moved into a realm I felt a little unfamiliar with. Nervous energy twitched inside me, but I didn't show it on the outside. I was on the stage, and I moved through my steps with sultry confidence, watching my own hands sometimes and making eye contact with him at others. This was part of my gift to him. He obviously liked seeing my body, even if, for the moment, he watched like one frozen, eyes wide and face carefully controlled.

The blouse eventually fell to the floor, followed by the skirt. I'd had bare legs earlier today but had covertly shape-shifted on thigh-highs while we walked to the bedroom. Left only in those and a cherry-red bra and panty set made of satin, I languidly moved my body in smooth and alluring ways as I played with edges and straps.

The stockings came off next, each one rolled down with delicate motions that let my hands slide against my own skin. Left in almost nothing, I savored the shining satin, trailing my fingertips over the bra and panty's surfaces. At last they peeled off too, and I was left in only my skin, left fully exposed and with a surprising heat burning in my lower body. I had turned myself on as much as him.

I stood there a moment, like I was taking in applause before an audience, then started to walk across the room.

"No," he said, voice thick and husky. His fingers dug into the chair's arms. "You'd better not get too close."

I stopped, laughing softly. "You don't strike me as the assaulting type, Mortensen."

"Yeah, well, there's a first time for everything."

"So you liked?"

"Very much." His eyes were drinking me in, ravenous and needful. "That was the best thing I've ever seen."

Pleased, I stretched out my muscles, holding my arms over my head a moment before exhaling and letting my hands fall.

As they did, I ran them down over my breasts and thighs in a careless gesture I didn't really even think about. Yet, as I did it, I saw his posture stiffen slightly and that fire in his eyes flare up.

A slow, dangerous smile spread over my face.

"What?" he asked.

"I don't think the show's over yet."

I sat back on the bed, then slid myself up so I was propped up against the pillows in full view. Watching him and his every reaction, I moved my hands up to my breasts, feeling them. But these were not the touches that came with a sensual undressing. These were caresses of a different sort. A more urgent sort.

I want to see you in the throes of orgasm, Seth had written in his missive. *I want to see your whole body writhing, your lips open as you drink in your own pleasure. Only yours, no one else's. Just you, completely given up to ecstasy.*

I stroked my breasts, cupping them, feeling their softness and curving shape. My fingers moved and stroked my nipples, teasing them further, moving in lazy circles. I ran my thumbs over them, reveling in their sensitivity. When my breasts were finally taut and aching, I let my hands travel down over my smooth and flat stomach, examining and lingering on every part until I reached my thighs. Parting them ever so slightly, I slipped two fingers between the waiting lips so I could stroke that throbbing knot of nerves, moaning without even realizing it. Something about Seth watching aroused me more than I'd expected. I was dripping with wetness, aching and scorching.

I slid my fingers over and over that burning, swelling spot, stoking the rapidly growing need. Arching my body, hearing the soft cries escaping from me, all I could think about was Seth's eyes on me. Doing this for him, was in many ways, more genuine than actual sex with Bastien-turned-Seth had been. This was as intimate as he and I could ever be. It wasn't exactly the same as the honest communication we kept talking about, but in a way, I was opening myself to him after all. Exposing myself without inhibition.

I kept expecting the succubus energy-need to pick up on this scam, but either the distance or the fact that I was doing this to myself continued to trick it. We'd found a loophole after all.

As my fingers continued to rub between my lips, bringing me closer and closer to that crest, I moved my other hand down and thrust a couple of fingers inside of me. This elicited a moan of yearning, and I opened my thighs further, letting Seth get a full view. Faster and harder both sets of fingers worked, touching everything, building and building up that delicious pleasure until I felt like I couldn't take it anymore. Like I was going to burst.

And then, I did.

Sparks and lightning shot through my body, radiating from my core outward until every part of me tingled with life. I cried out again, loudly, my body writhing against the sheets as spasms racked my muscles. What had started as an ostentatious show had become something more. Doing this for Seth—with Seth—had reawakened something sleeping inside of me. I had lost control; my own body had taken over.

When I finally calmed down, I lay back against the covers, my breathing shallow as I recovered myself. I could feel sweat all over me. And with that physical response, an emotional and almost spiritual one radiated through me as well. Like the experience had somehow lit a flame within me. One that hadn't died with the orgasm. One that had nearly gone cold once—long ago—but now shone fiercely.

A moment later, I heard Seth stand up. Gingerly, he moved to my side, just barely sitting on the bed. We stared at each other, neither of us speaking, our eyes conveying all we needed to each other. He reached out a hand, like he might stroke my cheek, then pulled back.

"I'm afraid to touch you," he whispered.

"Yeah. It might . . . might be wise to hold back on that for a little longer. Just in case it kicks in."

"I take back what I said earlier about the stripping. *This* was the best thing I've ever seen." He crooked me a smile. "No, you're the best thing I've ever seen. Everything about you."

I smiled back. "We might have found a workaround."

"For you maybe. As it is, I'm, uh, feeling a little . . . uncomfortable right now. I'm glad you were able to get a release, at least."

I suddenly sat up, energized. "Well, why can't you?"

His smile dropped. "What? Like in the bathroom?"

"No. Right here."

"You're joking."

"No." I could feel my lips turning into a mischievous smirk. "Fair is fair. Quid pro quo. I did it for you, now it's your turn."

"I . . . no. *No.* I can't do that."

"Sure you can. There's nothing to it."

"Yeah, but . . ."

"No buts. You're the one going on about openness and sharing."

"Whoa. That's not even the same."

"It is." I rolled over so that I was not quite in a pouncing position, but pretty close. I gave him a smoldering look. "How do you think I was able to do all that? I thought about you. I thought about you being over me while I spread my body for you. I opened up to you. I let you see everything. I wanted you to have that part of me. Nothing held back. And now I want to see the same." I leaned close, starting to tug his shirt off. "I want to see you come. I want to see you give in to that desire. I want to see your face when you touch yourself and think about me."

"And they say I'm good with words." He closed his eyes for a moment. "I can't believe you can have this effect on me."

I pulled his Spam shirt over his head. "I'm waiting."

Seth stared at me, then carefully and hesitantly began taking off his pants. He tossed them on the floor and moved on to his adorable flannel boxers. He paused there, clearly nervous, and then removed them in a quick motion before he could turn back. I looked him over admiringly, seeing him naked for the first time. As my gaze lingered between his legs, I had to work to keep a straight face. Bastien hadn't done him justice.

"This is going to be hard," he observed.

"It already looks hard to me."

"Stop making jokes."

"Sorry. Just relax, that's the key." I sat back away from him, putting some distance between us once again. "Drop the self-consciousness. Just give in to how you feel."

He nodded and took a deep breath. "Thanks, coach. Can you move over to your side—yeah. There. And then, the hand . . . yes, put it right there. Perfect." He shook his head, an almost comic look of misery and eagerness on his face as his hand slowly moved down. "I need a good view of you to pull this off, I think, so I can keep my eyes off me. If I pay too much attention to what I'm doing, the absurdity will hit."

"Well then," I said, getting comfortable. "Don't look down."

Please turn the page for an
exciting sneak peek of the third
Georgina Kincaid novel
SUCCUBUS DREAMS!

Chapter 1

I wished the guy on top of me would hurry up because I was getting bored.

Unfortunately, it didn't seem like he was going to finish anytime soon. Brad or Brian or whatever his name was thrust away, eyes squeezed shut with such concentration that you would have thought having sex was on par with brain surgery or lifting steel beams.

"Brett," I panted. It was time to pull out the big guns.

He opened one eye. "Bryce."

"Bryce." I put on my most passionate, orgasmic face. "Please . . . please . . . don't stop."

His other eye opened. Both went wide.

A minute later, it was all over.

"Sorry," he gasped, rolling off me. He looked mortified. "I don't know . . . didn't mean . . ."

"It's all right, baby." I felt only a little bad about using the *don't stop* trick on him. It didn't always work, but for some guys, planting that seed completely undid them. "It was amazing."

And really, that wasn't entirely a lie. The sex itself had been mediocre, but the rush afterward . . . the feel of his life and his soul pouring into me . . . yeah. That was pretty amazing. It was what a succubus like me literally lived for.

He gave me a wary smile. The energy that flowed through

me was no longer in him. Its loss had exhausted him, burned him out. He'd sleep soon and would probably continue sleeping a great deal over the next few days. His soul had been a good one, and I'd taken a lot of it—as well as his life itself. He'd now live a few years less, thanks to me.

I tried not to think about that as I hurriedly put on my clothes. He seemed surprised at my abrupt departure but was too worn out to fight it. I promised to call him—having no intention of doing so—and slipped out of the room as he lapsed into unconsciousness.

I'd barely cleared his front door before shape-shifting. I'd come to him as a tall, sable-haired woman but now once again wore my preferred shape, petite with hazel-green eyes and light brown hair that flirted with gold. Like most of my life, my features danced between states, never entirely settling on one.

I put Bryce out of my mind, just like I did with most men I slept with, and drove across town to what was rapidly becoming my second home. It was a tan, stucco condo, set into a community of other condos that tried desperately to be as hip as new construction in Seattle could manage. I parked my Passat out front, fished my key out of my purse, and let myself inside.

The condo was still and quiet, wrapped in darkness. A nearby clock informed me it was three in the morning. Walking toward the bedroom, I shape-shifted again, swapping my clothes for a red nightgown.

I froze in the bedroom doorway, surprised to feel my breath catch in my throat. You'd think after all this time, I would have gotten used to him, that he wouldn't affect me like this. But he did. Every time.

Seth lay sprawled in the bed, one arm tossed over his head. His breathing was deep and fitful, and the sheets lay in a tangle around his long, lean body. Moonlight muted the color of his hair, but in the sun, its light brown would pick up a russet glow. Seeing him, studying him, I felt my heart swell in my chest. I'd never expected to feel this way about anyone again, not after centuries of feeling so . . . empty. Bryce had meant nothing to me, but this man before me meant everything.

I slid into bed beside him, and his arms instantly went around me. I think it was instinctual. The connection between us was so deep that even while unconscious we couldn't stay away from each other.

I pressed my cheek to Seth's chest, and his skin warmed mine as I fell asleep. The guilt from Bryce faded, and soon, there was only Seth and my love for him.

I slipped almost immediately into a dream. Except, well, I wasn't actually *in* it, at least not in the active sense. I was watching myself, seeing the events unfold as though at a movie. Only, unlike a movie, I could *feel* every detail. The sights, the sounds . . . it was almost more vivid than real life.

The other Georgina was in a kitchen, one I didn't recognize. It was bright and modern, far larger than anything I could imagine a noncook like me needing. My dream-self stood at the sink, elbow deep in sudsy water that smelled like oranges. She was hand-washing dishes, which surprised my real self—but was doing a shoddy job, which did not surprise me. On the floor, an actual dishwasher lay in pieces, thus explaining the need for manual labor.

From another room, the sounds of "Sweet Home Alabama" carried to my ears. My dream-self hummed along as she washed, and in that surreal, dreamlike way, I could feel her happiness. She was content, filled with a joy so utterly perfect, I could barely comprehend it. Even with Seth, I'd rarely ever felt so happy—and I was pretty damned happy with him. I couldn't imagine what could make my dream-self feel this way, particularly while doing something as mundane as washing dishes.

I woke up.

To my surprise, it was full morning, bright and sunny. I'd had no sense of time passing. The dream had seemed to last only a minute, yet the nearby alarm clock told me six hours had passed. The loss of the happiness my dream-self had experienced made me ache.

Weirder than that, I felt . . . not right. It took me a moment to peg the problem: I was drained. The life energy a succubus needed to survive, the energy I'd stolen from Bryce, was almost gone. In fact, I had less now than I'd had before going to bed with him. It made no sense. A burst of life like that should have lasted a couple of weeks at least, yet I was nearly as wiped out as he'd been. I wasn't low enough to start losing my shape-shifting, but I'd need a new fix within a couple of days.

"What's wrong?"

Seth's sleepy voice came from beside me. I rolled over and found him propped on one elbow, watching me with a small, sweet smile.

I didn't want to explain what had happened. Doing so would mean elaborating on what I'd done with Bryce, and while Seth theoretically knew what I did to survive, ignorance really was bliss.

"Nothing," I lied. I was a good liar.

He touched my cheek. "I missed you last night."

"No, you didn't. You were busy with Cady and O'Neill."

His smile turned wry, but even as it did, I could see his eyes start to take on the dreamy, inward look he got when he thought about the characters in his novels. I'd made kings and generals beg for my love in my long life, yet some days, even my charms couldn't compete with the people who lived in Seth's head.

Fortunately, today wasn't one of those days, and his attention focused back on me.

"Nah. They don't look as good in a nightgown. That's very Anne Sexton, by the way. Like 'candy story cinnamon hearts.'"

Only Seth would use bipolar poets as compliments. I glanced down and ran an absentminded hand over the red silk. "This does look pretty good," I admitted. "I might look better in this than I do naked."

He scoffed. "No, Thetis. You do not."

And then, in what was an astonishingly aggressive move for him, he flipped me onto my back and began kissing my neck.

"Hey," I said, putting up a halfhearted struggle. "We don't have time for this. I have stuff to do. And I want breakfast."

"Noted," he mumbled, moving on to my mouth. I stopped my complaining. Seth was a wonderful kisser. He gave the kind of kisses that melted into your mouth and filled you with sweetness. They were like cotton candy.

But there was no real melting to be had, not for us. With a well-practiced sense of timing that you could probably set a watch to, he pulled away from the kiss and sat up, removing his hands as well. Still smiling, he looked down at me and my undignified sprawl.

I smiled back, squelching the small pang of regret that always came at these moments of retreat.

But that was the way it was with us, and honestly, we had a pretty good system going when one considered all the complications in our relationship. My friend Hugh once joked that all women steal men's souls if they're together long enough. In my case, it didn't taken years of bickering. A too-long kiss would suffice. Such was the life of a succubus. I didn't make the rules, and I had no way to stop the involuntary energy theft that came from intimate physical contact. I could, however, control whether that physical contact happened in the first place, and I made sure it didn't. I ached for Seth, but I wouldn't steal his life as I had Bryce's.

I sat as well, ready to get up, but Seth must have been feeling bold this morning. He wrapped his arms around my waist and shifted me onto his lap, pressing himself against my back so that his lightly stubbled face was buried in my neck and hair. I felt his body tremble with the intake of a heavy, deep breath. He exhaled it just as slowly, like he sought control of himself, and then strengthened his grip on me.

"Georgina," he breathed against my skin.

I closed my eyes, and the playfulness was gone. A dark intensity wrapped around us, one that burned with both desire and a fear of what might come.

"Georgina," he repeated. His voice was low, husky. I felt like melting again. "Do you know why they say succubi visit men in their sleep?"

"Why?" My own voice was small.

"Because I dream about you every night." In most circumstances, that would have sounded trite, but from him, it was powerful and hungry.

I squeezed my eyes more tightly shut as a swirl of emotions danced within me. I wanted to cry. I wanted to make love to him. I wanted to scream. It was all too much sometimes. Too much emotion. Too much danger. Our increased flirtation and sexual taunting fed a complication that didn't need any more stoking.

Opening my eyes, I shifted so that I could see his face. We held each other's gazes, both of us wanting so much and unable to give or take it. Breaking the look first, I slipped regretfully from his embrace. "Come on. Let's go eat."

Seth lived in easy walking distance to the assorted shops and restaurants adjacent to the University of Washington's campus. We got breakfast at a small café, and omelets and conversation soon replaced the earlier awkwardness. Afterward, we wandered idly up University Way, holding hands. I had errands to run, and he had writing to do, yet we were reluctant to part.

Seth suddenly stopped walking. "Georgina."

"Hmm?"

His eyebrows rose as he stared off at something across the street. "John Cusack is standing over there."

I followed his incredulous gaze to where a man very like Mr. Cusack did indeed stand, smoking a cigarette as he leaned against a building. I sighed.

"That's not John Cusack. That's Jerome."

"Seriously?"

"Yup. I told you he looked like John Cusack."

"Keyword: *looked*. That guy doesn't look like him. That guy is him."

"Believe me, he's not." Seeing Jerome's impatient expression, I let go of Seth's hand. "Be right back."

I crossed the street, and as the distance closed between my boss and me, Jerome's aura washed over my body. All immortals have a unique signature, and a demon like him had an especially strong one. He felt like waves and waves of roiling heat, like when you open an oven and don't stand far enough back.

"Make it fast," I told him. "You're ruining my romantic interlude."

Jerome dropped the cigarette and put it out with his black Kenneth Cole oxford. He glanced disdainfully around. "This place? Come on, Georgie. This isn't romantic. This place isn't even a pit stop on the road to romance."

I put an angry hand on one hip. "What do you want?"

"You."

I blinked. "What?"

"We've got a meeting tonight. An all-staff meeting."

"When you say all-staff, do you mean like *all*-staff?"

The last time Seattle's supervising archdemon had gathered everyone in the area together, it had been to inform us that our local imp wasn't "meeting expectations." Jerome had let us all tell the imp good-bye and then banished the poor guy off to the fiery depths of hell. It was kind of sad, but then my friend Hugh had replaced him, so I'd gotten over it. I hoped this meeting wouldn't have a similar purpose.

Jerome gave me an annoyed look, one that said I was clearly wasting his time.

"When is it?"

"Seven. At Peter and Cody's. Don't be late. Your presence is essential."

Shit. I hoped this wasn't actually *my* going-away party. I'd been on pretty good behavior lately. "What's this about?"

"Find out when you get there. Don't be late," he repeated.

Stepping off the main thoroughfare and into the shadow of a building, the demon vanished.

A feeling of dread spread through me. Demons were never to be trusted, particularly when they looked like quirky movie stars and issued enigmatic invitations.

"Everything okay?" Seth asked me when I rejoined him.

I considered. "As much as it ever is."

He wisely chose not to pursue the subject, and we eventually separated to take care of our respective tasks. I was dying to know what this meeting could be about, but not nearly as much as I wanted to know what had made me lose my energy overnight. And as I ran my errands, I also found the strange dream replaying in my head. How could it have been so vivid? And why couldn't I stop thinking about it?

The puzzle distracted me so much that seven rolled around without me knowing it. Groaning, I headed off for my friend Peter's place, speeding the whole way. Great. I was going to be late. Even if this meeting didn't concern me and my impending "unemployment," I might end up getting a taste of Jerome's wrath after all.

About six feet from the apartment door, I felt the hum of immortal signatures. A lot of them. The greater Puget Sound area had a host of hellish employees I rarely interacted with, and they'd apparently all turned out.

I started to knock, decided an all-staff meeting deserved more than jeans and a T-shirt, and shape-shifted my outfit into a brown dress with a low-cut, surplice top. My hair settled into a neat bun. I raised my hand to the door.

An annoyed vampire I barely remembered let me in. She inclined her chin to me by way of greeting and then continued her conversation with an imp I'd only ever met once. I think they worked out of Tacoma, which as far as I was concerned might as well be annexed to hell itself.

Others walked around—vampires, lesser demons, etc.— and I nodded politely as I made my way through the guests. It could have been an ordinary cocktail party, almost a celebration. I hoped that meant no smiting tonight, since that would really put a damper on the atmosphere. No one had noticed my arrival except for Jerome.

"Ten minutes late," he growled.

"Hey, it's a fashionable—"

My words were cut off as a tall, Amazonian blonde nearly barreled into me.

"Oh! You must be Georgina! I've been dying to meet you."

I raised my eyes past spandex-clad double-D breasts and up into big blue eyes with impossibly long lashes. A huge set of beauty pageant teeth smiled down at me.

My moments of speechlessness were few, but they did sometimes occur. This walking Barbie doll was a succubus. A really new one. So shiny and new, in fact, it was a wonder she didn't squeak. I recognized her age both from her signature and her appearance. No succubus with any sense would have shape-shifted into that. She was trying too hard, haphazardly piling together an assortment of male-fantasy body parts. It left her with a Frankensteinian creation that was both jaw-dropping and probably anatomically impossible.

Unaware of my astonishment and disdain, she took my hand and nearly broke it with a mammoth handshake.

"I can't wait to work with you," she continued. "I am *so* ready to make men everywhere suffer."

I finally found my voice. "Who . . . who are you?"

"She's your new best friend," a voice nearby said. "My, my look at you. Tawny's going to have a tough standard to keep up with."

A man elbowed his way toward us, and whatever curiosity I'd felt in the other succubus's presence disappeared like ashes in the wind. I forgot she was even there. My stomach twisted into knots as I ID'd the mystery signature. Cold sweat broke out along the back of my neck and seeped into the delicate fabric of my dress.

The guy approaching was about as tall as me—which wasn't tall—and had a dark, olive-toned complexion. There was more pomade on his head than black hair. His suit was nice, expensive and tailored. A thin-lipped smile spread over his face at my dumbstruck discomfiture.

"Little Letha, all grown up and out to play with the adults, eh?" He spoke low, voice pitched for my ears alone.

Now, in the grand scheme of things, immortals had little to fear in this world. There were, however, three people I feared intently. One of them was Lilith the Succubus Queen, a being of such formidable power and beauty that I would have sold my soul—again—for one kiss. Someone else who scared me was a nephilim named Roman. He was Jerome's half-human son and had good reason to want to hunt me down and destroy me some day. The third person who filled me with fear was this man standing before me.

His name was Niphon, and he was an imp, just like my friend Hugh. And, like all imps, Niphon really only had two jobs. One was to run administrative errands for demons. The other, his primary one, was to make contracts with mortals, brokering and buying souls for hell.

And he was the imp who had bought mine.

Eugenie Markham is the most powerful shaman around, a mercenary who spends all her time banishing spirits and fey who cross into this world. When a teenage girl's abduction takes Eugenie into the Otherworld, she learns about a startling prophecy—a prophecy that threatens her world and reveals secrets about her own past. Determined to stop the prophecy *and* rescue the girl, Eugenie assembles an odd assortment of allies: a bored fairy King who's into bondage, a cursed spirit who fantasizes about killing her, and a hot shape-shifter who is both literally and figuratively a fox. As the danger increases and time starts running out, Eugenie realizes her greatest threat may actually be her own nature and the dark powers awakening within her.

**Please turn the page for an exciting sneak peek of
Richelle Mead's
STORM BORN!**

Chapter 1

I'd seen weirder things than a haunted shoe but not many. The Nike Pegasus sat on the office desk, inoffensive, colored in shades of gray, white, and orange. The laces were loosened, and a bit of dirt clung to the soles. It was the left shoe.

As for me, well . . . underneath my knee-length coat, I had a Glock 22 loaded with bullets carrying a higher-than-legal steel content. A cartridge of silver ones rested in my coat pocket. Two athames lay sheathed on my other hip, one silver-bladed and one iron. Stuck into my belt near them was my wand, hand-carved oak and loaded with enough charmed gems to blow up the desk in the corner if I'd wanted to.

To say I felt overdressed was something of an understatement.

"So," I said, keeping my voice as neutral as possible, "what makes you think your shoe is . . . uh, possessed?"

Brian Montgomery, late thirties, with a receding hairline in serious denial, eyed the shoe nervously and moistened his lips. "It always trips me up when I'm out running. Every time. And it's always moving around. I mean, I never actually see it, but . . . like, I'll take them off near the door, then I come back and find this one under the bed or something. And sometimes . . . sometimes I touch it, and it feels cold . . .

really cold . . . like . . ." He groped for similes and finally picked the tritest one. "Like ice."

I nodded and glanced back at the shoe, not saying anything.

"Look, Miss . . . Odile . . . or whatever. I'm not crazy. That shoe is haunted. It's evil. You've gotta do something, okay? I've got a marathon coming up, and until this started happening, these were my lucky shoes. And they're not cheap, you know. They're an investment."

It sounded crazy to me—which was saying something—but there was no harm in checking, seeing as I was already out here. I reached into my coat pocket, the one without ammunition, and pulled out my pendulum. It was a simple one, a thin silver chain with a small quartz crystal hanging from it. New Age stores that sold more elaborate ones were ripping you off.

I laced the end of the chain through my fingers and held my flattened hand over the shoe, clearing my mind and letting the crystal hang freely. A moment later, it began to slowly rotate of its own accord.

"Well, I'll be damned," I muttered, stuffing the pendulum back in my pocket. There was something there. I turned to Montgomery, attempting some sort of badass face because that was what customers always expected. "It might be best if you stepped out of the room, sir. For your own safety."

That was only half true. Mostly I just found lingering clients annoying. They asked stupid questions and could do stupider things, which actually put me at more risk than them.

He had no qualms about getting out of there. As soon as the door closed, I found a jar of salt in my satchel and poured a large ring on the floor. I tossed the shoe into the middle of it and invoked the four cardinal directions with the silver athame. Ostensibly the circle didn't change, but I felt a slight flaring of power indicating it had sealed us in.

Trying not to yawn, I pulled out my wand and kept holding the silver athame. It had taken four hours to drive to Las

Cruces, and doing that on so little sleep had made the distance seem twice as long. Sending some of my will into the wand, I tapped it against the shoe and spoke in a singsong voice.

"Come out, come out, whoever you are."

There was a moment's silence, then a high-pitched male voice snapped, "Go away, bitch."

Great. A shoe with attitude. "Why? You got something better to do?"

"Better things to do than waste my time with a mortal."

I smiled. "Better things to do in a shoe? Come on. I mean, I've heard of slumming it, but don't you think you're kind of pushing it here? This shoe isn't even new. You could have done so much better."

The voice kept its annoyed tone, not threatening but simply irritated at the interruption. "*I'm* slumming it? Do you think I don't know who you are, Eugenie Markham? Dark-Swan-Called-Odile. A blood traitor. A mongrel. An assassin. A murderer." He practically spit out the last word. "You are alone among your kind and mine. A bloodthirsty shadow. You do anything for anyone who can pay you enough for it. That makes you more than a mercenary. That makes you a whore."

I affected a bored stance. I'd been called most of those names before. Well, except for my own name. That was new—and a little disconcerting. Not that I'd let him know that.

"Are you done whining? Because I don't have time to listen while you stall."

"Aren't you being paid by the hour?" he asked nastily.

"I charge a flat fee."

"Oh."

I rolled my eyes and touched the wand to the shoe again. This time, I thrust the full force of my will into it, drawing upon my own body's physical stamina as well as some of the power of the world around me. "No more games. If you leave on your own, I won't have to hurt you. *Come out.*"

He couldn't stand against that command and the power within it. The shoe trembled, and smoke poured out of it. Oh, Jesus. I hoped the shoe didn't get incinerated in the process. Montgomery wouldn't be able to handle that.

The smoke billowed out, coalescing into a large, dark form about two feet taller than me. With all his wisecracks, I'd sort of expected a saucy version of one of Santa's elves. Instead, the being before me had the upper body of a well-muscled man while his lower portion resembled a small cyclone. The smoke solidified into leathery gray-black skin, and I had only a moment to act as I assessed this new development. I swapped the wand for the gun, ejecting the clip as I pulled it out. By then, he was lunging for me, and I had to roll out of his way, confined by the circle's boundaries.

A keres. A male keres—most unusual. I'd anticipated something fey, which required silver bullets; or a spectre, which required no bullets. Keres were ancient death spirits originally confined to canopic jars. When the jars wore down over time, keres tended to seek out new homes. There weren't too many of them left in this world, and soon, there'd be one less.

He bore down on me, and I took a nice chunk out of him with the silver blade. I used my right hand, the one I wore an onyx and obsidian bracelet on. Those stones alone would take a toll on a death spirit like him without the blade's help. Sure enough, he hissed in pain and hesitated a moment. I used that delay, scrambling to load the silver cartridge.

I didn't quite make it because soon he was on me again. He hit me with one of those massive arms, slamming me against the walls of the circle. They might be invisible, but they felt as solid as bricks. One of the downsides of trapping a spirit in a circle was that I got trapped too. My head and left shoulder took the brunt of that impact, and pain shot through me in small starbursts. He seemed pretty pleased with himself, as overconfident villains so often are.

"You're as strong as they say, but you were a fool to try to cast me out. You should have left me in peace." His voice was deeper now, almost gravelly.

I shook my head, both to disagree and get rid of the dizziness. "It isn't your shoe."

I still couldn't swap that goddamned cartridge. Not with him ready to attack again, not with both hands full. Yet I couldn't risk dropping either weapon.

He reached for me, and I cut him again. The wounds were small, but the athame was like poison. It would wear him down over time—if I could stay alive long enough. I moved to strike at him once more, but he anticipated me and seized hold of my wrist. He squeezed it, bending it in an unnatural position and forcing me to drop the athame and cry out in pain. I hoped he hadn't broken any bones. Smug, he grabbed me by the shoulders with both hands and lifted me up so that I hung face-to-face with him. His eyes were yellow with slits for pupils, much like some sort of snake's. His breath was hot and reeked of decay as he spoke.

"You are small, Eugenie Markham, but you are lovely and your flesh is warm. Perhaps I should beat the rush and take you myself. I'd enjoy hearing you scream beneath me."

Ew. Had that thing just propositioned me? And there was my name again. How in the world did he know that? None of them knew that. I was only Odile to them, named after the dark swan in *Swan Lake,* a name coined by my stepfather because of the form my spirit preferred to travel in while visiting the Otherworld. The name—though not particularly terrifying—had stuck, though I doubted any of the creatures I fought knew the reference. They didn't really get out to the ballet much.

The keres had my upper arms pinned—I would have bruises tomorrow—but my hands and forearms were free. He was so sure of himself, so arrogant and confident, that he paid no attention to my struggling hands. He probably just perceived the motion as a futile effort to free myself. In seconds, I had the clip out and in the gun. I managed one clumsy shot and he dropped me—not gently. I stumbled to regain my balance again. Bullets probably couldn't kill him, but a silver one in the center of his chest would certainly hurt.

He stumbled back, surprised, and I wondered if he'd ever even encountered a gun before. It fired again, then again and again and again. The reports were loud; hopefully Montgomery wouldn't foolishly come running in. The keres roared in outrage and pain, each shot making him stagger backward until he was against the circle's boundary. I advanced on him, retrieved athame flashing in my hands. In a few quick motions, I carved the death symbol on the part of his chest that wasn't bloodied from bullets. An electric charge immediately ran through the air. Hairs stood up on the back of my neck, and I could smell ozone, like just before a storm.

He screamed and leapt forward, renewed by rage or adrenaline or whatever else these creatures ran on. But it was too late for him. He was marked and wounded. I was ready. In another mood, I might have simply banished him to the Otherworld; I tried not to kill if I didn't have to. But that sexual suggestion had just been out of line. I was pissed off now. He'd go to the world of death, straight to Persephone's gate.

I fired again to slow him, my aim a bit off with the left hand but still good enough to hit him. I had already traded the athame for the wand. This time, I didn't draw on the power from this plane. With well-practiced ease, I let part of my consciousness slip this world. In moments, I reached the crossroads to the Otherworld. That was an easy transition; I did it all the time. The next crossover was a little harder, especially with me being weakened from the fight, but still nothing I couldn't do automatically. I kept my own spirit well outside of the land of death, but I touched it and sent that connection through the wand. It sucked him in, and his face twisted with fear.

"This is not your world," I said in a low voice, feeling the power burn through me and around me. "This is not your world, and I cast you out from it. I send you to the black gate, to the lands of death where you can either be reborn or fade to oblivion or burn in the flames of hell. I really don't give a shit. *Go.*"

He screamed, but the magic caught him. There was a trembling in the air, a buildup of pressure, and then it ended abruptly, like a deflating balloon. The keres was gone too, leaving only a shower of gray sparkles that soon faded to nothing.

Silence. I sank to my knees, exhaling deeply. My eyes closed a moment, as my body relaxed and my consciousness returned to this world. I was exhausted, but exultant too. Killing him had felt good. Heady, even. He'd gotten what he deserved, and I had been the one to deal it out.

Minutes later, some of my strength returned. I stood and opened the circle, suddenly feeling stifled by it. I put my tools and weapons away and went to find Montgomery.

"Your shoe's been exorcised," I told him flatly. "I killed the ghost." No point in explaining the difference between a keres and a true ghost; he wouldn't understand.

He entered the room with slow steps, picking up the shoe gingerly. "I heard gunshots. How do you use bullets on a ghost?"

I shrugged. It hurt from where the keres had slammed my shoulder to the wall. "It was a strong ghost."

He cradled the shoe like one might a child and then glanced down with disapproval. "There's blood on the carpet."

"Read the paperwork you signed. I assume no responsibility for damage incurred to personal property."

With a few grumbles, he paid up—in cash—and I left. Really, though, he was so stoked about the shoe, I probably could have decimated the office.

In my car, I dug out a Milky Way from the stash in my glove box. Battles like that required immediate sugar and calories. As I practically shoved the candy bar in my mouth, I turned on my cell phone. I had a missed call from Lara.

Once I'd consumed a second candy bar and was on I-10 back to Tucson, I called her back.

"Yo," I said.

"Hey. Did you finish the Montgomery job?"

"Yup."

"Was the shoe really possessed?"

"Yup."

"Huh. Who knew? That's kind of funny too. Like, you know, lost souls and soles in shoes . . ."

"Bad, very bad," I chastised her. Lara might be a damned good secretary, but there was only so much I could be expected to put up with. "So what's up? Or were you just checking in?"

"No. I just got a weird job offer. Some guy—well, honestly, I thought he sounded kind of schizo. But he claims his sister was abducted by fairies, er, gentry. He wants you to go get her."

I fell silent at that, staring at the highway and clear blue sky ahead without consciously seeing either one. Some rational part of me attempted to process what she had just said. I didn't get that kind of request very often. Okay, never. A retrieval like that required me to cross over physically into the Otherworld. "I don't really do that."

"That's what I told him." But there was uncertainty in Lara's voice.

"Okay. What aren't you telling me?"

"Nothing, I guess. I don't know. It's just . . . he said she's been gone almost a year and a half now. She was fourteen when she disappeared."

My stomach sank a little at that. God. What an awful fate for someone so young. It made the keres' lewd comments to me downright trivial.

"He sounded pretty frantic."

"Does he have proof she was actually taken?"

"I don't know. He wouldn't get into it. He was kind of paranoid. Seemed to think his phone was being tapped."

I laughed at that. "By who? The gentry?" "Gentry" was what I called the beings that most of western culture referred to as fairies or sidhe. They looked just like humans but embraced magic instead of technology. The found "fairy" a derogatory term, so I respected that—sort of—by using the term old English peasants used to use. *Gentry.* Good folk. Good neighbors. A questionable designation, at best. The gentry actually preferred the term "shining ones," but that was just silly. I wouldn't give them that much credit.

"I don't know," Lara told me. "Like I said, he seemed a little schizo."

Silence fell as I held onto the phone and passed a car doing forty-five in the left lane.

"Eugenie! You aren't really thinking of doing this."

"Fourteen, huh?"

"You always said that was dangerous."

"Adolescence?"

"Stop it. You know what I mean. Crossing over."

"Yeah. I know what you mean."

It was dangerous—super dangerous. Traveling in spirit form could still get you killed, but your odds of fleeing back to your earthbound body were better. Take your own body over, and all the rules changed.

"This is crazy."

"Set it up," I told her. "It can't hurt to talk to him."

I could practically see her biting her lip to hold back protests. But at the end of the day, I was the one who signed her paychecks, and she respected that. After a few moments, she filled the silence with info about a few other jobs and then drifted on to more casual topics: a sale at Macy's, a mysterious scratch on her car . . .

Something about Lara's cheery gossip always made me smile, but it also disturbed me that most of my social contact came via someone I never actually saw. The majority of my face-to-face interactions came from spirits and gentry lately.

It was after dinnertime when I arrived home, and my

housemate Tim appeared to be out for the night, probably at a poetry reading. Despite a Polish background, genes had inexplicably given him a strong Native American appearance. In fact, he looked more Indian than some of the locals. Deciding this was his claim to fame, Tim had grown his hair out and taken on the name "Timothy Red Horse." He made his living reading faux-Native poetry at local dives and wooing naïve tourist women by using expressions like, "my people" and "the Great Spirit" a lot. It was despicable to say the least, but it got him laid pretty often. What it did not do was bring in a lot of money, so I let him live with me in exchange for housework and cleaning. It was a pretty good deal as far as I was concerned. After battling the undead all day, scrubbing the bathtub just seemed like a bit much.

Scrubbing my athames, unfortunately, was a task I had to do myself. Keres blood could stain.

I ate dinner afterwards, then stripped and sat in my sauna for a long time. I liked a lot of things about my little house out in the foothills, but the sauna was one of my favorites. It might seem kind of pointless in the desert, but Arizona had mostly dry heart, and I liked the feel of the moisture on my skin. I leaned back against the wooden wall, enjoying the sensation of sweating out the stress. My body ached—some parts more fiercely than others—and the heat let some of the muscles loosen up.

The solitude also soothed me. Pathetic as it was, I probably had no one to blame for my lack of a social life except myself. I spent a lot of time alone and didn't mind. When my stepfather Roland had first trained me as a shaman, he'd told me that in a lot of cultures, shamans lived outside of normal society. The idea had seemed crazy to me at the time, being in junior high, but it made more sense now that I was older.

I wasn't a complete misanthrope, but I found I often had a hard time interacting with other people. Talking in front of groups was murder. Even talking one-on-one was uncomfortable. I had no pets or children to ramble on about, and I couldn't exactly talk about things like the incident in Las Cruces. *Yeah, I had kind of a long day. Drove four hours, fought an ancient minion of evil. After a few bullets and knife wounds, I obliterated him and sent him on to the world of death. God, I swear I'm not getting paid enough for this crap, you know?* Cue polite laughter.

When I left the sauna, I had another message from Lara, telling me the appointment with the distraught brother had been arranged for tomorrow. I made a note in my day planner, took a shower, and retired to my room where I threw on black silk pajamas. For whatever reason, nice pajamas were the one indulgence I allowed myself in an otherwise dirty and bloody lifestyle. Tonight's selection had a cami top that showed serious cleavage, had anyone been there to see it. I always wore a ratty robe around Tim.

Sitting at my desk, I emptied out a new jigsaw puzzle I'd just bought. It depicted a kitten on its back clutching a ball of yarn. My love of puzzles ranked up there with the pajama thing for weirdness, but they eased my mind. Maybe it was the fact that they were so tangible. You could hold the pieces in your hand and make them fit together, as opposed to the insubstantial stuff I usually worked with.

While my hands moved the pieces around, I kept turning over the knowledge that the keres had known my name. What did that mean? I'd made a lot of enemies in the Otherworld. I didn't like the thought of them being able to track me personally. I preferred to stay Odile. Anonymous. Safe. Probably not much point worrying about it, I supposed. The keres was dead. He wouldn't be telling any tales.

Two hours later, I finished the puzzle and admired it. The kitten had brown tabby fur, its eyes an almost azure blue. The yarn was red. I took out my digital camera, snapped a picture, and then broke up the puzzle, dumping it back into its box. Easy come, easy go.

Yawning, I slipped into bed. Tim had done laundry today; the sheets felt crisp and clean. Nothing like that new sheets smell. Despite my exhaustion, however, I couldn't fall asleep. It was one of life's ironies. While awake, I could slide into a trance with the snap of a finger. My spirit could leave my body and travel to other worlds. Yet for whatever reason, sleep was elusive. Doctors had recommended a number of sedatives, but I hated to use them. Drugs and alcohol bound the spirit to this world, and while I did indulge occasionally, I generally liked being ready to slip over on a moment's notice.

Tonight I suspected my insomnia had something to do with a teenage girl . . . But no. I couldn't think about that. Not yet. Not until I spoke with the brother.

Sighing, needing something else to ponder, I rolled over and stared at my ceiling, at the plastic glow-in-the-dark stars. I started counting them, as I had so many other restless nights. There were exactly thirty-three of them, just like last time. Still, it never hurt to check.